Perfect
COMPOSITION

TRACEY JERALD

A Midas Series Standalone Novel

XOXO,
Tracey Jerald

Tracey Jerald

101 Marketside Avenue, Suite 404-205

Ponte Vedra, FL, 3208

https://www.traceyjerald.com

Perfect Composition/ Tracey Jerald

ISBN: 978-1-7358128-9-2 (eBook)

ISBN: 978-1-7358129-0-8 (Paperback)

Library of Congress Control Number:TBD

Editor: One Love Editing (http://oneloveediting.com/)

Proof Edits: Comma Sutra Editorial

(https://www.facebook.com/CommaSutraEditorial)

Cover Design by Tugboat Design (https://www.tugboatdesign.net/)

Photo Credit: Wander Aguiar

Model: Clayton Wells

PR & Marketing: Linda Russell - Foreword PR (https://www.forewordpr.com/).

*I'm dedicating this book to love, art,
and the men who brought them to me.*

To Wander Aguiar, Andrey Bahia, and Clayton Wells.

I'm forever grateful.

ALSO BY TRACEY JERALD

Midas Series

Perfect Proposal

Perfect Assumption

Perfect Composition

Perfect Order

Perfect Satisfaction (Coming Soon!)

Amaryllis Series

Free - An Amaryllis Prequel (Newsletter Subscribers only)

Free to Dream

Free to Run

Free to Rejoice

Free to Breathe

Free to Believe

Free to Live

Free to Dance

Free to Wish

Free to Protect

Free to Reunite (Coming Soon!)

Devotion Series

Ripple Effect

Flood Tide (Coming Soon!)

Glacier Adventure Series

Return by Land

Return by Sea

Standalones

Close Match

Unconditionally With Me – A With Me in Seattle Novella

Go to https://www.traceyjerald.com/ for all buy links!

PLAYLIST

Taylor Swift: "Love Story"
Billy Joel: "And So It Goes"
Toto: "Africa"
Marc Cohn: "Dig Down Deep"
U2: "Pride"
Amy Grant: "If These Walls Could Speak"
Stevie Nicks: "Edge of Seventeen"
Kelsea Ballerini: "Peter Pan"
Bruce Hornsby, The Range: "The Valley Road"
Taylor Swift: "Christmases When You Were Gone"
Edwin McCain: "I'll Be"
Aerosmith: "Dream On"

THE MIDAS TOUCH

In Greek mythology Midas, wandering one day in his garden, came across the wise satyr Silenus who was rather the worse for wear. Midas treated him kindly and returned him to his great companion, the god Dionysos.

In return for this, Dionysos granted Midas a wish. The king, not realizing the repercussions of his decision, chose to be given the magical ability to turn any object he touched into solid gold. Simple things, everyday things, Midas took for granted were instantly transformed by his touch into solid gold.

The full consequences of this gift soon became evident. At the barest touch, flowers, fruit, and water turned to gold. Midas became sick of this world he world surrounded himself with and sought to relieve himself of it.

Those finding themselves burdened with an abundance of perfection gifted to them by the gods often seek relief to reverse their fortune.

Except when that gift is love.

PROLOGUE
BECKETT

TWENTY YEARS EARLIER

The heat is so unbearable it's causing my clothing to stick to my skin, even at nine o'clock at night. I pluck at my shirt to peel it away from my chest. Then again, until a few moments ago, I didn't care much about the sweltering humidity.

All I care about is Paigey and the plans we're making to leave all of this behind. I jump and fist pump the air. Well, I care about a hell of a lot more than that. There's the fact she believes in my dreams. Hell, believes? She encourages them as we sit around the ruins of her family's original homestead and I play on the decrepit ashes of a piano that's missing half of its keys because that's all that remains of the original furniture her family carted here as they settled this land close to two hundred years ago.

There's a burn in the back of my eyes when I recall the way she whispered her love for me the first time. I know no one will ever love me the same way, and I'll never love anyone the way I do her. Ever. Paige is the other part of my soul, marked on my skin as surely as if she were inked there. In my head, I've composed a hundred songs to her—even if I've only managed to scribble down just a few on the pieces of scrap paper I've shoved under my mattress.

She's my heart's calling. And it has nothing to do with the way she gives herself so sweetly to me when we come together under the stars. A tingle runs up my spine as I remember the way her long legs wrapped around my waist before her hips rose up to meet my thrusts. The way her gem-colored eyes shone and her lips whispered my name as I slid inside her body.

"Beckett..."

It's part of the name someone else might have given me, but it's the man I'll become.

Someday.

When we're long gone.

She knows I need to leave Beau here in Kensington, and my Paige is already helping make my dreams come true.

I kick at the dirt ferociously as I make my way home to twelve hours of hell before I can see her in the school halls. Even a glimpse of her dark hair in the halls will give me enough oxygen to keep me going until we can meet.

Not long now, I think savagely as I pass through the bend in the chain-link fence behind the wall of trees between the back line of Paige's family property and the trailer park where my family lives. Just one more year until she graduates and we both can leave this town and everything it represents behind us. Parents who'd rather lose themselves in their misery or their bottles than acknowledge their children.

But I frown as I hear a raised voice coming from the direction of my folks' place. While not uncommon to hear one or the other yelling at each other, I catch wind of a name that should never be yelled from that direction.

Paige's.

As quietly as possible, I stop just beneath the open window and listen.

"...could make things so much worse for both of them. All I have to do is tell Paige the truth about how her mother died."

I hear my mother's gurgle—a clear sign she's been hitting the bottle early. "What's it matter to me?"

A hard fist slams down. "You keep your boy away from my daughter, Ava."

I stay in the shadows as Tyson Kensington, Paige's father, slams out the front, letting the door slap against the side of the trailer without a care. *What does he mean?* Paige told me her mother died of an infection they couldn't treat because she was pregnant with Paige herself. She cried inconsolably in my arms when she did.

Slipping my hand into my pocket, I pull out my cell phone and send a text to Paige. *Let's run away.*

Her response is immediate. *Okay.*

I'm not kidding.

Neither am I. I don't care anymore. I just want to be with you away from here.

Concerned about what I just witnessed, I press my hands against my eyes tightly. I have no doubt about my love for Paige. None. For me, this is forever. *It's going to be a huge change for you, bird.* My Paige. My little inspiration. I love calling her my songbird. The first time I did, she just laughed before claiming, "It's not me who carries the tune, Beckett. It's you."

"Then you're the inspiration even if I'm the composer," I pressed.

"What do I inspire?"

"My heart."

Jolted, I take stock of our assets. We're smart. We're hardworking. We're in love.

What else do we need?

I quickly type back, Start thinking about what to pack. Just one bag. Hide it. And when we meet tomorrow, we'll make plans. Serious ones, and then slip my phone into my pocket before heading inside yelling, "Is there any food?"

My mother slurs, "Where the fuck have you been, Beau Beckett Miller?"

I ignore her, but I bump right into my old man. While I'm the same height he is now, I don't have the same bulk he does as he works with horses all day on Tyson Kensington's farm. "Answer your ma, you little shit," he barks.

I shrug before ducking under his arm into the tiny kitchen. "Out walkin'."

"Until nine thirty?" he bellows.

"It's a nice night."

"If you like sweaty balls. Is that what you like, Beau? Sweaty balls?" my father jeers.

I ignore him before I decide if I want to try my luck eating anything in the bug-infested kitchen. *I swear to God, if I ever get out of this shithole, I'm never going to eat like this again*, I vow.

Suddenly, I'm slammed up against the counter. I shudder, not because of the chickenshit move my father's done countless times when he's tried to intimidate me, but because I'm fairly certain I felt a mouse scurry off behind me. Still, his eyes—the same light blue as my own—gleam almost eerily. "Got ya that time."

I decide to play along, hoping it will placate him long enough for me to get behind the locked door of my room. "Sure did. Now, how about letting me go so I can—"

"Right after you tell me what you're doin' with my boss's daughter." He leans in.

And that's when I smell it—the alcohol on his breath too.

Shit. One of them drunk I can deal with. Both of them takes much more finesse. I hold up my hands to ward him off. "Geez, Pa. Didn't know it was a crime to study with someone." I tell him part of the truth. Back in the beginning, Paige did help me study French when I admitted I almost failed the class the year before.

But that was then, and this is now, and studying is the furthest thing from our minds.

He jerks back. "Study?"

"Yeah. Remember that shit grade I got in French last year? Remember how you told me never to let it happen again."

His face relaxes. He even grins. When he does, I want to hurl as I'm hit with a full-frontal explosion of decaying teeth and bad alcohol. "Right. So Miss Paige knows French? Shouldn't be surprised and all."

"Nope. Not a bit. So, I got a test. Can I go study?" I ask hopefully.

"Sure. Go."

I try to keep my steps measured as I make my way through the small space to my haven when he calls out, "Hey, Beau?"

I subdue my expression before turning to face him. My mother's moved by his side. "Yeah, Pa?"

"I find out you're lyin', you won't like the results. You get me?"

I nod slowly. Oh, I get him. Which is exactly why I need to get Paige and get the hell out of Kensington.

Yesterday.

Before something can happen to either of us.

PAIGE

TWENTY YEARS LATER - FEBRUARY

@BeckettMiller... you're unbelievably awesome. And gorgeous. Ditch the blonde and marry me. I'd look good on the red carpet too! #beckettmiller #biggestfan #premier

— @LMozzo, Celebrity Fan

I'm sipping a lukewarm beer with my oldest brother after the Founders' Day Celebration when my middle brother, Ethan, hooks his arm around my waist. He tips his longneck at the television over the bar and yells, "That's going to be Austyn one day!"

"What is?" Immediately, he catches my attention when he mentions my daughter's name.

"Walking down some red carpet in some sequined gown, trying not to trip all over her heels."

I catch the long gown in question just as the artist drifts away and grin up at him. Shouting just to be heard over the noise at Rodeo Ralph's, I reply, "Your niece wouldn't be caught dead in something so sedate these days. Let me show you the pictures of what she wore..."

But even as my hand reaches for my phone, my voice falters

because even above the crowd celebrating the founding of our town like it's a national holiday, his face is right here.

In jumbo size.

Suffocating this room.

The closed-captioning at the bottom of the screen indicates his date for the evening is a new singer on the scene named Erzulie. And even though the volume is off, there's no sound needed as the swarm of people go wild when he holds his hand back into the limousine to assist her out.

I blink slowly behind my glasses when the blonde emerges, her long legs encased in sequined boots. She barely looks to be a few years older than Austyn in her voluminous gown covered in floral appliqués.

He looks like a more mature version of the boy I gave my heart and soul to, even if his unbuttoned tuxedo shirt flashes skin now carrying ink from his collarbone down to his ribs—all from a life I never lived with him.

It's only fair, I guess. Mine carries the scars from bearing the child he's never acknowledged.

Jesse—Ethan's and my oldest sibling—steps in front of me, blocking my personal nightmare—something few are privy to. "He doesn't matter, Paigey." His use of the nickname only close family and friends are allowed to use warms a gut that's burning with a combination of alcohol and bitterness.

"Jesse's right, sis," Ethan insists.

I lift my drink to my lips, sucking back more ale and ignoring the huge elephant in the room as the glamorous couple makes their way up the red carpet to the movie premiere. "Think I could get another one of these?"

"Paige, there's a guy I want you to meet. Good guy. New in town."

I stubbornly refuse to meet my brother's eyes, not even really hearing which one is trying to fix me up. Instead, I slide to the right to again get a better view of the big screen. The scrolling ticker at the bottom clearly indicates that at the Grammys next month, Beckett

Miller is nominated for Album of the Year while his date, Erzulie, is nominated for Best New Artist.

"I hope you get everything you ever dreamed of, you lying bastard," I whisper almost soundlessly. Finishing my beer, I turn my attention back to my concerned brothers. "I have a problem."

"We can tell." Ethan's face is like the thundercloud that threatened the kids riding their bikes during the Founders' Day Parade earlier today.

Jesse smacks him in the shoulder. "What do you need, Paigey?"

"Austyn called. She's coming home from school."

Both men relax. "For the weekend? That's great news!" Jess enthuses.

I slap a patently sweet smile on my face. "So glad you think so. But you're wrong. She's leaving it."

"Wait, why?" Ethan's face becomes concerned.

"The semester's only been back in session for a week. Nothing terrible could have happened. She'll want to go back." Jesse dismisses my daughter's concern.

"Then you can be the one to calm Daddy when she announces she's decided to cash out her college fund to try DJ'ing full-time." I pause for dramatic effect. "In New York City."

"Who gave her that cockamamie idea?" Ethan grumbles.

My eyes widen. "Why, apparently it was you, E. She saw how successful your website and business are doing and decided to mimic it on a grander scale."

Jesse reaches over and punches him. "Great move, genius."

"How the hell was I to know..." Ethan protests.

"Because music is all she's breathed since she was a little girl," I remind them. "I'm proud of Austyn for finding the way to make her dream come true. What I will not have is Daddy coming down on her like an overbearing boar. She is a strong woman now who is fully capable of making rational decisions."

"He means well," Ethan argues.

My heart softens. "I know. But when the two of you have children, you can decide if his persistent interference is well-meaning or stifling. Like this man you want me to meet. Who's the one who wants me to meet him?"

Jesse's gaze drops to his boots. I roll mine heavenward. "Precisely my point. It's time for a Kensington to make their mark outside of Texas."

"But do you think she can make it in music?" Ethan's eyes cast toward the big-screen television.

I reach over and grab his chin in my hands and jerk it back hard. "Don't. Don't you dare compare her to him. Not ever."

"It's kind of hard not to..."

"Not ever, Ethan. Not in your mind, not in your heart. She doesn't exist for him by his own choice." I release his chin. "Now, I think I'm done celebrating our forefathers. Despite how lovely the fireworks were earlier, I'm going to head home and worry about the kind of explosions our actual father is going to have when he hears his granddaughter is leaving college."

Setting my empty bottle down, I turn around and find myself engulfed in the arms of my oldest brother. For a moment, I let myself do something I so rarely do.

I lean on someone.

"It will work out, Paigey. No matter what, things will work out just the way they're supposed to. And besides, Dr. Kensington," he teases me, "you built yourself an impressive life here."

"You're right. I did. And I'm proud of it," I lie aloud. I've done it so often, I've convinced myself as well as everyone around me. For just a second, my eyes bounce off the television.

But what would my life have been like if I'd had *him*? The one man who made my heart sing?

Ethan shoves Jesse aside to give me a swift hug before I manage to escape them and worm my way through the bodies packed into Rodeo Ralph's.

But before I make my way down the street to my car, I can't help but turn around one final time to torture my heart. Beckett is at the entrance to the movie theater now with the lovely blonde. There's a look of pride on his face I'd have given my soul for when Austyn was eleven and she was declared a prodigy, a virtuoso by her music teacher.

Much like her father is. The thought works its way insidiously into my thoughts as I turn away from the image that won't leave my brain like any of the others since he ran off, leaving me to face our small town at seventeen, alone and pregnant.

Instead, I replace it by pulling up an image of my daughter in my mind. She's unmistakably ours, created from a young girl's heart and a young man's lust.

Shoving aside the bitterness and focusing on the miracle I've raised, I recall the day I asked her music instructor during a parent-teacher conference when a lovely composition soothed my ragged nerves, "Who's the composer? This piece is lovely."

He stood and held open the door before gesturing me through it.

The sounds of the harp became more pronounced as we moved outside his office. For some reason, I found myself wanting to hiss when his deep baritone interrupted the beauty.

But it was his words that held my tongue. "Like I said, she's a virtuoso."

"That's Austyn?" My whisper trailed away with the crescendo of notes.

"Indeed, Dr. Kensington." And through the windowed door, I saw her lost to the notes I knew were floating in her mind. It was in that moment, I realized how much of her father she has in her. The same dreamy smile tipped up her lush lips as her finger plucked away at the fine strings. Her long lashes fanned out, hiding eyes that held room for only one lover.

Music.

As I rush down the street to my car, the old wound opens enough to cause a trail of unseen blood to pour from me as I recall Beckett crawling from our bed of trampled-down grass and a saddle blanket to compose a song with just that look on his face. It wasn't long after, he left me and never returned. He never looked back, not once. Never for the woman he claimed to love forever and certainly never to find out about the miracle he helped create.

Instead, it's my blessing and burden to give her the wings to fly and catch her if she falls—the way I have from the moment she was placed in my arms.

And I'll do anything I can to make sure that she soars.

Anything.

BECKETT
NOVEMBER

If you can't take time to enjoy the scenery while you're dining, well, you're not opening up all your senses. Even if you are simply reheating leftovers at home, make every meal an experience. Pretend your favorite celebrity is dining with you. Set the table. Interact with one another. Embrace the experience.

— **Fab and Delish**

"It's good to see you." I hold my hand out to the dark-haired Broadway actor.

"You as well, Beckett." Simon Houde holds up a finger, and the hovering waiter comes rushing over to our table. "Something to drink?"

"Just some sparkling water." At Simon's arched brow, I toss him a careless smile. "Somehow I have a feeling I'm going to need my wits about me for this conversation." The reality about my life is I don't indulge in any vice to a degree that I'd become addicted to it. Not booze, not drugs, and due to my parents, I'll never enjoy a woman to the degree I'll lose myself in her. Not after the way my parents ruined my life.

Or the woman I abandoned to have it.

Simon and I exchange quips about his wife, who is my longtime financier, while the waiter is fetching my drink. "I consider myself a fairly knowledgeable man."

"I would agree."

I lean forward to make my point. "But when your wife starts in on the importance of diversifying my portfolio to include alternative energy futures, I swear I feel like I'm back in high school, man. I have to ask, does she talk like this at home?"

Simon bursts out laughing just as the waiter arrives. I lean back in my chair as my drink is poured. When the waiter steps away to the far corner of the private room we're in, Simon responds, "Sometimes, she talks to Alex like this. And sure, we'll talk about our finances. But after all these years, she knows better than to loop me in on a conversation about energy futures."

I lift my glass in a toast. "To your wife, one of the most crazy-brilliant women I know."

He does the same. We both take a quick sip, and then he declares, "Now, the biggest coup—aside from you agreeing to do the music score by the end of this lunch, of course—would be finding out if some smart, savvy woman has sunk her claws into you, Beckett."

Immediately, I shake my head. "Not going to happen."

"You can't tell me you play the field as much as the tabloids say. You'd be dead."

"And you would have had an affair nine times over with your favorite leading lady—who happens to be your wife's sister," I retort.

"True. Hey, speaking of which, let's look at the menu. I have to find something completely noxious for lunch."

I smirk. "Why? You and Evangeline have a kissing scene to practice later?" I make smooching noises in his direction.

"Tragically, yes. But let's order before we talk business." Simon calls the waiter over.

I lift my menu. "I'll take the halibut."

"And I'll take the tilapia. Extra cilantro."

The waiter clears his throat before clarifying, "Extra cilantro, Mr. Houde?"

The waiter is swallowing repeatedly—like he's trying not to choke over the very idea. I rescue him by shaking my glass. "That's all... Charles. And perhaps some more of the sparkling water when you have a moment?"

"Yes, sir. Right away." He scuttles off.

Simon pouts for just a moment. "I was going to tell him to add onions."

"You were going to give yourself heartburn. Now, let's talk business." Before Simon can say anything, I rattle off names. "ABBA, the Who, Paul Simon, Elton John, Alanis Morrissette, just to name a few. It's been done."

"But see, I believe you can dream up something that's next-level," he argues.

"You flatter me and I think give me too much credit."

"Evangeline doesn't think so either. We're so certain of what you're going to be able to produce, Beckett, we're willing to step away from any commitments next spring. That gives you close to nine months to come up with the book."

My heart starts pounding in my chest. "And you? What about you?"

"I'm so certain that you can do this, I want to talk Bristol into financing it."

Christ. I just clench my jaw. "And if I say no?"

"Then we'll figure something else out. But Beckett, you have a story to tell. What it is, we're not certain."

"You're giving me too much credit. I'm not even sure if I know what it is yet."

He flashes a smile that makes him look remarkably like his brother for just a second. "You know what you need to do?"

"What's that?" I ask.

"You need to fall in love."

"That is the very last thing that will ever happen in my life, Simon. I'll agree to do the music without a contract first. Trust me."

He bobbles his glass "Excuse me?"

I open my mouth to repeat what I said, but his hand slashes through the air. "That's complete and utter bullshit, Beckett. You have one of the biggest hearts of any guy I've ever met. You're funny, not all that bad-looking..."

"Are you planning on writing my online dating profile? Because if you are, be certain to mention I'm filthy rich due to your wife."

He flicks me off. "So, I don't get it. Is it the gold diggers? I mean, Bris knows some great—"

"I refuse to fall in love." My voice, devoid of emotion, is more potent for its absence of feeling.

"Care to share the reasons?"

"There's just one." I hold his gaze steadily when he finally lifts his eyes to mine.

"Oh, hell. There was a woman once, wasn't there? And you're not over it?"

I try to dodge the question with one of my own. "Must we keep talking about this?"

"With the ridiculous nondisclosure agreement you insisted your lawyer have me sign? Yes."

A flicker of amusement cuts through the memories of my life in Texas Simon has unwittingly aroused. My lawyer, Carys Burke, essentially threatened to cut off Simon's balls if he so much as breathes a word about our negotiation to anyone. "It's more because it's unfinished business. Maybe I need it to remain that way," I muse.

"You left someone behind?" he guesses.

"I never let her know I'd be leaving so suddenly. Never told her I'd never be back. Then, one night, I ran into one of her brothers at a club after one of my shows." The sick feeling of seeing Jesse Kensington washes over me. I reach for my water and take a sip.

"What happened then?"

"I asked how she was. He mentioned she had a beautiful daughter. And I felt those words like a punch to my gut."

"Beckett, how old were you when you left her?"

"Eighteen."

"Eighteen," Simon repeats. "And in that time, you didn't expect her to move on? Especially if you hadn't contacted her?"

"You have no right to judge the depth of what happened between Paige and me. You have no idea what happened between us. You..." I lash out until I realize Simon isn't doing any of those things; he was simply asking me questions. And now he's patiently waiting for the answers. "I don't know what I expected."

"Did you expect her to wait for you? Did you ask her to do that?" Simon presses.

"No. I expected her to leave with me."

"What changed all that?"

I shove myself to my feet and start pacing back and forth. Sunlight streams through the enormous windows of the restaurant. Wealth, fame, notoriety—I covered all the pain of leaving Paige behind with the things I earned. I don't need to pay millions of dollars to a shrink to tell me that. In the many years since the last time I saw her face-to-face, I've made my mark on the world in ways most people can't fathom. Yet, it means little when compared to the songs I wrote under the burning Texas sun for the girl who vowed to love me forever.

To know she gave another man a child... I whirl around and almost collide into Simon. "What happened to you, Beckett? I'm not asking as anything but your friend."

And I deflate. I can't shoulder this burden alone any longer, especially not if I plan on sharing the story of my life with the theatrical world he inhabits. When I'm done telling Simon everything, he sinks back into his chair. "Christ, Becks. You left because you love her."

"And I always will. Therefore my heart isn't mine to give."

Before I can say anything else, the door to our room is opened, and the waiter arrives back with the bottle of sparkling water.

⊕

A few hours later, and after I've endured my own indigestion from watching Simon inhale tilapia dunked in enough cilantro to torment

Broadway star Evangeline Brogan for the next week, I step from the trendy New York City restaurant. Slipping my phone from my pocket, I scroll through the missed notifications, texts, and calls until I land on one from StellaNova. Opening it, I think, *Don't get pissed.*

I stop walking and step out of the way of the pedestrians behind me before pressing it.

I'm immediately taken to StellaNova's website where there's a picture of me carrying a half-dressed Erzulie out of a hotel. You can't see my security team in the photo, though I know they're not far behind me. "God damn fucking..."

An elderly woman pushing a collapsible shopping cart rolls deliberately over my foot. "Watch your damn mouth."

"Sorry, ma'am." But even as I'm apologizing, I'm pulling Erzulie up in my list of contacts.

"'Lo," comes her sleepy voice.

"I am going to do everything short of murder you. You're too talented to be dead. I told you not to go to that frigging party," I shout in frustration.

"Becks? What's the problem?" Kylie Miles, the singer known as Erzulie, questions me.

"The problem, Ky, is the fucking paps got a picture of me carting your damn ass out of the hotel when you called me drunk off your ass. And do you want to hear the caption on this one?"

"Umm..."

I don't give her any time to decide. "Rock God and the Indie Goddess? Is this a match made in heaven or someone's idea of a sick hell. In this case, the daddy/daughter dating doesn't do it for us."

"Oh shit. Tell me it wasn't..."

"Yes, little girl. Your favorite of the bunch. StellaNova."

I jerk my phone away from my ear as she screams. When I jerk it back, I shout, "Do you get it now, Ky? Do you? I get you're suffering. Believe me, I understand that. But you know the rule I taught you to live by—nothing to excess."

She starts to cry. "I didn't drink that much, Beckett. I swear."

I start walking now, certain now I don't have to go kill someone who has become as close to me as if she was actually my little sister. Still, I'm brutally unsympathetic when I inform her, "Take your emotions out on the music, Ky. Now, I have to go have Carys deal with this for both of us. Do you realize how pissed she's going to be?"

"Oh, God. Becks, no. It can't be that bad."

"I suggest you haul your ass up out of bed and check your phone. You aren't in school, and this isn't playtime anymore, little girl. Your whole life is a damn business. And next time, figure out some way else to deal with the pain. Just like I told you after the Grammys when I had to hold you up when we got out of the limo and we dealt with these rumors then." I press End before nodding at the lead to my security team.

"It looks as if you boys may just come in handy for once."

"Sir?" Kane, my lead bodyguard, says.

"Never mind, Kane. Let's get going." After sliding in the back of my car, I call my lawyer's office.

"LLF, LLC," Angie's voice vibrates through the line.

"Is she free?" I normally have time to flirt with Angie in an attempt to build up her self-confidence, but not today. Not right now. Not after my emotions are scraped so raw on the inside.

"Yes. I just scanned this morning's feeds and prepared her. Carys has been waiting for your call."

A few seconds later, the husky voice of my ex-girlfriend comes on the line. "Tell me your security team was with you so I can at least threaten StellaNova with reporting false news."

My lips curve humorlessly. "Of course they were."

"Good. Now, go sing something. I have work to do." And Carys disconnects the call, leaving me once again disenchanted with too many things about the life I lead and no clue about how to fix it.

BECKETT

Someone sent me a tip they saw Beckett Miller at their local gym this morning. People, let me be clear once again. If you don't send a pic showing off his famous tats, then I don't believe you. #sorrynotsorry #infamousabs #wishitweretrue

— Viego Martinez, Celebrity Blogger

I slip the dumbbell back into the slot before blowing out a huge breath of air. "I can't wait for this last bit of the tour to be done so I can cut back a bit on these workouts," I say to my lead guitarist, Mick Ceron.

"What, keeping your abs in shape or the workout you do each day with the press?"

"Either. Both. Part of me feels exhausted over all of it."

"And you're what? Thirty-eight? I thought you were a baby, Becks. Now, I'm going to call you Old Man. What do you think, honey?" He directs the question to his wife.

She flaps her hand at him as the treadmill incline increases.

Mick laughs.

It's just before sundown in Toronto, Canada. Due to the overcast, the sun is barely penetrating through the windows of the gym we've commandeered. It's my absolute favorite time of day. It's that moment where the regrets of the day before disappear and hope of the night begins. At least it used to when there were things left to hope for, goals to reach.

Now, what's left?

Deciding if I want to be fresh for tonight's show, I'd better ease up. I start to stretch and ponder the question.

It's been almost eighteen years since Kristoffer Wilde caught me messing around on a piano I was supposed to be moving off the Small Town Nights stage. By then I was already making my name for myself in a whole different way even as I sweated away my pain every night, shoving hundreds of pounds of equipment beneath the often blazing sun that would beat down on me during summer tours. I knew I didn't want to live on the edge of sanity my whole life. I'd run away to avoid that very thing. So, I chose to distance myself from temptation and did what I knew I could do best—compose music.

But it wasn't enough. Frustration built up until one day, I overheard a conversation between Shane—the lead singer of Small Town Nights—and his business manager. They were talking about using a song Shane wrote in a commercial, and the numbers they were talking about astonished me. They were willing to pay how much for a twenty-second piece of music?

And suddenly, I had a focus. I wanted a piece of that pie.

I stopped existing for the moment and started thinking of a future beyond finding something cold to drink. I listened and found out that joining ASCAP would maybe get my music noticed by television stations, radio shows, and advertising agencies. At the hotel that night, I paid for internet access and then paid for my membership. I wanted my music to be found by whomever wanted to use it. And with more fervor than ever before, I wrote. A quick stanza here, a coda there. I held deep-seated dreams that maybe one of the songs I scribbled in between moving Shane's piano would be picked up for a hit television show.

Then it happened, though not quite the way I expected.

I crack open a bottle of water and chug most of it down as the drips of memories trickle along with it. It started with a request by some local car dealership. Then a few months later, a regional hair salon. But, hell, tears still prick my eyes when I recall the night the crew went out to wrap up the tour in Philly and the nationally broadcast dog food commercial came on with my song playing as the black Lab cantered through the grass. To this day, I can't spot a black Lab on the street without getting choked up. Those dogs don't know it, but they paid for the two best things in my life—my online college education and the battered upright I wrote my first number one single, "Run Wild," on. I still write every song on that baby to this day.

I'd been home in my apartment—a rare three days not on the road—and I'm not certain if it was the scorching temperature in the city or the vendor selling sunflowers, but it made me think of home. Of *her*. She's the only reason I can't fully blank out my past, the only bright light in the darkness that surrounded me day after day. Before I left, Paige was the only one comfortable enough to approach the wild animal I was quickly becoming, so fearless. So with a fifth of Jack and my memories, I took out my feelings about my life before I'd run away justifying I'd made the right choices, on the keys instead of on some nameless face I had no intention of learning.

Still pissed in more ways than one the next day, I shoved it all aside and focused on the future because I couldn't go back and change the past. Because even if I wouldn't admit it aloud, I knew I'd left my heart there.

As Beau Miller, I began to earn a tidy fortune once a syndicated game show picked up a snappy jingle I wrote. I invested it but kept working. And then the Holy Grail happened—a computer company picked up my music to be digitized to represent their new line of devices.

I was so dizzy with euphoria, I don't know how I managed to do my job that night. Mick and Carly commented on it, but I waved them off. We'd jammed together a few times, but this? This might be my ticket to finally escape. To run.

And it was due to a few notes of music composed together.

Alone on stage with Shane's piano. I sat down and began to belt out the song I wrote in my lonely apartment so long ago:

It's a calamity
What they did to me
No one else can see
I gotta run—run to be free

That's when I heard it—the slap of a single chair nearby as someone stood. But to my shock, instead of asking what the fuck I was doing, the person started to applaud. My fingers poised above the keys as his hawklike features came into view. "That's a shame."

"What is?" I challenged.

"You stopped." He nodded to one of the security guards, who steps back respectfully before granting him access.

While I gaped at him, he walked calm-as-you-please up the side of the stage steps. "I'm unfamiliar with that song."

Squaring my shoulders, I told him, "I wrote it."

"Really? Interesting." He leaned against Shane's piano as if he owned it.

"Mind if I ask who the hell you are?"

His face broke into a Cheshire-cat grin. "I'm not often asked that. Must say, it feels good. I'm Wilde. Kristoffer Wilde." Then his expression turns more serious. "You?"

I felt like my tongue was twelve sizes too big for my mouth. I was just some nothing mouthing off to a man who was everything to the music industry. On top of which, I was playing the piano and loafing off at one of his top acts' shows. Swallowing humble pie, despite the fact that in a not-too-distant day in the future I might be at an event where this man and I might be equals, I give him my name before apologizing. "I'll just get this piano moved now, sir."

He scoffed. "Sit down, Beau? No. That doesn't suit you. B? BAM?"

I sneered at that.

"Well, we have to find something better for you than Beau. You need a catchier stage name than that. What's your middle name?" Wilde demanded.

From belting out a song I wrote about running away, to this? I raised my tattooed finger and thumb to my head and squeezed. Hard. "I'm sorry. I don't understand."

"Are you a solo act? Do I need to get a house band to..." But we were interrupted just as Mick and Carly came bouncing out from backstage.

"Hey. Are you finished with that piano yet? I think they have open mic night at..." Mick started. Then his voice trailed off as he realized I was speaking with someone.

Carly had pulled out a pair of spare drumsticks from her pocket. She twirled them around her fingers before she started tapping them on the boxes. Then she too froze.

"And that answers my question." Wilde stepped around me and held out his hand. "Kristoffer Wilde."

"Mick Ceron," Mick managed.

"Carly Stolliday," she blurted before shoving her drumsticks under her armpits.

"Where's this place you were thinking of taking young Beau to play tonight? That is, if you don't mind a tagalong?"

"It's just up the road about a mile. It's called the Mess. Let's help you get this piano moved, Beau, before we..." Mick rushed out.

Carly was frozen in place. I remember hoping she'd snap out of it to hit some drums.

But Wilde just waved his hand. "I'll deal with this and will see you later. It was good to meet you, Beau."

"Yeah, sure." Then Mick and I grabbed Carly to drag her offstage.

"That was Kristoffer Wilde," Mick hissed.

"I guess so."

"You guess?" Carly unfroze finally to screech.

My head swiveled back and forth as we rushed away from the amphitheater. "Keep it down, Smash."

Mick hooked an arm around his wife's neck. "Yeah, baby, we do not need word of this to get out. Let's just go play and pray to every god we can think of."

Back then I didn't say what I was thinking—that I'd been forsaken by so many of them that I held out no hope of Kristoffer Wilde coming to listen to the three of us play.

Years later, long after Kristoffer Wilde signed me to Wildcard Records, our friendship survived through the traditional rock-and-roll excess and absurdity playing out in the media. Stories of alcohol and drugs, cheating spouses, and more groupies than any of the three of us could handle with any sense of morality.

Carly is huffing and puffing on the treadmill but still manages to get out, "It's not funny anymore, Becks."

I laugh before retorting, "The press is always funny, Carly."

"It really isn't," Mick agrees with his wife of close to twenty years. "You've taken the brunt of the gossip for so long. You've asked over and over if we wanted to become a group instead of just your studio musicians, but you never pushed, letting Carly and me fade away so we could raise our family in peace. Never doubt we appreciate it."

"But it's wrong," she interjects.

"It's fine." I wave off their concern. There are few people I'm comfortable with to call friends, and these two are part of that select group.

"Freaking social media is toxic," Carly grumbles.

"And here she goes," Mick sighs.

I grin even as Carly points a finger in her husband's direction. I'm just grateful she's not throwing things. She has wicked aim with those muscular arms of hers. "Our kids are starting to believe the crap about Becks in the media."

"They're young and impressionable," I try to soothe her.

"That's just it, Becks. They are that," Mick says.

I feel a twisted feeling in my stomach. "What are you trying to say, Mick?"

Carly and Mick exchange a complicated look. "Have you given more thought to that offer from Evangeline Brogan?" Carly asks as she slows down to a walk.

"About doing a musical based on my life? Like I said to Simon, it's been done so many times." I wave my hand in the air.

"But what they haven't done is figure out a way to tell the story of Beckett Miller," Mick counters my argument again. "You aren't a drama queen; you didn't grow up in a crazy period of music history. You could do this without laying your tracks on top of someone else's story. You were a lost boy, Beckett. How many people would relate to that?"

Mick's words cause my creative juices to flow, even as they strike fear inside my soul. "Too many," I acknowledge.

"For you, it's about the music and what inspired it. That's what would be your challenge."

I feel the trickle of sweat run down my back. "You both think I should do it?"

They nod. "We do. We could help when it comes to the composing. Besides, while I don't mind these one-off gigs, I don't want to traipse around the world with you. I mean, let's be real. You're a pain in the ass on tour. And the kids are getting old enough they need to understand our lives aren't constantly some crazed media frenzy," Carly states firmly.

"It will force you to stretch, to grow. And you need that piece to keep going, don't you, Becks? What are you so afraid of?"

Sitting down and composing the score to a musical about how fucked-up my life was before I broke my own heart to escape it? Realizing I can't find the words to convey how sorry I am for the mistakes I made? Questioning if I took the right path after all? "Nothing. Can't wait," I lie convincingly. "I'll slot it in after the last set of shows."

Carly squeals in excitement, which I'm shocked she has the breath for after running as hard as she did.

It's the water spilling over my hand from crushing the bottle beneath my fist that jolts me out of my head. Cursing, I reach for a towel and use my sneakered foot to mop up the mess. "Listen, I'm going to go grab a protein shake. Do either of you want anything?" When they both indicate they're fine, I turn and head down the hall to the small kitchenette to make myself a drink filled with nutrients that I hopefully won't throw up.

I need something in my stomach before I call Carys to start making arrangements about drafting a contract to damn myself to the past. At least for a little while.

But not right away. I still have a little more time to avoid composing the truth and having it sound as perfect. Even if it means leaving my heart somewhere beneath a piano underneath a burning Texas sky.

For the second time.

PAIGE

The Brendan Blake show is tonight at Madison Square Garden. And I'm at home with a double ear infection. I blame this on my mother for not getting me tubes as a kid. I'm arranging for my tickets to be transferred to @PRyanPOfficial. Sniff. Sniff. It just isn't the same. I need love, people.

— @CuTEandRich3

"Now that didn't hurt at all, did it, Rosa?" I smooth my hand over the perfectly plaited hair of the little girl whose ears I'm evaluating to make certain weren't damaged after multiple ear infections.

Her braids whip around my wrist, binding my heart to her little one firmly. She giggles. "No, Dr. K. It was just like you said—I sat in the room which was really quiet."

Because the Espositos are so anxious behind me, I encourage her to go on. "Tell your Mama and Papa what else you did."

"Nurse Dawn put these big puffy earphones on my head. They were enormous!"

I laugh, delighting in the little girl's oversized gestures. "Perhaps not that big?" I reach over and grab a pair and hold them up.

"That's them! Papa, you know your earbuds? These are a million times larger!"

Mr. Esposito chuckles, relaxing slightly. "What happened next, Rosa?"

"Then, I had to raise my hand when I heard sounds. Sometimes they were on the left, sometimes the right."

"And from what I'm seeing here, you did very well."

"But not perfect?" Mrs. Esposito asks worriedly.

"Few do, Mrs. Esposito. I think your primary care provider had every right to be concerned with the fact Rosa's had three ear infections in six months this year. If she gets another one, I will be advocating putting in tubes, more so to assist with infection prevention, but her hearing is well within acceptable ranges. I think…"

"I don't want tubes hanging out of my ears!" Rosa screeches.

I grin at the charming young girl. Walking over to the cabinet, I throw Dawn a quick wink before I reach for a few pieces of tubing I use just for this purpose and tuck them beneath the arms of my glasses. "You mean like this?" I whirl around and bounce them up and down.

Everyone laughs, except Rosa.

"What are you all laughing at? I mean, we're just talking about…" I deliberately let one of the tubes hit me in the face. "Oh, sugar. Did that fall out of my ear again?"

Rosa's eyes narrow on me. "You're making fun," she accuses.

I yank the tubes out. "No, honey, I'm not. I'm trying to get you to relax. First, because you don't need to have the procedure done. And second, because the real ear tubes go inside your ear and are this size." I pull out a vial to show her the actual size of an ear tube, the blue tubes barely a speck when compared to the long strands of tubing still attached to my glasses.

"That's like a chunk of my crayon!" she exclaims.

"What color blue?" I prompt her.

"Hmm." Her face scrunches as she runs through the colors in her mind. "It's Bluetiful!"

"And so are you, little Rosa. And you're healthy. So let's keep you that way, okay?" I give the Espositos information about signs to look out for to avoid ear infections before the grateful family leaves my appointment.

Dawn provides a small gift for Rosa and an information package for her parents while I make some notes in the tablet about her condition. "Since Rosa was my last patient for the day, I'm going to head out."

"Any big plans tonight, Paige?" Dawn asks.

I lean against the counter where she and our receptionist, Amie, have been chatting. "Does a command performance around my father's dinner table before I go out of town count?" I ask dryly.

Both women groan, though it's Amie who says, "I don't know how you do it, Paige."

"Do what?"

"It's hard enough living in the town you grew up in—"

"That is named for her family—don't forget that," Dawn interjects.

"—but then you raised your daughter there. Plus you dance attendance on your family whenever they call."

"I don't do that," I protest.

"I beg to differ," Dawn counters. "How about when Ethan needed help designing his store?" She mentions my brother's IT business in downtown Kensington.

I flick my hand to the side. "That's just helping family. Either of you would have done the same."

"That may be true, but you sure as hell wouldn't have caught me dead shoveling horse manure while my oldest brother went on a ten-day cruise," Amie counters.

"That was a good learning opportunity for Austyn," I try to reason.

Both women crack up. "Yeah, on what? How to become a smart-ass when Uncle Jess comes home with a T-shirt as a thank-you gift?" Dawn manages through her giggles.

I give in, a smile spreading across my face. I'm not the least bit upset. When you work closely with two women you respect and admire day after day, you learn a great deal about one another. And aside from one major secret which I've withheld from everyone except my family for the last nineteen years, they know everything there is to know about me. "God, I thought Jess was going to collapse when Austyn informed him that she'd have had more use for a fake ukulele."

"So what does Daddy K have you coming over for? Does he need a party for thirty to be arranged?" Amie teases with a smile.

I take no offense since both women adore my father. His gruff exterior hides a heart of pure gold. And despite the fact I'm the reason he's been a bachelor the last thirty-six years, he's been a rock to us all. "I'm flying to see Austyn in New York this weekend," I remind them both.

"Ooh! That's right!" Amie claps her hands together excitedly.

"Why?" Suspicion is rife in Dawn's voice.

It causes me to bristle a bit. "Because she has a big gig at some famous nightclub, and she's working herself up. So, the last time we talked, I offered to fly up if it would make her feel better. She jumped on it."

"Oh. Congratulations to her. That's great news." But there's something in Dawn's voice I can't quite put a finger on.

Ignoring it for the moment, I go on. "I suspect my father wants to worry about my welfare, Austyn's welfare, and remind me to convince her this DJ'ing nonsense is a fad. Of course, I'll spend the better part of the evening reminding him that I'm thirty-six and well able to take care of myself. Austyn is older than I was when I had her, so I'm certain she knew what she was doing when she made the decision to cash out her college fund to follow her dreams. And when all else fails, I'll remind him that just like he was there for me, I'll be there for her if things don't work out."

I hand over my tablet to Amie, who immediately plugs it in to transfer the data from the Espositos into our main database. "And with that, friends, I'm off. Rush hour should have dissipated enough for me to make the drive to Kensington in just under forty-five minutes."

Shrugging off my white coat, I start down the hall toward my office when Dawn calls out from behind me, "Paige?"

"Yes?"

"Has she asked recently?" Her face is filled with complicated concern.

I brace my hand against the doorjamb to my office. "Austyn? About her father?"

"Yes. I mean, I don't mean to pry. It's just, I'm concerned. For you."

In the years since Austyn's father crushed my heart, leaving me to rear his child alone, I've confided in no one but my family the truth about his identity. I have only told Dawn—who's been my best friend since I was able to go to college—that when Austyn asked as a teenager, I promised her I'd tell her when she asked me once she was of legal age.

I had my reasons. I still do.

But since she turned eighteen, she hasn't brought up the topic once. Part of me lives in a hyperstatic fear of the time she will. But despite the number of times I've practiced the words, I'm still not ready.

After all, how many people can lay claim to the fact their father is a rock god?

I push away from the door. "Trust me, I suspect you'll know when I finally tell her." Dawn frowns in confusion, so I clarify, "The shrieking. Probably at me, but I suspect it will be loud."

Dawn smiles in sympathy. "I'm here when you need me."

"Remember that bottle of tequila I gave you?" One night a few years ago when my dad was watching Austyn, I had a girls' night with Dawn. I handed her a bottle with a note attached that said, *Open when P tells A.*

"Of course I do. It's the bottle of booze Jess brought you from Mexico. Dumbass."

"Keep it handy," I prepare her before ducking into my office to drop off my coat and grab my bag. When I come out, she's disappeared, so I head out the back door, calling out a goodbye.

Once I reach my Rover, I sit for a few moments, letting it cool.

Dawn's words stir up the same questions I've been wrestling with since Austyn turned eighteen. How do I tell her the boy I fell in love with, who I gave myself to out of that love, who gave *her* her brilliant blue eyes and her desperate love of music, is none other than the media spectacle Beckett Miller?

Cringing, I put the car in gear and drive west in the direction of my home. I've spent too many sleepless nights lately wondering what her reaction will be. And I put all thoughts of Beau—no, Beckett, damnit—out of my head while I do so.

PAIGE

Who has plans with their outlaws for Thanksgiving? Can't wait to remind them, yes, I get paid to write this blog. I like my tattoos fine—why would I want laser removal? Maybe I'll lock myself in hubby's old bedroom and binge-watch *Planes, Trains, and Automobiles* and *Woodchipper Massacre.*

— **Viego Martinez, Celebrity Blogger**

"Paigey." My father stands to greet me as soon as I step into the kitchen. He immediately opens his arms, and I move into them sure with the knowledge I've had from the moment I was born, that unlike so many others in this world, I am loved.

From within my father's embrace, I spy the kitchen table where we spent many hours as a family eating as not. I was a lonely little girl, so I clung to my family in my early years. I built a false sense of security within my family bosom. Timidly courageous, cautiously fearless. A constant paradox, perhaps because I didn't have my mother as a steady influence, not that she left by choice. The infection she caught when she sliced her leg on a rusty piece of fencing did that. And because she thought her tetanus shot was further along and rejected her booster since she was pregnant with me, we both almost died.

When Austyn was old enough and I was going to college at the University of Texas, I debated going into obstetrics instead of otolaryngology. But it would have been an homage instead of a passion. And by then, I was already a parent who had faced the infant years of worry about too many ear infections impacting hearing loss. It left different scars than the ones on my heart. I remember rushing Austyn to the emergency room with high fevers and recall her being diagnosed with *otitis media*. As well the well-meaning doctors cautioning me about too many infections causing potential hearing loss.

And so my course in life was set.

"How was work today, honey?" my father asks. He pulls back, giving me an unobstructed look at his handsome face. In his mid-sixties, he is still incredibly handsome. The unattainable prince locked in the tower, I recall thinking in my perfectly plush bedroom growing up. Now, I wish there was someone who had caught his eye so his heart wasn't so lonely. Then again, I can't exactly throw stones at my father's choices.

"It was good, Daddy. Cutest little girl. Reminded me a lot of Austyn at that age."

"In looks?"

"No, with her intelligence. And then how sweet she was."

His hands squeeze my shoulders before he lets me go. He drops into his seat at our table and motions for me to join him. Kicking off my heels, I do with a happy sigh. "So many memories around this table."

"Good ones, I hope." I'd have to be absolutely deaf not to catch the anxiety in my father's voice.

I extend a hand toward him. "Wonderful ones."

"I know it hasn't been easy for you, Paigey. And sometimes I forget to tell you, but I'm proud of the woman you are."

Immediately, I sit up straight. "What's wrong?"

"Nothing." His lips twitch from side to side—a sure tell.

"You're fibbing."

"And you're my daughter. You're not supposed to notice these things."

"Please. How do you think I won that $100 off you in the poker game during the Founders Day tournament?"

"I raised children who have no respect for their elders," he declares.

"No, you raised three smart children who appreciated getting extra allowances when they were kids. Now the stakes are higher. Spill it. What are you keeping from me?"

"Sheriff Lewis came around today. Asked about you."

"Ahh." Flynn Lewis, our sheriff, fairly recent addition to our community of 1,574, and newly single father has caught a certain Kensington's eye. It's just not mine.

My father pounds his fist on the table. "Well? What's wrong with the damn boy?"

Sliding from my chair, I make my way over to the refrigerator and pull out the pitcher of sweet tea I know will be there—just like it's been there my whole life. I pull down a glass and lift it to my father without a word. He gives me a curt nod. I get down a second before I begin to pour.

Flynn Lewis is gorgeous with thick black hair and melty choco-late-brown eyes. He's got a body that would make someone swoon, I think absentmindedly as I place the tea in front of my father. Sitting back in my seat, I wait for him to take a sip before I answer, "Not a thing. So, when are you two going to go out?"

Tea dribbles out of my father's mouth as he sputters in response. Calmly, I reach for the napkins in the center of the table and hand him a few as a flush begins to ride his cheeks. "Not me—you! I think he'd make a fine man for you."

"I can find my own man. Thank you, Father." I lift my glass to my lips.

"Really? How many have you found since that boy left you high and dry? Thank goodness the rest of us were here, because he sure wasn't."

Every part of me freezes. My arm holding the glass, my mind causing my lips to move, and worst, my heart. I'm uncertain how long the silence stretches out between us, but when I can move, the first thing I do is find my shoes.

"Paigey..." he begins, voice filled with regret.

"Don't," I lash out. "I came here tonight assuming you had something to say to Austyn before I go to New York. To find out this is the reason..." I swallow my temper. I'm good at it; I've had years of experience. Calmly, I address my father, "Do you have any messages for her?"

"Tell her I love her. That I'm half tempted to hire security to follow her around that city if the stories she emails me are true."

I really can't wait to hug my daughter after hearing that. Then I want to know what the hell she said so I, too, can worry right along with my father. "Then if you don't mind, I think I'll go for a ride before I head home."

Pushing to my feet, I leave the remainder of my tea sitting at the table. Hurt and fury propel me toward the door when my father's voice stops me. "I just want to see you happy, Paige. I don't want you to grow old alone."

I don't turn around before I give him this much. "I know. And I love you. I always will."

But I still leave the house.

On the back of Shadow Under the Moon, simply my Shadow, I gallop across the fields without much thought to where I'm going. Fortunately, since he's taken over day-to-day operations of the farm, Jess doesn't bitch about the fact Ethan and I keep spare clothes in the tack room just for this reason.

There are days when it's just easier to compose your thoughts when you're on the back of a horse. At least that's true if your last name is Kensington.

Our family has lived in the town incorporated in our name since the late 1800s. Our relatives were among the earliest settlers who helped build the original town hall, the first church, and the original bank. Our family homestead was built about two miles from where Daddy's house stands today—still on Kensington land but as far away as you can get on the east border.

As much as I have Texas in my blood, if it wasn't for the blood of the people who've lived under the Kensington roof and are woven in my soul, I'd have left long ago.

There are too many demons I face every day by staying.

As if she knows why my heart's been in a state of repair for twenty years, instinctively the five-year-old quarter horse starts toward the east border.

It was fury that propelled me to seek out the old homestead the first time too. It was a mix of anger at him for once again telling the story about how he proposed to a mother I never knew in order to cheer up my older brothers, the innate guilt I felt over being born and taking away Melissa Kensington, and indignant because once again, he ended it by telling Jesse and Ethan "When the time's right, you'll go to the old homestead and carve the initials of your intendeds into the family piano. For years, it was done after the wedding by an actual engraver. Now, since the damned thing was the only piece of furniture that survived the fire in '72, Kensington grooms have done the deed themselves cause the old beast was too heavy to move."

I jumped on one of Shadow's ancestors and followed the clues Daddy didn't even realize he dropped in his story.

Tonight, I do just what I did that fateful night. I ride with the blazing Texas sun at my back for miles when I spot the stalks of green in the distance. Only when I reach the wall of sunflowers and rein in Shadow, there are two things missing.

Discordant music being played on the old piano.

And Beau Beckett Miller.

Aloud, I whisper not for the first time, "Why did you leave me?"

When no answer comes, just like it hasn't for so long, I whirl

Shadow around and head back toward the farm. I have things to do for my trip to go see my daughter.

I sure as hell don't consider her Bea...Beckett's. After all, he's not the one who raised her.

I was.

BECKETT

Beckett Miller opens his mouth and makes people's dreams come true. When he sang "Life In Sin," he touched my hand, and I swear I wept. All the parts of me did. His lyrics are pure sin, but when he looks in your eyes and sings them, they're worth praying to God over. #Boston #hetouchedme #handjob

— **Viego Martinez, Celebrity Blogger**

"I swear to you, I can't stop the media from writing what they do about me." Though inside I'm cracking up at the blogger's creativity. *Freaking hand job.* I shift restlessly in my seat. It's been so long since I've sought out female companionship—something I ruthlessly hold back from while we're on tour because I know without a doubt from previous experience it will end up in the press—the idea of the intimate sexual act has stirred dormant parts of my anatomy to attention.

"I swear to God, Becks, if you don't keep yourself out of the press, I'm going to actually have to work to defend your honor one of these days." Another of the few people I explicitly trust in to call my friend, my lawyer, Carys Burke, laughs at me.

"Cut me some slack, Carrie. You and I both know I could be

teaching kids to sing their ABCs and the press would find some way to sexualize it." I slouch even deeper in her tufted leather guest chair. Nibbling on the ankh, the very first tattoo I ever got, which is tattooed on my finger, I lose myself deep in thought. I spend way too much time in this chair doing this very thing.

"One of these days, you're going to look down and your ink is going to have disappeared." Carys's voice has transformed from humor to the care and concern. Our relationship is special, more than just attorney and client. Born from a potential relationship that went nowhere because we became each other's sanctuary from wounds we both were licking from loving people we couldn't have, in the end, she got the guy she always wanted, and me? Well, I somehow managed to gain a foothold into a small circle of friends who have never let me down. Outside of my music, they're the one constant I have.

So it's with the ease of friendship I use the finger that has wet ink on it to flick her off.

And the blasted woman just laughs.

My lips quirk as I try to explain to one of the few people who understand the real me, not the tattooed bad boy on their favorite social media site. "I honestly don't know what it is. I'm antsy, anticipatory. I haven't felt like this since the last time we were preparing to go on tour."

Carys pushes away from her desk and walks around until she's leaning against the front of it. "And that won't be happening for quite a while."

"No. Once we're done performing these last few shows locally, I'll be tied up with composing." I chew on the ink of a different finger as I contemplate the agreement I came in earlier to sign. Did I make the right decision? For Mick, Carly, and the rest of the band I usually employ? For myself? What kind of impact will this have on all of us for the years to come?

She tips her head. "Do you regret making the decision to score the show? You've been given awards for your ability to write music,

Becks. I would think this would be the kind of challenge someone of your caliber would be intrigued with."

I automatically reply, "No, I don't regret it." But inwardly, I'm quaking.

She laughs softly before holding out a delicate hand which has a blazing diamond band on it. I take it gratefully, gently, between mine. "Liar," she chides.

"Of course I'm lying. I'm terrified. I'm about to lay my soul on the line for people to judge me."

"Haven't they been doing that for years?" she counters.

Just as I'm about to explain the difference, a door opens and closes behind us. I whip my head around before relaxing. Instead of letting go of Carys's hand, I squeeze it tighter merely to annoy her husband and senior paralegal, David Lennan. "Not quite in the same way, my delicate goddess," I drawl.

Carys giggles, and David—predictably—growls, "Becks," before he approaches his wife to hand her a file.

Even after all these years of closeness despite their rocky beginning, the home they've made, the beautiful son they share, I find David's unnecessary possessiveness over his wife when I'm in her presence charming. Because the reality is, while I don't envy him the woman, I covet the relationship they share, the unshakeable bond.

It's something I deliberately walked away from twenty years ago when I saw nothing but blinding pain instead of blooming roses in my future. I scratch the back of my hand where more ink rests—the only tattoo I've never, nor will I ever, explain.

"Well, this is interesting." Carys's words interrupt my thoughts. A frown pulls her brows together.

"What's that?" I ask more out of politeness than anything else. The reality is, I'd rather be at home in my music room with my old upright, trying to pour out some of the emotion I'm feeling into this musical score.

"Apparently, Angie noticed Redemption is trending heavily on the feeds. I wonder why?"

"I asked Ward. He said he was there a few weeks ago. Nothing out of the ordinary." David props himself next to his wife.

I let out a full-throated laugh. "Your baby brother-in-law should know better, Dave."

"David," David impatiently corrects me, not for the first time in the many years we've known each other.

Carys ducks her head to the side to hide her amusement. But not before she intercepts the wink I toss her way. Once Carys and I became friends, I promised her I'd annoy David by calling him "Dave" once for every missed opportunity he had to pull his head out his ass about her. I don't care about the fact they're now blissfully married. By my count, I've got a good four more years of tormenting him to look forward to.

Letting him off the hook for now, I flick my wrist. My Breitling glints in the afternoon sun as I explain, "Marco tells few people about his plans for the club."

"Louie," David assumes correctly, naming the doorman who also happens to be a silent partner in the club located just between Fort Washington and Manhattan.

"Yes. But also his brother. And since I had lunch with Simon just before the Toronto show—" I'm name-dropping Marco's brother, the famed Broadway actor who is often paired with Evangeline Brogan.

David interrupts me. "*You* had lunch with Simon Houde? Christ, I'd have loved to have been there for that. What did you two talk about?"

My mind blanks. I drag my gaze to Carys for help. She shakes her head imperceptibly, chastising me without words about having to keep secrets from her husband. Blithely, she says, "I'm certain Simon is just a fan of Becks, David. And with these shows in New York being the last few he's doing for a while..."

David's suspicion recedes. "Right. Carry on."

I clear my throat. "As I was saying, Simon indicated Marco was bringing in a few guest DJs over the next several weeks. Apparently, his regular guy in the booth got married. So, he thought this would be a good promo opportunity."

Carys's expression is wistful. "It sounds like a lot of fun."

David runs his hand over her hair. "We could try to go if you want."

She shakes her head. "Ben's been fussy when we leave him lately, even with people we know. Besides, I supposedly turned this part of my job over to Ward. It would have just been a nice night to have gone out—just the two of us."

"Right. You, me, and a few hundred others all scrambling for VIP passes at the eleventh hour."

Carys has the good grace to look chagrined. "Well, yes. But at least we know Marco, and it wouldn't have been an issue to have been issued one. Plus, we would have heard some potentially magical talent. You know Marco has a great ear."

And even though I'm being taunted by an enormous challenge issued to me by an eighty-eight-key mistress, I hear my own voice. "Well, it's not as if I won't drop by. If there's anything impressive, I'll be sure to report in."

"You just want to avoid working," Carys teases me.

"You'd be right." I lean forward, displaying the well-muscled body I've kept honed all these years.

"Music doesn't get made that way!"

Shoving myself out of the chair, I make it to Carys's office door before I respond. "Neither does lack of inspiration. But we'll see which happens first in this case. I'll drop by if I see anything of interest for you at Redemption."

Before either she or David can respond, I slip out of her office.

With years of practice, I ignore the paparazzi that follow me with each and every step I take on my way back to my Upper East Side penthouse, knowing my security team will ward off any true threats. I love New York, but I miss the freedom of open spaces where I could walk for miles and never see another soul. Never speak to another soul. Unless I ran into her. Then, it wouldn't be long before speaking—hell, thinking—was the last thing on either of our minds.

My pulse thrumming, I nod brusquely at the doorman, who races to open the door. Striding toward my private elevator, I touch the biometric pad and enter the code I had installed a few years ago after a crazed fan somehow managed to bribe the then doorman for the code and leave herself waiting naked in my elevator. It didn't take long to handle her, but it truly made me realize I couldn't walk around the city any longer without protection.

I don't begrudge a single dollar I shelled out to Hudson Investigations to help me keep that hot little disaster out of the papers. In fact, I ended up putting them on permanent retainer. I whirl around and meet the eyes of one of their security experts, Kane McCullough, who nods and steps back as I enter the elevator, knowing his counterpart has been prowling my penthouse upstairs for the hour I've been outside of it.

I almost miss the days where I had nothing more than a couple of pairs of torn Levis and stained tees to my name. Instead, I have my clothes custom-tailored in London and Rome twice a year. I buy shoes and boots that are where the leather is specifically fit for my size 14 foot. And, most importantly, I no longer worry about where my next meal is coming from.

Or what I'll have to endure to get it.

Shrugging away the memories isn't as easy as sliding off my jacket, but I won't allow them into the nearly 10,000 square feet of space that overlooks Central Park. I tip my chin up at the other body-guard from Hudson, who swaps spots with me and quietly descends in the elevator.

And when he does, one thought goes through my head as I take in my home as I make my way over to the floor-to-ceiling windows.

Mine.

And no one can take it away. Nothing can. Even if the words and notes stopped flowing so smoothly, I'd still have this. I have friends. And in the off-the-rocker chance I ever fell in love with someone—I snort derisively at the thought—there's enough socked away that no one in the next six generations should feel any pain.

At least not the kind I did.

With that mental reassurance, I make my way to the most sacred place in my home—my music room. And I struggle with telling a story that for the first time I won't sing.

Even if it's about me.

PAIGE

There's big doings happening at Redemption tonight. If you're not already inside, well, too late. This might be the best music played since I last heard Beckett Miller played live!

— **Moore You Want**

"Mama!" My head whips around as soon as I clear the security check at JFK. Then she's hurling herself into my arms. My Austyn, my true home.

There's a tradition in my family I've carried on with the ball of energy twirling us around the airport terminal as if we haven't seen each other in forever instead of the few months since she moved to New York. Dating back to my female ancestors being born along the long journey from Kentucky before eventually settling in Kensington, no matter where the female child was born, that's where her first name was derived. According to my father, my mother, Melissa, thought it was a lovely tradition and had fully intended on continuing it. Which is how I ended up with the name Paige. My mother was visiting some friends in the nearby town when she was rushed to the local emergency room while eight and a half months pregnant with me.

Austyn, although technically born in Kensington, was a slight deviation from tradition. But since I had no intention of burdening her with carrying her father's last name, I made the choice to name her for the nearby city where I intended to build our lives. And while I didn't fully succeed from escaping the long reach of my family's good intentions, I helped my daughter do just that.

And that's all that matters.

"Let me get a good look at you," I demand, pulling back. I clasp her face between my hands and scan each feature with the thoroughness and pride of a mother before I declare, "Your gramps is going to have a coronary over the hair color." Since leaving home, my daughter has bleached some of her chestnut-colored hair and turned it rainbow-hued.

She cups my face before smacking her lips to my forehead. "Let him. It will do him good. He's too stuck in his ways."

Recalling the stilted conversation we had just before I boarded the plane, I caustically say, "You have no idea how true that statement is, darling."

Austyn wraps an arm around my waist. "Let's get your bags, Mama. Then we can head into the city."

"I hired a car so we wouldn't have to deal with a cab," I inform her.

"Good. Once we get you settled, we can swing by my place and get my bag."

"Your bag?"

"Surprise! I'm going to stay with you."

I almost trip stepping onto the escalator down to baggage claim. "There goes any rest I planned on."

"And the room service bill," my daughter agrees cheerfully.

I carefully step off and wait for Austyn to do the same before I tell her, "I wouldn't have it any other way."

Her light blue eyes sparkle. "I know."

The next night after a day of wandering around the city my daughter has fallen in love with, my hotel room at the Plaza palpitates with her nerves. I spent the night adjusting to the new time zone and relaxing while Austyn went off to the first of three sets she planned on playing. But I clearly recall waking just as the sky was lightening when I heard her open the door to my suite.

Today, I just wandered up and down Fifth Avenue, convincing myself I really didn't need anything from the magical stores lining both sides of the street. Even though I lingered longer than I should have admiring a pair of flawless diamond earrings in the window of Cartier, I couldn't force my legs to walk inside the brass doors to inquire about the price. Maybe one day I can justify splurging on something like that just for myself.

By the time I got back, Austyn had ordered up lunch. I caught her up on the things she's missed in Texas: work, our family, and old friends. She laughed when I passed along her grandfather's message about security and growled when I reluctantly shared what happened with Sheriff Lewis. "When is he going to realize you're a grown woman?"

"I am? Somehow I thought I was pigeonholed into being a daughter and mother forever," I murmured.

She flung a french fry in my direction. "Cute. One day, you're going to be knocked sideways by a man who realizes you're so much more than that."

"It hasn't happened yet, baby."

"Doesn't mean it won't."

"Bet it happens to you first."

Austyn snickered. "Doubtful." Then she caught the time on the small gold clock practically buried beneath our plates. "Geez, is that the time? We need to start getting ready."

With that, we each took over one of the suite's two bathrooms to get ready.

Now, fully dressed and ready to leave, I'm calmly relaxing on the couch as I fondly watch Austyn tap out a rhythm on a counter, then a glass, before picking up her guitar and strumming a few notes before she settles and starts jamming to something only she can hear. Such talent in such tiny little hands. The song takes on a Spanish flair that reminds me of the serenading mariachi musicians who play at our favorite tapas restaurant back home in Texas.

Only Austyn plays so much better than anyone I've ever met. Well, save one.

I'm startled by the abrupt end to the song long before it should. Then again, I think wryly, why should I be? This is my baby girl. She never stayed in one place for long; she dashed from pillar to post. She never could find one music she loved; she fell in love with all of it. And, much to my chagrin, it was often played at decibels way too loud for me to understand much of it.

Tonight, I'm bracing myself for more of the same as she takes the booth at some club called Redemption here in the city. But there's something different about this one, something that suddenly has her flipping over suitcases while screeching, "It's a red boot, damnit."

My eyes dart over toward the chair where she slipped on the first one, something I can very clearly see from where I'm perched on the edge of my chair. After I calmly point out the maroon army boot she's been searching for, I rub my hands up and down my bare arms as Austyn dashes across the room to snatch it up as if a thief was going to break into our room and steal it. "Honey, you seem rather anxious. Why is this event so different than all the other shows you've played? I might be biased as your mother, but you're wonderful."

She whirls on me, her multihued braids flying around her head. "Mama? Really? Are you asking me that right now?"

Oh, where did my little girl with her brown pigtails go? My heart aches for a moment when I remember the mornings before the school bus would arrive and Austyn would sit in my lap patiently for me to do her hair. Now, she's as tall as I am, so smart and mature, and has an exuberance I'm almost eclipsed by.

Much as I was by her father.

Shoving that thought in a box and slamming the lid tightly

closed, I push a little. "Austyn? What's so different about this gig than the others?"

And just like all the other times I've said the word "gig" in my native Texan drawl, since she started playing them regularly after dropping out of college, Austyn giggles. "Mama, you're a nut."

"I appreciate that coming from you, sweetie."

She drops the boot, but I take careful note of where it is, knowing we'll likely have another mad hunt shortly if I don't. Grabbing both of my hands, she squeezes them tightly before confessing, "There were some pretty serious people in the audience last night."

"And there haven't been in the past?" I'm confused. Even though my family supported me having Austyn at seventeen, I willingly gave up a lot of the freedoms I want her to experience. I want her to embrace the highs and lows of life and know that no matter what path life may take her, the people who love her will always stand behind her. Namely, me. I may not always appreciate what she does, but always I will love her.

But for my normally laid-back child to be going off the rails, something big is happening. I lean forward and cup her cheek. Her facial structure is almost a mirror of mine, even if her eyes and lips are his. I let my thumb rub over her cheek when I realize her mind and heart must be as well since they're the only two people I've ever loved with this all-encompassing madness. "Talk to me, Austyn." I've said the words a million and one times since she was a little girl and could understand that I would stand behind her hopes and her dreams. That she could run to me with anything in her heart.

And no matter what, I'd never run away.

"Louie said when I was done that there were some big-name music bloggers." Austyn names the man she described during our chat earlier as "super funny and kind, but so tall, Mama. I think he's even taller than Rodeo Ralph."

And since the restaurant owner in Kensington stands at six and a half feet tall, I had a very clear mental image of this "Louie" I'm due to meet in a few hours.

"Austyn Melissa Kensington, are you starting to have doubts

about the choices you've made?" I do the one thing I know to get my daughter focused. I challenge her.

She tosses her head like a riled filly in the fields of our farm not far from where I met her father twenty years ago. "No, ma'am."

I glance down at my watch. "Then you'd better get a move on, young lady. I believe you said the car was going to pick us up in..."

"Shit. Thirty minutes!" Austyn springs up and dashes off.

"And watch your language! We're not at the club yet," I call after her.

A trill of perfectly pitched laughter precedes "Whatever, Mama."

I flick off an imaginary piece of lint from my black pants before wincing as I hear a crash in the bathroom. "I wonder if my makeup is going to survive Austyn's anxiety," I mutter. Fiddling with a heavy gold ring I slipped on earlier, I try to let go of my own emotions. Not because I'm worried. No, my daughter is able to take on the world and conquer it. But I thought I'd have more precious time before my baby became an adult.

I'm just not ready, even though she's been shouting her intentions since she was seventeen. And who but an audiologist should hear people? The thought has my lips curving as I get to my own feet. The silk of my slacks slides down over my legs, a mere whisper. My deep plum tie-front shirt was approved by my daughter as appropriate for the trendiest nightclub in Manhattan. Pushing up my glasses, I slip in a few necessities into my purse just as Austyn dashes back calling, "You don't need a lot, Mama."

"Oh?" I flip open my wallet and pull out my ID, credit card, and some cash.

"Remember I told you Marco mentioned in passing that everything's on the house? And don't forget the no cell phone rule."

"Right." No cameras are allowed in this mysterious nightclub. I still slip in my other essentials. I refuse to rely on an unknown man's passing words of largesse. "I just hope the security at this place is tight."

"For good reason. Geez, Mama. You wouldn't believe the kind of celebrities that patronize this place." Austyn snatches up her iPad and does a quick survey around the room before asking me impatiently, "Are you ready? We have to go."

Now it's my turn to roll my eyes. "Yes, darling. I've been ready."

Sheepishly, she grins as I stroll to the door in the glittery slingback sandals I'm certain I'll be dying to kick off by the end of the night. "Sorry about the crazy."

I cup her cheek as I pass by her. I rub my thumb over the apple of it. For just a moment, I'm transported back to the moment I first held her in my arms. I forgot in that moment all about the times I asked her father's family about where he was. The certified letters I was advised my father's attorney sent to his address that were returned unopened. I had the most important piece of him I'd ever need.

His child.

Together, we make our way to the elevator, gushing about the opulence of our temporary home away from home. "I really wish you could spend more than a few days here."

I tuck my arm around her waist. "Honey, I'll be back up for almost two weeks at Christmas. I have patients I have to see. Besides, by then we'll know if you're going to be permanently based here in the city," I point out logically.

We step out into the cool November night. I verbally berate myself for not bringing a wrap as the cool air flutters through my thin shirt. Austyn wraps her arm around me and laughs, even as she jumps up and down to keep her legs warm in her miniskirt. "You get used to it, I'm sure."

"I'm not certain how," I respond doubtfully. Fortunately, our car pulls up in the circular drive. And blessedly, there's heat coming out of the vents.

Austyn and I spend the car ride catching up on her last job in Miami. I bemoan, "Why couldn't I visit you there? I could have put on a swimsuit and lounged by the pool."

My daughter chokes on her laughter. "Because then Gramps would have insisted on hiring security to accompany you."

"You're lucky he hasn't with you. This time I think he was serious," I warn her.

"And I still think he's leaning toward Sheriff Lewis because then he won't have to worry about security for you."

I scoff.

"Mom, you're a babe. Want my opinion?"

"Oh, this should be interesting. Go for it."

"I think if you didn't live in the town named after our family, you would have married a long time ago."

I arch a perfectly groomed brow at her. "It's not like I lacked for dates while you grew up."

"Dates, yes. Someone special in your life, no."

"I had you."

"You deserved more," Austyn argues, something she's been doing more and more of late.

"I had the world, Austyn," I correct her, not for the first time. And I also know I'm lying to both of us when I remind her, "I had a family who supported me when I got pregnant with you. I was able to study for and build a fulfilling career. And yes, when it was appropriate, I did enjoy dates."

"You didn't fall in love." Austyn's head turns away when she admits, "I kept waiting for you to. Like Sari's mom and stepdaddy did."

I swallow, trying hard to battle against the ache blooming in my chest. I can't tell my daughter it was impossible to fall in love when I never really fell out of it despite how young I was. Instead, I share, "I'm not opposed to it. If the right man strolls into my life, I promise you I'll give it a chance."

"And I swear I'll compose sonnets to it if you do."

Exasperated, I demand, "Have I been so unhappy? Have you?"

"No, but you're a beautiful, giving woman, Mama. I just want you to know what it's like."

"What what's like?"

"To experience when every second of your soul sings." Austyn reaches over and grips my hand just as we exit the tunnel. "That's what music is like for me."

I don't correct her and tell her I experienced that with her father.

That would just make her more infuriated with the fact the man who produced half of her cells walked out of my life without a word when I was seventeen, leaving me alone to face the speculation and whispers of an entire town, pregnant and alone.

And though I've protected her from the knowledge, maybe it's been because I've seen him cavorting on the covers of every gossip rag without a damn thought to what his daughter might think that has kept me from doing the same.

But right now isn't the time to give her the truth. I twist my ring back and forth, the streetlights glinting off the matching one hanging from around my daughter's neck—a gift I bought us both for her eighteenth birthday. The inscription I had put inside was *Nothing else matters but us.*

The first time Austyn asked me about her father, she was fifteen. And all she asked was whether he was a good man. It was right after I had seen a picture of Beckett on the cover of some tabloid with a singer from some band. They were wrapped around each other in ways that should have been kept in a bedroom. Hell, maybe they were in a bedroom.

"He was," I told her truthfully.

"Will you tell me more about him?" Beckett's eyes in my face looked at me pleadingly.

Warring emotions pulsated through me. And what came out of my mouth was almost desperate. "When you're eighteen, you can ask me anything you want—including his name. Until then, I'll just say this. He won't be back in our lives."

That's when I knew a pain worse than Beckett leaving. Because I saw him leave my daughter too.

PAIGE

I can't believe I'm IN at #Redemption! Now I can see what all the buzz is about with this #Kensington. Hey @CuTEandRich3 are you still waiting in line? Hahaha!

— @PRyanPOfficial

"Are you sure there's nothing else I can get you before we begin letting in some of the patrons?" Marco Houde's deep voice, with its hints of Paris nights whispering through it, comes from behind me. I turn and smile into his handsome face and feel nothing.

Absolutely nothing.

Not even when he lifts my left hand and observes quietly, "I still find it difficult to believe you're Kensington's mother. You don't look much older than she is."

I pull my hand away gently before joking, "The color in her hair didn't set us apart?"

"You could carry the same look quite easily, Dr. Kensington."

Not completely immune to the flattery, I blurt out, "Paige. That's my first name."

"Please make it Marco." He lifts a hand and stops a passing wait-ress, his obsidian eyes not wavering from my face. "Dr. Kensington's tab is being picked up by the club tonight."

"Of course, sir."

"Thank you, Donna."

"Do you need anything right now, Dr. Kensington?" she inquires politely.

I've been drinking water, but I decide tonight's a night for a little recklessness. Turning to Marco, I ask, "What would you recommend?"

"Please bring Dr. Kensington tonight's specialty."

Donna offers me a quick smile before bustling off. When she does, I demand, "What did you just order me?"

"It's called 'Liquid Lingerie.'"

Gulp. Deciding it's time to make myself clear, I inform him, "I don't mix business with pleasure, Mr. Houde."

"I wasn't aware we had any business together, Dr. Kensington."

I hold up my hand and state firmly, "My daughter is my business. I put her hopes and dreams ahead of my own."

Something shifts across Marco's face. "I hope your daughter real-izes the treasure she has in you."

"I like to think it's the other way around," I point out gently as the music begins to play. Wincing, I reach into my pocket for a pair of disposable earplugs. I offer a pair to Marco. "Would you like some?"

He throws back his head and roars with laughter just as Donna returns with my drink—a deep cranberry red to match the walls. Marco reaches for that, as well as the water bottle on the tray, before thanking her. While he holds both drinks, I quickly pinch the foam ear guards and slip them into my ear. I sigh in relief once they're in place. Reaching for my drink, I ask, "What's in this?"

"Simply a cranberry martini." Just as I'm about to take a sip, Marco places a hand gently on my wrist to stay me. "Shall we toast?"

"All right." I wait while he opens his water. "How about to a long and lucrative relationship between you and my daughter?"

"To fruitful business relationships." Our drinks come together as the music changes and, if I'm not mistaken, gets louder. I can only hope Austyn has her headphones on in the booth. When I say as much to Marco, he grins. "Definitely a mother. It's attractive on you, Paige."

I roll my eyes before turning to look over the railing at the people congregating on the dance floor. Then, before I can stop myself, I ask, "What level acoustic fabric do you use to reduce the sound to help with your patrons' hearing?"

Marco barks out another quick laugh before joining me at the rail and walking me through the soundproofing procedures he and his partner—the enormously tall but softhearted Louie—undergo to ensure they retain their proper licenses. After a while, where I make a few suggestions for improvement, like adjusting the speaker location and installing a limiter on the amplifier, that he takes into consideration, he excuses himself to deal with a VIP at the door.

I lose myself in the club and the music for an untold amount of time.

It's like a wicked fairy tale come to life, I think. Dark mulberry velvet—what I now know to be ridiculously expensive velvet acoustic fabric—drapes every available surface. What's not covered in fabric twinkles. Every time the spotlights twist and turn on the crystals in the room, they glitter like shiny new diamonds.

The club is luxurious in a way I've never experienced in my entire life, and I grew up blessed by a father who showered me with love and provided our family with ample money. But in the end, we lived in a small town. I spin in a slow circle, catching sight of some exhibitionist dancers. This wasn't available in the tiny town of Kensington.

Not by a long shot.

An old saw about not being in Kansas anymore floats in my head. *Wrong state, Paigey,* I can hear my father snap, his Texan pride leaping at me. No, I'm not.

Austyn begins laying her own tracks over Toto. My hips sway back and forth in time to the heavy thumping of beat of the drums. Then her powerful voice—prerecorded—comes out over the microphone, singing the popular song in French, just as guttural.

Austyn's alto rips down into the soul, somehow reminding the people listening to her there's more out there. Her lilting tone layered on top of the original makes the crowd think the song's about two lovers separated instead of what David Paich himself stated, which was that it was about a young man's love of a continent.

But here, in this club where I'm drinking a cranberry vodka martini out of a glass I easily recognize as Waterford with a name that exudes sexuality, the crowd goes wild. Then again, ever since high school, they always have when my daughter plays.

My smile splits my face in two as the warmth of motherly pride washes over me. I can't wait until Austyn's break where I can tell her I'm so glad I flew here to be with her. But just as the song ends and the next one picks up, I hear from right behind me, "...Beckett Miller."

And all the warmth I felt a moment ago crystalizes into absolute fear.

No. It's not possible.

What the hell is he doing here? Tonight of all nights? Fury makes me whirl around to find two girls who are wearing almost identical sequined dresses. "I deeply apologize. But did you just say something about Beckett Miller?" I ask. I keep my voice pitched low, knowing I have less of a chance of being overheard.

"Oh, my God, yes. He's coming through the VIP entrance," one says dreamily.

"All that inked hotness..." The other begins to fan herself.

I want to fan myself, too, but to stop the nausea churning my stomach. Now, I really wish I'd stuck to water. But only one thought pulsates through my mind.

Get to Austyn.

"Right. Do you know how to find Marco?" I inquire politely.

"Talk about hotness," Number One says.

"I think I see... Yeah, he's down on the dance floor. You can't miss him." Number Two points past me.

I whirl around and find she's right. Marco's gliding across the dance floor like he's made for it. Damn, I curse inwardly. It was too much to hope he'd be making a lap. "Thanks for your help."

"Hey, no problem. Where are you from? Love your accent," Number Two yells out as I scooch past them.

"Texas," I call back. But I quickly forget about the two girls not much older than my daughter. I scan the top level for stairs and stride to them as quickly as I can. Making my way down them in the blasted sandals, I find myself on the fringes of the dance floor.

In what feels like forever but is actually seconds, Marco is in front of me. "Paige, what's wrong?"

"I need to speak with Austyn."

His eyes drift upward to the DJ booth. "She's due for a break in a few moments. Come, dance with me, then I'll take you up to her."

"No, I'll just...wait!" I'm tugged onto the dance floor just as Joan Jett comes blaring from the speakers. *Oh Austyn, you have no idea how perfect this song is right now.* But I don't have much time to relish the soul-deep connection I have with my daughter because I'm too worried about the fact I need to get to her. Because my time just ran out here in a club while she's working.

I'm not certain who I hate the most in this moment as I'm being whirled and twirled around the dance floor: the patrons of Redemption who stand back to watch the little show Marco's putting on, Marco himself for not directly taking me to my daughter, or myself for sparing Austyn the name of her father all these years so she didn't grow up with a festering bitterness I had no way to address despite the love we Kensingtons showed her.

It's not her fault her father left town and never looked back. Not once.

It's not her fault that despite my falling pregnant at seventeen, he never acknowledged his daughter. Ever.

It's not her fault her father made it his life's mission to appear on the cover of every tabloid once he "made it" in the music industry. Unable to know myself what was truth or fiction, I chose to shield her from it all.

But tonight, I'm not going to let Beckett Miller ruin my baby's life just by showing up at the same club. He had a chance to be a father. He's had nineteen years to show up.

Tonight is not the chance he gets to pick up the instrument and determine if he can play it. Not when it's my daughter who wrote the lyrics to the tune when she first cried after she came out of my body.

I'll be damned if I let him.

BECKETT

Not nice at all, @PRyanPOfficial! Remember those tix to Brendan Blake? At least the line's moving (Taps foot impatiently). But, OMG! Beckett Miller just strolled up! And I got a photo! Suck it, Ryan!

— @CuTEandRich3

I'm swarmed by people all vying for my attention the moment I step across the threshold. I'm just grateful Louie came in with me as well as Kane. "Thanks, guys," I tell them both gratefully as they lead me to the VIP section.

Kane nods before heading out the side door to watch the stairs that lead to the dance floor.

"You know, it would be helpful if you called in advance, Becks. Then I could plan for the..."

"Handsome motherfucker about to grace your presence?" I offer.

"No, the onslaught of screeching," Louie grumbles even as he moves around to the bar to pour us each a vodka on the rocks.

I chuckle as our glasses make that distinctive ping that fine crystal does. I've learned that over the years since I left Texas. I've learned so many things about money I never would have learned if I stayed.

Including the simple matter of having it.

After taking a large glug of my drink, I wipe the back of my mouth on my hand. "So, tell me about this DJ. Decent?"

"She makes me want to stop listening to the crap you put out."

My eyebrow quirks. "Seriously?" Since Louie's always backstage at the shows whenever I'm in town, I don't take the comment seriously, but there's an underlying compliment there he rarely uses.

"Oh yeah. For such a tiny thing, she's got some massive talent."

I flick my eyes upward. "Lou, bud, in comparison to you, I'm tiny."

His gold tooth flashes. "That's true. But this little girl's only up to about here." He aims for a place on his chest that puts her at about five foot six.

"Okay. She is small next to you," I concede.

He just pours himself another drink, ignoring me. I grin. It's rare to be treated just like one of the guys, but when you used to have sweat pouring down your back at music festivals next to someone sweating under the summer sun moving around someone else's drum kit, a bond forms.

And close to twenty years ago, that's what happened when my life first intersected with Louie Scott's, after I hitched a ride out to get away from Kensington and my heinous family. He was a beast on that first summer tour, hauling speakers around like they weighed nothing more than a shoe box. He never cut me any slack, giving me the chance to regain some of my pride. But when we parted, he stopped me to say, "I live in New York. When you're done running, come find me."

I found him working at Club, an exclusive hot spot long before Redemption existed. Even though with my advertising earnings I could have sought him out much sooner, it wasn't until much later I actually did. With Mick and Carly by my side, we hit up the trendy club. Through Wildcard, my music was landing me on charts all over the world. I wanted to see if Louie wanted to be a part of it, but he had a different dream. And together with Marco, they built it.

Louie refills my glass, this time with club soda. "I'm just sayin' last night was one of the best nights we've had. And Marco's take is this little girl might push tonight into being the best night we've had in club history."

I pause in lifting my drink to my lips. "No shit."

"None at all."

"Well, damn." I wander to the front of the VIP area and concentrate not on my old friend but on the music.

I set aside my glass as the tracks laid over one another blend seamlessly together. "She's damn good," I remark.

"Just wait."

A tingle of awareness travels through my spine as song after song plays. I close my eyes and just listen, as always the music grabbing me and hurling me into a metaphysical plane few have the ability to join me on. Unlike the house DJ, this artist somehow manages to almost haunt me, weaving her own music into the original. And yet, unlike others of her kind in a club like this, she doesn't speak. She doesn't use a lot of talk to pump up the crowd. It's all about the music.

I'm about to ask Louie for more information about her for Carys when Toto begins to blast. He shushes me. "I was hoping she'd play this again. Dude, you're in for something. Just listen."

So, I do.

And as the song continues to play, I get the eerie feeling I'm in a haunted hell. Because my heart knows the voice singing in perfect French on the track. She's my soul's one true regret—the only thing I left behind I wish I could have scooped up and carried off into the night they marked me with their words.

Paige.

But her family was Kensington, Texas. Somehow, I knew if I'd made off with the crown princess, they'd have hunted me down and dragged me back. I couldn't have brought her with me. I just couldn't.

Rubbing my arms, I manage to get out, "What is this DJ's name?" I know it's not possible, but I still pray my heart isn't thumping against my rib cage hard enough to alert him.

"Oh, sorry, man. I thought I told you." Louie bends down.

That's when I spy her. At least, I think I do. The damn lights flash on the stairs for a millisecond before they dash away. I snarl in frustration, wanting them to hold in place. She's flying down the stairs toward the dance floor. Marco twirls away from his current partner and approaches her as the song changes to Joan Jett. The two of them glide across the dance floor as if they've danced together before. *How can this be possible?* I shake my head hard to knock some sense into it. There's no way she's here. She's probably back in Texas, married with three kids by now instead of the one daughter I know about. I grab my drink and take another long swig to regain my equilibrium.

Louie says something, but I don't hear him as I swallow furiously. "Sorry, man. Didn't catch that." I rattle my glass, indicating I'm dry.

"On it. But keep listening to Kensington. I'll try to see if I can arrange an introduction before the night's over." He snags my glass and walks away.

And it's a good thing too because my knees give out slightly. *The DJ's name is Kensington?* Wildly, I search the dance floor for the woman who I'm now certain is Paige. But she's gone. Just like she is in my dreams when I wake up.

My head snaps toward the DJ booth. Yeah, I'll take that introduction. Because unless I'm mistaken, that's her daughter in that booth.

An arc of pain I wasn't expecting strikes me as Louie approaches with my drink. The music changes. I frown as it isn't the same caliber of what was just on.

He laughs. "Sorry to offend your auditory senses, Becks, but even DJs get a potty break."

I flush with embarrassment. "Right."

"Kensington will be back on in fifteen."

I throw out, "Maybe I'll do a lap around the club in the meanwhile."

Louie groans. "Must you? You know you'll just be mobbed, and I'll have to be the one to shove people away. I've been having such a good night."

"Suck it up," I voice unfeelingly. I need to do something with this energy, or I'm going to go mad and do something stupid that will land me on the front page of every tabloid. Like approach the new wunderkind DJ and ask, *How's your mother? And your father? Are they happy? Does your mother ever mention me?*

Because that would be a really brilliant move, Beckett, I think to myself derisively.

Louie strides past me and warns Kane what we plan on doing. Kane moves into the VIP area so he can keep an eye on the place while we walk around. "All right, rock star. Let's do your lap."

I clap a hand on his shoulder and give it a squeeze. "Thanks, my friend."

"You'd better be glad I like you, Becks," he grumbles.

Within minutes of stepping out of the VIP area, we're immediately swarmed by my fans. Even though I normally appreciate the seclusion of my own area, right now I need to be distracted. From myself.

Or I just might go mad until I get that introduction.

PAIGE

I had the nicest dream. On one side of me was Marco Houde, and on the other was Beckett Miller. Oh wait, it wasn't a dream. That was me for about .02 seconds at the bar at #Redemption last night. Glory be, I almost had to go home and change. Then I slapped myself silly when I realized I'd never get back in.

— Sexy&Social, All the Scandal You Can Handle

We're in the town car heading back toward the Plaza with Austyn chattering away. She's high as a kite about the tracks she threw down, the people she got to meet after the show. And since I hung out in the booth with her the rest of the night, I know one of them wasn't Beckett.

Thank God for small miracles.

Austyn's wired as we step from the car. "Want to go grab something to eat? Check out the modern sculpture park?" She twirls around, hair and skirt flying out in all directions.

Exasperated and emotionally on edge, I'm firm when I shoot her down. "Austyn, it's four o'clock in the morning. I've been up since yesterday at 8:00 a.m. I want to find my bed—" Where I'm certain I'll be worrying instead of sleeping. "—not traipsing around the streets of New York. Cut your mother some slack. We can do both of those things in a few hours."

Her face falls just like it did the first time I told her she couldn't hunt around in the Kensington fields to find a dilapidated piano that was the sole remaining remnants of a fire that burned down our original family homestead. The very same piano her father dared to carve his initials and mine on just before he took my virginity next to it, swearing, "I'll love you forever, Paige." Acid churns in my stomach. I reach for her hand. "I was so proud of you tonight, baby. But I need to sleep. Then, I want you to show me everything that you love about this place. I want to see New York through your eyes."

Excitement replaces disappointment. "You got it, Mama. I hope you brought comfy shoes."

"Darling, I'm on my feet most of every day. There are few pairs I own that aren't."

Austyn grins. "So, not to be nosy, but I can't say I didn't notice you and Marco Houde on the dance floor earlier."

"Austyn," I warn.

"He's a dish," she declares as we reach the elevator bank.

"Not my type."

"Hot? Wealthy? Single?"

I use the key card to access our floor before answering with complete honesty. "A smooth talker. Been there, had one, don't need another. And that man has those signals flashing off him like crazy."

Austyn is quiet until we enter our room. But the moment the door closes, she asks, "Mama, you were seventeen when you had me. I know you don't regret it. But so much was stolen from you. Do you resent it?" *Do you resent me?* Her underlying question is obvious.

I step right up to my daughter and press my hand to either side of her cheeks. I stare into her eyes—his eyes—and speak the truth. "I wasn't ready for you, but you're a miracle, Austyn. Never, ever doubt my love for you. Every decision I made from the moment I knew I was carrying you was made with your well-being first."

I love when she smiles, and I feel it against the palms of my hands. "Even when you argued against Gramps to cash out my college fund?"

"Austyn, your talent is undeniable. I've experienced nothing like it." Except maybe once. "If I didn't support you, what would you have done?"

Her full lips curve upward. My heart thumps against my chest. I've had that smile in my heart since I was barely seventeen. I just pray I don't lose it when I tell her what I now know I'll need to. "I'd have done it anyway."

"Right. You're just as stubborn and hardheaded as the rest of us Kensingtons. This way, I don't worry as much if you're okay. Now—" I yawn deliberately. "—can we save the rest of our heart-to-heart for after coffee?"

"Of course."

I lean in and kiss Austyn. "Good night, baby." I turn to make my way to my room, but I'm stopped when Austyn calls out my name. "Yes?"

"Were you really proud tonight?" Anxiety and a need for reassurance twist her features.

It's a shot to the heart because the look is quintessentially her father's. Every time he'd compose a new song on the piano in the field, he'd expose the same vulnerability. But where I had a few months of lies with her father, I know our daughter truly values my opinion. "So proud, baby. You're magic."

Her face relaxes into a grin. "Sleep well, Mama."

"Dream big, baby," I return.

"Don't worry. I already am." Then Austyn disappears into the door behind her.

I know. And I want nothing and no one to harm those dreams. On that thought, I drag myself wearily into the room.

✦

I twist and turn in the bed before I fall into a space ripe for dreams.

I'm determined to find it today.

Daddy told the story again at the dinner table last night. Ethan, Jesse, and I all loved the fact that he brought Mama out to the original Kensington homestead to propose. But he said the location was a secret. It wasn't written down, and the markers were only passed along to sons.

I call bullshit. She was my mother too, damnit. I should get to see where Daddy proposed. After all, if it wasn't for me, Ethan, and Jesse...

I put my head down and ride. Hard. And I think of the clues that Daddy unwittingly gave away.

We rode for what felt like hours.

There's the most beautiful stone fence nearby we sat on for hours. Just talkin', so get that thought out of your heads.

It springs up on you like magic.

When I lay awake last night, recalling every word Daddy spoke, I stared at the picture of my mother I keep on my bedside, willing her to tell me. Please, Mama, I want to know. I need to know.

And as Sunflower gallops over the hard earth, through the fields she was named after, I hear disjointed music. Reining her in, I pause, trying to make certain I'm not just hearing something my heart is wishing for.

Then, there's a discordant slam that carries over the wind due east that makes my head jerk. I begin walking Sunflower in the direction of the somewhat harmonious music. My pulse starts hammering against my ribs when I realize we're passing through an old stone wall, painstakingly put together by my ancestors.

And maybe twenty yards away, someone's playing the ancient piano.

Gotcha.

I wake up with a jerk, breathing hard in the hotel room. Then I hear screaming, and I race from my bed, not bothering to put on a robe. "Austyn, what is it?" I yell.

"Mama! I'm in all the news feeds. People loved the show last night!" She's holding her phone like it's the winning lottery ticket.

I clutch the back of the sofa, trying to get my bearings from the dream and my daughter's exuberance. "I thought you were being stabbed."

"No, that would be a different kind of screaming. I could demonstrate."

I groan. "Please don't. I think this hotel is lovely and would like to stay in it a few more nights."

Austyn is about to retort when her phone beeps with an incoming text. "Crap."

I frown. "What is it?"

"You know the guy who was checking my sound last night? Trevor?"

"I met about eighty new people yesterday, Austyn."

"Fair point. He was the guy walking around the club with the mic making sure the sound was good from random locations in the club. If it was off, I could adjust it from the booth."

I recall the fair-haired young man in glasses holding an iPad. "Yes. Now I recall him. What's wrong?"

"Slipped off the sidewalk this morning when he was trying to read the reviews. Ankle's jacked. He's at Urgent Care. I bet I can't find anyone who can do that on such short notice."

"Is he professionally trained?" I query as I go over to the room service menu and debate whether we should stay in or go out to eat.

"No, just a friend. The software is actually a lot like your... Mama." Her tone of voice isn't lost on me.

"No. Anything is a no before coffee. You know better than that."

"Then let me take you to breakfast, and then I'll ask," she practically purrs. Her expression, so dejected before, has already lightened considerably.

Crap. I know that whatever it is, I'm going to say yes.

⊕

"You know I didn't pack for a second night of going out, Austyn," I say as I stir my coffee. I can feel myself caving over eggs Benedict.

Austyn waves her hand as she chews. After swallowing, she declares, "I have a dress for you at my apartment, Mama."

I raise an eyebrow at my daughter's multihued catsuit with a sheer duster over it before glancing down at my more conventional jeans and corduroy blazer. Austyn clarifies. "More traditional clothes, Mama. Here in the city, I can wear whatever. It's not like at home."

Reaching across the table, I capture her hand. "Honey, don't be anyone but who you are whether that's here or at home. I love you whether that's with multicolored hair and fun clothes or not."

"Then you won't mind if I get a tattoo."

My breath hitches slightly as I recall the ink that now decorates her father's skin. It brings up everything I swore last night I would tell her. "Austyn..."

She laughs. "Just kidding, Mama. I'm not ready to get ink of any kind yet. I believe that if you're going to do something that permanent, it needs to mean something."

"That's not..." I begin, but we're interrupted by the waiter offering us a refill on coffee. And when he departs, Austyn launches into an explanation of the sound software.

I frown thoughtfully. "It sounds like when I conduct an audiometry exam."

"Only instead of examining one small patient, think of the entire club as your patient."

"And the software is on your iPad?"

"Yes. It's the only software on there. I had to show it to Louie and Marco before they'd let it into the club." She scrunches her face.

"Dramatic much?" I chastise her.

"It was annoying, Mama. I had enough to flip out about with getting ready for the tour that I didn't want to wipe my device."

"I think that instead of sightseeing today, our time would be better spent at the Apple Store." I dab my mouth with a napkin. I reach for my purse to pull out my wallet when I get a good look at the tears on Austyn's face. "What is it?"

"I'm so lucky. Other friends of mine—like Trevor—they don't have their families' support as they try for their dreams. They're here eating fifty-cent meals because their parents said if they wanted to chase this lunacy, they were cut off. And here you are, stepping up. Having my back."

"I always will. No matter what. Under any circumstance. You're a part of me."

"I hope you know, Mama, I don't take a single thing you've sacrificed for me for granted. Not a damn thing." Her light blue eyes blaze at me. "And I know you tried to contact him the only way you knew how over the years. You need to know that even if *he* was in our lives, he couldn't have been a better parent, a better person, than you are."

Tell her now, my conscience nudges me. But I hold my tongue for the moment. Austyn will ask when she's ready. It's up to her to ask.

But what will happen when she does, I don't know.

But I suspect it will be a good thing I'm heading home so I can shatter once again in my safe place.

BECKETT

Did Beckett Miller sleep in his clothes, or were they strewn about someone else's floor? He was without his usual flair this morning outside Rockefeller Center.

— **Moore You Want**

The last forty-eight hours have been some of the most heinous of my life. And I've endured quite a bit in thirty-eight years. I recall Angie's words when I told her about my suspicions. "How are you still standing? How are you not shrieking this to the world yet?"

I don't know how I didn't crush her fingers when I choked out, "I'm trying to do the right thing. That's why I came here first. My inclination is to go charging in like a raving lunatic and demand answers, but I can't because of who I am. The reputation I've cultivated. I won't do that until I know for sure. I could be wrong, Angie, and if I am, I could do so much damage. I need you to get Carys out of whatever she's in today. I need your help."

That was yesterday after Carys had dealt with a potential nude photo scandal by her other mega-star client, Erzulie. I sent the singer a voice text message. *Thanks for the break. At least I'm not on the front page today.*

Erzulie promptly sent me the middle finger back.

I followed up by recommending to her that she contact Hudson Investigations immediately for assistance—that they could likely figure out who did this in a matter of hours.

She promised she would, and I began to relax. That was, until I went to Redemption.

And my heart fought for a way to beat.

How could my body forget what being close to Paige Kensington was like? From the first time I saw her standing on the foundation of her ancestors, peering down at me like a queen, I was enraptured. I'd already lived a thousand lives in hell, and she was the balm to all of my wounds. But I left her behind despite promising her I'd take her with me. And swearing that oath by taking a liberty I never should have.

Louie and I were approaching the entrance of the sound booth on our way back to the VIP section as Marco was escorting the woman he'd been dancing with toward it. And like a perfect storm, the door was flung open. A young woman looked quickly in both directions before a smile spread across her face.

Then she dashed off into the woman's arms.

Arms I'm certain I've been held in beneath the burning Texas sun after I made slow, sweet love to her.

Arms that tightened around me as I promised to love her forever.

A vow that I've never broken as much as it may appear otherwise.

Paige Kensington whatever-her-name-is has held the entirety of my heart since the moment she listened to the school outcast about his home life and offered some real suggestions about how to make it better.

The younger of two women spun the older around in a circle, and I got a good look at the young woman's face. My mind hurled me back to the sunflower fields surrounding Paige's family's old homestead, despite the rainbow hue of her hair. There wasn't a doubt in my mind she's Paige's daughter.

But what almost toppled me over was when the spotlight hit her face and I saw her eyes. A trick of the light in the club or, God help me, are the eyes in that face the same light blue I see in the mirror every damn day?

Pacing back and forth at my condo, I anxiously wait for word about Angie's and Ward's—Carys's younger brother and partner—night at Redemption.

Yesterday, they agreed—albeit Ward reluctantly—to head to the nightclub to talk with the young DJ. During a long planning session that had me sharing about my past, and not just the parts that included Paige, we all agreed my making an approach wasn't the wisest decision. Hell, I have to have two guards at any time following my movements because of who I am. I've always resented the necessity of my security team, but no more so than right now.

I can't take it anymore. I snatch my phone and text Angie. *What happened last night?*

There's an interminable wait before I get a response from Carys, not Angie. We're on our way in. She's taking notes. Take a deep breath and meet us at the office in an hour.

An hour. I can handle that. But first: *Is Angie okay?* Angela Fahey has suffered due to her own past from the vicious hands of the press. I thought I understood her backbone and the word "humility" until yesterday when she volunteered to do this for me.

Carys's response of *She will be* doesn't do much to reassure me. "Crap," I say aloud. I immediately head out the door after calling for security.

✦

My nerves have me bouncing my leg up and down in the limo. I haven't been this anxious since the first time I took the stage, opening for Mastodon. The stop and go of the morning traffic in Midtown churns my morning espresso so hard, I'm terrified it's going to come back up as a frappe.

Then, as my driver pulls to the curb, I see them, the paparazzi. As soon as they see my vehicle, they swarm to it like locusts.

"Fucking hell, not today." I quickly slide on my sunglasses to protect my eyes from the flashes that still manage to pop through the blackened window like flashes of lightning.

"Mr. Miller, please don't exit the vehicle until we secure the space," Kane calls out.

"Right. I know the drill." I should after years of this shit.

Kane nods before wedging himself out of the vehicle. I hear shouts, screams, cheering. Taking a few deep breaths, I prepare myself for the moment that door's flung open. Because then I no longer get to be just me. I'm a commodity. I gave up everything to be this, to have this.

And this is a large part of the price.

But was I the only one who paid? The thought works insidiously into my mind. Thoughts of the two women at the club flash into my mind. And I can't generate the trademark smile I normally greet the paps with. Instead, I duck my head and allow Kane to get me from the limo to the door. "Thanks, man."

"Just doin' the job, sir," my shadow addresses me.

"For all that's holy, Kane. Didn't I say it clear enough the first twenty times? It's Becks. If you can't manage that, Beckett. I mean, you know everything about my life."

"No offense...Beckett. But there's some things I don't *want* to know about your life." He leans in. "I mean, really? Of all the things you could be addicted to...decades music?"

My lips twitch. This was what I needed to face the meeting ahead of me. "Some of the best lyricists in the world rocked it out in the '80s and '90s, man."

His head shakes back and forth tragically like I've ruined his image of rock stars. I clap a hand on his shoulder. "I'll probably be a few hours. And no, I won't leave the building."

Just then, a Muzak version of one of my favorite singers comes over the lobby sound system. A slow grin crosses my face as a pained expression transforms Kane's. "And with that, I'm out."

I whistle as I pass Security and head into the elevator. When I enter the office, Angie's not at her desk. Shrugging, because I'm expected and I've done this a million times before, I fling open the heavy wood door to the inner sanctum. Muted voices are heard from the direction of the conference room. It isn't until I get close that I hear Angie say to Ward, "Thank you. That was sweet."

I laugh as I saunter in. "Ward? Sweet? Jesus, did Houde pump some kind of herbal essence into the air last night?" Then I get a good look at the deep bruising beneath Angie's eyes, and my voice hardens. I knew this was going to be too much for her with her background. "Screw it. I don't care if the damn paps make up secrets to sell about me. Someone better tell me why Angie looks like she didn't sleep a wink."

Ward jumps in. "We had a bit of an altercation last night."

"I hope you punched the fucker who got in her face."

"Kind of hard to do that to myself," Ward says sheepishly.

I've been looking for an excuse to expend some of the frustration over this situation. I back my arm to throw a punch. "Then allow me."

But just as my arm is about to swing forward, I feel like I've pissed on myself. I yelp and jump backward. I glance down, and the front of my white silk shirt and trousers are wet with Angie's coffee. She yells at me. "Stop it, Beckett! It's *fine*! I handled it. Okay?"

Her fingers poke me in the chest, stunning me. We've been friends for years, but it isn't until recently she's been comfortable with any type of physical affection—hell, any kind of touch for that matter. She jabs a finger directly in my heart. "And just to let you know, you have *much* bigger issues to be worrying about."

The tension that had been stripped snaps my spine straight. "Why?" What did she find out last night? Is Kensington my daughter? My heart trips in my chest faster than any drumbeat Carly's ever managed to rip out on a set during her solos.

Angie doesn't pull her punches when she says, "I could be looking at her right now."

Somehow through the murky tension that fills the room at her declaration, I manage, "You spoke with Kensington, then?"

"No." There's a slight pause where I try to grapple with the ramifications of what she's saying. "But I met her mother."

"Paige? You talked to Paige?" This might possibly be worse. The familiar feelings of longing rise up inside of me. I quickly tamp them down to focus on the conversation.

Angie confirms, "She's lovely." Her eyes are trying to communicate something more to me, but I'm not getting it. I'm still struggling with the fact it was Paige at Redemption. With her daughter. I don't know what to think, what to feel.

Carys and Ward are involved in a small squabble to the side. I don't tune in until Carys asks gently, "Did you get the NDA?"

Angie shakes her head.

"What happened?" I manage a tortured whisper. Then, realizing I sound like a selfish bastard, I cut her off before she can speak. "No, don't say anything else. Thank you, Angie. I realize it must have been terrifying for you. You have no idea how much I appreciate it."

Chest heaving, lips trembling, Angie whispers, "It wasn't. It was incredible. Exhilarating. Everything I thought it would be, until—"

"Until it wasn't?" I shoot a dirty look at Ward, who doesn't say anything to me but has a lot to say to Angie.

But as the story starts to unfold, I realize Angie's words hold true for something else.

My life.

Because I'm now more certain than ever that when I left Texas to escape my abusive family, I left my then seventeen-year-old girlfriend pregnant. And it appears she raised our baby to become a remarkably talented young woman.

"Her name, by the way, is Austyn. That's not available on her website."

A brief flicker of a smile crosses my face. "She followed family tradition, then." At the confusion around the room, I explain, "Paige's family has a long-standing tradition. It's complicated, but whenever a firstborn female child is born, they're named after the city they were born in. Paige told me she was born in Paige, Texas—about forty or so miles from Austin. Her mother was visiting her maternal grandparents. There were...complications. Paige lived; her mother didn't."

"Oh, God. That poor family." Carys reaches for David's hand.

"I guess Austyn was born in an Austin hospital," I conclude.

"Well, Dr. Paige Kensington," Angie begins, but I jump all over that.

"Wait, Paige is a doctor? What kind?"

"An audiologist."

I jerk back, stunned Angie has the answer. "What the hell? Did you two bond in the restroom or something?"

Ward and Angie exchange an amused look. "Something like that. As I was saying, Dr. Kensington loves her daughter tremendously. When I spoke with her, she—Paige—was assisting Austyn with sound. I approached her thinking she was using an iPad in the club which I knew was against the rules."

"Angie, you're too damn smart to work here," I declare.

Carys shoots me a fulminating glare. "Bite your damn tongue, Becks. Or I'll triple your fee for this fiasco."

"How is this my fault?" I yell. For once I didn't instigate the outrageousness that might hit every scandal sheet. No, that's not entirely true, I admonish myself. I fell in love with the perfect girl for me.

And I left her.

Pregnant and alone to raise our daughter.

Christ.

"Are you kidding me right now?" she shouts back.

I send an apologetic glance in her direction before turning back to Angie. "What else did you find out, love?" I'll take anything. Any little bit of information.

"Just that she—Austyn—cashed out her college fund to give this —and I can only assume Paige meant DJ'ing—a try. Oh, and her mother is proud of her."

"The last one I'm not surprised about." But the college one has me frowning. I have a ludicrous amount of money. And if I'm right, then neither Paige nor Austyn ever need to worry about it ever again.

Steepling my hands together, I ask the room at large, "So, what's next? What should I do?"

"Something you're so good at," Carys declares.

Eagerly, I lean forward, awaiting my orders like a young corporal from his general.

"Wait." Carys's words deflate me.

"There has to be something..." I protest.

"Wait, Beckett. We have to do this right. Not just for you, but for that family. There can be no uncertainty. Do you understand me? I need to have someone start looking into things and this isn't a priority for them."

Unfortunately, I do.

PAIGE

Crying in public is something that happens. Don't deny it; it's happened to all of us. We were not surprised to find some of the top places to do so being your car or at airports, but some people seek out the religious section of a bookstore. Really? Over self-help? I'm not judging; I just don't appreciate why one section version another. What's wrong with self-help?

— **Beautiful Today**

Austyn shifts her weight back and forth as we wait for the car that's going to take me back to the airport. We spent the rest of my trip preparing her for the next bit of hers—her tour across varying clubs in different cities with a break over the holidays. "Don't be nervous, baby. You're going to be fantastic. No, miraculous," I reassure her.

She opens her mouth and closes it, a sure sign of nerves.

"Austyn, what is it?"

Her head shakes back and forth.

"Austyn Melissa," I stress her full name.

"Mama, you said I could ask." Her words come out in a rush.

Just then, a black town car pulls up. The driver hops out. "Ms. Kensington?"

"Yes." My voice is weak. But then, I'm answering them both.

"Mama?" Austyn's voice is laced with agony.

I wrap my arms around her and hug her hard. "I'll be here for Christmas. For two weeks."

She buries her head against my shoulder, her lips at my ear. "And we'll talk then?"

"Yes. I'll tell you anything you want to know then." After all, even with my promise, after knowing how close Beckett was, there's no way I won't have her armed with the knowledge of who her father is. Not anymore. I just want to have all of the information with me to substantiate my claims.

"Can you answer a question for me? Just one?"

I inhale sharply. But I whisper, "Yes."

"Do I know him?"

Hesitantly, I nod. After all, who hasn't heard of Beckett Miller?

Then I burst out laughing when she demands irately, "Tell me it wasn't Mr. Stevens, my chemistry teacher. I always thought he perved on you."

"Darling, he's like Gramps's age."

"And who knew if he preyed on some of his students."

I pull back and press a kiss to each cheek. "Trust me, it wasn't him."

"Well, now I can go on this trip happy."

"And that's the only thing I've ever wanted—your happiness." My words are serious.

"I love you, Mama. Save travels." She throws herself back into my arms.

"I love you too, baby. And same to you. I'll meet you back here soon." I hold her tightly, knowing it will all change soon.

Everything will the moment I loosen my arms and she steps away.

But finally I must when the driver clears his throat. I cup Austyn's face and brush the apple of her cheek a final time. "Don't forget to use that new iPad to call your mother on occasion. Or if you can't manage that, an email will suffice."

"I'll even email Gramps to keep him off your back," she vows.

We both laugh before I force myself to move over to the car. I slide into the back, and the door closes. Austyn immediately starts waving, as do I.

I keep up waving until I'm out of the Plaza's circular drive.

Two months. The countdown starts now.

Putting my face in my hands, that's when the tears start to fall in earnest.

⊕

Later that night, I let myself into my home on the outskirts of Kensington. Leaving my bags where they are, I immediately head into my office where I keep a biometric safe.

When Austyn was a teenager, I explained to her I chose to take an extra step to protect the privacy of my patients when I was working on their information at home since there were times I did have celebrity patients. This wasn't a lie as I've treated members of varying Texas sports teams for hearing issues.

But since the safe was only able to be accessed with my fingerprints and passcode, it also gave me a place to store the information about Austyn's birth father.

I don't hesitate to open it now.

The brown accordion folder sits on the very top shelf. I don't touch it—not yet. I don't need to know what's inside. My cheeks flushed the day my father presented me with its contents years ago—first a photo of Beckett and me kissing behind school. Letters from his lawyers to the Millers—at my bequest—after I found out I was pregnant. All sent back unopened, except the very first. That one was never received back. I would understand why when my father's attorney produced a letter originating from the Millers demanding a monthly stipend to keep quiet about who the baby's father is.

Canceled checks they cashed every month once Beckett became a household name.

I haven't looked inside it for years—not since the Millers died in a gas explosion when Austyn was five due to a faulty line in the trailer park. It was a tragic accident that impacted more than one family. While I didn't feel much at their demise, other than relief that my father could stop paying them hush money about who my baby's father was, I expected Beckett to return to attend his parents' funeral. Stoically, I prepared myself and my family to deal with him then, but he never showed.

Slamming the safe shut, I move over to my file cabinet. I pull out a folder of news clippings from Dallas and Houston showing him fronting the stage to sold-out shows, but never here. So many clippings of Beckett himself—some good, some bad. All of them from the front page where they couldn't be avoided when I saw them in line at the grocery store. Or when something particularly crazy hit the national news. He never even returned to the Austin area with his band, I think bitterly.

No, he abandoned me and the child he must have known he made.

Now, it's been twenty years since I've seen him—nineteen years of raising our daughter with that microscopic piece of hope in my heart that somehow the boy I loved will emerge from that public shell and return. "There's something you don't realize, Beau, Beckett, whomever the hell you are now. I'm no longer the naive girl who trusted her body to the first boy who told her 'I love you.' Motherhood changed me. The moment the light of hope dies in my daughter's eyes when she realizes who her father is, so will my love for you."

I move away from my desk and leave my study to go get my bags.

And while I'll finally be free, what will be the cost?

PAIGE
DECEMBER

Alison Freeman-Marshall, COO and General Counsel for Amaryllis Events, was spotted having a breakfast meeting with the social coordinator for the Museum of History. Could this be where Amaryllis Designs is hosting its next Fashion Week?

— Jacques Yves, Celebrity Blogger

"Oh, my God! Mama! You are not going to believe this!" Austyn shouts through FaceTime.

"Believe what?" I'm curled up in my lounge chair reading.

"I was contacted to have a conversation for legal representation."

I toss the book aside as my blood pounds through my veins. "Like an agent?"

"I don't know. It must be. God, Mama. I'm over the moon!" Austyn's dancing, still holding on to her iPad.

"Austyn, stop moving. You're making me dizzy," I caution.

"Oops. Sorry! I feel like a soda that's been opened where all the little bubbles come rushing to the top."

"Or like the bottle of champagne I see in the background? Hmm?"

She shifts to the right, and the champagne and glasses disappear.

"You didn't see those. You don't know what those are. I don't know how those got there."

I burst out laughing. "It was a good night?"

"Mama, this whole tour has been a rush. I know it seems like it was a whim, but the more we're getting media attention from these social influencers, the more the places are jammed. It's such an amazing high." Austyn's eyes are sparkling.

"Is it everything you wanted?" I ask softly.

"Almost."

"What's missing?"

"You. I want you to be here, to feel this."

"I did that night at Redemption, baby."

"It's not like that, Mama. This...it's different now. Like I was born to do this."

Pride and searing jealousy fight each other for the premier place in my heart. Pride wins. "Then that's all I want for you."

We talk for a few more minutes about her upcoming trip to San Antonio, then Chattanooga, and how "I'll be back in warm weather finally."

"You chose that, baby. Aren't you the one who said you'd adjust to New York?"

"But New York isn't Milwaukee. Or Detroit. Or..."

I cut in. "I get the idea. You're cold and you're busy." Then an idea hits me. "Do you want Gramps to check out this attorney?"

"Hell no. He'd have them investigated and up on a rack before I could make a decision about them. I'll look into them when I have the time."

I reach for my iPad. "Hold on a moment, baby. Satisfy your mother's curiosity. What's the name of the attorney?"

"Mom," Austyn groans.

"Austyn, if you're turning into a big name, let's weed out the ambulance chasers, shall we? I'm just doing a web search."

"Oh. Okay. Let me get the letter. Close your eyes."

"Why?" I say in exasperation.

"Because it's in my room. And, um..." Austyn flushes to the roots of her hair.

And my baby isn't alone. "Austyn, the smart thing would be to put the tablet down and then to go get the letter," I manage to grit out.

"Right. This is why you're the mom." She drops her iPad next to the champagne bottle with the two glasses.

"I'm also the mom who got knocked up at seventeen, so I hope like hell you listened to all my lectures about protection," I mutter.

Soon she's back and scooping up her device. "Here it is. I'm so glad Travis had our mail forwarded."

I clear my throat delicately. "Is Travis..."

Austyn averts her eyes. "No."

"Is that a bad thing?" I wonder aloud.

"No. It's just...no." Her voice is firm.

"For a later time, perhaps?" I suggest.

"Christmas," she agrees. "Oh, the name of the law firm is LLF, LLC."

I type it into my tablet and get a very slick website. I quickly scan it and read the partner profile. My eyes shoot to my hairline when I read the profile of the senior partner, Carys Burke. "It says here the senior partner used to work as the chief counsel of Wildcard Records..."

"I'm going to faint, Mama. Wildcard? Are you kidding me?"

"What does the letter say, Austyn?"

"Hold on. I'll scan it and send it to you."

"You still have to teach me that," I mutter.

"At..."

"Christmas. I know." I wait while my daughter scans the letter and sends it to me in a text. "I'm putting you on hold, honey. I want to read this."

"Okay."

I click on the message and start reading.

Request for Confidentiality
Re: DJ - Kensington
Dear Ms. Kensington,

As an experienced entertainment law firm with close to twenty-five years' combined experience working with exclusive clients, your work sparked our interest not only because of the talent you so clearly demonstrate but because of the legal aspect in protecting it.

My firm brings a comprehensive set of skills we believe will be critical to protecting your best interests including contract negotiations, social media mediation, and talent management. In addition to my well-developed resume, my interpersonal skills and compassion have afforded me with excellent decision-making skills I feel would be an excellent guide for you.

I would appreciate the opportunity for us to sit down face-to-face at your earliest convenience to determine if representation is something you seek and if LLF, LLC is the right firm to do so. Of note, it is important to understand that while references are available on our website, specifics about what services we offer to those clients will not be discussed without a non-disclosure agreement being completed.

Thank you for your time and consideration,

Carys Burke

Senior Partner

LLF, LLC

I pick up my tablet and click on the discreet link titled "Clients." I immediately recognize the heavy hitters this woman and her firm represent: Zappata, Mastadon, Erzulie. Then, I let out a gasp when I spy his name just above that of his band's.

Beckett Miller.

The tablet falls uselessly out of my hands. "How? Why? Why now?" I moan aloud. Why does he suddenly give a damn about a grown daughter when for nineteen years, he couldn't care a single iota about her existence?

I want to drag my knees to my chest and start rocking, but Austyn's screech of "Mama!" stops me.

I flick my phone back over to video to find her anxious face staring at me. "Baby, promise me you won't contact that law firm."

"Mama, I'll promise you the world if you'll get that look off your face."

I push up in my chair and leap over my fallen device. "How would you like some company in San Antonio?" Mentally, I'm already shifting patients and canceling appointments.

"I'd love it. But Mama, why?"

"Because, honey. I thought it could wait until Christmas, but it can't. You have to know everything."

Austyn's face blanks. "Are you saying that letter has something to do with...him?"

"We'll talk about it—"

"Just tell me!" she snaps.

"Yes. I'm almost a thousand percent certain of it."

"Can you tell me if the success I've been having lately does?"

"No, your success is your own. In my opinion, you're more talented than your father dreams of being." I'm in my closet pulling down clothes to pack.

She scoffs. "You're just saying that because you're my mother."

I don't deny it. "Damn straight, but I'm not lying about the rest. That's all on you, kiddo."

She lets out a relieved breath. "Okay. You and me after the show?" She puts me on hold and then comes back to rattle off the address of the hotel she's book at.

"Yes. And if we could perhaps lose your...companion?"

Austyn's chuckle is music to my ears. "Don't worry, Mama. I'll take care of that."

"Bless you."

Her face turns serious. "No, I should be saying that to you. You gave me your life, and you're still doing everything to protect me. I love you more than anything—including music."

With that, she disconnects the line before I can respond. I sink to the floor, still holding my phone, and curse out the one person who deserves it.

"Damn you, Beckett. Why the hell do you have to step in it now?"

I don't know how long I sit there before I push to my feet and continue to pack.

San Antonio is still warm by the time I arrive after dinner the next night. I immediately drive to the hotel in the historic district and text my daughter to let her know I'll see her after the show.

Carefully, I lay everything out on the desk—a timeline of heartbreak for her to follow.

I wait for her to arrive, nervously drinking a pot of coffee.

When the knock on the door comes after one thirty, I'm as prepared as I can be.

I fling open the latch after checking to make certain it's Austyn. And she immediately crashes into my arms. We stand in the open doorway for a few moments, clinging to the last moments of her ignorance.

Finally, I draw her into the room. "I'd like to tell you a story before you look at everything I've laid out."

"Mama, I feel like I've waited my whole life for this."

I take her hand and bring her to the sofa.

"It started with Gramps telling the story of how he proposed to Grams."

"He always tells that story," Austyn murmurs.

I smooth a hand over her head. "True. But I don't know what made that day so different. Maybe it was because he wasn't just telling it."

"What was it, then?"

I've given this a lot of thought over the years. "It was their anniversary. Your Uncle Jesse and Uncle Ethan were missing her something fierce. And, of course, so was Gramps. But no one could see how much I was hurting."

Austyn immediately picks up why. "Because you were alive and she wasn't."

"Yes, darling. It's...difficult...to know your very breath has caused someone else's to cease. To know if I wasn't inside Grams, they could have tried different drugs to stop the infection. A cut from a fence she let go too long." My voice trails off, wonder and bitterness filling it. "I still don't understand why."

"Umm, Mama? You've met Gramps, right? He'd have had her bedridden for months over a scratch," Austyn says drolly.

"Have I mentioned how much of a smart-ass you are?"

"Must be from my father's side of the family." She gives me her usual response.

"No. It's from ours." Then I take a deep breath and tell her the first piece of truth. "Your musical talent comes from him. The night I met him, he was at the old homestead. Somehow, he found the old piano, and he was playing a song I'd never heard."

She inhales sharply. "He was a musician?"

"He still is."

She absorbs that blow. "Okay."

I give her a moment before I tell her, "The first thing I ever said to him was, 'You know you're trespassing?'"

Austyn stares at me mutely a moment before asking, "What did he say?"

I remember it as if it was yesterday.

BECKETT

Conversation starter: you've suddenly won a major lottery. Do you keep or change your name and phone number? Discuss.

— Moore You Want

"You know you're trespassing," I say haughtily from my perch on the stone foundation.

"I know," comes the mumbled response.

Good Lord above. He doesn't even have the decency to look in my direction, and he's playing our piano. I bend my knee to stomp my foot when I catch the side of his face.

I know him.

He's Beau Miller from Kensington High.

Entranced by the way his fingers are racing up and down the keys, even if they sound odd with the missing keys, I lower my foot. There's a haunting beauty to the music without the right keys there. But someone who plays as well as he does must know that. Instead, I wait until his fingers stop moving before I begin to clap with enthusiasm.

Much to my surprise, he flushes before he turns his back and starts to walk away.

I jump off the foundation and chase after him. "Hey! Where are you going?"

He stops moving. "Like you said, I'm trespassing."

I whip around until I'm facing him. Even with his head ducked down to his chin, I'm shorter than he is. "So, who cares. According to my Daddy, so am I." I can't quite hide the bitterness in my voice.

His head cocks to the side. "How can you be trespassing on your own land?"

"Because I'm just a girl." I stress the last word.

"That doesn't make any sense..." He shakes his head, causing his over-long hair to flip in front of eyes the color of the Texas blue sky. "Damn, I know I've seen you around."

"Paige. I'm Paige Kensington."

His mouth twists slightly. "That's right. Princess Paige. Matriarch of Kensington." He swoops low for a bow.

My temper fires. "I'm not like that."

"No, but some of the guys think that."

"Then they're stupid. And so are you if you believe everything you hear." I start to move away from Beau Miller.

But he catches my wrist. I don't know if it's because my anger is so close to the surface or because it's him, but my pulse flutters.

He steps closer. "You're right."

"About what?" I demand.

"So far? About everything." He jerks his head. "How about we sit on the wall and talk and you can tell me all about who you really are?"

I pull my wrist back and cross my arms. "I know who you are, but we've never formally met."

This time when his lips curve, the funny feeling causes my stomach to clench. "Beau Miller."

I finish telling Austyn the story of how her father and I first met. Her eyes are wet. "He was playing the piano."

"He wasn't just playing it, baby. He was making magic on it," I correct her.

Her hand reaches for mine and grips it tightly. "My father's name is Beau Miller."

I hedge. "Legally, yes."

Her head tips to the side, causing her rainbow-hued braids to brush her midriff. "What does that mean?"

I hand Austyn her baby book. She flips it open. The first page has the confirmation of my pregnancy. "Can you imagine Gramps's reaction when I told him I was pregnant? Especially when he didn't know I was dating anyone?"

Her face loses all color. "Oh, God. Mama, you must have been terrified."

"I was more terrified for Beau, if you want to know the truth." It's funny how in the years of bitterness, I forgot that until the words came out of my mouth. "But after hours of screaming and yelling at me, I finally crumbled and told him the name. He packed me up into his car, and we drove over to the Millers'." I don't mention at this point he already knew the name. She'll find out soon enough.

I reach for her baby book and put it aside. "There was exactly one reason I asked you to wait until you were eighteen until you asked me for your father's name."

"Why?"

"To protect you," I explain simply.

"Is he an axe murderer?" she half jokes.

"You might wish he was." I stand and reach for her hand. Leading her over to the desk, I explain, "Gramps confronted the Millers only to find out your father—"

"Biological father, because Uncle Jess and Uncle Ethan were more fathers than anything this man ever was," she corrects me.

I press a kiss to her cheek. "Be sure to tell them that the next time you're home. Your biological father had left town."

"You have got to be kidding me," my daughter hisses.

"You knew this, Austyn." My voice holds a note of exasperation.

"But knowing the story of the piano, the pieces I've put together in my head over the years, he had no guts if he left you, Mama."

Her words warm me momentarily. I touch the letters from Daddy's lawyers. "Over the first few months of my pregnancy, Gramps's attorneys tried repeatedly to contact your father. They used an investigations firm to locate him. The Millers claimed he didn't want to be found. Later, it became abundantly clear why."

"Can you explain it to me?"

"I will." My hands are shaking when they touch the checks. "Do you remember the fire that hit the trailer park when you were very young?"

"Vaguely. Why?"

"Your biological grandparents were in it. They died." She gasps. My voice is like ice when I explain, "But at least Gramps was able to stop making payments to keep their silence about who your father was."

"Excuse me? He was paying them?"

"Yes. By then, your father had started to become 'someone,' and they were threatening to go to the media. I refused to let your childhood be marred with that kind of scandal. I told Gramps I'd leave. I'd take you and leave if that's what it took. He refused and gave in to their demands."

"The fire..." Austyn asks hesitantly.

"Was a gas explosion. A freak accident. Ruled that way by an outside arson expert. Gramps knew this would all come out, so the fire chief called in two experts to rule on it." And thank goodness my father had that foresight. I lay my hand on the closed file. "Do you want to read about it?"

"No! But Mama, didn't he come home when his parents died?"

"He didn't. I expected to have to deal with your father then, but he never showed up. At least not that I was able to ascertain." My hand moves to the last pile.

The photos of me and Beckett.

"Before I show you these, before you react to the man who is your father, I want you to understand down to the depth of your soul what your life would have been like if you knew who he was before you were the woman of character standing before me. Even though I resented every dime he paid his family, Gramps claims he did it to protect us. He didn't do it for the Kensington name; he did it so people assumed I had a wild weekend fling. He did it so people would never associate the gossip rags with my daughter. So you would never be heckled by mean little shits."

I lift my hand from the photos.

Austyn reaches for them, but she doesn't lift them. "Gramps had you followed?"

My laugh only holds a slight resentment toward my interfering father. "He browbeat me for the name of who the baby's father was, but he already knew. He wanted me to admit to it, to my failing."

"Falling in love isn't failing at anything."

I love that my daughter feels that way. "Then let's just say he wanted to know why I went from being a snotty teenager to being one with a dreamy smile on her face."

My daughter lifts the pile. Her intake of breath leaves no air in the room for me. I stand as still as a statue as she flips through the 8x10 glossies.

When she's done, she carelessly tosses the pile on top of all the other meticulously laid-out information. "Well, he always has been a photogenic bastard, hasn't he?"

I reach for her. "Austyn..."

"Beckett Miller is my biological father." Her voice is flat.

"Beau Beckett Miller is, yes," I confirm before my head drops. Why didn't I realize how much it would hurt to admit my shame to the one person who I swore shouldn't suffer for my mistakes?

There's an eerie silence in the room. Her footfalls don't make a sound. My eyes drift to see her feet are planted firmly in place. I follow the path upward to find her arms akimbo, her jaw tight. "I can't believe you kept this from me."

"There were reasons..."

"None of them are good enough right now! How could you not tell me sooner?" she shouts.

I recoil at the lash of her anger but keep my own temper in check when I respond calmly, "Did you really want this burden while you were growing into the woman you are now, Austyn?"

"It would have been better than answering 'I don't know' all the fucking time to my friends when I was asked if I knew who my father was. It would have been better than the fake support I endured. Knowing would have been better than not."

I spring to my feet. "Would it? Would it really? Would it have been better when you confided in just one of your friends, and every time they saw his face on a tabloid they gave you such a pathetic look of sympathy you wanted to curl up and die? Or maybe when it was when he was on the cover of StellaNova as the Sexiest Man Alive? Or maybe walking down the red carpet with a different beautiful woman? Because trust me, baby girl, that's exactly what I've endured from your uncles for years."

She falls back a step. "So Uncle Jess and Uncle E know?"

"Yes. And you want to talk about feelings, Austyn? Deal with those," I yell.

She nods as she moves further away from me. "At least you had them to confide in. Who the hell did I have?"

Frozen, I can't move a muscle as she races for the hotel room door. It isn't until long moments later when I'm finally able to choke out, "You had me."

Right before my legs give out beneath me and I succumb to tears.

I wait the entire next day without hearing from Austyn. I analyze the situation from her perspective, and after all that's been said and done, I come to the same conclusion I did when she asked me about her father a few years ago.

I wouldn't have done anything differently.

I opened the door for her father to walk through. When he chose not to come through it, I wasn't subjecting my daughter to the innuendos and speculation that Beckett seems to thrive under. Moving over to the file of clippings from last month alone, I flip through them.

All-night booze fest at Beckett's! Cops called by building security.

Beckett in a love triangle with favorite lead guitarist Mick and drummer Carly.

What's the real reason for Beckett Miller deciding not to tour this year?

My fingers flip through article after article; every blip and bite about his life fills my hands. Finally, I get so frustrated, I hurl them across the room. "When am I going to just be able to let you go? When does the pain end?"

"Mama?"

Shit. I didn't even hear the door open. I keep my back to the door even as relief fills my voice. "Austyn. I'm so glad you're back."

"I had to be completely clearheaded before I could say what I needed to say."

I turn around. "Say it."

"Right now, I just need you to be my friend and not my mother. Can you do that?"

"Yes." God, it's going to be next to impossible, but I'll do it.

"I don't know how she did it. But Paige Kensington has always been my protector, my sword, and my shield."

"Austyn." The tears come up on me swiftly.

"No. Just listen. It took me being alone banging on a piano to realize you gave me my music—not him. You could have been like so many others would have and taken away something that reminded you of the person who walked away, but you didn't."

"I couldn't." My arms lift helplessly.

"Because you love me."

"Because when you love someone as much as I love you, it's impossible not to give them your whole heart. You'd live for them; you'd die for them. There's nothing you wouldn't do to make things perfect for them. And for you, that's music."

Austyn rushes forward and wraps her arms around me. "I'm so sorry, Mama. So, so sorry."

"You have nothing to apologize for," I whisper as I stroke her hair.

We stand for long moments communicating with broken sobs, the clenching and release of arms, and the synchronization of our hearts. It's a beautiful melody only the two of us can fully understand.

After long moments, my daughter lifts her head and wipes her eyes before asking, "Will you answer something for me?"

"I'll try."

"Are you still in love with him?"

I give my daughter the truth I've shared with no one aloud and rarely myself in the darkest of nights. "Oh, only every part of me that loves you."

Austyn winces. "Mama, that sucks in the worst way."

"Tell me about it, baby. I've lived with it since before you were born."

Her lips tremble. "And do you think things would have been different if he came back?"

My hands raise before dropping helplessly at my sides. "Austyn, if I did, our lives might have been very different, or they might have turned out just the same. I have no way of knowing. What I do know is I didn't want you broadsided every day of your life with the same feelings I've had—swept away wondering about what-ifs and shoulda, coulda, wouldas."

Austyn lets me go to walk around the room restlessly. "I'm sorry, Mama."

"Stop, Austyn. We can't change the past."

Her eyes—his eyes—are damp when they meet mine. "For you, I wish I could."

"I know." And for one moment, I let down the walls I've held up for so long. Then, I snap them up tighter than before, bringing us back on track. "But Austyn, this doesn't address the issue of why I told you sooner rather than later."

Her brow puckers in concentration. "No, it doesn't. It had to do with that letter from the attorney."

I step on top of the papers I threw around the room—and God, if it doesn't feel good to step all over Beckett—to snatch up my cell phone. "Sweetheart, they represent your father."

"What? I don't understand."

"I think we need to do some research into this firm before *we* meet with them when I'm up for the holidays. Because a Kensington would never go into a meeting where they're signing any sort of binding legal documents—"

"—without Gramps investigating the hell out of them," Austyn concludes. Her smile might be her father's, but the intent behind it is pure Kensington.

And so I lean forward and give her a big smooch right on her lips. "Exactly."

BECKETT

Jack Daniels or Cristal? Rumors of a party at Beckett Miller's are surfacing, but the details are unclear. All I know is I wish I was invited regardless of what was served.

— Viego Martinez, Celebrity Blogger

"So, how was your weekend in Memphis with Mick and Carly? I'm assuming you got back early," Carys asks.

"Hardly, or I would have killed someone," I growl. I'm seething with fury as my security team accesses the closet where my internal recording devices are stored. "My place is trashed."

The "What?" is screeched so loudly in my ear, I have to pull my phone away to preserve my hearing. "Yeah. There's booze puddling all over my fucking floors. Art is completely ruined. Only thing that's not destroyed is the music room, but that's likely because I have the place locked up like Fort Knox." I make my way over to the master suite. "Fuckers even went at it in my room," I call out over my shoulder.

"We're on it, Becks," Kane calls out.

"I need to find a place to crash tonight and hire someone to completely redo everything tomorrow." Then a thought occurs to me. I ask suspiciously, "What did you mean you assumed I got back early?"

"Beckett..."

"Carys, tell me."

"The 'party' at your place was all over social media. Cops were called. You're getting slapped with a disturbing the peace charge."

"Are you kidding me? I wasn't even here!" I shout.

"And we'll be able to defend that once the security team..." But I stop listening to Carys as Kane comes out shaking his head, eyes blazing in anger.

"You've got to be fucking joking, Kane. What did they do? Use a kitchen knife to pick the..." My face flushes when he lifts his arm and my broken Grammy is in his hands. Before he can speak, I grind out, "Are you telling me that whomever was in this place used one of the crowning achievements of my career to smash the keypad lock your team installed on the server room holding the data we need to prosecute them?"

"Yes." On some level, I appreciate his simple, no-nonsense answer. But it doesn't cause my fury to abate. If anything, it flames it more.

"I suggest you get building security to figure this out before I call Hudson and get all of you fired for oh, say, gross incompetency?"

Kane frowns. "Someone has to stay with you."

"Someone has to come with me because I'm sure as hell not staying here. One more minute in this place and I'll be arrested for murder."

Carys is silent during this exchange. There's murmuring on her end of the line before, "Do you want to come here?"

My heart swells with warmth despite the cold fury that wants to take over. "No, honey. But thank you. Tell David thank you as well. I'll go to a hotel."

"Come for dinner tonight at least. I have some things I want to discuss with you I don't want to do over the phone," she urges.

I'm about to board the elevator to take me back down to the lobby.

I stop in my tracks, and Kane almost crashes right into me. "Is it going to piss me off? I'm not sure I can handle much more right now, Carrie."

"Actually, it might calm you down a bit. Be here at six." Before I can even agree, she disconnects.

I turn to the lead of my security team. "I'll be finding a suite of rooms to check into, then heading to the Lennans' for dinner."

"Understood. And we will figure out who did this, Becks. That's a promise."

"It'd better be." With a final sweeping glance around my trashed home, I step into the elevator and head down.

***

I choke on the Scotch Carys poured me earlier. "What do you mean LLF is under investigation?"

A smug little smile crosses her face. She nods at David, who has just entered the room from putting their son, Ben, to bed. "You tell him, honey. You're the one who noticed the emails."

David perches on the arm of the chair Carys is sitting in. He reaches past her for his own drink. "How often would you estimate people inquire about the validity of the recommendations on our website?"

I scoff at the idea of someone questioning my recommendation. "Um, never?"

David smiles, probably the first true one he's ever aimed at my direction. "Actually, slightly more frequently than that. A lot of times it has to do with our clients."

I put it together quickly. "People trying to use you all to get to us."

"Exactly, which is why I'm in charge of responding to all of those inquiries. We have a formal letter that goes out which Carys drafted for just such a circumstance." He toasts his wife, who assumes a modest look.

"I knew there was a reason I paid you a ton of money, Carrie." I lift my drink to her in a salute as well.

"No, you pay me a ton of money for innumerable reasons, Becks. For this, you pay David. Go on, honey. Tell him," she urges.

David takes a sip of his drink before he notes, "We received an inquiry in the last few days from a different email address on every single one of our recommendations."

"What's so..."

"Except yours."

My body freezes in the process of lifting my drink to my lips. "Really? Isn't that interesting. Does it have anything to do with my place being trashed?"

Carys shakes her head, making my hackles rise. I demand, "How do you know?"

"Because I contacted our friendly investigator myself when David brought it to my attention." Her face takes on a fierce countenance. "I don't like coincidences." Carys puts her drink down with a snap. "Now, I can think of only one reason why someone would want to validate the law firm where Beckett Miller is listed as a client—one who gives us a glowing review. Especially when we've taken on no new business in the last two months."

My heart begins thundering in my chest. "No new business, eh?"

"None." She tips her head back to bestow a beaming smile up at her husband. "Make his day a whole lot better, my love."

"If I must." David sweeps a hand over his wife's hair before sharing, "The investigator traced all the emails back to the same IP—one in Texas."

My hand is shaking so hard I have to put the glass I'm holding down. My eyes dart back and forth between the two of them. "You're kidding."

"There is no way I'd even come close to joking about this, Becks. It appears there are people who are very protective of that girl," Carys informs me.

"I can't believe it. I just can't wrap my mind around it. After so long without hearing anything, to be given this enormous lifeline." I surge to my feet and hold out my hand. "Thank you, David."

He cautions me, "This doesn't confirm anything. Don't go putting the cart before the horse."

I nod, but inside I'm already making mental adjustments to my life.

My heart.

Kensington has to be my daughter. She just has to be. Now if I can just figure out why Paige never told me.

PAIGE

If you haven't checked out Saks' new line this year, do so. DJ Kensington was spotted shopping there. Her edgy style screams Stella McCartney with a twist of McQueen layered with Free People. It's young, vibrant, and in-your-face—just like she is.

— **Eva Henn, Fashion Blogger**

I take an inordinate amount of time dressing. How ironic Austyn and I found a dress at Saks with what our shopping assistant called "the Kensington stand collar."

This Kensington sure as hell is here in New York to take a stand, all right.

I smooth my opaque thigh-highs one last time before slipping on a pair of simple leather pumps with a distinctive red sole. I finish the look with a pair of diamond studs and my gold signet ring. After I slide the heavy ring on my right hand, I give myself a head-to-toe perusal. "You'll do, Paige."

"You'll more than do, Mama." Austyn's standing in the doorway of my bedroom. The only thing that remotely resembles my outfit are the red soles of her Christian Louboutins—an early Christmas gift—

and her matching gold signet ring. Though for her, the skinny hombre leggings beneath the uber-short, sheer shift dress work. And it shows its own kind of power when combined with the lift and twists of color in her hair.

"So will you, my darling." I move over to my briefcase and slide all of the paperwork I carried with me from Texas into it. Picking it up, I step up to her and ask one final time, "Are you sure you want to do this?" I don't want Austyn to look back and regret.

There have been far too many of those.

Her hand comes up and grips my wrist. "Mama, no matter what, I'll have my music. Even if the lot of them get together to blackball me, nothing and no one can take that away from me."

I try one last time to get her to listen, "But Austyn, you could have..."

"More. It's a possibility. But at what cost?"

"None. I've told you over and over, I want you to be happy."

"Then you want this for me. If I'm lucky, I'll get the chance to look him in the eye—just once—to tell him he lost out."

"He certainly did," I murmur. I drag my thumb over her brow, around her eye, to her cheek. "He missed out on you."

Her breath shudders out. "Then let's go. I have a date with my mother tonight for dinner. Maybe we'll find her some hot guy."

I shudder. "Now you sound like Gramps."

"There are worse things," she throws cheerfully over her shoulder as she enters the living room of our suite.

I close my eyes and say goodbye to the boy I loved before I go confront the man. "I really did love you." And for just a moment, I want to stop Austyn. I know I've told her that Beckett's home life wasn't the greatest, that that's why he sought out the piano, the music, and me.

But for her, it doesn't matter.

He made a promise to me he never kept. He left me and through me, her.

"Mama? Are you coming?" Austyn calls out.

And I feel my feet move, one in front of the other. In just a few hours, it will all be done.

And maybe I'll be able to move on.

It's only taken twenty years.

Heels clicking in time against the marble floor, we enter the building at Rockefeller Center. After passing security, we board the elevator. Once inside, Austyn barely breathes. I reach over and clasp her hand with my free one. "Calm, baby."

"How can I?" she asks just as the elevator door opens.

We both exit. But before we pass through the frosted glass doors, opaque but for a Celtic symbol, I remind her, "Because nothing is holding you here. You are not bound by a contract." *Nor by a vow you made in your heart*, I amend silently.

She visibly relaxes. "You're right." She reaches for the door and pulls it open.

I'm surprised to find a familiar face behind the desk. My head tips to the side as I try to recall the name of the magnificent redhead.

She stands and holds out a hand first to my daughter. "Kensington." She then turns to me, her eyes warm. "Dr. Kensington. May I take your coats?"

As we shuck our outerwear, the redhead continues. "It's unusual we're meeting like this again, but can I take a moment to thank you?"

"You're welcome..." I flounder as I hand over my coat.

"Angela. Please call me Angie. Everyone here does." She turns to Austyn to take her jacket. "Your mom is kind of a badass."

Austyn relaxes fractionally even though she's obviously confused. "I know."

"I was in a predicament one night when I heard you play at Redemption. She was fearless."

I open my mouth to wave off the praise when the wood door behind Angie opens. The man in question from that very night steps out. "Angie, honey, have you...Kensington. Dr. Kensington. Welcome to LLF."

My voice is frighteningly frigid when I ask, "Tell me you're not Carys Burke." The website I looked at didn't include any pictures of the personnel.

He takes no offense. His face creases into a soft smile. "No, Dr. Kensington, I'm not."

"Good."

"I'm her brother, Ward."

My body goes completely rigid. I move subtly closer to Austyn.

"Dr. Kensington, what you saw that night isn't what you thought." Angie's feather-soft voice captures my attention. And when I search her face, I don't find a victim. I see a survivor.

Trusting my instincts, I hold out my hand. "Mr. Burke."

He shakes it. "Thank you, Doctor."

"For?"

His gaze slides over Angie's smiling one. His lips curve slightly. "For making me see what I should have long ago."

Angie blushes before she picks up a tablet on her desk. "Let me just text Carys and tell her we're ready out here. Okay. Will everyone follow me? We're going to gather in the conference room."

The heavy wood door is opened by Ward, and we step across the threshold.

My first impression is opulence. Warm, rich wood is intermixed with open, spacious glass. If it wasn't for the very enormous desk set off to the side, I'd think I was in the lobby of a fancy hotel with the small sitting area off to the side. An attractive man stands and holds out his hand. "Hello. My name is David Lennan. I'm the senior paralegal here at LLF, LLC. Welcome."

Austyn shakes his hand first. "Mr. Lennan."

"Please make it David. We're all on a first-name basis here." He releases my daughter's hand and holds out his hand to mine. "David."

I hesitate briefly before I give over. "Paige."

"Welcome, Paige. Carys is just wrapping up a call. We have everything set up in the conference room. We thought we might be more comfortable there instead of crowded in her office." He gestures us forward.

Angie and Ward fall in step behind us as we all make our way into the bright space dominated by a highly polished mahogany table. At the head of the table are files neatly stacked. Notepads and pens are laid around at every other chair. Assuming that to be the spot where Carys will sit, I deliberately seat myself at the foot. Austyn drops down next to me, her back to the magnificent view of the city skyline.

"Can I get either of you some coffee? We also have an espresso machine, so any sort of latte wouldn't be a problem," Angie offers.

"Regular coffee is fine for me. Black," Austyn pipes up.

"I'd be grateful for some. With cream if that's not too much trouble." My lips tip up slightly.

"None at all. Ward? David?" When both of them nod, she disappears, closing the door behind her.

David smiles at us. "Based on your website, Kensington, I understand you're from Texas?"

"I am."

"I grew up in Tornado Alley myself. It's one of the things year after year I don't really miss about living in New York."

Austyn laughs. "I haven't been here a full year to appreciate that part of it yet."

"There's a pleasure about being able to sleep through the night because there's no sirens waking you up at all hours."

"I don't know about that, David. Despite the quality of my hotel, I heard quite a few sirens on the street last night," I quip to ease the rising tension as we wait for Angie to come back with coffee.

Or Carys.

His smile is genuine. "Angie mentioned you're an audiologist?"

I flush. "I handed Marco Houde a pair of earplugs at his nightclub the night I went to hear Austyn play and suggested he put them in."

"Mama, you didn't," Austyn groans. Her head falls forward into her hands.

Ward and David chuckle.

I'm about to defend myself, but the door opens. Angie comes back in carrying a carafe of coffee, cups, and accoutrements. I jump out of my seat. "Let me help you with that."

"Oh, there's no need. I'm used to hauling around boxes of files. Especially because that one"—she nods at Ward—"finally sent his files to off-site storage."

Ward's comment of "Slave driver" is murmured with such adoration, any lingering qualms I had about him fade away. It helps he stands and lifts the tray out of her arms before asking, "How much longer is Carrie going to be?"

"She was just..." Then the door opens again. And a woman whose tiny stature might be described as almost fairylike strides through the door. The room goes static by her presence. I realize why when she reaches the head of the table and sets her portfolio down. "Thank you, Angie," her husky voice rasps. Aqua-colored eyes peruse Austyn first, lingering on her eyes and lips. Then they flicker over to me. "Kensington, Dr. Kensington. I'm Carys Burke."

David interjects before I can reply. "We've dispensed with formalities, Carrie."

She nods but doesn't retract her words, her eyes remaining locked on mine—making the choice mine. "As David said, we've dispensed with formalities. It's Paige and—darling?" I face my daughter.

"Austyn. That's my given name. There's a story behind it."

A smile breaks across Carys's face. She reaches for a file from the stack next to her and flips it open. "I hope I'll get to hear you tell the tale before we're done with what we have to cover today."

She glances downward for a moment before she asks, "So, should we talk Austyn's legal representation?"

Austyn's head whips toward me, lips rolling inward. I drawl, "Let's just cut to the chase, why don't we? We all know we're here to discuss her father."

"So, you're prepared to discuss Beckett Miller?"

I simply lift my own briefcase on the table and unlatch the locks. "I believe I said I was prepared to discuss her father." I leave my words ambiguous.

Carys's smile turns ferocious. "Excellent." Her head turns toward her assistant. "Angie, perhaps now would be a good time to pour for everyone while Dr. Kensington prepares what she brought with her."

My head tips in acknowledgment toward the woman at the far end of the table. I begin to pull out my own set of files. But I still take time to say, "Thank you," to Angie when she places the fine china cup of coffee in front of me.

After all, there's no need to be rude when you plan on decomposing the people who support your greatest enemy—the man you've loved your entire life.

PAIGE

Erzulie broke down on stage last night during her show when she was singing a rendition of Stevie Nicks' "Landslide." According to a member of her crew who gave a quote, it was "uncomfortable. She's been getting progressively worse." Apparently, the indie goddess is beating back some serious demons.

— StellaNova

"Before we get this discussion underway, I have something to say," Austyn declares.

Everyone's attention turns toward her, especially mine. "What is it, baby?" I ask.

"I've dreamed of being a professional musician my entire life. My mother has supported that dream, even letting me cash out my college fund to try to make it a reality. She's encouraged me, feeding my soul. Knowing what I only recently found out myself, it would have been easier if she made very different decisions from the moment she found out she was pregnant with me. The moment someone begins talking to her with anything less than respect, this conversation is over in any capacity—personal or professional. Am I understood?" She directs her last comment to Carys.

"Perfectly. You're awfully brave, Austyn," Carys remarks.

"No, my mother was. She was seventeen and pregnant. And she didn't have to make the decision to have me," my daughter shoots back.

My fingers knot together. "That wasn't an option. At least not to me."

I feel Austyn's hand cover mine. My eyes fly to hers.

Carys clears her throat. "Can I ask some...delicate...questions?"

I nod, unable to look away. "There's nothing I've kept from my daughter, Carys."

"Beckett Miller is her father," she states.

"That wasn't a question, Counselor," I shoot back just to be contrary.

One of the men—judging from the location of the sound, her brother—chokes back a laugh.

"*Is* Beckett Miller her father?"

I shake my head no.

"He isn't?" Carys's voice is laced with shock.

"I can confirm that *Beau* Beckett Miller is her biological father. By all accounts, I would assume they are one and the same, but since I haven't had a conversation with Beau Beckett Miller in close to twenty years, I cannot confirm that information."

"Lord save me from doctors who would make excellent witnesses," Carys mutters.

"I've been on the stand a few times," I offer.

"I'd have been certain of that even if it wasn't for the investigator's report." She taps the pile next to her.

I'm not surprised in the slightest she had us investigated, but Austyn is indignant. "You had someone look into us?"

Carys smiles so widely it's like staring into the mouth of a shark. "Your mother did the same. Didn't you, Paige?"

"I had your firm looked into, not you personally. I wanted to validate your ethics before I brought my daughter here. You'll be pleased to know everything I read was impressive," I correct coolly.

"As a parent, I would likely do the same. As the owner of this firm, I do consider the distinction fair. As the lawyer who represents Beckett Miller, I'm still suspicious."

"As am I. Tell me why I should encourage my daughter to sign away her confidentiality rights to a firm that also represents her biological donor?"

Carys opens her mouth to respond, but I plow over her. "Just know something, Carys. I have little faith in promises, even those made in writing."

"I can see how you might..."

"My father hired an investigator back then to find him—so I could tell him." I hand the file to David, who immediately flips it open. His jaw locks as he begins reading.

"David?" Carys queries.

"He did."

"And?"

David shakes his head. Carys's shoulders slump. "What happened next, Paige?"

I can feel myself get lost in the memories. "At first I refused to name who Austyn's father was."

"Why?"

Confused, I ask, "He left me. Did it matter?"

"Some would have argued it might have, Paige." Carys's voice has softened.

I shake my head before I'm transported back. "My father did at first," I whisper.

"Did he?" David murmurs, but I barely hear him.

"You will tell me right now!" my father thunders.

"Why? He's gone. He left. Why does it matter?"

"Because I will know how far this treachery of yours goes, Paige. We need to determine what to do about that aberration you carry." He flings his hand toward my stomach.

I back away from him. "You dare? This is your flesh and blood."

"Never," he hisses.

"Then I swear this. If you make me give up this baby, it will be the only time I get pregnant. I swear I will never have another baby. Ever."

I take great satisfaction as the blood drains from my father's face.

My whole body shakes as the long-ago memory is plucked from my head. Austyn's squeezes my fingers so tightly, there's pain. "Gramps really said those things to you?" Her voice is filled with tears.

"Baby, I never meant for you to know any of that. Those were words he said because he was furious I'd been careless."

"Are you sure about that, Paige?" This comes from Carys.

"Of course I am. He's my father—Austyn's grandfather. He's loved her from the moment he first held her. You have no idea the things he's done for her. So much more than her biological father ever has."

"Like what?" Ward challenges.

"In the early days, he helped simply by giving me a place to raise her. I grew up well-to-do. I'm sure you know that." I nod at the stack of files still towering next to Carys's elbow. At her chin tip, I continue. "But he could have cut me off, made it impossible for me to finish my education. Instead, I was able to get my degree and go on to one of the best medical schools for audiology in the world."

"What made you choose audiology?" David asks.

I smile before pulling a hand away from Austyn's to run it over the shell of her ear. "This one. She had a number of ear infections as an infant. I was in my early years of med school, debating if I wanted to go into obstetrics, and became fascinated by the entire process of audiology. Now I just embarrass her by offering people earplugs at her shows."

Austyn squirms as the tension in the room lessens slightly when Angie giggles. David smiles before ducking his head back into the file.

"Why obstetrics?" Carys asks.

"As an homage to my mother. She passed away due to an infection she contracted when she was pregnant with me. Overall, I think I made the right choice as my specialty is working with young children."

Carys makes a noncommittal sound before querying, "David?"

"Investigation, yes. Same firm as the one in our files, but the data's incomplete. They had his social security number, knew he was writing and being paid for his early compositions, but didn't provide the information about his permanent residence? That was either shoddy work or..."

"Deliberately incomplete," Carys finishes grimly.

David nods in concurrence.

"What are you trying to say?" Austyn cries out.

David closes the file and hands it over to Carys. "What your mother gave to me was an investigation conducted by your grandfather's investigation firm looking for your father. Either the information was incomplete at the onset—which was then passed along to your grandfather—or your mother was never given all the information."

"That's all the information I have," I whisper faintly. My eyes scan the room. "I swear it."

"Paige..." Carys begins.

"No. You don't understand. My father searched for Bea—Beckett, damnit. My father did that so he could stop paying his parents!" I shout.

Carys pushes to her feet and leans toward me. "Excuse me? Payment for what?"

"They knew. The lawyers wrote them, and after the first one, they sent the letters back. They knew she was their grandchild, and they had not...one...thing to do with her. But oh, once he started hitting the tabloids, they started blackmailing me about her parentage. And my father paid."

"You can't be..."

I shoot a file filed with copies of canceled checks across the table. "Every single month. My family paid for my decision to have my daughter and to keep her parentage quiet. Beckett's fame made things quite difficult. Then they died in an explosion at the trailer park where they lived—a gas explosion."

Ward whistles aloud. Carys shoots him a filthy look. "Hush."

"Carys, it sounds to me like…"

"I know!" she snaps. She sits back into her chair, dragging the file with her. She flips through pages of canceled checks. Finally, she closes her eyes, pain dashing across her face. "Paige, Austyn, I don't know how to tell you what you need to know."

"Just do it. It can't be worse than what I already know."

"Most of what you've been told is partially the truth."

I suck in a deep breath to calm the heat of my first words which is to accuse Carys of being a damn liar. "What evidence do you have to substantiate that?"

Austyn doesn't speak. She just clutches my hands as I confront the attorney whose job it is to protect her father at all costs.

Carys rests her hands against the stack of files next to her. "I hired my own investigations firm to look into the past—Hudson Investigations. They found everything you just showed me, plus a lot more. What I need to know is how much do you want to know the truth?"

"How can I trust this Hudson Investigations?"

"I'm certain you've heard about the case of the Supreme Court justice whose daughter was sentenced to prison for stalking?"

The inside of my mouth gets dry. "That was them?"

She nods. "They've also been involved in cases involving relatives of US senators and clients of ours, not including Beckett. They do pro bono work involving missing children and some hostage situations."

"I can pull up their website if you'd like to contact your investigator to validate their credentials," David offers.

But it's not the credentials they're listing out for me that convinces me. It's the terrible concern on all of their faces. "Will someone please take Austyn out of the room while I read the files?"

"Mama, what?" Austyn yells.

My head whirls in her direction. "I made most of the decisions about your life based on the information your grandfather placed in front of me. Please, give me this, Austyn."

Angie stands. "Come on, Austyn. Let's give your mother a few moments."

After my daughter has been escorted from the room and I'm left with the Burkes and David, I ask outright, "How much of my life is a lie?"

Carys tells me bluntly, "Your love for your daughter and your degrees are the only things I wouldn't be suspicious of."

My insides twist. "Right. Can I have the first file?"

Carys hands it to David, who passes it to me. "This one might be the worst."

"Why?" I ask as I flip it open.

I should have waited for someone to answer me before I did.

There's a picture of my mother on one side. And a T-boned car on the other. I suck in an enormous breath. I scan the date on the photo. Then I lift the file closer, certain I'm reading something wrong.

It's the day before I was born.

"How can this be?" I ask aloud.

Carys sighs. "Your mother didn't die of an infection, Paige."

The file clatters to the table. "How did she die?"

"She was hit by a driver who ran a red light."

As soon as the words leave Carys's mouth, I'm flipping through the police report to see who drove the car. And I swear I'm having heart palpitations when I see the name Ava Miller.

Because that's Beckett's mother.

"Oh, God. He did consider her an aberration." Tears begin to well in my eyes.

"Who did?"

"My father."

"Yes. I'm beginning to believe so" is the last thing I hear before I begin learning the truth about my own past from a complete stranger.

Two hours later, we still haven't let Austyn and Angie back into the room. There's no more files to read. Ward and David left the room some time ago. My heart is in pieces. Carys has come down to sit next to me to offer me moral support. After all, no one in this room is going to hurt me.

No, the person who deliberately hurt me is someone I have to face when I head back to Texas.

"When he overheard your father threatening his parents, Beckett made the decision the two of you had to leave if you were going to have half of a chance at the life you had planned together. His whole life in Kensington had been subject to the whims of two parents who became alcoholics when he was a young boy, but he never knew why. When he finally put the pieces together, he never wanted you tainted with that. Somehow, his parents figured it out. He's still not sure if they found a bag, the money he siphoned away—he just doesn't know. But after they found out he was intending on leaving with the one girl he shouldn't be, the daughter of the woman whose life they ended, they threatened him—only after physically doing some harm."

"He claimed he was in a fight," I whisper.

"He wasn't. It was his mother slapping him around while his father held him down. Then...they switched."

"Oh, God." I shove my face into my folded arms.

Carys runs her hand up and down my back. "That's when he realized it was never going to work. He didn't leave because of you, Paige. He left to protect you from what he endured."

"What are you hiding from me?"

He smooths my hair away from my face. "Everything. But soon it won't matter. I hope."

"Why didn't he tell me?" Faster and faster, tears leak from my eyes into the sleeves of my dress.

"Because he loved you. He wanted better for you than he could possibly give you." It's such a simple statement, but with it comes every memory of those months when I knew my heart.

I lift tormented eyes to meet Carys's compassionate ones. "What?

A life of ceaselessly loving him? Of being unable to stop because I love our child the exact same way? And now what am I supposed to do? Go home to a town where my life was built on lies to do what? Wither away in the sun?"

I push wearily to my feet. "Let's bring the others back."

Carys does the same. "Are you sure?"

"It's time to settle this."

Austyn storms into the room, her face set in lines of fury until she takes a good look at mine. "Mama." She rushes forward and wraps me up tightly. "What did you do to her?"

Carys doesn't say anything to defend herself. She waits for the others to file in and for the door to close. I smooth the hair away from my daughter's face, cataloging each and every feature that's mine, that's Beckett's. "From the moment I knew I was carrying you, the love I've had for you has been surreal. You were my reason for not giving up on life after your father left; that's how much love I had for him."

I hear a sniff behind me, but I focus only on Austyn's damp eyes. "I was wrong, baby. Maybe today, maybe tomorrow, I can forgive myself for making the wrong decisions. All I can say to defend myself is I trusted. One day, I hope your father understands that."

"Mama, what do you mean?" Austyn whispers, her hands coming up to grip my wrists.

"Your father was trying to protect me when he walked out of my life. And your grandfather..." I feel bile surge up, trying to take over. "For now, you just need to know your father will be overwhelmed to know you, Austyn. In a good way, I promise. Carys is going to help with that."

"Where are you going to be?"

My jaw tightens. "Dealing with your grandfather."

"Let me come with you," she begs.

"No, baby. Stay. I..." Swallowing past the knot of pain, I push the words out. "...believe what they told me. Trust Carys. She only has your best interest at heart." Whereas my father only had his.

"Paige, please, wait. There's so much to discuss." Ward's voice is laced with urgency.

I ignore him, focusing only on Austyn. "You're safe here. Don't worry—I'll handle everything back home. Just promise me you're going to fly. Soar. Rain down magic with your music." I glance over at Carys. "You'll represent her legally?"

"It would be my honor."

I nod at the evidence I brought with me. "Keep those. If something happens, you might need it to protect both of them." Smoothing a hand over Austyn's cheek, I pick up my now empty briefcase and leave the conference room without looking back.

And I easily ignore the eruption of voices as the door closes behind me as I hurry out of LLF. I'm too busy searching for a flight back to Texas.

It's time to confront my father once and for all.

BECKETT

If a celebrity walks by another celebrity on the street, do they acknowledge each other? I mean, after all, even when we offer them a friendly smile, they ignore the rest of us. #ScrewHolidaySpirit

— Jacques Yves, Celebrity Blogger

It's my favorite season in New York—Christmas. There's something incredible about the fact people are willing to drag their loved ones into the city to stand cheek by jowl in front of a tree that has 30,000 lights on it, but I can't seem to get into the spirit.

I ping Angie to see if Carys is available, only to be told she's in a conference all day. I frown before I type back, *Ward?*

No, and before you ask, David is busy as well.

Then why are you free?

I'm out running an errand. Then I'll be back.

Maybe I'll stop by.

The dots move next to her phone before she tells me, Today is NOT a good day, Becks. What about tomorrow? Unless it's a real emergency?

It's not, but I'm feeling festive.

Yeah, that's not the mood around here.

Angie's words have me sitting down in front of my upright. My mind goes back to the first Christmas when I was wandering through Nashville after a show. I was so tempted to pick up the phone and call Paige. My soul was miserable without her. And just as my fingers hit a G chord on the piano, I use the other to fiddle with a melody as I sing:

I'm so cold and lonely without you
I don't want a blue heart, baby
But what I want won't fit under a tree
When the gift I need is you with me

I fiddle for a few hours, recalling the emotions behind how I felt returning to my shithole of a hotel with a pack of Slim Jims and a Coke alone instead of the warm arms of the woman I loved. Finally, when it's done, I stretch. I recall something David said to me that night I was at their place when Carys was with Ben. "Beckett, you're never going to be done with the love you have for Paige Kensington. Every moment the two of you shared is a part of who made you the man you are."

"So you're saying I'm always going to be like this? Even though she's moved on?" I lashed out.

"Would you want to give up those memories?" he asked me logically.

"No! I just have to figure out how to cope..." And I stopped myself.

"Exactly. You just said it. For so long, you haven't coped with your past. You've ignored it. But you can't do that."

"It would be easier."

"Not if this woman turns out to be your daughter," he challenged me.

I nodded to give him the point. He continued. "Even if you were to move on and fall in love with someone else, the boy you were may have created a life with your first love. If that's true, there will always be a part of you that will have some feelings towards her."

"Any ideas about how to do that?" I asked.

"Follow your heart. Follow your soul. And above all, if it turns out to be true, listen."

The hours I've spent at the piano have helped the wounded part of me. I feel almost buoyant as I slip into a suit and silk shirt. Quickly calling down to my security team, I announce, "I'm heading out."

"Any particular destination?" Kane asks.

"Rockefeller Center." I hang up before I can listen to his squawking about the number of tourists. I need to feel the energy emitted from Christmas present after I've just spent hours in the memories of Christmas past. Right before I hit the Down button on the elevator, I smile at the new interior of my home. It took about ten days, but even I can't tell there's a thing out of place. Sure the furnishings are different, but I feel like my place has a fresh start. Nothing and no one has been in here.

With a satisfied nod, I press the Down button and use my thumbprint to activate the elevator. With a chuckle, I recall Colby Hunt's comment when he called to advise me I needed to return to my condo for the installation. "Think of it like a roach motel, Beckett. Even if they manage to get in, they'll never get out."

"Who knows? One day that might come in handy." I laugh aloud as I swoop into the elevator that will take me to the first floor.

✦

I send the recording of the new song to Mick while I'm in the car. He immediately sends me a thumbs-up, which I know means he'll listen to it later. I also shoot off a text to Erzulie asking if we're still on for dinner. Her quick *No. Have to get back to you* concerns me. I make a mental note to ask Carys if she's connected with the young singer lately since her negative press in the fall.

I frown before texting back, *Tonight was important.* And it was. I was going to try to talk her into meeting with Kristoffer Wilde after some recent events had happened to her. Despite the fact Kris tends toward more commercial acts like myself, Brendan Blake, and Zapatta, Erzulie has that appeal on the indie circuit. She's got the same allure of a young Stevie Nicks, Sarah McLachlan, and Annie Lennox with a bit of Brittany Hölljes tossed in. "The kid could go far," I mutter aloud..

"I'm sorry, Beckett. Did you say something?" Kane asks.

"Nothing to worry about."

Within moments, we pull up alongside the curb outside Carys's building. I let out a sigh of relief. Whether it's the cold weather or the presence of the tourists, I don't care. But for once the paps aren't clustered around the entrance. I start to open my door when Kane growls. "Oh, for Christ's sake, it's just..." Then I see someone stumble out the door, wiping her eyes.

And there's no keeping me in the car.

I fling open the door and sprint toward the woman, who is somehow managing a fast clip in Louboutins. "Paige! Damnit, Paige! Stop!" I holler as I bob and weave past confused and annoyed citygoers.

The woman in question comes to a halt, whirling around. Her lips part as I catch up and grip her upper arms. "Bec—Beckett." Her voice is stilted, eyes dilated.

I shake her slightly to bring her into focus. "What's wrong? Are you okay? Did someone hurt you?"

She opens her mouth to respond, but before she can, I trample all over her words. "Come on. I have friends with an office in this building. They can help. I swear they're wonderful people. They'll protect you."

She braces her hand against my chest. Unthinking, I left the first four buttons undone in what has become my trademark move while dressing. Her cool hand lands against the center of my chest, causing us both to gasp. She goes to yank her hand back, but I grip her wrist and look down. It's her left hand, completely bare of rings. My heart thumps so wildly, I'm certain she can feel it.

She begins to tremble. And suddenly the impact of her daughter's stage name hits me full force. I step closer. "Dr. Paige *Kensington*? You've never married?"

Paige responds distractedly, "Not that it's any of your business, but no. I haven't."

"It's my business when your brother taunted me years ago about *your* daughter after I saw him in a club in Dallas, bird." I immediately slip back into calling her my little songbird.

Paige lets out a small cry of despair. Because of the memories? I wonder. Her free hand flies to her mouth. "Him too? Who hasn't..." She tries to twist away, but I've still got a hold of her hand. "Please, please, let me go."

"Tell me, Paige," I demand, needing the answers more than I want to protect her from the pain. "Tell me the truth, right now."

Her ridiculously clear green eyes have tears pouring from them. "That's what I came here to do, only it was me who learned too many of them. My...our...Austyn is upstairs in Carys's office. Please be kind. There's been too many shocks for all of us today." And with that, Paige rips her hand from mine and dashes away as fast as she can in stilettos.

Leaving me standing there with a gamut of emotions—too many to name. I tip my head back and glance upward, trying to ground myself, wondering what the hell happened.

And what I'm about to walk into.

⊕

"Uh-oh," Angie murmurs when I stride into LLF a few moments later with my security team hard on my heels, which is where they've been since Paige ran from me less than ten minutes earlier. An unbearable ten minutes Kane spent blistering my ears about the insanity of running off without the protection I pay a small mint for.

As I shrug off my outer jacket, I order them, "No one leaves."

Grimly, Kane nods before taking a post by the door. I throw my coat across the waiting room chairs and storm to the imposing mahogany doors.

"Damnit, Becks. You can't go in there." Angie throws herself in front of them, trying to block my entrance.

I skewer her through with a look. "I just ran after Paige down on the street. She was destroyed even before I had words with her.

There's no way in hell you're stopping me from walking through those doors, Angela."

She curses under her breath. "Give me two minutes to prepare them. Promise me."

I lift my arm and shift my shirtsleeve so I can view my watch face. "Go."

Angie slips through the doors. I hear a distinctive snick of the lock. I'd be faintly amused at her lack of trust if it wasn't for the fact my daughter's just beyond those doors, and I'll kick them in if I have to.

One minute and thirty-eight seconds later, the doors are unlocked, but instead of Angie opening them, it's David. "You're a pain in my damn ass on a good day. You know that?"

I'm about to blast him until I get a good look at his face. It's filled with fatigue and worry. "What happened?"

"The truth happened, Beckett. And it wasn't pretty."

I swallow the lump building in my throat as we move toward the closed door of the conference room. I confirm what we'd already guessed. "Paige kept Austyn from me."

"Yes, but it wasn't because she wanted to. It was because she was fed a bunch of bullshit from the one person she should have been able to trust." David stops just short of opening the door.

"Who?" My question may be simple, but the answer is everything.

"Her father. He's been lying to her from the moment she was born."

"Motherfucker!" I shout.

Of course, that's when David flings open the conference room door. Immediately, Austyn surges to her feet. And despite my age and the life I've led, I flush like an errant schoolboy over the fact cursing is the first words my daughter hears directly from me.

BECKETT

Do you think Beckett Miller goes on Santa's naughty or nice list? I know where he should go! Right in the middle—of my bed, that is.

— Sexy&Social, All the Scandal You Can Handle

"What the hell are you doing here?" she snarls when she sees me. Immediately, she turns on Carys. "Was this a setup? Was Mama supposed to be involved?"

Carys shoots daggers at me with her eyes. "No. In fact, I believe he was given explicit instructions that today was not a good day for one of his drive-by visits."

I have the grace to feel abashed. "I..."

But before I can apologize for my intrusion, Carys lambasts me in front of my own child. "My colleagues and I have worked tirelessly for this day. Does that penetrate through your thick skull?"

I grit my teeth. "It does."

"Are you sure you understand that? Because first, Angie and Ward went to listen to Austyn play—putting Angie at significant risk, which fortunately hasn't caused any harm, knock on wood." Carys leans over and knocks on the conference room table. "Then, my firm was investigated because of *you*. Where I had to hire my own investigators to find out why."

"I know all of this. And if you're so pissed, bill me for the last," I snap.

"Then let me catch you up on something you might be missing, Beckett. When I tell you don't come in, there's a damn good reason! You may be my largest client, but you're not my only one. And you could have broken any of the potential ten different confidentiality clauses I insert into the contracts I make other people sign—some of which are on your behalf—just by stepping foot into this office." Before I can butt in, Carys holds up a hand. "I'm not surprised by this, mind you. But I have no compunction about sitting back and letting Kensington rip into you since I'm officially her attorney of record. And you just interrupted a very private meeting between me and my client. Now before you say a word, think very hard about how you would react if that happened to you and it was because you just dropped in *after* you were advised not to do so." Carys taps her fingers on the table behind her, waiting for my response.

I have such conflicting emotions rioting through me: chagrin, humiliation, and regret. Because she's right. I'd have torn the arm off whoever walked into the door, and she damn well knows it. I open my mouth to acknowledge my mistake when I hear the most annoying sound in the world.

A slow clap.

"If I hadn't hired you to be my attorney already, Carys, that would have convinced me," drawls Paige's and my daughter. "Does anyone win an argument with you?"

Carys twists her head slightly so she faces Austyn. "Not when it matters. Like I told you, I'm damn good at what I do."

"Well, that will be one thing to relieve Mama's mind," my grown daughter whispers.

And hearing the word "Mama" is what does it. Anger overrides everything else. I curse the lifetime of opportunities I missed with this precocious woman because of a wealth of mistakes and lies, none of which my fame or my wealth can get back.

By the time I'm done, Austyn's expression has changed from hostile to pensive. "You truly didn't know? Before we came here, Mama thought you must have. Then something happened before she left. It wasn't until she"—she nods at Carys—"explained everything she told Mama that I realized you both got rooked."

David coughs. The expletives stop tumbling from my lips. It's all I can do to force myself to nod as a knot the size of a cantaloupe swells in my throat.

"I figured if Gramps was bein' nickel-and-dimed by your folks because they knew, then you probably knew. My one true regret in finding out about all of this is thinking you just didn't give a shit about me or my mother the night she told me who you were when she's given up her whole existence to make sure I could be me." Her expression becomes so protective, so fierce, I'm almost thrown back from the sheer force of it.

And the memories.

Because it's almost a replica of Paige's as she whispered to me the last night we were together before my parents beat the crap out of me. The night before we were both going to run away. *"I'm not afraid of hard work, Beau. I'll work and go to school."*

"I don't want you to support both of us, bird. I can write anywhere."

She snuggles against me as our still-warm bodies lie entwined against one another. "We'll figure it out. As long as we're together, we can do anything. Be anything. Just as long as I have you."

I raise a trembling hand to my mouth. I feel like I've been kicked in the stomach as the realization sets in.

Paige was someone. She did do what she had to do. Because she had a piece of me with her.

Christ.

I tune back into the conversation to hear Carys placate Austyn. "I don't think he feels that way."

Austyn says to Carys hotly, "I won't sit here and listen to Sexy&Social's favorite darling malign my mother. It's bullshit. You *saw* her reaction. She wouldn't even let me see her break down like that."

Paige broke down? Then I recall the tears on her face when I confronted her on the street and groan. "Oh, shit."

Austyn surges to her feet and stalks around the table. "What did you do?" she demands.

"I ran into Paige downstairs," I confess.

David bangs his head against the door. "As if this couldn't get worse."

Carys bares her teeth at me. "And you said?"

"I demanded the truth." Then I jump back a foot because the two women in the room hiss at me so loudly, I'm afraid they're about to unsheathe their claws next. "She was already upset!" I shout over their belligerent yelling.

"I don't have to guess if you made things worse," Carys demands.

"All I did was..." But I feel the blood leech from my face when I recall chasing Paige down the street and what I revealed about Jesse. Subdued, I acknowledge, "Yes. I made things worse."

Austyn lets out an impressive-sounding shriek. I can't help but note, "You even screech on pitch."

"Give me a pen, a folder. Something. I need to kill him." She turns and reaches for a stack of files Angie likely put together with military precision when Carys wraps her up in her arms.

And my daughter starts to cry.

An ache so enormous, it makes those first few nights I spent without Paige when I left Kensington pale by comparison, opens inside of me. "No, please. Stop. I'm sorry. I'm so sorry."

I feel the warmth of David's hand come down on my shoulder in encouragement. I fumble out, "I had no idea until I heard you play that night at Redemption."

"You're full of it," Austyn manages.

"It was like hearing your mother speak French all over again. Did she tell you she used to try to help tutor me?"

"She did?"

"When you sang, I felt chills down my spine. Your mother's voice was surrounding me; it was like a dream. Then, I thought I was having delusions when I saw her racing down the stairs at the club." I swallow hard.

"The dance," Austyn whispers. She wraps her arms around herself.

"I was going to talk with her. And then I saw you, Austyn." I try to piece together the emotions I felt in that moment.

"Do you know my name from these?" She lays her hand on top of Carys's files.

I don't pretend. "Yes. And because your mother told me your name downstairs."

Another long, slow blink. "She did? What else did she say?"

"To be kind to you, that you've had too many shocks today." *God, Paige hasn't changed a bit, has she?* I think to myself. Or at least I think I do.

But when a smile—my smile, I realize with some surprise—crosses my daughter's face, I realize I might not have been so circumspect. Austyn announces, "Well, obviously, Beckett is on Team Mama and not Team Douche."

"He'd better be. Because she didn't deserve a damn thing that happened to her. Or to you," Carys declares. "Don't worry about your mama, sweetie. We're all going to protect her. Right, Dad?" She skewers me with a look that easily says, *Don't mess this up.*

I manage to push out around the boulder that's lodged against my vocal cords, "Right. I swear, Austyn, I'll do everything I can to protect your mother."

She lets out a huge sigh of relief, her body sagging into Carys's.

I blurt out the first of a million questions I have for my fully grown daughter. "So, you were born in Austin?"

Carys emits a light chuckle. "Finally, I'll get Austyn's version of the story."

Austyn shakes her head, a small, sad smile lifting her lips. "Actually, no. I was born in Kensington. Mama used to tell me she had a big fight with Gramps about it. She said there was no way in hell she was naming her child Kensington Kensington. Mama said she informed

Gramps she would either name me Austyn or after my father—his choice."

For a brief moment, I think about all the battles Paige must have fought for this girl, but I shove the thought aside when Austyn leaves the safety of Carys's embrace. She takes a tentative step toward me. Then another, until she's standing right next to me.

And I realize I was right that night at Redemption: she has my eyes.

My own burn when she holds out her hand. "Austyn Melissa Kensington. It's a pleasure to finally meet you."

I take her hand and tug her slightly. With a small cry, she flies forward against my shirt. I bury my head against her multihued braids. "The pleasure is definitely mine, Austyn."

Her arms tighten around me hesitantly before she lets go. And I'm not ashamed of the tears that fall from my eyes that everyone can see. What I'm devastated by is that Paige isn't here to understand. I don't blame her, though I plan on finding out every detail about what happened from Carys.

What I need to find Paige for is to thank her profusely for the gift she just brought to my life.

But where did she go?

PAIGE

People are more aware of the loss of loved ones during the holiday season. Here at Beautiful Today, we encourage you to take time to remember those you've lost. If you don't feel like participating in a holiday event, don't. And above all, take time for you.

— **Beautiful Today**

The plane lands with a bump on the tarmac in Austin. I never even bothered to check out of the hotel in New York since I plan on flying back to my daughter just as soon as I get this confrontation over with. But I couldn't let this fester inside me, not when I have so much more to deal with. Instead, I hopped on the last flight out of New York back home.

It's almost 11:30 p.m. by the time I pull up to my father's front door, but I don't care about the late hour or the inconvenience of waking him. I've had hours in the air to reread the files I asked for Carys to send to me.

And I'm more than prepared to say some things to this man who manipulated so much about my life.

Pulling up in the circular drive, I shove my car in park, leaving the engine running, lights on full blast. I don't grab a thing except my iPad before I storm up to the front door still wearing the same dress and heels I slipped into this morning. I immediately start ringing the bell and alternately pounding on the heavy knocker over and over until I see the lights turn on in the hall foyer.

That's when I stop and step back.

My father flings the door open, a snarl on his lips before he sees me. Then his face smooths out. "Paigey! What's going on? Come in. Why didn't you use your key?"

I don't move an inch from where I'm standing, even though my body is quaking. "How could you?" It's the only question I want answered.

"Paigey, what on earth are you talking about, girl? Come inside your home and talk..."

"This place will never be home to me again." A silence falls between us as I flick my tablet on and quote what I read earlier. "*After many years of travel with only a PO Box, Subject has identified a primary living residence in New York, New York. Inform client of new address for updated records.* Austyn would have been three at that time. Three. When I finally told her who her father was, do you know what she asked me?"

"No." He doesn't say anything else. His gaze is steady on mine. He doesn't deny or defend himself.

"She said, 'Knowing would have been better than not.' It wasn't your choice to make. It was mine, his, *ours*. Even if you hated me for my mother's death," I fling out.

His head turns to the side, pain leeching into it. And his actions become clear. "That's it, isn't it? You hate us both because we were alive and my mother wasn't?"

"Paige..." He twists his head back toward mine. But I step away, away from the man who manipulated my life while he claimed to love me, love my child.

"How could you look at us every day and live with your lies and your hate? How could you believe that's what my mother would want for me? For Austyn?"

My father's face is haggard. "You have no idea how hard it's been living without the person you love."

"I don't? At least you didn't believe the last thirty-seven years Mama left you because she didn't love you. Try living with wondering if you weren't enough of a woman while the man your heart is longing for parades on national television with one woman after another. That's pain, Father," I drawl.

"I didn't do it to hurt you."

"And that's just another lie. Lie, lie, lie. All you've done is lie to me. From the moment I could cogitate, that's all you've done," I shout. A car pulls up in the driveway behind mine, but I pay it no attention. "You've lied to me about how much you love me, how much you respect me. You've lied to me about every fact of my mother's death, including the fact I'm the damn reason for it, but we both know that's not quite the whole story, is it?"

Tears well in his eyes, but I pay them no mind as heavy footsteps fall on the stairs. "What's going on, Paige?" Jesse demands.

"Oh, good. I can tell you to kiss my ass at the same time." I seethe, whirling on him. "How dare you taunt Beckett with Austyn's existence when you saw him in a club in Dallas?"

"What the hell did you do, Jess? When the hell was this?" my father roars.

"None of this is your concern anymore, Father. I'll protect my daughter and myself from whatever is necessary," I inform him haughtily. I whirl back to find Jesse stunned. "Now answer me, you ass. What gives you the damn right to talk about her to him?"

"How did you find out?" is his only response.

"I'd like some answers too, Paige," comes my father's response.

"You want to know? Fine. I didn't trust the slick law firm that was suddenly contacting Austyn to represent her legal interests as they also represent her father's. So, I had your investigator do some digging."

My father's eyes close. If anything, his face turns a pasty white.

"Right. When I got to New York armed with all the information you gave me over the years, they came back at me with oh so much more. I was blindsided by how much you betrayed me, Father. You knew from the moment he was put on a steady payroll where to find him. You knew," I hiss.

"I did it to protect you," he tries to make me believe.

"You did it to hurt him, to hurt me! That's all you cared about. You did it to perpetuate a cycle of pain because that's all you felt when you looked at me. All this time, I was alone raising my daughter."

"You had us, Paige," my brother reminds me.

"And look at what good that did me." Jesse falls back a step at my harsh words.

Tears trickle down my face. "If it was just me, I might find some way to forgive you. But despite both yours and E's help, it was me raising my daughter. Alone. It was me wondering if I was woman enough every time I entered into a new relationship—when I had time. It was me wondering *when* they were going to leave, not if. But I could have known, had answers, if he"—I jerk my thumb toward our father—"had just told me the truth. Starting with the fact that it was Beckett's mother T-boning Mama and not a damn infection that killed her. Isn't that right, Daddy?"

Jesse's head whips toward our father. His voice is shocked when he asks, "Dad?"

Our father's face contorts, but he remains stubbornly silent.

"How did you find this out, Paige?" Jesse demands.

"It's a damn police record, Jesse. The day before I was born, Mama was in an accident."

"That's..." He's about to deny my words when something changes. "I remember now. She picked flowers in the field with Ethan that morning. Put them in a white pitcher on the counter. How could I have forgotten?" Jesse moves closer to me as he stares in horror at our sire. His hand grasps for mine as wounds of his own start to bleed.

I let him take it because I know how it felt in New York to bleed when no one else is there. But my anger at Jesse is still simmering just below the surface.

"Jesse, you were so young," our father tries.

"I was five, Dad. And she was gone. Would it have mattered if it was a virus or a wreck? No. All that mattered was Mama was gone."

"What neither of you two realize is she was the love of my life. It was my job to protect her! To protect this family!" he shouts.

"And that gave you the license to interfere with mine? Even to the point of leaving me and my daughter in the dark?" I fume.

His maniacal eyes shift toward me and drift downward. "Anybody else, Paige. Why did it have to be him."

"What's he talking about, Paige?" Jesse asks.

"The person who crashed into Mama was Beckett's mother. That's why—despite knowing everything about where he was from practically the beginning—he never told me how to reach him. Just think, Jesse, our father would rather pay blackmail to the people who killed Mama than..."

An eerie shiver races down my spine when my father starts to laugh. "Blackmail? Darlin', that wasn't blackmail. Let's just say that was a thank-you to them for never acknowledging their biological grandchild. After all, it wasn't hard to convince them to accept it as it came with a legal agreement I would drop the wrongful death civil suit against them."

"You sued Beckett's parents about Mama?" I confirm slowly, the picture becoming clearer.

"You're damn straight I did!" he roars.

"How long had it been in court, Father?"

His brow furrows. "By that point? Sixteen, seventeen years. What does it matter?"

Enough time for all of us to be punished for an accident or fate. Dropping Jesse's hand, I stride forward and succinctly declare, "She'd be ashamed of you."

He sneers, "You never knew her. Despite the stories, you never knew your mother, girl."

"No, but I did. And Paige is right, Dad. Mama would have been damn ashamed. I know this because I am. Come on, Paige." Jesse steps forward to take my arm.

He guides me down the stairs to my waiting vehicle.

"Now wait just a damn minute," our father calls after us.

We ignore him. "I'm furious with you, Jess," I grit out.

"That's for later. Are you staying at your house tonight?"

I nod. "For a few days. Then I'm heading back to New York. I need to be with Austyn."

"Fair enough. I'll drop by." When I shoot him a menacing look, he holds up his hands. "I swear, I'll give you a few days. But I really want to know what happened in New York."

I twist my body to the still-shouting man on the front porch of the place I once called home. "Every part of my life has been shaken by this."

Sadness pinches the corners of his eyes. "Paige, I never meant..."

I lay my hand across his mouth. "Just save it, brother. I can't right now."

He nods before backing away. I slide into my car and put it into gear. Almost on autopilot, I drive back to my home. When I reach the community of cookie-cutter houses I raised Austyn in, I pull into the garage and drop my head to the steering wheel.

What do I do? How do I go about fixing two decades of deceit perpetuated by my family?

Are there even enough ways to apologize to Beckett for the years he missed with Austyn?

Unable to process what to do, I drag myself from the garage into my house, seeking the oblivion of sleep.

BECKETT

It's like watching the privileged abandon the *Titanic*. All of the celebrities are fleeing New York for the holidays. Our sincere hope is the employees at Teterboro, La Guardia, and JFK are being treated with kindness and respect.

— Stella Nova

Edited to add: Sorry, Newark! Didn't mean to leave all of you out!

A few days after the confrontation in LLF, I arrive unannounced at the offices to find a battle royale going on with the women ostracizing the men as they plot out their demise. "What did you do this time, Dave?" I ask Carys's husband.

He mutters something unintelligible, clearly more surly than usual. Ward, the cheeky bastard, has no problem informing me, "He passed along work Carrie earmarked for him to me to be double-checked. Now we're both up a creek because Angie figured out we were billing incorrectly."

"How in the hell did you manage to rook that up? Do I need to request an audit of my account?" I demand.

Ward holds up a placating hand. "Nothing of yours, Becks. I swear. Angie looked at all the billing on our flight back from Montana and..."

"Montana? What were you doing out there?"

"Kris's holiday party. You know, the one you RSVP'd for and missed?" Ward says pointedly.

I always reply I'll attend the owner of Wildcard's holiday to-do at his winter residence in Bigfork, but usually something or another always comes up. "Kris always understands." I wave off his comment with a flick of my hand.

"Must be nice to have a boss that understands," David finally speaks. When he does, his voice is so glum both Ward and I shake with our laughter.

"Do you want me to find out just how bad it is?" I offer. After all, I do owe David a solid after he found out the information about the firm in Texas.

He momentarily brightens. "Would you? The last time I poked my head in there, Carrie was threatening my annual bonus."

I stifle the laugh threatening to erupt as I straighten my obnoxiously awful holiday suit I decided to don this morning. "Just call me Santa."

His normally serious countenance splits with a wide smile. "Not a chance in hell."

I stroll to the conference room door and fling it open. "Ho, ho, ho, darlings. Who else is getting in the holiday spirit?" I proclaim.

Angie drawls, "I can just imagine the headlines tomorrow. 'Who wants to sit on this Santa's lap?'"

"Are you volunteering, Angie?"

"Fuck you, Becks" is yelled by Ward from behind me.

Then Carys announces, "Ward, David, we're ready for you both now."

"And that's my cue to go," I declare.

"Oh, no, Becks. Stay. Please. This impacts you as well." Carys's smile when her brother and husband walk in can only be classified as pure malice. When everyone's seated around the conference table,

Carys preens. "Bad boys generally get coal. This season, David, Ward, you both are getting Becks."

They groan unanimously. I demand, "What the hell did I do wrong?"

She turns on me. "I'm sure you'll think of something."

I wink, my good mood going unperturbed. "I always do, don't I?"

And that's when Ward says, "Shit."

"'Tis the season, brother. Enjoy your present." Angie taps at her watch insistently. "Now, the lot of you, get out. Angie and I have an important meeting we have to attend."

But just before we all exit the conference room, there's a commotion at the door. "Let me by, you *goons*! I'm here to see Carys."

"I'm sorry, do you have an appointment?" one of my security details asks my daughter calmly.

"This is an emergency. I shouldn't need one," she snaps.

Just as Austyn is about to shove at a bodyguard who easily could hurt her, I bark out, "Mitch, leave it."

"But sir..."

"It's fine. Austyn, what's wrong?"

She scans the room until her eyes settle on Carys, and they marginally relax. "I can't get a hold of Mama."

Carys shoots a look at Angie. "We'll delay a few hours."

Angie murmurs, "Of course. Austyn, can I get you some coffee?"

"Thanks," she says gratefully.

Carys guides her into a chair. "When was the last time you spoke to your mother, Austyn?"

"Here. Right here. But I know she flew home to Austin. I managed to get a hold of my Uncle Jesse briefly the day after, but now I can't. He said she confronted my father. He showed up because as foreman to the Kensington Properties, he could see a car pull up and not leave. He was worried about my grandpa."

A sick feeling churns in my gut. "What did Jesse say, Austyn?"

Her face turns up to mine, and now I don't see what's mine but everything about her that's Paige. "She yelled at him, accused him of lying her entire life. Uncle Jesse said it was bad, really bad. And Grandpa showed no remorse, none."

"Does your uncle know where she was going next?" Ward asks. His fingers are on his phone.

"Just to her house. But every time I've reached out, she doesn't answer."

"Maybe she's just absorbing everything," I hear myself say.

Including the web of lies that's been wrapped around both of us for decades—first around her, then spun from her around me. God, it's time to cut through them to free both of us.

"You couldn't possibly understand." There's frustration in every word spoken by Austyn. "There isn't a day where I don't connect in some way with my mama. Whether it's just a funny emoji, a GIF, a news article, something. She's always been that person I can tell anything to. Hell, when I got the letter from all of you, I immediately contacted her while I was on tour on a video chat, buck-ass naked, where I'd just—"

Angie coughs loudly, interrupting my daughter's rant. I affect a stern face. "There are some things we don't need to know, young lady."

"See? Mama didn't care. Well, she did, but she trusts my instincts. And right now, they're screaming at me there's something wrong."

Before I can do something to worsen the situation, Carys interrupts. "What do you think happened?"

"That's just it, I don't know. I've tried home, her office. No answer. I've sent texts; they're delivered, but she's not responding."

"It could be she's just processing everything," I point out logically.

Austyn shoots me a filthy look, which reminds me of the ones Paige used to hurl in my direction when I would say something insane. I want to cower and beam at the same time. I hold up my hands to placate her. "Right. I get it. That was ridiculous. Tell me what you need and it's yours."

For a moment, stunned incredulity replaces the abject worry before suspicion sets in. "Why?"

I fumble for a response. Fortunately, David saves me. "Becks cares for a number of people. I'm not surprised he'd volunteer to help."

To my shock, that agitates Austyn more. "Oh. I thought it was because he's..."

"Your father? Damn straight it's because I am," I growl.

Belligerently, she whirls on me. "Well, it's been three days, and I haven't heard a word from you. I thought you might reach out to me. It's not like they"—she flings her arm out to encompass my legal team—"are going to just drop your cell number in my lap so we can just skip off to a basketball game."

I sneer. "I hate organized sports."

"Me too."

"I much prefer rodeo," I announce, likely shocking everyone in the room.

"Same. If I can't see it at the pens, I love watching it at Rodeo Ralph's."

I frown. "You're too young to get in there." Rodeo Ralph's is a dive bar located in downtown Kensington and has been around since I was a kid.

"He's turned it into more than just a bar. Now you can get food there."

"Really? Is it any good?" The idea of the behemoth of a man cooking sends my stomach reeling while simultaneously intriguing me.

Austyn smirks. "No, it totally sucks. I go just to get a free beer on occasion."

I bark a laugh. "How does your mother feel about that?"

She rolls her eyes. "Ask her yourself."

"Trust me, I will. After we find her." I turn to Ward, who's texting on his phone. "Can you do me a favor? Have my plane fueled and ready on standby at Teterboro in two hours?"

"I already texted your pilot. He said closer to three because of holiday traffic."

"Wait. What's happening?" Austyn's head swivels from one of us to another.

"We're flying down to Austin to find your mother." And while I'm there, I can lay some old ghosts to rest.

"Shut the hell up," Austyn breathes. "I just came in here hoping one of you would call her."

Carys chuckles. "That's what I was going to suggest, but your father is obviously taking control of this show."

I lift my hand to flick her off, but damnit, I have an impressionable nineteen-year-old looking at me like I'm her hero. Not because I'm the rock god, Beckett Miller, but because I'm willing to drop everything and help her mother.

Of the two, I'd give up my career in music just to experience the second for eternity.

I clear my throat. "Right. Wheels up in three hours. Austyn, do you want to pack and then meet me here so we can get to the airport, say in two hours?"

She gestures behind her. "I already packed. I was going to head out to JFK to get a flight if I couldn't get anyone to take me seriously."

"Right." Just that alone tells me how serious her concerns are. "Then why don't you ride with me to my place, I'll pack a couple of days' worth of clothes, and we'll head out."

"Hold on, Beckett. You're planning on staying? In Kensington?"

Grimly, I reach for my daughter's hand and press it firmly against my chest. "I made your mother a promise to come back for her. It's taken me too long to keep it." Especially knowing she needed me this whole while. The guilt that wants to suffocate me is like a tidal wave.

But I'm not left to drown in the emotion. Instead, I'm poked in the chest by Paige's and my offspring. "Damn straight. Now, let's go. I've heard about some legendary parties at this place of yours. I'm dying to see it."

"Those are a thing of the past," I inform Austyn as I push her out the door. "I intend on becoming a model of propriety."

Carys chokes on air. David calmly thwacks his wife on the back.

With Austyn in front of me, this time I do give them the middle finger. But I have a goofy smile on my face when I do. Therefore, I'm not surprised when they all burst out laughing.

Carys shouts just as I'm about to close the door, "Let us know how Paige is!"

"We will," I call back.

Then I close them out and focus on the part of my heart that manages to live and breathe outside my body—my daughter.

BECKETT

I can only speculate Beckett Miller was headed to his home in LA. Sources indicated he and another passenger boarded a plane early in the day at Teterboro. And there goes New York until after the Grammys.

— Sexy&Social, All the Scandal You Can Handle

"Did you ever fall out of love with her?" Austyn asks me after the pilot announces we're descending into a regional airport in Austin.

"What day is it?" I ask in return.

"Thursday."

"Nope. It's a day that ends in y," I quip.

Austyn doesn't even crack a smile. "If the two of you who had such intense feelings for each other can't make it, I'm afraid for the rest of us. What hope is there for love?"

"Whoa, whoa, whoa. Where is this coming from?" I'm as unprepared for this as much as I was for the dick pic that appeared on her iPad when she was in the bathroom earlier and her cool "Please, Beckett. I've seen more of your naked ass in the tabloids than one child should see of their father. You seeing a random cock shouldn't shock you in the least."

"Nothing is ever forgotten once it hits the internet." God, I of all people know that.

She shrugged nonchalantly. "And that's why we have Uncle E."

That piqued my interest enough to distract me away from the men's genitalia on her Liquid Retina display. "What is Ethan doing these days?"

"Well, there's what his storefront says he does, and then there's what he really does."

"What's the difference?" I asked.

"One means I don't ever have to worry about pics like these associated with my name. Ever." She tapped her pad.

I barked out a laugh. Then. Now I'm not laughing as we eat up the miles in seconds, but it's still not fast enough to get to Paige.

Long minutes go by before red-rimmed eyes meet mine. "There's you and Mama, two people who each nurtured this unshakeable love, but other people who had nothing to do with it came in and managed to take it over. What kind of hope does that offer the rest of us?"

I school my face over what Austyn unwittingly gave away. I won't know if she spoke the truth until we land and I'm standing in front of Paige again, but if she's right... "You said it yourself."

"What do you mean?" Confusion mars her beautiful face.

"Other people. I did it first, your mother next. We allowed other people to come into our relationship. If I'd just stuck to the plan, then the only two people to make or break us would have been the only two people who mattered. Her and me."

The wheels of the plane touch down just as I finish. Austyn's hands cover her face to hide her tears. "I just hope she's all right."

"I'm sure she is."

"Thank you for bringing me." Austyn drops her hand and reaches for mine.

I hold her hand until we're given permission to deplane to the waiting SUV. As for me, it's time to go find Paige and demand answers for what she put our daughter through.

Our daughter. A crazy smile lights my face. I've sung in front of tens of thousands of people, and yet, following Austyn off that plane, I don't think I've ever quite felt quite so alive.

⊕

The caravan of SUVs comes to a stop on the outskirts of Kensington in a modest but pretty development. "Is this it, Ms. Kensington?" Kane calls from the driver's seat.

"Yes. That's her car." Austyn reaches for the handle, but I quickly lean over and stop her.

"Kane, go." The former Marine jerks up his chin before sliding from the car. The other Hudson agent remains in the car with us. Before the chambers of my heart can fully rotate in sequence, the locks on the car are engaged. Several other men from the other vehicles have done the same, breaching the fence to slip into Paige's backyard. "I just pray like hell she's not in the back."

"I hope so too. What the hell is going on, Beckett?" Austyn shouts. Her fingernails dig into the skin of my hand.

"They're making sure she's safe," I tell her brutally, not hiding the truth from her.

"But...why? Mama's an audiologist. Why would someone want to...you?"

"Money," I inform her succinctly. "I have quite a bit of it."

"Mama wouldn't care about that. She'd tell you to donate it to some charity. It's what she tells Gramps constantly."

I smile faintly, remembering she used to do that when she was seventeen. Still, I give Austyn a moment to reason it all out. Her brow forms a V. "But why would they want to hurt her because of you?"

"It's not necessarily because of me anymore, Austyn."

Her jaw drops. "No. Just keep your...no. That's not why...I don't want your money!" She shoves at me.

I wrap my fingers around hers, still uncertain of my rights to do more. "I..." But I'm not given a chance to say more as we're interrupted by Mitch. "Kane says you're clear. Leave the bags; we'll bring them up. "

I let go of Austyn. "Let's go find out what's going on with Paige."

The moment I say the words, her fingers are on the door handle.

The two of us hurry under the watchful eye of the security Kane coordinated. Austyn unlocks the front door, yelling, "Mama? Mama? Where are you?" as she dashes from room to room.

But my eyes are caught by the kitchen table. Albums of photos are stacked to one side, scissors and glue to another. "What on earth..." I murmur.

"Don't touch that!" Paige snaps.

My head whips around. Her dark hair is pushed back by a bandana, much like she used to wear it while riding. She's wearing a ratty UT Medical School T-shirt over a pair of short jean shorts. Her face and feet are bare. And her arms are loaded down with more albums. Her eyes go wide when she spies Austyn. "Honey? What's wrong? What are you doing here?"

"Mama? How can you ask me that? You haven't answered your phone in *days*!"

Confusion puckers Paige's brow. "What day is it?"

"Thursday," both Austyn and I answer.

Her bright green eyes widen comically behind her glasses. Shoving the albums in my direction, she races to find her phone. "I was supposed to... Crap, it's my turn. They're going to be so upset. We were supposed to talk about what to do about...well, about things."

"What happened, Mama?" Austyn asks.

Paige ignores her. "They would have called the house if something important changed. They know my head's still reeling."

"Paige, are you okay?" I drop the books into one of the dining room chairs.

"I..." For the briefest of moments, our eyes lock. In hers I see agony, grief, and determination.

"That does it." A few quick strides and I'm standing directly in front of the woman who with a few words made me want to be a better man. Lying in my bed on so many empty nights, I'd have flashbacks to the moments of the two of us before my life went to shit, before I clawed for it to become something Midas himself would envy.

And I still missed the one thing I needed to make it perfect: the love of the woman who built the music in my soul.

"Paige, bird, talk to me, please. What happened?" I cup her cheeks.

She visibly shudders. "He lied. About so, so much. I..."

I hush her. "Carys told me. I hope that's okay."

Her bitter laugh echoes the pain rattling around inside her chest. "Of course. I left her everything I had in the event he tried to worm his way out of it and smear your good name."

I tip her chin up and smile. "We have a daughter, bird. I think we both know my name isn't entirely good."

Her body collapses against mine as sobs take it over.

I scoop her up in my arms, holding her high against my chest. Her face burrows against my neck. "Oh, God, Beckett. I'm sorry. I'm so, so, sorry."

I declare, "Beat it, Austyn. Me and your mama have things to discuss."

Paige's head whips up. "No. Wait. We don't have time. Jesse's going to be here soon."

I hear one, two doors slam. "Too late. Kane will verify it's him and bring him to the door."

Paige's legs drop down, sliding down the front of my body. Every inch of her warm body scalds mine. I hold her branded against me. "We need to talk."

She nods frantically. "I know. But we have to get to the hospital first."

"What?" Austyn and I shout together.

Fresh tears well up in Paige's eyes. She turns from my arms and walks straight to Austyn's as the front door opens to Jesse Kensington. His face first displays shock, then a sort of resigned acceptance to see me. He walks across the room. "Beau."

"It's Beckett these days." I can't prevent my eyes from drifting to where Paige and Austyn are embracing. "For more than just your sister."

"Beckett," he immediately corrects himself. "I owe you a long-overdue apology."

"What's going on?" I ignore his attempt to make amends for the moment.

He takes a deep breath. "My father. He had a heart attack the day after Paige lit into him. He's in critical care. We've been taking shifts going..."

I hear my daughter let out a hoarse sob. With that, it takes me three strides to cross the room to wrap her and her mother up in my arms. "It will be all right. I promise," I croon in their ears.

"You can't promise that," Paige begins.

"Yes I can. For the first time, we're all together. Therefore, it's going to be all right. It has to be." I hold Paige's eyes as I try to communicate with her that there's no need for her to ask for forgiveness. None at all.

Her lips tremble as she whispers, "You're right. It has to be."

And with that, I clutch the pieces of my heart I lost and the piece I never knew I was missing just a little closer, afraid if I let them go, they'll disappear and I'll never feel this whole ever again.

PAIGE

Be festive, my ass. I just got dumped right before Christmas. This is such bullshit #airingofgrievences

— @PRyanPOfficial

"They say the surgery will take between three to six hours and depends on how severe the damage is once they get inside." I repeat the surgeon's words later that night to my brothers, my daughter, and Beckett. "They can't perform an angioplasty, which is where they use a small balloon to widen the artery. He has more than one that's diseased, including the left main coronary artery, which is severely narrowed or blocked."

"Christ," Ethan mutters. "How the hell did this happen?"

"We'll work on figuring this out after. The good news is that if all goes well with the surgery, and if he follows doctor's protocols, he should remain symptom-free for as long as ten to fifteen years after this procedure. The bad news? He's going to have a six-to-twelve-week recovery period. I'm sorry, baby. But when you go back to New York, I'm going to have to ask you to send my things back." I can feel

Beckett's eyes pierce me with that announcement, but I can't handle glancing in his direction.

Austyn snorts. "Like I plan on going back with this news?"

"Austyn, you have work commitments," I try to reason.

"And you don't?" she shoots back.

I decide now is as good a time as any to make the announcement I had already come to days earlier. "I'm closing down my office." Immediately, there are protests from my family members. I hold up a hand. "There are other reasons why I'm making that decision." *Namely, my father's investment when I want nothing of his*, I think bitterly, but I hold that back. "I'll be using the time I'm here in Kensington to refer my patients to other doctors, maybe see if I can get someone interested in purchasing the entire business as is."

Beckett stands. "Paige, can I speak with you a moment?"

I hold up a finger to ask him to give me a second. "So, that's it. Surgery is tomorrow. Due to his age, he'll be the first one in at 7:00. I'll be heading down to the hospital at five."

"Will they let you scrub in, Mama?"

"Unlikely, darling, though I'll ask. I'd be surprised if they grant me that request since it's Gramps, but I'm certain I'll receive more frequent updates since I know everyone on staff." I push to my feet. "Now, I'm not in a mood to cook."

"Ralph's?" Austyn proposes.

I sigh. "Young lady, we are not going to a bar with crappy food just so someone can try to pick you up to get you a beer. If you want a drink, have one here. I'm too tired to argue. Besides, your father has enough security personnel here to drive all of us in four separate directions in the event of an emergency. But, for the love of all things, pick out some decent food." I walk in Beckett's direction and then past him toward the covered lanai. He follows me out, and I shut the door.

Immediately, I become anxious until his gorgeous face splits into a smile. "You handle her beautifully. She was talking about Ralph's on the plane."

"I don't know how she knew to come back to Texas," I wonder.

He passes a hand absentmindedly over my hair, much the same way he did when we would sit in a field not so very far from here. "She just did, bird. She marched right into Carys's office demanding help because you weren't answering your phone." His eyes narrow on mine. "Why weren't you?"

"Between being at the hospital, then napping, then working on something... I meant to. But I hadn't slept until after yesterday when..."

"When what?"

"When I knew it was safe. When I felt like someone I could trust had my back," I confess.

"Christ, Paige. It was that bad?" A muscle ticks in his jaw.

I nod before whispering, "He called her an abomination. How could I ever have forgotten that, Beckett?"

And before my eyes, the boy I remember surges inside of the man I've only seen on television or in glossy magazines. "To you, for you, part of me will always be Beau." He brushes a piece of hair away from my face.

"But that's not who you are. Not really."

"Paige..."

"Not anymore."

"Don't say that."

"I understand what Austyn's doing here, Beckett. Why are you?" I ask bluntly.

"Because we were worried."

"I find that..."

"What?"

"Unusual. Odd. Absolutely surreal if you want to know the truth."

"You find it odd I would care about what matters to our daughter so quickly?" He appears as if I've wounded him.

I shake my head. "No. Austyn is so dynamic, so warm, just so incredible, I have little doubt it took you the same amount of time to fall for her it took me."

Certainly it's curiosity that prompts him to ask, "And that was?"

"Her first heartbeat," I respond instantly.

His lips curve slowly. I ignore the way my own heart trips the way it did all those years ago when that smile was mine alone before I saw it directed at how many women in the media. And had to ignore the ache it left in my gut afterward. "It looks good on you," he concludes.

"What does?"

"The beauty and fierceness of motherhood."

I toss my head back and laugh. "Oh, please, Beckett. There's no need to tell me pretty little lies at this late date."

"I wasn't..." he protests. I just hold up my hand to stop what he was about to say. "What I said was nothing less than the truth," he defends himself.

"Don't," I plead shakily.

He squares his shoulders. "What would you say if I told you my feelings never changed?" His fingers dance along the back of his tattooed hand nervously.

My stomach roils at both the trite pickup line and the tiny seed of hope that gets flamed. I hate myself for feeling anything, so my voice is guttural when I reply, "Please don't. I have enough on my plate without looking back."

Beckett winces but doesn't say anything.

Damn my soft heart. I rush to add, "It's just hard. I loved you so much."

"And I loved you. God, a part of me always will."

"Same." Somehow, I have to find the strength inside me to cut these bonds between us—except for those he now has between him and Austyn. Whatever little nugget of guilt he has about me needs to be dissolved so he can be free to live the life he was meant to lead. And inspiration strikes. "Say goodbye, Beckett."

"What?" he bursts out loudly.

I wish I could hold my hand to my chest to stem the bleeding. Instead, I whisper, "The reality is we're not the same people we were. Maybe this was always the way it was going to be."

"You can't..."

"Give me the kiss you should have given me twenty years ago. Then leave. Go. I'll send Austyn back to New York in a few days."

"You're trying to get rid of me?" he confirms incredulously.

"You clawed and dreamed your way away from here. Maybe if..." Then I regain my wits and start to back away. "Never mind. What a terrible idea. Just put it down to my being..."

Before I can get another word out, he hauls my body back against his. His tattooed hand surges into my hair, tilting my head just the way he used to when we'd be in a field of trampled-down, sun-warmed grass. His other arm bands tightly around my waist. But just like the first time he ever kissed me, I'm lost in the ferocity of his eyes.

It wasn't the first time our lips met that I understood why the blue is the hottest part of the flame.

Without breaking my gaze, Beckett dips his head and nips at my lower lip, causing me to gasp. Instead of immediately plundering inside like every other man whose lips have met mine, he takes his time, sweeping his tongue across my lower lip, drawing it in between his lips. Savoring the taste, savoring me.

Just like he always did right before he made me forget the universe existed.

Tilting his head, he fits his mouth to mine and deepens our connection. Our tongues duel back and forth, brushing up against each other, twining together.

If it's possible for a kiss to say more than words, ours would declare all the apologies, forgiveness, and wishes we would hope for the other. Tears mist in my eyes at the gentle beauty of the moan that escapes his lips.

My fingers score up his pecs as they make their way to his neck, his hair. My body melts into his to accept him—any part of him—against me. The beauty of this offering makes me long for things I can't want any longer and remember the perfection of the past with searing clarity. I can't prevent the shiver that racks my body. It's always been more than desire with this man; it was an all-consuming love.

And I love him enough to let him go back to his life, not be tied to the town he fought to escape.

Eventually, he brings me back down. I wrap my arms around myself to protect what's left of my shredded emotions. Turning away, I murmur, "I should have known better than to have done that."

"It wasn't a mistake, Paige," he replies hoarsely.

"Chalk it up to a naive heart, Beckett. I'd just appreciate if you wouldn't say anything to anyone." I twist my head around. "Even in song."

Indignant, he starts, "I would never…"

"'Guess Now I Know Better'?" I quote one of his song titles.

He flushes.

"'Live the Dream'?" I name another which is all about how stifling living in a small town is.

"That was about this place, not you," he replies hotly.

That's when I remind him. "Aren't you the one who said to me within minutes of meeting me I was the ruler of all I surveyed." I spin in a small circle. "You escaped, Beckett. Don't let yourself get trapped again."

He opens his mouth and shuts it without saying a word. Then he storms off the lanai, slamming the door behind him. A few moments later, I hear the front door slam as well.

And that's when I sit down in the chair sightlessly, knowing I did the right thing.

I let him go so he could compose the life he was meant to live. Even if it was meant to be without me.

And for just a moment, I allow myself the luxury of a strong woman's tears. I figure one day I'll be able to look back on this moment and equate it to waking from a perfect dream.

Even if that day is on my deathbed.

"Be happy, love. That's all I ask."

Hours after Jesse and Ethan have left and Austyn's stopped badgering me about where her father's gone, I drag myself to the dining room table again.

Pulling out the photos album from the time Austyn was five, I flip rapidly through it. Carefully, I select a few of my favorite shots and remove them. Tugging the new album closer, I slip in the photos and then tag them in my precise handwriting.

Austyn at her 5th birthday. All she wanted that year was drums, much to my dismay.

Austyn playing the recorder at school.

Austyn on her first pony. She named him Clef—after a treble clef, of course.

After I finish, I carefully add the stickers beneath the correct photos when I hear his deep voice ask, "What are you doing, bird?"

I screech, and the pen I'm holding goes flying. Beckett's standing in front of me, expression completely neutral. "How the hell did you get in here?"

He holds up Austyn's key ring. "Did you really think I would just leave?"

I can't prevent the bitterness from seeping into my voice. "You did the first time."

He doesn't bother to hide the wince on his face.

I scrub my hand over my face. "I'm sorry, Beckett. I'm tired, and that wasn't fair. I understand why you left. I can even say with complete truthfulness I might have made a similar decision under similar circumstances." I stand and bend down to retrieve my pen.

His smile is crooked. "Are you talking about the first time or after we kissed senseless—something, for the record, I think we should do again?"

I blink at him, unable to believe his audacity. I'm seriously tempted to hurl the pen in his direction. Fortunately, he speaks before my temper gets the better of me. "You're being generous again, but we both know the truth. I never should have left—then or now."

I snap back up. "Why are you trying to make this difficult?"

"Why are you trying to make it so easy for me to go?" he counters.

"Because somewhere between hating you and running into you on the street in New York, I was slapped in the face with a dose of reality! That all the cock and bull I'd been fed about you, about myself, was as bad as most of the media reports about you likely are."

He rubs his thumb across his full lower lip, causing me to catch sight of the rose tattooed on the back of his hand. I jerk my chin up. "That's an unusual tattoo for a badass rocker."

He tips his hand slightly. "Do you know I've never told anyone why I got that tattoo?"

"Sorry, I didn't mean to step on any boundaries."

He continues as if I haven't spoken. "That's because it's about you, bird. The rose reminded me of your beauty and, of course, Texas. It's not filled in because it's meant to represent the unfulfilled promise of love." His eyes meet mine. "Our love. What I sacrificed for the rest of it to happen. So, no, I'm not going to let you make this easy, Paige. From the moment you told me you were trespassing on your own land because you were a girl, it's never been easy."

"Stop. Please stop." I rub my hand over my forehead.

"I can't. Deep down I always believed you were too good for me."

"I think we both know that's not true. Look at who my father is, what he did to all of us." I jerk my head to the side.

And the next thing I know, his hand is gently turning my face up toward his. "Did you teach Austyn it mattered who her parents were?"

"Of course not," I respond indignantly. "I..." My voice dies as I realize I'm caught in my own trap.

"The first time I said I left to protect you, I was wrong. This time you're trying to protect me. And you would have been just as wrong. Why don't we take time to learn who we are as adults before we ruin something that could be the most beautiful thing either of us has ever created?"

Without thinking, I take his tattooed hand and drag it down to my stomach before whispering, "I've already carried the most beautiful thing we've ever made. I'm not sure how we could possibly top it."

I'm suddenly crushed in his strong arms, being rocked from side to side. I can't make out all the words, but I can make out his repeated thank-yous.

After long minutes, I pull back and rest my forehead on his before admitting, "I'm glad you came with Austyn. I'm so happy you didn't leave with this between us."

His crooked smile crinkles the corners of his eyes. "I never left. I just gave your brothers a break and took a rotation with your father so they could be rested to be with you tomorrow."

Stunned at the generosity of this man whose whole life was changed by my father, I wonder aloud, "How could you think you were never good enough for me?"

He opens his mouth, but I quickly press my finger against them softly. Pulling back, I whisper, "Thank you. Now, I need to get a few hours' sleep."

"Do you want me to sleep on the couch?" he asks, completely serious.

The very idea of multi-multi-millionaire rock god Beckett Miller bunking on my couch sends me into uncontrollable giggles. This is the same man who was once quoted as saying, "I don't intend to leave this planet with Sir Paul and Andrew as the only musicians on the billionaire list. Just wait and see." Once I regain my breath, I shake my head. "I do have a guest room."

"Good. Then Kane can take the couch."

Beckett picks up the duffle he must have dropped by the door when he came in. As I lead the way down the hall to the first-floor guest room, I probe gently, "So, security everywhere you go?"

"Trust me, bird. It can be a royal pain in the ass." He drops his bag just inside the room before admitting, "Though I'll be glad to have them when Austyn's around. I don't want anything to happen to her."

I lay my hand on his heart and let him in on a secret. "The first lesson of parenting?"

He ducks his head. "Yeah?"

"Something is always going to happen to her. The trick is knowing how to be there for her. You flying her here—knowing she needed to be here despite your reservations at coming back to Kensington? You're doing a great job, Dad. I always knew you would." My fingers trail away as I step back. "Sleep well, Beckett."

When I start to climb the stairs, I hazard a glance back. He's still standing exactly where I left him with the same goofy look on his face.

BECKETT

Ward Burke was spotted coming out of a jewelry store last night. He wouldn't devastate my heart like that, would he?

— Sexy&Social, All the Scandal You Can Handle

"How did it go?" I jump up from the couch the moment Paige walks through her front door.

"Not as well as expected." She heads into the kitchen. I immediately follow her.

After she ducks into her refrigerator, she holds up a pitcher of tea toward me, and I nod before continuing our conversation. "What do you mean?"

"They had to do surgical repair of the valve due to stenosis."

Without thinking, I remark, "Your brains have always been one of the sexiest things about you, Paige, but right now I need you to stop speaking Pig Latin. Can you translate what that means, please?"

Before she can answer, Austyn says, "The things I always wondered about my parents, and now I'm not so sure I really want to know."

I'm agog as Paige pulls down a total of five glasses. "You seriously wondered what I used to allure your father to me? This one leaves me stumped, Austyn. Should I feel offended or flattered? I assume since we do look alike it wasn't about looks since you basically look at my face when you look in the mirror."

"No. It was more general than that—you know, sex in general. But that's before I knew who my father was. Now that I actually know, it's creeping me out a bit."

Paige calmly keeps doing what she's doing without a reaction when Ethan enters the conversation with ease. "That's for damn sure, kiddo. I mean, think about what it took for your grandmother and grandfather to..."

"Thanks, Uncle E, but no. Just no."

"Oh, but come on, Austyn." Jesse's tired voice joins in mocking my daughter. "Your Grams and Gramps had to have had sex at least three times."

"This conversation is not going in the direction I wanted it to," Austyn announces.

"When does it ever with those two around?" Paige shrugs.

"You're no help, Mama!"

"Listen, kiddo. We have a rule. These are the questions you ask me in private. I'm sure as hell not answering these things in front of your uncles, let alone your father. Try again later." Paige sets a glass of tea in front of me.

Almost by rote, I lift the glass to my lips. "You actually talk about things like...like..."

"Sex?" Paige offers helpfully.

"Well, yes!"

All four Kensingtons laugh robustly. Ethan slaps me on the back. "We men will take you on the lanai later and we'll tell you all about when little Miss A had sex education in the fifth grade. Funniest damn day of my life."

Paige smirks while Austyn shrieks. "It was not funny!"

Jesse deadpans, "Would you rather we tell your father or your future husband?"

She whirls in my direction. "Enjoy your night with Uncle E and Uncle Jess. I'm going to—"

Paige interrupts. "Do some laundry if you want clean clothes that don't look like they're from the Kensington Borg."

I come damn close to spewing tea across the immaculate island as I listen to Paige disparage her hometown even in the smallest way.

"Good call, Mama." Austyn races over and presses a kiss to Paige's cheek. "Though I could have raided your wardrobe."

Paige's smile is filled with malice. "Not if you want me to keep to myself when you started your period."

The screech Austyn emits likely scares cats away for miles before she takes off running from the kitchen. Soon there's pounding up the stairs. Nobody speaks for a moment until they hear a door slam. Paige's energy deflates like a balloon. "Good. I didn't want to worry her."

"It's not like she can't look it up online, Paigey," Jesse argues.

"True, but if she follows true to form, she'll be angry at me for a while, lie down, and sleep. When she wakes up and is more rational, I'll explain everything. She's just too emotional to listen without over-reacting," Paige counters.

Jesse lifts his glass to acknowledge his sister's words.

"Tell her what?" I ask.

"The damage to her grandfather's heart was significant. They ended up having him on the heart-lung machine for much longer than they intended while they not only replaced a valve, but also repaired an aneurysm near his stomach that was ready to burst." She slams her fist against the counter. "Damn him. This was so much worse than a simple blockage."

"What are his chances?" I ask quietly.

"The next twenty-four hours are critical. After that, we'll find out how much brain and motor function he lost." She whirls on her brothers. "And you both know there's no way I can go back to work now."

"I wish there was some way I could argue otherwise, but..." Ethan's hand lifts and falls.

"I've never seen anything like the way you cut through the crap at the hospital to get us answers, Paige." Jesse's voice is filled with pride. "He would be too, if..."

She waves her hand. "This changes nothing with him. He's merely another patient."

"What if it changes everything?" I ask.

Paige looks at me incredulously. "Beckett, he stole twenty years from you—all the time I was pregnant with Austyn and her entire life. How can you even ask that?"

"Because maybe this will change him, make him realize what he almost lost. If it doesn't, then you can still walk away. But Paige, don't throw it in the trash." I take a sip of tea to let that sink in.

"I can't have this discussion right now." She rubs her temples to alleviate the stress.

"No, right now, you need to sleep and you need to eat. Same goes for you two." I jerk my chin in the direction of her brothers.

"Wish I could, but the horses don't wait for anyone." Jesse takes a long pull of his tea before moving to the sink to dump out the rest.

"I don't have that problem. I'm going to find my bed," Ethan declares.

"Alone?" Jesse taunts as the two make their way to the front door.

"Maybe." And without another word, the two older Kensingtons disappear wordlessly, trusting a drooping Paige alone with me.

I set my tea aside and reach for her hand. "Come on, bird. Let's get you in the direction of your bed."

"Beckett, I have too much to do. I have to remain awake in the event the hospital..." An enormous yawn overtakes her.

"Will they call?" I ask logically as I guide her to the stairs. With a small nudge, she trudges up.

"Sure. I have my phone right here." She pats her rear pocket, drawing my attention to her perfect heart-shaped ass.

I clench my teeth at the overwhelming surge of lust that floods me. "Then up you go. Take a nap."

"Help yourself to whatever. I'll be down in like an hour. Tops."

Hoping it's more like three, I head back to the couch and resume

my search for the best restaurant in the area that either delivers or does takeout. When I find it, I pick up my phone and call Kane. "Hey, I need a favor."

⊕

Three and a half hours later, I've started reheating the mouthwatering Italian when I first heard movement upstairs. Now, two women are laughing uproariously at something I can't hear, and part of me aches to be let in on their secrets. I yell, "If the two of you don't hurry up, I'm eating all this food from Murray's myself."

The laughter not only pauses, but Paige and Austyn make enough noise clamoring down the stairs they sound like a herd of elephants. "Did you say Murray's?" Austyn demands.

"He doesn't have to say it, baby. Just take a whiff. God, it smells like a miracle in here." Paige inhales deeply.

I do the same and get a faint scent of her perfume. She's right; it does smell like a miracle. My cock stirs beneath the zipper of my jeans. I clear my throat. "Right. So I wasn't sure what you ladies liked, so I ordered some of everything."

"That might be an understatement," Paige murmurs. But the smile twitching at her lips tells me she's teasing.

"Okay, so I went a bit overboard," I allow.

"Beckett! There are seventeen pans of food here. For three of us!" Austyn is doubled over laughing.

"Well, if the two of you don't mind, I thought I might invite the guys inside to grab a plate."

"Your security team?" Paige asks.

"Hell yeah! Eye candy! That's dessert before dinner." Austyn cheers.

Paige rolls her eyes. "Obviously you're not longing for Mr. iPad."

Mr. iPad? Is this woman code for something?

"Mama, he was a distant memory before I met you in San Antonio. I'm just glad he didn't get up in the middle of our conversation and embarrass us both." Austyn dismisses some random dude while checking out the Italian I had brought in from a nearby town.

I rub my forehead before shoving my hands through my hair. Part of me is enthralled by the openness of our daughter's relationship with her mother, but on the other hand... "Do you realize the kind of trouble she can get into out there?" I demand of Paige.

The quirk of her brow before she gives me a head-to-toe perusal tells me she knows just the kind of trouble her daughter can get into. "I do. I've already warned her all about the bad boys. Too bad *your* daughter didn't listen. Go tell your security team they're welcome to eat in the dining room, the lanai, wherever they're most comfortable."

Ouch. I wince as Paige makes her way toward a door in the kitchen. At first, I wonder if she's escaping me and my big mouth, but then she pulls out a ridiculous number of paper plates. "Austyn, grab these."

"On it, Mama. Do you want to use real silverware?"

"No. And call your Uncle Jesse to make certain he's eaten. E's at the hospital with Gramps."

"Righty-ho."

I text Kane to let him know to come to the house before sidling up next to Paige. "What can I do?"

An arm reaches out with a package of napkins. Instead of checking out her ass again—something I commend myself on—I try to peek inside. "Is this the magic closet? What else is in there? Horse feed? Cotton candy?"

Paige straightens, and I love the pink flush that makes the light dusting of her freckles pop. She's holding a two-liter of soda. Both things remind me of those afternoons we spent in the sun before we'd ride her horse back to the Kensington barns before sneaking around the side to dash into town. After grabbing a fountain Coke, we'd sneak around the side of the building and make out just like normal teenagers on a date.

"Funny what I just remembered this very instant," I murmur.

Paige's face, which had begun to relax into a smile, closes up.

"And my problem is I've never been able to forget. Here. Put this on the table."

"Crap, Paige."

"Let me by, Beckett. The past is nothing—nothing but past."

But our past isn't nothing. It's a whole lot of everything. And we have to find a way to bridge the divide between then and now—if not for us, then certainly for our daughter.

When the doorbell rings and Paige scuttles by me to answer it, I tamp down the jealousy I feel when she smiles up at members of my security team, welcoming them into her home. Yeah, I just started tonight with a tasty course of denial.

I don't know how long I'll be able to keep feeding it to myself.

PAIGE

Two words, people: special order! It is not the teenager at the grocery store's fault that your Domaine Valette Pouilly-Fuisse is not available at your local Stop & Shop! It's yours. Own your mistake and stop ruining someone else's holiday by spending twenty minutes ranting at the poor kid.

— StellaNova

"Dr. Kensington, do you have to work while you're here?" Beckett's head bodyguard, Kane, asks me as he passes me the pan filled with garlic bread.

"No. I always close down my office for two weeks around the holidays. Normally the other doctors and I rotate who will be on call for emergencies over the holidays. Since they knew I intended on visiting this one in New York"—I nudge Austyn seated to my right with my shoulder before handing her the pan, which she eagerly accepts—"I'm not expected back until after the first of the year."

"Before you go back, we need to have a conversation about your security."

I had just taken a bite when he said that. From my other side,

Beckett calmly whacks me on the back repeatedly to help dislodge the piece of bread I'm now choking on. "Maybe some better timing next time, Kane?" he suggests with some amusement. Damn him. I glare at him. "What? I'm not the one who suggested it."

"But you're not saying, 'No, Kane. That's a ridiculous idea. Why would Paige need security?'" I mimic his distinctive voice that has spent too many nights in my dreams.

He looks momentarily startled. "Do I really sound like that?" Everyone else around the dining room table tries to disguise their amusement poorly. Then he shakes his head to regain his train of thought. "Sorry about that, bird. It's like I told Austyn right before we came in—was it just yesterday?"

Austyn nods and moans as she shoves in another bite of bread. I don't fail to notice she attracts the attention of more than one of the men around the table. I wonder if her father does. Flicking a quick glance at him, I notice his jaw harden. "This should be interesting," I murmur.

"What? Our conversation about your personal security or mine with Kane about him replacing his entire team with eunuchs?" Beckett says so calmly that Kane just snickers.

"Get used to it, Beckett. I have a feeling you're in for a rough ride."

"And I'll be talking with your bosses about you too."

"Why do you need security?" I ask suddenly. Everyone but Austyn freezes at my question. "I mean, I know you're fairly notorious, Beckett, but I count...eight people? Isn't that a bit overkill for the man StellaNova declared the decade's rock god?"

His fork clatters to his plate. "I honestly don't know how to respond."

Austyn reaches over and pats him on the shoulder. "It's okay. I'm sure *Rolling Stone* will change their mind about you one of these days."

The look he sends in her direction is so filthy I can't help but chuckle. "Welcome to my pain. I blamed you—often—for her smart-ass mouth."

His look changes from one of disgust to pleased. "What else did you blame me for?"

"Her stubbornness, irascibility, and willfulness."

"Hey now," Austyn protests.

My head whips around, and I narrow my eyes at my recalcitrant daughter. "Potty training, dressing for school, or missing curfew. Your pick."

"How about none of the above and I offer to clear the table?" She shoots me a breathtaking smile.

A hand taps me on the shoulder. I whip around and find the identical version of that same smile behind me on her father's face. It's overkill to my already overwhelmed senses. "How about you cut her some slack for the moment—" He jerks his head toward the security team still seated around the table. "—and I'll address your curiosity if you get your cell phone."

"My cell phone?" I'm confused, but I give in as I push back my chair.

Austyn quickly begins clearing the table of dirty plates and offering new ones to anyone who is still hungry. I snag my phone off the counter and shake my head over the amount of leftovers. "Beckett, I hope you have a large appetite."

"Kane's relief team will eat it."

I whip my head around to the other man. "Your what?"

He shrugs. "We have to sleep sometime."

I hold up my phone. "And this is supposed to explain?"

Beckett holds out his hand. "It will if you hand it over."

I clutch my phone to my chest. "Are you crazy? There's a thing called privacy."

He rolls his eyes. "Fine. We'll use mine since we have the same model."

I don't know why something so trivial sends a warmth through me when millions of people received the same phone after the last upgrade. I watch Beckett's tattooed fingers quickly power down his phone. The long fingers I remember gliding over my skin are covered with ink, ink I'm sure carries memories. Memories I never shared with him.

Suddenly Murray's doesn't sit quite right with me, and I want just a few moments alone.

Then with a press of a button, he starts his phone back up. A familiar song—the company's jingle in electronic format—plays when he does. He tosses his phone onto the table. "That's why."

"That's why what?" I've been so absorbed in his hands, I've forgotten what we were even talking about.

He points at the phone. "That's why I have a security team. I invested wisely after I made the money from that."

I'm still confused. "So, you're saying you bought some stock?"

"No. Paige, bird, I wrote the music."

"The music," I repeat. I follow the line of his arm where it rests on his phone. Then I fall a step back and gape at him. "You wrote the jingle for the computer company?"

He grins, this time with excitement, his mask completely dropped. "God, I wish you could see your face."

"What? Why?" He cocks his head.

"You're so giddy. You deserve to be," I quickly add. "But it's like this is a perfect score on a test or something and you're racing home to share it."

He traces the cover on his phone. "I don't have a lot of friends."

I scoff. "Whatever, Beckett. You're a rock star and probably a billionaire or something."

"Finding people to hang with isn't the problem. Everyone wants a piece of you when you have money." His voice is both sardonic and lonely. Before I can tell him that his money means less to me than my father's did, he asks seriously, "Does my money change things?"

And I blurt out, "If it were up to me, I'd tell you to educate a thousand doctors. Then send them to the far corners of the globe where they can save a thousand lives. Then those lives can help raise fields of crops to feed a thousand villages. Money is worthless. True gold is found in the actions of what people do."

His fingers reach out and tuck a piece of hair behind the arm of my glasses, trailing down my ear. "There she is."

"Who?"

"*My* Paige. I've missed her."

I shake my head as I push to my feet to head into the kitchen. "You have a million people who slid into your life, Beckett. Until... this, you forgot all about me."

"Wrong. I never forgot about you."

"Try pulling the other one."

"I'm a man who may be expected to be the world's best friend but who is very alone in it." Beckett stands and follows me.

"Right. That's what I'd call it."

"Don't believe everything you've read about me. Ask me if you have questions about my life, Paige, and I'll do the same."

I begin to put lids on the food, avoiding him.

He slaps his hand on the counter. "Ask me, Paige. What's the worst thing you read? What's the worst thing lying between us being friends again?"

I whirl on him. "The things that lie between us are not because of the things printed. They're because of the fact I had things to hide—because I was alone in this. Part of me doesn't give a shit that I hid the accusations of drugs, the parties, or the women from your daughter. The part of me that does is the part that would have resented it if you were *here*. If you had a hand in raising her. That's the part of me that resents you. What little girl should know her absentee father is off touring a strange land doing God knows what with God knows who?"

His eyes drift shut as if the pain is too much to bear. "That's why you never told her."

"Kids learn to dish out crap young. You're damn straight I protected Austyn by not telling her about you until she was of age. Can you imagine her growing up in a world where some little shit came up to my pigtailed princess with a tabloid sheet of her daddy's ass hanging out after he banged some groupie when he got caught by some tabloid? I'd have killed them." Ignoring his pale face, I forge on. "So, no. I don't believe everything I've ever read about you. But don't you stand there and expect me to accept the fact you've spent the last twenty years missing me when you're some shit-hot guy who can be with anyone you want. Because you obviously didn't want to be here."

With that, I shove past him and out of the kitchen. I've made it to the stairs when I hear him call out, "Paige? Who showed you those tabloids? Since I know that shit ended very early in my career…"

I interrupt him. "Haven't you figured it out, Beckett? Only three people knew you were Austyn's father. And they made damn sure to protect me." I jerk up my chin. "Much like your guys here."

With that, I dash up the stairs and prepare for another day where I'll sit by my father's bed and fetch him ice chips, praying he lives so I can kill him when he's better.

Hours later, I toss and turn in my bed. Too much weighs on my mind, and acid churns in my gut. I want a drink of milk, and I need some time out on the lanai.

Just to be.

Just to sort things out.

With a heavy sigh, I slide from my bed and zip up a thin sweatshirt. My mind just won't shut off. It's a few days until Christmas. I'm hopeful my suitcase will arrive tomorrow from the Plaza with Paige's gifts.

As quietly as I can so I don't disturb Kane, I make my way down to the kitchen and pull out the milk and grab a clean glass, careful not to disturb him as I make my way out the back door before sitting in my favorite chaise.

"One more burden to carry. How many am I supposed to bear?" I ask the quiet night air.

And suddenly, I can't handle it any longer—the residual fear of Beckett finding out about our child, my realizations about my father, his heart attack and subsequent operation. And the one thing that has my emotional barometer jumping like crazy—Beckett giving a damn enough to bring Austyn to Texas. No, that's not quite right.

That is well within what I could imagine him doing. It's him staying here by our sides that doesn't fit. My tears begin falling faster, hotter.

And then I hear his voice behind me. "If you'd let someone help you, it would be easier."

I whirl around, brushing the tears off my face. "How long have you been there?" My arms wrap around myself protectively.

"Long enough to know you need a friend. Talk to me, Paige. Please." And there's something poignant about the way Beckett says that last word that makes me relax slightly.

"What do you want to know?"

"Will you tell me about our daughter?"

I can feel each and every muscle in my body start to relax, especially my heart. "It would be my pleasure." I scoot over on the double-wide lounger and pat the space next to me. "Sit down. This might take a while."

He hesitates for just a moment before he joins me. "What did *you* feel when you found out you were pregnant? Were you scared? Happy?"

"Both," I respond immediately. "Like I told you, I loved her from the moment I first heard her heart beat."

"You never thought about..." His voice trails off.

I shake my head but realize he likely can't see that in the shrouded darkness. "It may be the right decision for some. I respect that. But it wasn't even an option for me."

I feel his hand reach for mine. He squeezes my fingers tightly. "If I haven't said it yet, thank you."

My head turns in his direction. "For what?"

"For making a life-altering decision at seventeen and upholding it beautifully. Not all of us do that." And for just a moment, I want to fall into his arms because the regret that laces his voice is impossible to miss.

I can't let myself, not when I'm as emotionally stable as a new foal on her first legs. "Austyn's the best thing to happen in my life." I redirect the conversation slightly.

"And I'm certain she'd say same the same about you. What was all that before with you giving her a choice about stories?" His voice is quizzical, not judgmental.

I chuckle. "When Austyn started to grow into her personality, it was next to impossible to get her to do anything without yelling all the time or reasoning with her. Even then, I would have to threaten her because she'd push me too far. It could be exhausting."

Beckett drops an arm around my shoulders. As naturally as breathing, I snuggle back into my place—the spot right against his pec where I can hear his heart beat and smell his scent. I frown a tiny bit when I realize it's different. It's not the smell of sunshine; it's more refined. Sophisticated. I debate pulling away but realize that I need to lean on him for just a moment.

Just one last time.

I know he's not mine, just the moment is. And that makes my voice quieter when I continue. "Because she's a perfectionist, she doesn't like her faults being called out. So, when she starts to go down a path with a wild hair, I can rein her in pretty easily."

His lips come down on the top of my hair. Another long-ago careless intimacy that's no longer mine. I start to squirm, but his arm tightens.

Time, distance, even other people can't make the heart want what it truly desires any less. In fact, all it does is intensify the need when it comes in contact with what causes the blood to flow through it again. "It was a long road, but we made it. I'm proud of the woman she's becoming."

He's silent as we sit there. "I never had that. But then again, when I learned what they did to your mama, I was glad I never had their stamp of approval."

My heart twists inside me. I whisper hoarsely, "I haven't even begun to process everything I learned."

"Paige, maybe he had a reason. Don't throw your whole life away," he begins.

I hold my hands up to my ears. "How can you say that? No, the time for him to tell all of this to me was when I was crying waiting for you to come back to me."

He rips my hands away. "It took a while, but I am back."

And his words fuel my anger, causing me to jerk away from him. "We're not a damn song lyric, Beckett. This is life. You weren't pining away for me for the last twenty years. It's been thrown in my damn face every time I walk into the grocery store to buy food to feed our child."

He vehemently disagrees. "You only think you do. What those damn paps can't tell you about are the lonely nights where I regretted leaving without saying goodbye."

I scoff. "For what? The first day? Week?" Before he can speak, I scramble off the lounger.

"And what, Princess Paige? You sat in your castle chaste and lonely?" His lash of anger whips at me as he surges to his feet.

I hold up a hand with three fingers and wiggle them in his direction. "Over twenty years, buddy." Then I start quoting some of the women he's been associated with this year alone. "Storia, some media personality, the designer Soy, your drummer Carly, the lead singer for CyberG—I can't recall her name—and Erzulie!" I sneer. Then I jerk up my chin as I scoff, "Plus the groupies, I'm sure."

He shakes his head as he takes measured steps toward me. Uh-oh. I back up until my back's against the frame of the house and there's nowhere else to go.

His dark head lowers slightly before he taunts, "Does it help to keep lying to yourself about me to deny how you still feel about me?"

"Are you insane?" I sputter

He merely smiles right before his lips capture mine.

Instinctively, my body responds. My hands sink greedily into his thick hair, pulling him closer. My body molds into his. Despite the years, the way his body has become harder and mine softer, they still seem to be made for one another.

If it wasn't for the squawk of the radio, I don't know where the kiss would have led. I'm not certain if I shoved Beckett back or if he jumped away, but either way, the flush of embarrassment warms my cheeks.

Without a word, I run back into the house, uncaring this time if I make enough noise to wake Kane. I left my room seeking solace, and now I need the safety of it.

But what tonight's interlude has solidified in me is I have to leave Kensington. I can't live forever with the specter of Beckett Miller everywhere I turn. I need to be somewhere he won't turn up and break my heart ever again.

BECKETT

Caleb Lockwood, Keene Marshall, and Colby Hunt walked out of their building. Each were on cell phones. One was smiling, one was snarling, and one was laughing. Match the man with the call.

— **Sexy&Social, All the Scandal You Can Handle**

"I frankly don't give a fuck. I'm not coming back to New York until I have everything settled down here," I tell Keene Marshall, one of the co-owners of Hudson Investigations, the next afternoon while Paige is at the hospital after a morning where I think Antarctica might have been warmer than the temperature in her house. Thankfully, we had Austyn as a buffer between us until Paige left, whereupon my daughter decided she was going to go help her uncle exercise the horses at Kensington Stables, begrudgingly taking one of my security with her.

Paige wouldn't even consider it when I suggested it. Then again, even if there had been an axe murderer standing outside the door with fresh blood dripping from his weapon of choice, I think she would have dismissed anything I said, I think glumly.

"You have two teams of eight down there to do what? Eat barbecue? Chase after a neighborhood dog? What the fuck, Beckett? Normally, you can barely tolerate a team of two and you're prancing around Manhattan. Kane won't tell me a damn thing outside you're safe where you are."

I make a mental note to give Kane one hell of a bonus, but I also appreciate Keene's frustration. "Is Kane's phone secure?"

"Do I look like an idiot? Do you think I'm sending any of my guys into the field with you as the principal and not equip them with the best tech there is? Sam can bounce a call off...why the hell does this matter?" Keene demands.

"I'll give you the full story, but I can't use my cell."

Keene's silent. "Hang up. I'll call you back."

Less than five minutes later, Kane opens Paige's front door, holding out his phone. "It's the boss." He doesn't appear unduly concerned.

"Thanks, Kane." He slaps his phone in my hand. When I take it, I grab his forearm. "Kane, I mean it sincerely. Thanks."

"Don't know if you mind my weighing in, but if I were you, I'd hit up the one resource who might know how to fix the shitshow from last night."

I challenge him. "Yeah? Who's that?"

"Your daughter." Just as I'm about to blast him, he smirks in a way he could only have learned from working at Hudson as long as he has. "Press '6' to take Keene off hold."

I do, right before I tell Kane, "You're an ass."

He flicks out his hand before he walks back out Paige's front door.

"Tell me I didn't just ask Sam to move a satellite for you to tell me your bodyguard is an asshole. He keeps your ass alive," Keene barks in my ear.

Talk about a mental distraction. "Did Sam move a satellite?"

"Beckett," Keene warns.

"I mean, because that's some pretty cool shit."

"God damnit, Beckett," he thunders, not intimidating me in the slightest. Fortunately I know the two badasses who own Hudson

Investigations, Keene Marshall and his best friend, Caleb Lockwood, are two of the best men in the world.

"As you likely know, I have a daughter," I blurt the news out. "I'm in Texas because something happened to her mother's family. I needed to be here."

My news is met with dead silence. I ramble on to fill the silence.

"She's nineteen years old. Her mother and I...we were just kids. God, Paige. She went through this all on her own." I rub my hand along the back of my neck as I pace.

Finally, Keene speaks as I hear the tap of his fingers on a keyboard. "Is that your daughter's name? Paige?"

"No, Paige is... Austyn—with a *y*—is my daughter. Why am I even telling you this? It's not like you don't..."

"Stop talking." His voice is eerily calm. Then, I hear him speak to his aide, whom I've met on the few times I've been up to their offices. "Tony, I want whoever ran the background check and trace for Carys Burke to be in my office in the next five minutes. After I brief Caleb, show them in. While they're in here, run their personal finances. Make certain if anything is out of place there's a dead body to back it up."

I start panicking. "What the hell are you saying, Keene?"

"Nothing. I do not need you freaking out. Right now, I do not suspect there is anything wrong. But I am running a full internal investigation against the analyst who performed the check for Carys. Anything that pulled up your legal name should have been flagged and been sent to me or Caleb."

"And it wasn't." I watch as Kane accepts a phone from one of the other guards. He turns it on and immediately snaps to attention. Kane's eyes immediately lock onto me before he nods. "What's happening outside?" I demand.

"Where's your daughter and her mother?" Keene asks, not answering me.

"Austyn went to her family's farm to ride horses—Kensington Stables. It's about twenty minutes away from here."

"Did she take one of the security team?"

"Mitch," I reply immediately.

"What about her mother?"

"No, she's not with her. She's at the local hospital with her father. Tyson is in the cardiac care unit." I quickly bring Keene up to speed as to why the three of us are even here in Texas.

"I'm going to send someone down to the Plaza to see if the paps are camped out there. Seeing if they're at your place is a waste of time since there's never a time they're not lurking around. In the meantime, I think it would be best for Kane to send someone down to the hospital to be with Paige."

"She will never go for it," I say swiftly, already striding over to the hook where she pointed out her spare house key.

"Make her go for it," he urges.

"That was my plan."

"Make it happen." His voice is cold.

"Christ, Keene." I scrub my hand over my head.

"Don't do anything dumb," he warns.

"Me?" My smile is grim as I exit Paige's house before I walk directly up to Kane. He shakes his head. I glare at him without speaking until finally he relents and types on his phone. Three other team members come out of nowhere. He points to the rented SUV.

"Yes. Just wait until we find out—"

I press End on the call and hand the phone back to Kane. "Your boss is going to be a douchebag when he calls back."

Kane shrugs. "Phone etiquette isn't his thing."

If it wasn't for the fact I'm terrified the paparazzi may have already found out about Paige due to a leak at Hudson, I might have busted a gut at Kane's dry sense of humor about Keene. But there are more pressing matters. "You were briefed?"

"Just enough to be told not to let you out of my sight, but I'm assuming we're including Paige and Austyn in that order?"

I smile grimly as I slide into the back seat of the eight-person vehicle. "Damn straight."

"Mitch will secure Austyn. I assume Paige is still at the hospital?" But I know he's not asking me. He turns to one of the agents, a man named Quinn, who responds, "Yes. I'm tracking her phone. It hasn't moved from its present location."

"Then we're off." Kane turns on the vehicle and throws it into gear.

It isn't until we're a few minutes down the road that he asks me, "Any idea what we're facing there, Beckett?"

And I answer with complete honesty, "I have no idea." Because I don't know what's going to be worse—my showing up at the hospital because the paparazzi found out or Paige just seeing me after our fight last night.

But I'm about to find out.

⊕

When I enter the Heart Specialty Care and Transplant Center at Singer Memorial Hospital with only Kane beside me about twenty minutes later, I'm prepared for anything. What I'm not prepared for is the overwhelming sadness that again engulfs me knowing the long road Tyson Kensington has ahead of him if he makes it past these first few critical days.

And my heart gallops when I glimpse Paige curled beneath an oversized UT sweatshirt lost in thought, staring out the window in the nearly empty reception area. She's about to rearrange her entire life for a man who tried his damnedest to destroy it.

What would she do for a man she loved?

Last night, I let frustration get the better of me. I pushed when I should have been patient, resented when I felt her pull back. And laughed at her bitterness. But honest to God, her green eyes weren't sparkling with anything but pure jealousy.

And I'd be lying to myself if I didn't admit my own when she held up those three fingers. *Mine*, I think savagely, disregarding the small voice inside of me that warns me to slow down. She and Austyn are mine to protect, mine to love. And if it weren't for the man lying in a bed on oxygen, they always would have been.

"Not if I'd been the man I should have been," I hear my own voice admit.

"Excuse me? What the hell are you doing here?" Paige hisses. Nervously she glances around, but I dismiss the elderly woman crocheting with her back to us as no threat. Even so, I absently notice Kane station himself so he has a good vantage point to watch all of us.

Instead, I move closer and wrap Paige up in a tight embrace. "We need to talk."

Her arms snake around my waist hesitantly as she whispers almost inaudibly, "What happened?"

"Is there somewhere private we can talk?"

She pulls back and searches my eyes. After just a second, she breaks away and starts walking down the hall. I follow, giving a subtle nod to Kane. Within moments, Paige leads me into a private family room. "This is about as private as we can get, Beckett. What happened?"

I quickly recount my phone call with Keene. To my surprise, she doesn't shout. Instead, she drops into an armchair with a sigh and rubs her head. "This was always a possibility. I always knew that from the moment I realized who you'd become."

I sit down on the couch near her and hold out a hand. She lays hers in it. "I won't let anything happen to either of you."

Her smile is a little sad. "This is going to break Austyn's heart if it happens."

"Having it come out I'm her father?"

Paige nods.

I ignore the hurt that floods through me before I grate out, "Why?"

"Oh, Beckett." Paige begins tracing "her" tattoo with a finger with her other hand. "I now know the real reason you didn't get this colored in." There's a ghost of a smile around her mouth.

Just as I'm about to ask why, there's a knock at the door before it swings open. Kane pops his head in. "They're looking for Paige. It's time for her visit with her father." Just as quickly as he enters, the door closes.

She stands. I quickly follow suit. She informs me, "I'll listen to what you and your team have to say about security." Just as I'm about to thank her, she holds up a hand. "Within reason, Beckett. My father's room is off-limits." Her doctor voice is firm, authoritative, and sexy as hell.

"Agreed," I capitulate immediately.

She holds my gaze a moment before shifting to the door. Her hand has just touched the handle when I call out her name. "Yes?"

"What did you mean before when you said you knew why I hadn't got this colored in? I told you my reason."

The ghost of a smile floats back. "Because you're completely transparent to me, Beckett Miller. You're upset thinking your daughter doesn't want to announce you're her father. That's not it. She wants to become a success based on her merit, not riding someone's coattails. Otherwise, I'm fairly certain she'd be shouting it from our rooftop. I've only recently learned of some less than friendly support she received about not having a father all these years. The man you are—dropping everything to be with her? That's absolutely the kind of daddy I'm sure she's been dreaming of."

And with that, Paige slips out the door to go see how her father's heart is healing. What she doesn't know is she's taking mine along with her while she does.

Christ.

BECKETT

You know what I'm having a craving for right now? Barbecue and potato salad. Blame Food Network. They were having a marathon on best barbecue places in the nation. Here's a top ten list of spots in the city for you to order some catered if you don't want to go to the trouble of firing up those smokers in the middle of winter.

— Fab and Delish

The next day, I slip on a Henley and ask Austyn what she has planned for the day.

"Nothing, why?"

"Let's do something."

"Like what?"

I haven't thought much about it. "You choose."

Much to my surprise, she directs the security team to drop us off in the center of downtown Kensington.

Kensington is an upscale suburb that screams Americana located west of Austin. The town fathers were determined to maintain its quaint charm even throughout the decades, which is why it feels like I've stepped back in time with the black-and-white store signs for modern eateries like Subway and Rodeo Ralph's mixed in with high-end dining and shopping.

Even though I've been gone twenty years, it appears some things never change. I stroll with Austyn as the smell of smoked barbecue makes my mouth water. "Despite everything that forced me to leave, this was probably the thing I missed the most," I confess.

"The monotony?" Her voice is dry.

I bark out a laugh. "No, kid. Of all the things I don't miss it's the monotony. Although you should embrace your roots." Thoughtfully, I raise a tattooed hand to my jaw and say aloud, "There were good things about living here. I was just too mired down to recognize it. Your mama, and hell, I should have come back for the barbecue if nothing else."

"Barbecue? That's why you should have come back" She practically trips over her indignation beside me.

"I'm kidding." I hesitate, wondering how much I should tell her, before realizing she already knows most of it. "I didn't realize it wasn't Kensington, per se, that was so bad. It was my personal situation. And maybe if I'd reached out to a teacher, someone, I could have changed it. Changed the past. Back then, my family was shit. And it wasn't until the end I knew why."

"I still don't know why."

Crap. I would have thought Paige would have shared. "My parents caused an accident. Then they spent the rest of their lives drunk to avoid caring about the repercussions of it."

"That's tragic in so many ways," Austyn murmurs.

You have no idea. "They weren't like your mama. They weren't present in my life. They didn't worry whether or not I was home, so it was easy to slip out of the house. God, I remember on days like Founders' Day, I'd walk miles to get to town. And then I'd just sit by the band and listen to them play for hours."

"Does Mama know this?"

I nod brusquely. "I told her when we were...we were. Austyn, I don't want you to ever believe I didn't love your mother." *I always will.*

She stops in her tracks. "Beckett, get real."

I'm offended. "Who are you to tell me what I did and didn't feel?"

"I'm not telling you what you felt; I'm telling you that you still have the same feelings for her now. Gee, am I the only one who realizes the two of you can't be in the same space without the air sizzling?"

I can't formulate words. Austyn pats my cheek. "Don't worry about it. I think it's because I'm a part of both of you I can read you both so well."

And there's that burning sensation pricking the back of my eyes. I slip on a pair of sunglasses. "I need more." The words are out of my mouth before I realize they're there.

"What do you mean?" Her head tilts to the side the same way Paige's does.

Hooking an arm over her shoulder, I guide my daughter to our first stop—to find her mother. "It means I want her to care about the man I am today, Austyn, not the memories we share because we're both connected to you. Christ, I sound like I'm composing a love song."

Her peal of laughter draws the attention of several people. A few wave. She waves back. "Somehow, I don't think that's going to be a problem."

My hope soars. "You don't?"

"Nope."

"What makes you say that?"

"Because, you're the only man I've ever seen drive her absolutely out of her mind." Just as we reach the line at Nina's Barbecue, Austyn reasons, "No one else has, and no one ever came close to winning her heart. So it must be the start of something enormous."

God, I hope so. But I just shake my head at my daughter before informing her, "You're insane."

As the line shuffles forward, she primly informs me, "I'm told I get that from your side of the family."

I can't prevent the bark of laughter that escapes. Nor the gurgle of my stomach as the wave of barbecue scent reaches our nose.

"Who's he?" I nod curtly at the man currently chatting up Paige around the town square next to the gazebo. One of his hands is tucked into that of an adorable little girl, which makes my heart ache with the idea of what mine must have looked like when she was that age. What, five? Six?

Austyn leans into me to get a better look. "Oh. That's Sheriff Lewis. He's been sweet on Mama for a while." Her face takes on a peculiar look. "I know Gramps and Uncle Jess have been tossing him her way."

My gut clenches as Paige ducks beneath the other man's arm. "Are they..." I can't finish the sentence. Probably because I don't want to admit to myself I'm stooping so low as to ask my daughter about her mother's love life.

Austyn snorts. "Please. If Mama wanted to tap that, she's had plenty of opportunity."

"Christ." I rub my hand over my forehead. "Do you come with a manual I can study? I really am a fast learner."

She bumps my shoulder in a friendly way. "You'd have to be. Mama doesn't tolerate morons. Say, is it true you have a college degree?"

"I do. Say, do you plan on going back to finish yours?"

"How did you know about that?"

I tug at one of her braids. "Your mother spilled the beans to Angie, who told all of us at Carys's office."

She looks unperturbed at the gossip flow I just alluded to about her life that's likely not to be stifled. "Someday. Maybe. When did you finish your degree?"

"I had enough credits I was able to finish it online after I saved up enough money. I wanted to have something to fall back on."

"Good on you. Maybe I'll go that route later. After I've earned the money. I don't want Mama or Gramps paying for it."

It's my turn to bump her back. "What about my helping you out?"

"That's cool of you to offer, but that's *your* money, Becks." The way she emphasizes "your" sets my teeth on edge.

"I missed out on so much that I want to give you the world, Austyn." *Much like I want to give it to your mother,* but I leave that unsaid.

She lays a hand on my bicep. I imagine the delicate fingers fly across a board as mine do piano keys. It's astounding to realize that I had a hand in creating this fascinating woman. A funny look crosses her face. "Don't you realize I've been given that already? And I don't need your money to get it."

My confusion must show because she grins. "You'll figure it out. I'm just hoping I'm around when you do. Oh, she's ready to be rescued. Mama." She jumps up and down, whistling between her fingers.

My eyes are forced back to the couple who were in conversation as they blur together in a haze of laughter and color. Every muscle in my body tenses.

And what does my darling daughter do? She laughs before grabbing my hand and dragging me toward them. I glare down at her. "Do you think if she wanted me around she wouldn't have taken off this morning?" That I haven't ached to do this very thing since I woke up to a bed all on my own.

"I think you're a chickenshit because you won't give up some of your pride to do something that makes you look foolish on the off chance it eases her mind."

My head rears back as my dainty child takes me to task. "That's not... You're wrong," I state more firmly.

"Then prove it to me, Beckett."

I ask honestly, "Prove what?"

"That you're man enough to go over there. Prove you want her for more than just recreating a memory." She rises on her toes and jabs me smack in the heart. "Prove yourself."

She's right. Just like a carousel. We're going up and down, and we're both afraid to get off and see what's beyond it because what happens when the world stops spinning?

Austyn drags me so quickly through the throng of people, more often than not, I'm apologizing for colliding into people. The people of Kensington are surprisingly generous. They take our mini stampede in stride. But I'm still left stunned when she suddenly chirps, "Partner switch. Mama, shoo. I need to chat with Sheriff Lewis."

And suddenly I have Paige within arm's reach.

Her face is flushed brighter than the setting sun. "I can't believe she dragged you across the square like that."

"I'm not quite certain of how it happened either." I catch her under her elbow before tucking her against my body. "But I'm grateful for it."

Paige's breath catches as our bodies rub against one another as I guide us through the maze of people on our way out the square. Sliding my hand forward, I twine my fingers in hers, unwilling to let her go. I don't know what makes me do it. I bring her arm above her head and slowly spin her around so close every soft shift brushes her hip against my groin.

It's better than the memory of the first time when I kissed Paige Kensington, homecoming queen, because I know what it's like to have something infinitely more precious in my hands than just her body.

I've held her heart.

That's when I trip over my feet. What the hell was I thinking all those years ago, never coming back to make certain she was happy? What excuse did I have?

"Are you all right, Beckett?" Her hand tightens in mine to make sure I don't fall. Just like she never let me down all those years ago.

Paige, who's been betrayed by everyone from me to her brother, to her own father, and yet she still cares. Paige, who did the best with what she had—enduring the whispers and stares from this small town. Becoming a doctor right away to make certain Austyn would always have food on the table and a roof over her head. Paige, who raised our child to become this remarkably talented young woman. Paige did all that.

What did I do?

Spying a break between the people out strolling, I quickly drag her off the square and away from the hoopla.

"Where are you taking me?" Paige begins to struggle.

"Just somewhere we can talk."

"What if I don't want to?" Her words strike a chord deep inside of me, triggering a memory of us by the piano in the field.

"What if I don't want you to just be my friend, Beckett? What happens to us then?"

I stop playing the music I know down to my soul I composed for the girl with the spring-green eyes and the spattering of freckles across her nose. Slowly, I rise from the drywall bucket I remembered to bring with me so I could push down on the pedals as I played, now that I know the damper pedal actually still worked.

She scrambles to her feet on the low part of the wall, but she still doesn't match my height as I approach her. Gently, I smooth a lock of her long dark hair away from her sun-kissed face. "Then we won't be friends anymore."

Her lips tremble, but she tamps down her emotions. "Fine." She begins to whirl away, but I catch her hand.

"What we'll be is this." And I kiss her for the first time.

I'm jerked from the precious memory as Paige yanks her arm away. I make a grab for her wrist. "Paige, I really need to speak with you."

"That's your problem. Here's one for you: I don't want to listen."

Baffled, my grip loosens enough where she's able to step away. The setting Texas sun illuminates her face much like the first time I kissed her. "Why?"

"Listen to me carefully, Beckett. I survived you once; I need to be able to do it again. Before, you left me, here, and never came back. After what you said last night, I figure that's your plan, and that's okay. But I live here. I raised our daughter here. But now I realize I'm worth more than what I've permitted myself. I need to stop treating myself as if I'm not good enough for a man to stand at my side. Because I am. And unless you're willing to be that man, I think it's best if you don't confuse the relationship we do have—parents." With that, Paige turns and heads quickly back in the direction of the town square.

I scrub my hands over my face. "God, what kind of damage did I do."

A male voice answers. "Untold."

I drop my hands and find myself face-to-face with Paige's brother, Ethan. I didn't realize we were standing in front of his store when we stopped. Other than a few flecks of gray hair, he looks just the same from when we went to school together. "Hey, E."

He jerks his head as he holds open the door. "Why don't you come in and sit for a spell, Beckett? We can...catch up."

"Is that a euphemism for you're going to try to beat the crap out of me?" I ask aloud even as I step through the door.

"Try? Man, it's going to take a team of guys to hold me back from doin' just that very thing."

Just then, Kane and Mitch come running up. They both blast me with murderous looks. "Next time you decide to do something so utterly stupid as get lost in a crowd, we're activating your tracking device," Kane says acidly.

I rub my hand along the back of my neck, where the damn thing lives. Meanwhile, Ethan doubles over with laughter. "How much would I have to pay you guys for access to the code to track him just for the fun of it?"

"You don't have that kind of clearance, bud. Friend or foe, Beckett?" Kane confirms.

"He's my daughter's uncle," I reply honestly.

"Right. If you attempt to kill him, we have to take you down, but he's handled himself in enough bar fights. We're good with anything fair." At those words, Kane turns his back pointedly on me.

"I might have a bro-crush on your security team—that is who they are, Beckett?" Ethan asks.

"Yes, they're..." I don't even get the question out, before Ethan's taking a shot at my face with a solid right hook.

"You asshole. That wasn't for getting my baby sister pregnant. That was for breaking her damn heart."

I dab my lip with my fingers and come away with blood. "Feel any better?"

"Somewhat."

"Then do you think we could actually talk? There's a lot I need to explain."

"Like why you're still here?" Ethan challenges.

"No. Like why I'm not planning on leaving anytime soon."

BECKETT

I don't need a sludgy-colored snow for the holiday season. I need Beckett Miller. I'm debating buying a ticket to LA to see if I can find him.

— Sexy&Social, All the Scandal You Can Handle

Ethan and I came to an understanding of sorts after he took a few shots at me. And that was before ranting at me for a good thirty minutes about how much harm I did to Paige. I cut him off by saying, "Don't throw any more punches and I'll make you a promise. One I intend to keep. I won't hurt her."

"Oh good. That means I can let out this pent-up frustration somewhere. Because there is no way you can promise me that."

Laconically, I drawled, "And see, growing up I always thought Jess was the one with a stick up his ass. What has you so bent out of shape, E? Woman issues? Maybe I can offer some advice."

He dove at me, but fortunately I sidestepped him. "This is about you and Paigey, you dickhead. You have no idea about what it was like for her—"

"I'm getting a good idea—"

"—even when you were here. You were so intent on your problems, your issues. Do you know the way the old man treated her?" And for the next thirty minutes, Ethan told me things I never knew about the woman I loved that she never shared about her hierarchy in the Kensington family.

I left forgetting about the swelling of my lip, more intent on seeking out Paige. But after a silent ride back to her home, leaving Austyn, who declared, "I need to do some Christmas shopping. You do you," I prowl through the front door to come up short at the sound of a familiar tune.

And a fitting one after my conversation with Ethan.

"Bruce Hornsby," I comment as I close the door. "Brilliant musician. Just as brilliant lyricist."

Paige's head snaps up. For just a moment, her guards are down, and I can read everything Ethan told me I'd find there: loneliness, sorrow, and pain. *Damn, she puts up a good front.* I lean down against the back of the sofa and give her a chance to gather herself. And it's almost painful to see her strap on the shields she wears. Because I now know she's worn them her entire life.

Does she even realize she's doing it anymore? I wonder. But instead of asking that, I remark, "I forgot you played."

"There's a lot about me you no longer recall, Beckett," she replies truthfully.

"If you let me, I'd like the chance to change that. I think there's a lot we don't know about who we are now, Paige, that's worth knowing." I push away from the couch and make my way over to her. "I want the chance to get to know you, this you. Not the girl I fell for years ago, not the mother of my child, but you."

For a moment my heart beats wildly out of control. She leans forward, resting her arms on the piano until our faces are close—too close. I could lean forward a few inches and kiss the breath out of her body.

And then her brows lower in confusion. "I don't understand."

"What do you mean?"

She swings her legs around and pushes to her feet. "I understand you came here for Austyn. I am thrilled to do anything I can to facilitate that after what my father...what he did." She swallows with difficulty. "But the two of you have formed a bond. That's terrific, that's great. Why don't you whisk her off to some fabulous destination for the holidays, and I'll deal with the mess here. Then we can sit down after and..."

And the light dawns. "You're punishing yourself. You've been doing it your whole life, punishing yourself for things you can't control."

"Where do you get these delusional ideas?"

"From Ethan. He filled in the gaps about why you would devote your life to a man who ruined yours," I tell her bluntly.

Her face pales. "You don't have the right to say these things to me. You left. You left! You left and never came back! And I'm the one who was whispered about. I'm the one who they talked about. And I'm the one whose child he called an abomination..." Her shoulders hunch, and she turns away.

My hands slam down on the keys, the furious clanging rising in the air between us.

"Beckett, whatever Ethan told you, he only knows part of it. You were right that first day we met. I was Princess Paige." Her face, ravaged with tears, meets mine. "I *had* to be. If I wasn't, I was reminded *she* gave up her life for me."

"Fucking bastard," I growl.

Paige starts to automatically protest, but her words die before she can give them voice. "Yes. He is. But he's the only parent, only grandparent, left. And I confronted him, and this happened. I'm a doctor. I took an oath. Maybe to most those don't mean much, but to me, promises, vows, and oaths are things you stand by. Your honor is at stake. And it's my duty to make sure I do everything possible to ensure he's well."

Her words ping through my head. *Promises, vows, and oaths are things you stand by.* I catch her shoulders in my hands.

She tips her head back. God, she's so beautiful it always made my heart ache to look at her. But now, knowing her father held her as responsible as my parents for her mother's death, I feel shattered. Back then, she was ready to run with me—to write the words to a new life together.

And I broke the biggest one of all. I promised I'd take her with me when I left. I thought I knew better by leaving her, but I was so wrong. But despite the long road that led us back to where we started, we're here now.

"I want to be here for you when your courage isn't enough to get you past your fears," I whisper hoarsely.

Her eyes drift shut. Her hands come up between us and rest on my chest. "I wish I could believe that."

Then without another word, she turns and walks away, leaving me standing there making a silent vow to never leave her alone again.

She just doesn't know it.

After dinner that night, the conversation between Paige and Austyn turns to what is going to happen if Tyson makes it out of the hospital. I take up residence at the piano and absently start playing.

"Can't Gramps rehab at the house?"

Paige shrugs. "I don't know, baby. It's doubtful. He's going to need round-the-clock treatment. And since he hasn't been out of bed since surgery, his muscles have atrophied quite a bit. I'm thinking a medical rehabilitation facility is the best way to go, but Uncle Jess and I are discussing all of the options. A lot will depend on his mental state of mind as well."

"Is it a question of money? You know Tyson can have whatever he needs," I pipe in.

Both women turn to me in shock. Paige manages to regain her voice first. "Beckett, that's incredibly generous of you, but..."

"No buts, Paige. He's important to both of you."

Her eyes narrow. "At the cost of what? A few moments alone to express your displeasure with his life choices?"

I shrug carelessly. "It wouldn't be amiss."

Paige slams her hand down on the arm of the sofa. "Damnit, Beckett, he needs rest."

My fingers become more agitated on the keys. "He needs to own up for his decisions."

Paige yells, "Don't you think I know that? Of all of us, I'm the one who was berated by the damn bastard every single day I lived in that house." Her voice drops. "'Oh, don't wear jeans that tight, Paigey. You'll look like a tramp.' Or how about 'Why not an A? Your mother would have got an A. Too bad she isn't alive to teach you. Guess you'll just have to make do with your old man.' Or my favorite. 'Whoa. I don't know nothin' about that woman stuff. Here. Take some money and go down to the store to get whatever it is you girls need. Sweet Melissa, I know she didn't have your problems with cramps and the like.' So, if you think I don't remember what it was like even before I told him I was pregnant, you're so wrong. But love isn't perfect. It can be filled with anger and hostility. It's also riddled with patience and forgiveness. The heart has ways of finding its rhythm."

Silence descends between the three of us.

"Do you think it's just that way with a parent or with lovers too, Mama?" Austyn probes gently.

Paige's lips part in shock. She tries to find the right words to answer Austyn. But I find them instead through song. One of my favorites by Imagine Dragons about not breaking and being let down comes out of me. If memories had title songs, this one would be mine and Paige's.

When the last note finishes, Paige declares, "Sometimes it isn't that easy, baby."

I retort, "And sometimes it is, Austyn. Other things get in the way."

"Time," she sniffs.

"Pride." I roll my eyes.

"Life."

"Stubbornness."

"People."

"Busybodies." My voice is despondent.

She looks right at me when she says, "Ultimately, what your father and I are trying to say is if the person matters enough, none of these things will matter. The heart will find a way around them."

I cheer up. "Listen to your mother, Austyn." I resume playing before bringing us back to the previous topic. "I was serious about Tyson, Paige. Whatever he needs."

Out of the corner of my eye, I see her mouth open—likely to refuse—when Austyn elbows her in the ribs. I suppress a smile. I instead hear a gritted "Thank you, Beckett. It's appreciated. I'll speak to Jess about it—he holds my father's medical power of attorney."

I mutter, "Stupid ass," because only Tyson Kensington would be stubborn enough to not give the medical power of attorney to his doctor daughter over something she had no control over. I twist slightly and catch Paige running her hand over Austyn's hair. "So, that's where we're at."

"I have to head back after the holidays," Austyn worries.

"I figured as much."

"I don't want to leave you alone, Mama."

I start to interrupt that she won't be but close my mouth before anything comes out. Paige shoots me a quizzical look. I stare back blandly. She ignores me and focuses on our daughter. "You need to get back to your life, and I'll be making plans."

"You're really going to do it," Austyn wonders.

"Do what?" I ask.

"Mama's discussing selling her practice," Austyn announces.

"She said that when we first arrived."

Paige coughs, hoping our daughter will get the clue and not go on. No such luck.

"In addition to all of this, she's been researching jobs in places outside of Kensington!" Austyn announces like the Tooth Fairy has signed a contract with Santa Claus for the next ten years.

Paige groans. "You really can't keep a secret."

Austyn looks stricken. "Oh no. Was it supposed to be one?"

"The part about my moving was!"

"The cat's out of the bag now, Paige," I drawl. Then I enjoy the flush that starts rising in her cheeks as a smile broadens mine. "Though personally I'll be thrilled if you're close by."

Paige shoves to her feet. "This isn't about you. It about me trying to figure out who I am at this late date."

"Paige, sweetheart." I swing my legs around to face her, but her temper's been nudged too far.

"I'm not your sweetheart." The pronounced silence following that declaration almost echoes in the room. "I realized long ago when you gave parts of what you promised me away, I was never yours."

And with that, she hurries up the stairs.

Austyn looks at me askance. I stop playing and push the stool back. "I'll go fix it."

Her laugh is a bit watery. "Last door at the end of the hall."

I take my time heading up the stairs, composing what I'm going to say to try to make Paige understand she doesn't corner the market on emotions, that what I felt for her then, now, isn't disappearing. What we felt for one another is still alive; it just needs to be nurtured.

Like a song. Like a child.

With those thoughts crawling around inside me, I lift my hand to knock. I hear her call out a weary "Come in."

I enter. She doesn't turn from the painting she's staring at in despair.

"No one ever had from me what I gave to you." Even I can hear the mingled anger and sadness. It's a combination I know well.

"Close the door," she entreats me. I step in and do what she asks.

She cuts her eyes to the side. "I meant with you on the other side."

"I never gave anyone else close to the depth of emotion I gave to you," I semi-repeat as I make my way to her side.

But I can tell she's barely listening, so engrossed is she by the framed images of two women that hang side by side.

I don't say anything until I'm standing right next to her. "It's a beautiful picture of your mother."

"How can I miss her this much when I never knew her? Not really?"

Her barely audible words lash through me. "You do know her, bird. You absorbed a part of her soul. Of course you miss her."

Her breath shudders out. "Thank you for that."

I tap my fingers against my lip. "I feel like I know the face in that print."

"It's Adele Bloch-Bauer. It was a painting done by Gustav Klimt. It's ironic, isn't it? I guess I learned about them both the same way— one I heard about every day of my life, and the other I studied about in an art history elective in college. Lectures. That's how I know them both so well."

I cock my head to the side. "It was in different colors."

"The first in the series was often referred to as *Golden Lady* or *Lady in Gold*. It was a commissioned piece of art that was stolen during Hitler's pillaging of art during World War II."

"That's not it. I mean, it is, but it isn't."

"What do you mean?"

"Do you remember the first time you ever showed me a picture of your mother?"

Even as I ask her the question, I'm swept back to the lazy day in the meadow instantaneously.

"What was she like?" I run my fingers through Paige's as I hold the framed photo she tucked beneath her shirt as she rode to meet me.

"From what Daddy says, perfect."

"She was like you, then."

"Ha, ha, funny. We both know I'm not that." Paige lets go of my hand to roll into my side.

"To me you are, Paigey. Never doubt that." I curl up slightly to press a kiss against her lips. "She must have loved flowers."

"What makes you say that?"

I flip the frame in her direction. "She's surrounded by them. And isn't that your mailbox? I've walked by how many times. There's no flowers there anymore."

She swallows hard. "He never told me she loved flowers."

"Has he ever brought you any?" I ask gently.

She shakes her head.

"When we leave this place, I'll bring them to you. I promise." Then I lay *the picture to the side before I pull her back into my arms.*

I begin wiping away Paige's tears that are flowing from her eyes unchecked. "It's not a surprise you'd relate to a beautiful painting because the artist surrounded her with flowers, Paige."

"There's so much more to the story than that." She gently steps away.

"There always is. Anything related to love is always complicated —even composing songs about it." I open his mouth to say more but close it quickly.

My eyes drift over the frames before they latch back onto hers. I was ready to confront Paige about the emotions between us as I walked into her room, but nothing prepared me to confront the emotions of the past that still lie between us. "All this just reminded me, I still owe you flowers." Then I turn on my heel and stride out of the room.

I've barely crossed the threshold when I hear her plaintive "What on earth is happening?"

But I'm very much afraid I know already. As a boy, I was determined to protect the woman I loved twenty years ago, and the man I am is a million times more determined to right wrongs and protect those I care for.

PAIGE

I feel like singing Taylor Swift's Christmas song on repeat.

— @PRyanPOfficial

@PRyanPOfficial, get over it. She didn't deserve you. Plus, you're bringing down the party. I'm halfway across the room and I can feel your vibe.

— Viego Martinez, Celebrity Blogger

"Could you possibly have more things delivered?" Beckett jokes as he hands me another box from the online retailer I'm certain I'm single-handedly supporting.

Ignoring him, I place it with the others needing to be wrapped. It's Christmas Eve. There's been little change in my father's condition in the last week since the surgery. I'm riding a teeter-totter of emotions as I visit. He tries to speak, gets frustrated, and turns away.

It's a damn metaphor for my life.

Today, I begged my brothers to take an extra shift at the hospital since I have a million gifts to wrap and Christmas Eve snacks for close to twenty to prepare. There are so many bodyguards around, I feel uncomfortable even going on the lanai anymore. But fortunately, the threat of exposure has been nipped in the bud, Beckett assured me the day after he visited me in the hospital. His presence in my home has been noticed by few, if any. And fortunately for all of us, his security team blends well.

I ask Beckett, "Is this what your life is like all the time?"

After I ask him, he shrugs. "You get used to it. I'll take the guards over the paparazzi."

"Why's that?" I pull down a bowl, add a strainer, and dump the Vienna sausage in to drain.

"Because if they can't find the truth, sometimes they make shit up." His blue eyes hold mine when he repeats very succinctly, "Like Storia, Lucia—who was the name of the media personality—Soy, my very happily married drummer Carly, the lead singer for CyberG, and Erzulie, who is just a few years older than Austyn and is like a little sister to me."

I flush to the roots of my hair. "It doesn't matter to me," I lie.

Beckett makes his way around the counter. "Really? I guess I'll be the bigger of the two of us to admit the no-name three have kept me up the last few nights."

I snicker as I roll out strips of crescent dough.

He makes a tsking sound. "You don't believe me?"

"Because I'm simply irresistible." I strike a pose before I reach for the deli cheese I lay down in between the dough and the sausage.

Beckett whirls me around. His fingers brush my hair away from the base of my neck. The feel of them against my skin sends shivers racing up my spine. "What...what are you doing?"

"Following a simple holiday tradition." His finger follows the whorl of my ear until it touches the delicate mistletoe earring I'd slid in that morning.

"I...I'm sure..." I stammer, but I get no further when Beckett's head lowers not to my lips but to whisper in my ear, "Beneath the mistletoe, is it?"

Then his lips lay siege to my rapidly beating pulse just beneath my ear. I'm paralyzed by the feeling welling up inside me. If I close my eyes, I'd swear we were in a field of sun-warmed grass. I'd believe the next thing about to happen would be him sliding my shirt over my head just as...

With a final flick of his tongue, he nips at my ear. "Maybe if you're a good girl. Santa loves giving gifts to good girls."

And not giving the first shit my hands are covered in dough, I shove him in the chest. "Get out of my sight before I murder you!" I shout.

He laughs, the idiot. He has no idea how close I am to deathly impulses—mainly out of embarrassment that I whispered all of my innermost thoughts aloud.

"God, I'm such an idiot," I moan, my face falling forward into my hands.

Then I do scream, because despite shoving Beckett, my hands have dough stuck on them. And it ends up in my hair. "Great. Just great. I am not taking this as a positive sign for tonight."

Quickly, I wash my hands and pop the first rounds of appetizers into the refrigerator to chill before baking. Then I race upstairs to shower and scrub my head hard.

Maybe it will shake something loose like my sanity, which I fear I'm losing.

Because the longer he stays, the more I fear I'm feeling things for the man Beckett Miller's become. He's kind, considerate, and overprotective of those he cares about. "And let's not forget he's hot as fuck," I mumble as I towel dry my hair.

There's a knock on my door. I call out, "Who is it?" Damn, I didn't use to have to do that. I used to be able to just yell "Come in" to Austyn. "The man has everything jumbled up," I grouse as Austyn comes in.

"Who is it doesn't mean come right in, kiddo. What if I was doing something personal?" I lecture her.

She rolls her eyes before flopping back on my bed. "Like what?

Taking care of business because you're hot and bothered—again—over my father?"

I open and close my mouth like a fish. "I hope that muzzle I bought you for Christmas fits because even if it's too tight, you're wearing it anyway."

"Should have gone for the ball gag. I hear they're more comfortable with the same result."

"I raised you to be smart, independent, and discreet. What happened?"

She shrugs. "Blame my birth father. You always used to."

"Yeah. I'll blame him," I say with relish.

"Or just bang him to see if the sparks are still what they used to be. I mean, if a man as hot as he is attacked my neck like Dracula in the kitchen..." Austyn fans herself.

I flush. "You saw that?"

"Mama, anyone entering or exiting the house in the 9.2 minutes it lasted saw that. And even if they didn't, they'll see that," Austyn points in my general direction.

My mind blanks for a moment. Then Austyn's words click. I race into my bathroom and spot the purplish-red mark on the side of my neck. My scream of frustration echoes off the still-steamy tiles.

Austyn leans against the jamb. "I mean, I'm not saying I'm speaking from experience here—"

I shoot my daughter a filthy look.

"—but guys try to avoid marking women they're not interested in, Mama. And I do mean seriously interested in. Think on that." She turns to leave when I call her name. "Yes?"

"Come sit with me for a moment." I crawl onto my bed with my daughter. "I want to preface this by saying I don't have a crystal ball."

"Oh-kay."

"But you're a part of this now—the biggest part of this," I start. But before I can continue, Austyn's already shaking her head.

"No, Mama. That's where you're wrong. We're all connected because of you." She reaches out and touches my heart. "You kept us both alive inside you here for twenty years, but I got to live inside you here once." Her other hand presses against my towel-covered stomach. "So, I'm not the connection; you are. And if you want to explore what you're feeling with the other person who has always lived in your heart, don't ask me for permission. Don't ask me for forgiveness. You don't even have to ask me if I'll support you."

Her words resonate deeply within me. "Would you? If I asked you to support me."

"Mama, I'd support you if you wanted to have a mad affair with the sheriff, Rodeo Ralph, or my father. If they make you happy, I'd give you my blessing to be with any or all of them."

I open my arms, and she falls into them. I kiss the top of her head. "If I haven't mentioned it yet, I love you."

"I love you too, Mama." We're both silent for just a moment before Austyn asks, "So, are you?"

"Am I what?" I try to fob off her question.

"Going to have a mad affair with my father?" Her eyes are bright with inquisitiveness.

I grip her chin, place a smacking kiss on her forehead, and announce, "I'm not telling."

Austyn begins to protest. "But I tell you everything."

"I'm the mother. That's how it should be, darling."

"That's a load of crap. We have a different kind of relationship. We're special."

"That we are." And despite the crazy road that led us here, I wouldn't change a single thing about the relationship I have with my daughter. Ignoring her dramatic sighs, I roll off the bed and make my way to my wardrobe to figure out what to put on to punish Beckett. There's no reason he should get to enjoy seeing his mark on me.

Not just yet.

⊕

For a night that many consider traditionally somber, my house is filled with lots of laughter. I love it. Right now, restrained emotion is the last thing I'm feeling. I want to sit on Santa's lap and make wishes I know might never come true. I want to feel a child's belief about Christmas Eve. I want my daughter and her father to find balance so they each have one another.

For a brief moment, I close my eyes and let the discordant sounds whisper over me as I make a wish on the most important star of them all that's shining down upon all of us—the Christmas star.

As I wander in and out of bodies, Jesse gives me a toast from where he's talking to Mitch near a window. I smile as I pass him. But my steps falter on my way to where Austyn is sitting at the piano with her father.

I didn't think wishes came true so quickly. Shifting out of their line of sight, I study the way their two heads bend toward one another. Beckett's head tips back in laughter. Austyn shoves him in the side, almost knocking him off the piano bench, which is apparently just what she wanted. Casting a sultry glance over her shoulder at Mitch, she begins to sing "Christmas Wrapping."

My eyes drift to where the mysterious guard stands with my brother. He lifts his drink to hide his smile from Austyn, but from where I'm standing, I catch the flash of dimples before he manages to control it. Judging from the way Jesse's face tightens, he didn't miss it either. He glares at me across the room.

Ah, what can I say, big brother. We Kensington women like our men difficult. I try to communicate that in the shrug I give to him.

He rolls his eyes and lifts his beer to his lips.

Austyn finishes with a flourish and to a round of applause, including, I note, verbal exultation from her father and nonverbal communication I don't want to interpret from Mitch.

Then Beckett bumps her over. "Okay, kid. My turn."

Grandly, she stands. "At least I have the courtesy to give way when another artist is playing."

Beckett rolls his eyes before his lock on mine, proving he knew where I was the whole time. Ignoring our daughter, he dances his long fingers along the keys before his deep voice launches into one of the most heartbreaking Christmas songs of all time: Taylor Swift's "Christmases When You Were Mine."

His voice croons softly about the combination of heartbreak and the holiday season. I could try to claim it's the perfection of his voice singing the powerful words that holds me immobile, but I'd be lying. It's the expression on his face, tortured yet hopeful.

It's a mirror of what's in my own heart.

Maybe it's the emotional upheaval causing my walls to crumble, but I feel them fall brick by brick. It's an avalanche inside my chest. I try to find an anchor in the room, only to find all of my usual supports enthralled with Beckett. Wildly, my eyes find his again, realizing his never left mine. He arcs his brows as he sings about loneliness and Christmases when I was his.

The song ends, and the room explodes in applause, freeing me from my internal meltdown. Just as I'm about to seek out some sanctuary, Ethan loops his arm around me. I sag against it in relief. "I'd ask how you're doing, but I don't think I have to," he observes.

"I'm fine. Fine. Everything's just fine," I babble.

"You're about as fine as when you realized he left the first time." He nods at Beckett, who's still playing at the piano, only now the tempo's more upbeat as Austyn's joined him. "Before you were left behind hurting, Paigey. This time, I wonder if it's not the other way around."

I whirl on him, incredulous. "Are you crazy? He's him, and I'm just me."

"That's exactly my point, darlin'. You're you. And all signs indicate that man's crazy about you. Don't be as careless with his heart as he was with yours. As much as I hate to admit it—"

"You're taking his side? For the love of God, you punched him, E!" I exclaim, before darting a look around to make sure no one overheard us.

He shrugs as if that's not important. I grit my teeth against male posturing when he continues. "I'm beginning to think he really left because he believed it was the only option. And as much as I still hate him for never coming back for you, it doesn't mean he stopped loving you. It just makes him a stubborn idiot. Don't be like Beckett."

My hands find my hips. "Is this the right time to talk about this?"

"Didn't seem like there was a better one with—hey, Beckett. Merry..." But he doesn't get a chance to say much else as Beckett drags me away.

PAIGE

However you celebrate and whoever you celebrate with, may you find peace tonight.

— **Beautiful Today**

"Would you mind letting me go?" I rip my arm from Beckett's hand as we reach the sanctuary of his room.

He slams the door once we cross the threshold and lets me go so abruptly, I almost trip on my heels. I reach out for the dresser for balance when I spy the open package in the center of the bed.

And the tissues around it.

Damn.

Beckett prowls toward me with what I see now are red-rimmed eyes. I try to understand his mood. "I didn't mean to anger you."

"I'm not angry. Far from it." He stalks me.

"Then I didn't mean to make you upset before the party." I skirt around the chair and his bag. "You know the drawers are empty if you want to..."

I don't get to finish my sentence before Beckett snags me around the waist and hauls me to him. He draws both of us toward the bed and flops backward on it until we're lying right next to the gift I'd left in there earlier in the day.

Beckett doesn't make me wait long before he tells me exactly what he thinks about it. "I've won awards for my music, made more money than I know what to do with. And there are few possessions I would die to protect. This became more important than any statue, any painting, any anything, Paige." His fingers reach out to brush the album I so painstakingly put together about Austyn. His eyes well up with tears. "You gave me our daughter's childhood."

My own fill. Hoarsely, I whisper, "I've been working on it every night since I landed. It wasn't fair. It just wasn't right he stole that from you, Be—"

He lays his fingers across my mouth. "You know what to call me."

And with the emotion swirling around us, I don't care what else has changed. Sure, in the last twenty years, his cologne is different. I'm sure my perfume is as well. But don't I know the man holding me enough to trust him with my heart, my words? After all, we created a life between us. So, I brush his fingers aside and whisper, "Beau, he was wrong."

His eyes close on an exhale so deep I can feel it waft over my hair. "And hearing my name from your lips means as much to me as the album you put together."

"Why?"

His magnificent blue eyes pop open. And in the tears I see swimming in them, I hear the words of the song he sang to everyone just a few moments ago. "With you, it's different. I'm not just—"

"Beckett." I finish his sentence for him, understanding. My hand comes up to cup his cheek.

"Maybe if you don't call me that, it won't feel like you're punishing me," he admits.

I push up on an elbow. I frown. "But that's who you are now. You left to become him. You should be proud of him."

And then the man I've always loved breaks my heart for the second time in our lives. "How can I be proud of that man after what he did to you? He made you promises he didn't keep. No wonder you barely tolerate him." Tears run unchecked from his eyes when he whispers, "He's no better than your father."

"No. Beau Beckett Miller, you just stop and listen to me." I scramble to my knees and tug him to a sitting position.

He begins to babble. "There's no tangible proof I can give you, Paigey, but I swear I'm not as bad as the press says. I didn't do drugs like they claimed I did. That's a fucking out-and-out lie. Hell, I don't even drink that much because of the shit with my parents. But of course, I can't say dick about that because then they'd be swarming down here hitting up everyone who lived here for a damn story."

"Beau..."

"No, I'm no fucking saint—far from it—but I swear to you, I swear on Austyn, I'd have come back as fast as Shadow used to carry you to me through the fields if I'd had the first fucking clue. I had no idea until that night at Redemption."

"Honey..." I try to interrupt again. But he's on a roll. And I know this burst of emotion has to run its course.

"She's a damn miracle, Paigey. I wish I'd known. I wish I'd known five, ten years ago. I wish I knew the minute you knew, the minute you suspected. When did you suspect? And I only wrote those songs because Jess taunted me with you moving on. I couldn't believe..."

We could be here all night unless I do the one thing I know will shut him up.

I kiss him.

Within seconds, I'm being flipped on my back. Beckett's immediately taken over the kiss. His fingers curl around the back of my neck, holding me firm. His lips don't just brush against mine, as I did to calm him during his diatribe—they devour mine. His tongue pushes past the barrier of my teeth as his head slants so our mouths connect much as our bodies always did.

Perfectly.

I'm trapped beneath the softness of the bed and the hard wall of his chest. Heat rushes through me as I feel the weight of him bearing down on me. My nails dig into his biceps through the silk of his shirt, feeling the power of the man instead of the boy as our tongues meet, heat flares, and the lines between what I knew of right and wrong explode into a symphony of need.

The music only he could play in me.

I strain against him for more, so much more than a kiss. I need it, need him. I want to remember the feeling of his hands skimming across my skin, his teeth against my nipples, him sucking... A broken moan leaves my lips when he lifts his lips from mine. "Don't stop," I plead.

"Sweet Paige," he croons before sitting back.

My body weeps in anguish at the loss of his until my brain puts together what he's doing.

My body arches into the air when his long fingers make deft work of the remaining buttons of his shirt, freeing them. I want to reach up and touch each inch of muscular skin that appears, but that damn bitch reason forces me to voice one final attempt at sanity. "Are you sure this is a good idea?"

As he shrugs off his shirt, I get my first full view of the beauty of the art that marks the passing of time on his body over the corded strength that he's kept honed over the years. "If dreams coming true are a good idea, then yes. It's the best idea I've had in a long damn time."

I suck in a breath, knowing I'll never be the same after tonight. Then again, why should tonight be any different? I sure as hell wasn't after he took me the first time when I was seventeen. With full cognizance of what's about to happen, I sit up. His hands fist and clench while I tug the hidden zipper down at my side.

That's when Beckett stays my hand. Our eyes meet and hold for an eternity and a heartbeat; they're one and the same. His hand slides under the hem of my dress before he slides the skirt up my thighs as he begins prowling up my body. Lifting it up and over my shoulders, it becomes tangled in my glasses and hair for a moment. When I finally pop out, I inanely whisper, "Here I am."

Beckett's eyes close before his forehead drops to mine. "Here we are." Then his mouth seeks mine, a certain power that's always crackled between us igniting.

His hand cups my breast, still nestled in the lacy fabric I slipped into earlier. Using his thumb, he rubs the edge back and forth, causing the nipple to protrude. I break my lips away from his, gasping, "Beckett."

But he shows no mercy—not that I really want any. I become transfixed as he ducks his head and draws an excited whimper from me when he takes a nip from the exposed curve of my breast while his other hand begins plucking a different rhythm with my other nipple. As he braces himself above me, I'm a mass of writhing nerves. It's heartbreakingly familiar and yet so different every time his calloused fingers touch me. This man brings alive all of my senses, even as he destroys them.

I slide my own hands over the rippled edge of his abdomen, forcing him to withdraw his ministrations for a moment as I steal some of his own breath. The light blue of his eyes is eclipsed by the black of his pupils when I ply his nipples with the same torment.

We spend long minutes rolling each other across the bed, each of us intent on pleasuring the other. I spend an inordinate amount of time on the too-sensitive skin around the word "Live" inked on his chest while he divests me of my bra. Then his mouth sips one of the peaks deep.

I moan, tightening my thighs on his hips the minute he does. The wicked heat of his mouth surrounding my nipple causes my clit to pulse with a matching ache. "Please," I beg.

He reaches behind him and slips a hand into his pants. Pulling out his wallet, he tosses it somewhere near my head. *Thank God* is my barely coherent thought. But if I thought Beckett taking a few moments to stand to shuck his shoes and pants would speed things along, I was wrong.

Because he drops to his knees by the side of the bed just before dragging me to the edge of it.

I feel his breath scald me against my slick folds before he runs a finger down the center of them, parting me. Then he proceeds to remind me he wasn't only a virtuoso at music. Hot kisses, quick flicks, combined with his fingers drive me higher and higher. So close to an edge I've been to only with him.

"Beckett," I cry out.

Quickly, he surges up, wiping the edge of his beard with his forearm before reaching for his wallet. Control is held on to long enough for him to slip on protection. Then I feel the head of his cock hone in where it belongs, where it's been missing—inside me. "Look at me, Paigey," he rasps.

I can barely lift my head, every inch of my blood pooled around him. But I manage it. "What is it?"

That's when he thrusts inside of me. "This is home. You will always be where home is."

Tears prick my eyes as he begins the push and pull, his length dragging along the sensitive tissue inside of me. Over and over, I'm taking a ride I've ridden so many times and yet I'm on for the very first time.

I feel the ripples of the beginning of my orgasm along his erection. He increases the pace of his thrusts, the sweat dripping from his hair. Civility is torn away, this essential mating taking us back to who we've always been.

Paige and Beckett. One of life's beautiful songs.

As we crescendo, his fingers twine with mine. I tighten my legs around him and hold on with all my might, knowing that even if I can't hold on to him forever, I'll always have this.

And therefore, I'll always have a piece of Beckett to love.

PAIGE

Celebrity tattoo artist Kitty made a public service announcement the other day. Before you ink something permanently into your skin, be certain you're not going to regret it later. This is why she refuses all appointments between Christmas and New Year's. Considering her clients include the likes of Beckett Miller, Brendan Blake, and Small Town Nights, she's serious when she locks those doors.

— Moore You Want

I trail my finger over the circular letters of the words "Live the Dream" on Beckett's chest. "Is this odd?"

He flattens my hand down, pressing it against the thundering of his racing heart. "What?"

"Us. This." I shift my legs beneath the sheet against his since one arm is trapped beneath his body, and I'm not anxious to move it.

Beckett barks out a laugh. "Why?"

"Perhaps because it happened so fast?

"I've been trying to woo you since I first got here."

"Is that what you call it?" I think back over the last few days where

Beckett's done nothing but been here for me and duck my head so he can't see my lips curve.

"Intense wooing."

"My home, my life invaded by security," I begin.

"By me. Rekindling the spark. Stoking old fires."

"Oh, you stroked something all right," I think aloud. But I don't beat myself up too much when I realize what I said as he roars with laughter because the sound is too precious. It rarely happened back then, and now, I ask, "Do you laugh?"

"Not the way I did with you. Nothing worked the same as it did with you."

I roll my eyes.

"I wasn't kidding just then, Paigey." Beckett pulls away just enough so he can roll to his side and face me. He captures my hand in his before pulling it to his heart again. "This certainly didn't work the same."

I snuggle down a little before confessing, "Mine didn't either. How could it when I had part of your soul tied to mine every minute of every day?"

His eyes close as if the weight of my words causes him both pleasure and pain. "I should have come home."

"You were home—wherever that was," I remind him.

His thick lashes lift off his cheeks. "No, I've been on the road running from home since the last time I saw you spread out before me."

I lean forward and press a soft kiss to his lips. "That's sweet."

"That's the truth."

"Beckett," I begin. He arches a brow at me calling him by his chosen name. The light catches off the nose ring he now sports. Determinedly, I go on. "I've learned the hard way love is just a sound your mouth makes unless it's backed up with actions and feelings."

His body freezes. "Are you deliberately insinuating something, Paige?"

I shake my head back and forth. "I'm telling you where my head is at. In the course of a few weeks, I went from despising you to being terrified of you to this. My emotions have whiplash."

But instead of causing him to back away, his body softens against mine. "You know what they say about love and hate."

"Don't quote old idioms back at me," I warn him, cutting him off before he can tell me the old saw about love and hate being two sides of the same coin. Because I know it well as I've lived it since the day he left me behind.

"Seriously? You just said 'idioms' while naked. Your brain has always been one of the sexiest things about you." His lips quirk into a smile that I'm sure has melted more hearts than I want to know about.

Frustrated, I slap the mattress. "We have to figure out what this means."

Beckett simply picks up my hand and kisses it. "I already know what it means."

"Then tell me, oh wise one," I shoot back, sarcasm dripping from every word.

"I have a better idea." Beckett rolls me to my back.

And then he does something so much more personal than touch my body. He touches my soul.

I left you there, all alone
To fight the wind, On your own
Standing tall. Standing proud.
Without me.
The secrets I keep
Swore I'd keep
Take a deep breath, I'll be back around
At least, that's what I said.
One month, two
Why am I so blue?
Can't forget a single thing
I should laugh, and sing, and dance
Maybe I'll find a new romance

And our promise of love will just drift away

The tears drip from the corners of my eyes as Beckett finishes the rest of the song that's obviously about the emotional turmoil he had about leaving. But finally, I whisper, "You should have told me."

"I know that now."

His simple words desecrate me. "We could have been together."

His head drops until our noses brush. That touch of gold brushes against my skin, reminding me of too many experiences he's had without me. "How could you have left me behind? Knowing who and what he was, how could you?" I lash out.

"Forgive me, Paige. All I could think of was..."

"Yourself?" The word escapes my lips unbidden. We both gasp, and Beckett even rears back.

For just a moment, I'm about to apologize until I realize I'm right to feel the small amount of resentment I still hold. I need him to address this before we can move on. Yes, by his accepting our child, by doing whatever he's needed to do to stop his life and be here for us while we're dealing with the fallout of my father, he's mostly atoned for whatever misplaced hurt I've endured because he carried the burden of my own father's betrayal so I didn't have to. Except one.

He still left me behind. And despite whatever part of my heart that will always belong to this man, I'm afraid to completely give the rest over to him until I know the reason why I was forsaken.

So, it's with bated breath I wait for his reply.

His fingers fidget with mine. "When I left... I don't remember much clearly, Paige. All I remember feeling was pain, agonizing pain. I was so bruised, I could barely lift the bag I packed." His strong face contorts in pain.

"What was in it? What did you pack?" I ask in an effort to distract him from remembering.

Instead, it does just the opposite. He buries his face in the crook of my neck. "I had some jeans, tees, briefs, and the like." I feel him swallow hard. "And..."

"And what?"

"And I'd bought you flowers just like the ones in your mama's picture. It was so stupid, but they were in the bag. I smelled those fucking things on my clothes for days after I left. And all I could think about was you and what you must be feeling."

My body jerks at his confession. "You bought me flowers?"

"They were dust before I finally threw them out."

I lick my lips, wetting them, before I ask something I need to know. "Have you ever bought anyone else flowers?"

He pulls his head back. His face is serious. "Just once. And it wasn't that long ago."

My heart starts free-falling in my chest until he finishes, "They were for Angie."

I blink in shock. "Carys's Angie?"

He nods. "I put together who she really is. And if someone was ever deserving of flowers, bird, it's that woman."

I frown, recalling the night I met her at Redemption. "Something happened to her."

"It's her story to share fully, but yes."

"And how does that man factor in?" Before Beckett can think I'm gossiping, I explain, "He scared her that night. I mean terrified her."

He cups the side of my cheek. "It wasn't Ward who scared her; it was the past. And it's fine."

My brows come together as I frown. "You're certain?"

"Well, considering I almost decked him and she stood in front of him to avoid him taking my fist, I'd say so."

I begin shaking with silent laughter. "Because that would have looked so good in the media. I can just see it now—"Rock God Beckett Miller decks 'Winsome' Ward Burke over a woman."

If anything, his face becomes more serious. "You do realize that about seventy to eighty percent of what's written about me is utter crap?"

I sit up and draw my knees to my chest. He does the same. "Honesty?"

His fingers reach for mine again. "I expect nothing less."

"I didn't want to. I wanted to believe you were some man-whoring ass who had everyone pandering to him. It made it easier to hate you."

His fingers rub back and forth over my knuckles. "And now?"

"Now, I'm feeling as much guilt and am probably more sorry than you are. I'm an adult, an educated woman, and a mother. I could have hired the investigators myself years ago, just like I did to protect Austyn from your law firm. And I'm kicking myself because what would have happened then?"

His fingers tighten on mine. "Neither of us can know, Paige. I made the best choices I could; you trusted people you believed in. And look where it brought us."

And my lips curve as my foot encounters his hair-roughened leg beneath the sheets. "Back where we started."

His lips twitch. "Well, maybe in better accommodations. Did I ever tell you about what a bitch it was when you'd be on top and I'd feel the rocks beneath my back? It will be a pleasure not to have to deal with that."

Deciding we've had enough serious talk for now, I dive and take him to his back—much the same way I did when I had just turned seventeen and felt like I could fly every time he was near. "Why don't we see if it makes a difference in a bed?" I suggest.

A wicked smile crosses his handsome face before he takes my suggestion and puts it to practice.

BECKETT

What's the best gift you ever received? For me, it was a second chance.

— StellaNova

I woke up alone but feeling better than I have in twenty years. I latch onto Paige's hand as she passes me another gift—the sneak. All that online shopping I teased her about and it was gifts for me—which causes her to blush furiously.

Instead of being disturbed I woke alone, I tugged Paige's pillow against me and held it close against my heart, absorbing her essence deeper into my every heartbeat. After last night, there's nowhere she could go I wouldn't carry her with me. My lips curve at the thought.

Then the weight of an adult woman drops like lead into my lap. "Merry Christmas, Beckett!" Austyn looks ridiculously adorable wearing a crocheted elf hat complete with ears.

I squeeze her tight. "Your mother keeps piling gifts in front of me. I don't need things when I already have been given the best gift ever."

Her eyes crinkle much like I imagine mine do when I'm up to no good. She teases, "What's that?" leaving me to wonder if she knows where her mother spent the night.

I press my lips to her brow and whisper, "You."

Much to my surprise, Austyn's lips begin to quiver. Fortunately, that's when Santa's little helper unceremoniously drops another gift in her lap. "For your father," Paige announces. She winks at me over our daughter's head.

I jiggle Austyn before I mouth, "Thank you."

Her emerald eyes, which were determined doling out gifts, noticeably soften. "Austyn, get off your father's lap and finish giving him your gifts."

My head whips down in surprise. "These are all from you?"

Her lips tremble a second more before the doorbell rings. She bounces up as quickly as she landed. "I've got it!"

Paige takes her place, perching on my knee. "Merry Christmas."

I wrap my arm around her waist to hold her there. "Merry Christmas. Would it traumatize her if I kissed you good morning?"

"Unlikely, as she caught me coming out of your room to start making cinnamon rolls as is our normal Christmas tradition," Paige says dryly right before her cheeks flush.

I feel a warmth in my own, but I still take advantage and press my lips against Paige's, who responds warmly. After I lift my mouth from hers, I bury my face into the side of Paige's neck and snicker out, "Busted."

"Totally. And my brothers are going to notice too," Paige predicts.

I frown. "Why do you say that?"

"I had to put on makeup." At my confusion, she explains. "It's Christmas. I never wear makeup."

"Why did you wear any at all? You're beautiful without any gunk."

Paige leans forward and brushes her cheek against my beard. Then her voice drops to an intimate level. "It feels great against the inside of my legs, honey, but I've learned it leaves marks in other areas." With that, she stands and leaves the room to go greet her brothers.

Just watching her walk away stirs my dick into hardening again. I don't immediately follow so I can attempt to try to get my now raging boner under control.

But there's no ditching the crazy-happy smile on my face. Nor would I want to.

After a few moments where I pray mightily that each and every package set in front of me forms a time machine that allows me to relive the last twenty-four hours over again in perpetuity, I stand and follow the voices into the kitchen. Immediately, Jesse punches my arm, and Ethan places me in a headlock. Both shout, "Merry Christmas," before Paige's "Seriously?" and Austyn's "Is this for real?" causes them both to cease tormenting me.

Both Kensington women have their arms crossed, a leg kicked out, and a foot tapping. "You look like warriors," I declare, making my way between them. I bestow a kiss on each of their heads before reaching for a mug to get coffee.

Jesse growls. Ethan chokes.

"Oh, get over yourself, both of you." Austyn flounces away, leaving the four adults in the kitchen.

Jesse holds up a hand. "I don't have much to say."

Paige interjects. "Good."

I smooth my hand over her back. Ethan growls at the gesture. I use my other hand to flick him off.

"But what I will say is this. My father was both right and wrong. Paige was worth protecting, yes. But not for the reasons he did it. She was worth protecting because of exactly who she is."

And because I agree with him, I hold out my hand. "And that's everything."

Jesse hesitates only for a moment before he shakes it. "Yes."

Ethan isn't so tactful. "Don't fuck this up."

"I don't plan on it."

Paige wedges between all of us and declares, "If any of you expect a day filled with merry and bright, you will cease this conversation as if I'm not here. I am a grown woman. I am not a child who needs coddling from any of you." Her fierce gaze rakes over me as well.

Ethan opens his mouth to say something when he takes an elbow to the gut from Jesse. "Right. We'll go pile our gifts up with the others."

Paige groans. "We're going to be opening gifts for hours."

Ethan calls over his shoulder, "Like this is anything new?"

We stand together as they begin doling out package after package —most for Austyn. Paige sighs dejectedly. "Nothing I can do will convince them she doesn't need *things*."

"What does she need?"

She rests against my chest. "Up until now, I'd have said stability, but every day I'm learning we find stability in happiness. And your daughter found it in much the same way you did."

"With music," I deduce.

"Yes. That's why my gift to her isn't material, per se. It's a dream."

"What does that mean?"

Paige smiles up at me. "You'll see. Get your coffee, Dad. You're going to need it." She picks up a plate of enormous cinnamon rolls and heads back into the fray, shouting, "Did someone get trash bags from the garage?"

"On it," Ethan yells, jumping up from behind his smallish pile of gifts.

Paige reminds us, "All gifts are numbered. If they aren't, then you'd better ask if there's a special order."

"Christ, you're organized," I mutter.

"If I wasn't I'd have lost my mind long ago," she replies sweetly. "Now, if we want to finish sometime before supper is on, everybody go ahead and dig in!"

Austyn doesn't hesitate. Immediately she dives for the bag with *#1* printed on it. And immediately laughs when she pulls out an empty Christian Louboutin shoe box. "So classy, Mama."

"I paid a fortune for those heels. I hope they're not being worn by your roommate."

Austyn snickers. "No, because even though I was worried about you, I packed them."

Paige beams at her. "I raised such a bright child."

"And a fashion-conscious one. Do you think I would violate my one and only pair of dream shoes? Please." She sniffs at her mother.

I immediately make a mental note to find out what size both Paige and Austyn wear so I can buy them hoards of the famous designer's footwear. Meanwhile, I tear into my first bag and yank out a University of Texas sweatshirt. Immediately, I stand up and yank it over my head. It's about two sizes too big. In other words, "It's perfect," I declare to the room at large.

Flash! Austyn takes a picture with her phone. "Mom, I'll AirDrop you all the photos later."

"Thanks, honey. Oh, Ethan. How did you know I needed new running shoes?"

Ethan nods at Austyn, who grins at her uncle. "Jess, thanks for the gift card to the computer warehouse."

"Like you need more parts. But still, if it makes you happy. Hey, who do I have to thank for the Yeti cup? This thing will keep my drink cool for hours when I'm working." He turns the black mug around in his hands.

I raise my hand. Everyone gapes in my direction. I get a bit defensive. "What? I can't think of a few useful gifts? I did use to live here, you know."

Paige's emerald eyes beam joy at me. I hope mine communicate back at her before I jerk my head to the side, indicating she should dig in her pile for another present. With a shy smile, she does.

I'm stunned as I unwrap a mug embossed with a recent picture of Austyn, a photo book of candids she must have put together from her phone, and a Kensington T-shirt from her website. The last, I vow, "I'll wear this onstage."

"You'd better! I need some free advertising," my daughter shoots back. She squeals in delight as she opens her own T-shirt that comes with a promise for front-row concert tickets and backstage passes to Brendan Blake's next show in Manhattan. "Now, this is the gift that keeps on giving! Right on, Beckett!"

Ethan lets out a war whoop before he dashes over and hugs his sister, who has given him a tree decorated in gift cards to the Apple Store. "I'll take one of these every year!"

"And I will too," Jesse declares. He waves his own tree of gift cards before leaning over to press a kiss to Paige's cheek. "You're the best."

But Paige is frozen as she holds the open box in her hands. I gnaw on my lip anxiously, hoping she'll appreciate the meaning behind it. "I know they're not..."

"Hush." Carefully, she lifts the bouquet of roses made out of sheet music up. Her eyes are glistening when they meet mine. "How did you do this?"

"There's an amazing store online I found." I give her the name. "The artist can make flowers from books, letters, and it turns out, from sheet music. I wanted to give you a part of me no one else has."

Paige carefully turns the bouquet. "I don't understand how..."

"I wrote out a few of my songs and express mailed them so they could be included." I hope she'll leave it at that.

I should have known better.

Austyn scrambles over next to Paige. She leans down and starts reading the music. I can watch her piece the music together in her head. She frowns. Her head snaps up to mine. "I don't recognize the music. Is it new?"

I shake my head. "No. In fact, it's older than you are, kid."

Paige's hand flies up to her mouth. "Beau..."

Austyn's head whirls in her direction. "Mama?"

"You didn't?" Paige's voice cracks.

I push aside the abundance of presents I've been given and make my way over to the only two gifts I need. Crouching down in front of the woman my heart has never stopped yearning for and the daughter she gave me, I confirm what she's thinking. "I promised you I'd give you flowers. And it all started with this song. I thought they'd be a perfect gift."

And as Paige launches herself into my arms, I'm quick to catch the bouquet of flowers Blooming Books handcrafted after I overnighted the sheet music—after Carys confirmed the artists signed one of her infamous NDAs, of course. Paige would be devastated if it were ruined. I hand the delicate flowers to Austyn while I hold Paige to me. Murmuring into her hair, I whisper, "I want to make up for every Christmas you weren't by my side."

Her breath shudders. "It's going to take some time to get used to."

"What will, bird?"

She leans back in my arms and scans the room. Jesse and Ethan are studiously ignoring us. Austyn is absorbed in the flowers, still trying to follow the notes on the sheet music. I bite back a chuckle, knowing I'll get the chance to bring her to New York and show her my music room and recording equipment there. But Paige's words bring my focus exactly back to where it belongs—on her. "Feeling this happy. I'm afraid to believe in it."

I squeeze her so tight, she squeals a bit. "Then although I never make them, it appears I have a New Year's resolution after all."

"What's that?"

"Doing my damnedest to make you happy." And I lower my head down to hers to kiss her, not caring who is watching. They'd better get used to it anyway. I don't plan on giving up this woman willingly.

Not ever again.

PAIGE

Someone claimed they spotted Beckett Miller in a small town in Texas. I laughed. I mean, what the hell would he be doing there?

— **Sexy&Social, All the Scandal You Can Handle**

The day after Christmas, I received a call from the hospital. My father's condition has improved enough he's throwing out autocratic orders like a king to his waiting court. And one of them is he wants me to dance attendance upon him.

Alone.

"I can handle this," I said stoutly to Beckett and Austyn before I left the house.

"You shouldn't have to, Mama. What he did affected all of us," Austyn argued.

"I second that," he growled. His arm was slung over our daughter's shoulders.

"See? It's two against one," Austyn claimed.

"Since when did this family become a democracy?" I asked, bemused.

"Since Dad stepped into it. Apparently I win more arguments this way."

We all burst out laughing at her audacity. Then Beckett dropped his arm from around her and came to me. He pulled me into his arms and studied my face for long moments before declaring, "Sorry, kid, but I'm changing my vote. Your mother is a fierce woman; she's got this."

To which Austyn replied, "Well, I know that. It's just..."

And I shivered as I turned in Beckett's arms—like it was one of a million dreams I was afraid to voice—to face our child. "Just what, baby?"

"You shouldn't have to be alone. We should be with you."

I tapped Beckett's arm. He let me go, and I immediately went to her. I pulled her into a tight embrace. "Don't you know, you always are? It's how I was coping until you were actually here."

Her "Isn't it better we actually are?" made my head swivel in Beckett's direction.

He merely cocked a brow, repeating her question without saying a word.

So I gave them both the same answer. "Yes, it is."

A few minutes later, I was out the door with a member of Beckett's security team trailing behind me. "Nonnegotiable, bird," he growled before pressing a kiss to my lips.

I let out a burst of frustration just as I turn into the hospital parking lot. So many things for us to talk about still, but we'll get there eventually. We have time. We found each other again. And even with the added strain of our current circumstances, my soul feels so light it feels like I could scale mountains. Admittedly, I still worry about Beckett and Austyn. They still have their own paths to travel, but this time together has been good for them, I think as I put the car in park.

But my father made so many decisions easier for me. I no longer feel the choking bonds to tie me to Kensington that I would have if Beckett and I had reconnected without his deception. There's no choice in staying here any longer. Even if Beckett and I hadn't reconciled the way we did, I'd be looking for something new, something far away from a lifetime of lies.

I begin making a mental list. After the new year, I'll begin looking at what it will take to sell my business to a suitable audiologist. Ideally, it would be perfect if my practice went to someone who wanted a slightly slower pace. Pressing the button for the elevator, I think about Dawn and Amie. I wonder how they're going to react.

Then I snicker. What am I worrying about? If they knew there was a man involved, they'd likely board up the windows and wrap the parking lot with tape, declaring it condemned. Oh, boy. What on earth does Beckett want said to people? Are we keeping this between ourselves? I step off the elevator and pass the nurses' station with a quick wave. Lifting my hand to my mouth, I begin chewing my thumbnail. "That's just one more thing to talk with him about. Great."

"Talk with who about, Paigey?" I hear in a raspy version of a voice I thought I knew as well as my own.

And there he is. Standing with the aid of a volunteer, but damnit. Even after everything, I can't stop the relief that washes through me seeing him stand. "Father," I acknowledge.

"You can go. My daughter will help me the rest of the way," he orders.

With that one sentence, it occurs to me he's always been like this: commanding, demanding, and expecting. And alongside that realization comes another.

He expects me to just forgive him.

As a doctor, I've agreed with my colleagues about many things. One of them is being an advocate for loved ones to be close after a major medical procedure. It's so critical, the NIH has run studies on how active involvement of family caregivers has the potential to improve patient outcomes. But while it documented the family caregiver's attitude, nothing would have prepared them for the bitter resentment and fury surging through me.

All because I'm standing here.

The volunteer hesitates since I don't make a move toward him.

Finally, I break the awkward tension. "Why don't you get Mr. Kensington settled back in his room? Then I'll be in to speak with him."

Shock crosses my father's face, so it's easy for the volunteer to steer him away from me.

I stomp off down the hall, needing a few moments to just breathe. I've seen him so many times unresponsive since surgery, I didn't expect the emotions that would return like a shot full broadside when he was on his feet. Slipping into one of the private rooms, I run a shaky hand over my hair. "It's almost worse than the night on the porch."

I begin pacing back and forth in agitation. I have to get myself together before I walk into that room. I deliberately dredge up the conversations during the first few months I was pregnant with Austyn.

"Are you sure you don't want to get rid of it?" my father asks me.

"It's my baby. It's a..."

"Mistake. It's a mistake, Paigey. One no one needs to know about."

"I'd know. I'd always know."

He storms up to me so fast, I almost trip backing away from him. "You're going to know anyway, girl. What in the hell were you thinking?" he roars.

I'm afraid of answering what's in my heart.

No longer shaking, I stride to the door of his room and knock. The volunteer opens the door, starts to say something, but then quickly excuses herself.

I don't give my father time to speak. I launch in with deadly calmness. "I was thinking I was in love. I was thinking I loved every piece of the boy who gave me that child. And the child that lived beneath my heart would help me live the rest of my life without him. And if you had loved me that way, maybe you wouldn't have asked me that question."

He opens his mouth to speak, but I don't let him. "You called her an abomination, you bastard. You asked me to abort her. You lied to all of us—starting with me, Jesse, and Ethan. Then, let's add in your granddaughter and Beckett. Yet you expect me to forget? To forgive?

To move on as if your own actions merit me kowtowing to your every whim?"

"It would be a shame for me to let your colleagues know you've been uncooperative, Paige. And you're a doctor..."

"Do it!" I shout. "Just do it. All you're doing is solidifying the decisions I've already been making."

"Which are?" His head tilts quizzically.

I shake my head, not giving him any more information—certainly not any more of me. "I do have one question. Why?"

"Why what?"

"Why did you never rise above her death and love me?"

His eyes glitter. "You just said it, Paige. Her *death*. She died, and I loved her with everything I had."

"That's a lie, and we both know it." I think back to the affection he gave my brothers growing up. "Why?"

He mulls over his response for just a moment before finally admitting, "Because you lived."

The answer causes my eyes to burn, but no tears fall since I was certain of it already. "What's horribly sad for you is you never realized you had a piece of her with you. *That's* why I was so adamant about carrying Austyn."

His head whips to the side as if I've slapped him. "Paige..."

"No. I'll arrange nurses, things you'll need when you go back to the farm, things like that. I won't leave that burden to my brothers. But that's it. I'll figure out the business financials—" I stretch the truth slightly. After all, selling my business is certainly one way of handling it. "—but this is where it ends. Right here. I'm no longer at your beck and call. I refuse to be punished for her death."

I walk to the door and put my hand on it. "As a doctor, I suggest you get some professional help"—I hear a scoffing noise behind me, but I plow on—"before Jesse or Ethan have children."

"So what? You're going to keep Austyn from me?"

I look back over my shoulder and really take a good look at his haggard face. "No, you did that all on your own."

I open the door. I'm just about to step through when I ask him a final question. "How do you think Mama would have felt if she'd have lived and I'd have died?"

I don't wait for him to respond before I shut it firmly behind me. Instead, I walk directly to the nurses' station. My voice sounds husky to my own ears when I declare, "Mr. Kensington may need to be checked on in a few. He may be experiencing a bit of pain."

"Thank you for letting us know, Dr. Kensington. Should we let you know if his condition worsens?" the nurse asks me.

I shake my head. "Contact my brothers. I'm off duty."

And I hurry as fast as I can to the elevator. I need to get out of this hospital and get home.

⊕

An hour later, tucked under a blanket with a glass of tea in my hands, I'm finally able to discuss what happened. Austyn is curled next to me, and Beckett? He's pacing in front of us like a caged lion. His fury is a living, breathing thing. I've just finished relaying what happened in my father's hospital room.

"So, what are you going to do, Mama?" Austyn takes my free hand.

I set my tea aside. "I've been giving that a lot of thought. I'm definitely leaving Kensington. But I need to determine where to go. I mean, I could move to the city."

Beckett's face brightens before falling considerably when I murmur, "I'd get to keep my patients that way."

"You meant Austin?" he says flatly.

"Well, yes. What did you think I meant?" I stammer.

He opens his mouth and then closes it. His eyes drift to Austyn, who issues him a defiant look.

"If you want to ask her, ask her."

I rub my temples. "Will one of you stop talking in riddles? God, it's like having two children right now."

Beckett squats down in front of me. "We..."

Austyn clears her throat loudly.

He amends. "I think you should give serious consideration to changing your plans."

I frown. "You mean, don't sell the business?"

"No. I understand why you feel the need to disassociate yourself from something your father loaned you the capital for once you had the right buyer."

"It isn't an easy decision to make. But I can't be here having built my life around lies and not become bitter about everything in it. Including medicine."

"Of course not. You have too big of a heart for that, Mama." Austyn dismisses my concerns.

The tightness in my chest begins to ease a bit. "Thank you, both."

"For what?" Beckett takes my free hand.

"For at least trying to appreciate what I'm feeling."

His eyes sparkle much in the same way Austyn's do when she's about to propose a half-baked plan I'm going to shoot down in 0.2 seconds. Uh-oh. I brace when his beautiful lips open. "Then why don't you consider this. Come with us."

"And do what? I need to work for a living."

Frustration crosses his face for the briefest of moments before it disappears. "I know. Come to the East Coast and look for a job."

My mind blanks. All I can do is stare at him. Then he says something that shakes me to my core. "It's time for you to live the life you were meant to live. Not the one Tyson Kensington wanted to control. So, take the pen. It's time for you to write your own life song."

My head whips back and forth between them in shock. And a wave of realization washes over me. I'm going to be thirty-seven years old and I'm about to be truly free to start my life for the first time. All the energy I spent on trying to keep a copasetic relationship with my father can be expended on the people who truly matter. My brothers, Austyn, and maybe, just maybe, Beckett.

But most importantly, I can give it back to myself.

And that's why I squeeze both of their hands and declare, "I'll think about it."

Austyn and Beckett have the same reaction. They hold their

hands up, waiting for the other to slap it. Then they look at the other in confusion. So, I do the deed and pronounce them both "Goofballs. Now, who's hungry? I suddenly just got an appetite."

Austyn leaps off the couch to start pulling leftovers out for dinner, but Beckett lingers behind. He cups my face, tattooed fingers tracing my features gently. "You're not just saying it? You really are going to consider coming to New York?"

"Yes."

He wraps me up tightly in his strong arms. And until Austyn calls us, that's how we stay. Just like we'd stand for hours in the field near the heart of my ancestors.

BECKETT

Beckett Miller is reportedly going to be a performing artist at this year's Grammy Awards. Though the gorgeous bachelor has been MIA for the last few weeks, we can only imagine that's due to the holidays. We can't wait to see what's in store for music's greatest night of the year!

— Viego Martinez, Celebrity Blogger

"When the hell are you coming back?" Carys demands.

"I don't know. Frankly, what the hell does it matter? You'd think you'd be happier without me there."

"For the most part, I am," she returns without hesitation. I grin. Then she goes on. "But I will admit—just this one time—it was much more convenient when you used to drop in so I could handle your legal issues."

I sit up with a snap from where I'm lazing on a lounge chair with Paige. "Tell me someone hasn't broken into my place again."

She tugs on the sleeve of my shirt and frowns up at me. I shake my head and stroke my hand down her arm until our fingers twist together. Pulling her hand onto my lap, I brace for Carys's next words.

"No, it's just you're you, Becks. People want you for things, though God knows why."

"Because I'm wantable," I shoot back with my normal arrogance.

Two women's laughter echo in my ears—one through the phone, one from the body next to me. I grin with unrestrained happiness, something I haven't felt since I was last lying next to this woman. "So, what's on the table?" I ask Carys. I squeeze Paige's hand and am comforted by her return of the simple affection.

God, if I let myself, the resurgence of fury toward her father could come back so easily for stripping us of all these years. What would it have been like to have shared my first gold record with her? My first platinum? The first red carpet? My mind wanders back when I think about what I bought with my first million. The first time I shuffled into Bristol Brogan-Houde's office at UBS with practically every dollar I'd ever made, begging her to turn it into more. Would we have had a couple of kids then instead of just Austyn? My breath catches at the very idea of watching Paige grow round over and over with my seed growing inside her belly.

I growl, which Carys must take as a sign to continue. Thank God. "ASCAP reached out. Your songs are wanted for a ridiculous number of commercials."

I shrug before realizing Carys can't see me. "That's nothing new."

"No, but—" She drops the name of the luxury carmaker that I happen to own. "They don't just want the song; they want you."

"Now, that *is* interesting," I admit. "When?"

"Yesterday."

"No can do." I shoot it down immediately. I'm not leaving Paige this soon.

"Yes, you are," Carys declares.

I throw my legs off the lounger and shove to my feet. "What the hell gives you the right—"

"The Grammys contacted Wildfire. Kris and I spoke earlier in the week. He wants you to agree to present Best Album of the Year, since you're not nominated for it."

"That's in early February this year." I immediately discount the argument.

"Um, hello, Beckett? Are you even thinking right now?" Carys shouts. "This isn't just about you presenting, you jackass; they want you to play. That means getting your ass back to New York and practicing before you fly to Los Angeles like a good little boy, walk the red carpet, and keep your fans happy."

Right now I wish I could tell my fans to kiss my ass. There's exactly one of them I give a shit about. But then Carys drops a bomb I wasn't expecting.

"And Kensington is trending."

I freeze. Every molecule of every cell in my body stills. "What do you mean?"

"I mean, people are pleading for Marco to get her back in the booth at Redemption. Hell, there's a new hashtag of #KensingtonGrammys going on. Your daughter has made quite the name for herself on TikTok, and with her tour backing her up, proving she's the real deal, there are some very interested people looking at signing her." Carys waits a heartbeat before emphasizing, "*Very*."

"Like who?" I whirl around and find Paige's eyes glued to me.

Carys rattles off all the major players and ends it with, "And Kris casually asked me if I'd heard her while she was in New York. When I told him I was her official legal representation, he said he'd be talking with me later."

I lift my finger with the ankh up and begin chewing on it. Thinking. Paige raises a brow. I tell her, "It's my way of thinking things out."

"Ah. Does the ink ever fade?"

Carys laughs in my ear. "If you screw this up, I'm dumping you as your lawyer. She's the best thing to ever happen to you."

At that, I drop my hand and stare directly into Paige's eyes before replying to Carys, "I knew that twenty years ago, and I still managed to fuck it up. She's the reason why it worked back then too." Then I hang up the call without addressing any of her issues.

After I slide back into the lounger, Paige lets me get settled before observing, "Conversations between you and Carys appear to be contentious."

"Only when she wants me to do something I don't want to," I say sulkily.

"What's that?" She tips her head back, and I'm instantly distracted by her jewel-colored eyes.

"Hmm?"

"What does Carys want you to do?"

I hedge.

"Beckett," she snaps.

"Do a commercial," I admit begrudgingly. Then I tell her the name of the manufacturer, and her jaw drops.

"No freaking way. I've always wondered what it's like to drive one."

I pull her on top of me. "Good. Come to New York and you can drive mine."

"Seriously? You own one?"

"No." I wait half a heartbeat. "I actually have a collection of them at my house in LA."

"A collection of them?" she repeats weakly. "Christ, Beckett. I'm really not going to get used to this. Go...donate some money or something. Okay?"

I bury my hand in her hair and whisper a kiss along her lips. "Already done."

"What do you mean?" Her mouth puckers in suspicion.

I wriggle a bit. I hadn't planned on telling her.

"Beckett!" she snaps.

"An anonymous donation of one million dollars was just donated to Doctors Without Borders," I blurt out.

She blinks up at me.

"And another was sent to that organization that delivers animals to help villages."

She still doesn't say a word.

"And there might have been an endowment to the University of Texas."

Her mouth gapes.

I shift uncomfortably. "Didn't you say if it were up to you, you'd educate doctors and then send them around the world to save lives? And then feed the world? All I did was help speed the process along a bit."

"You heard what I said," she whispers incredulously.

I nod.

"And you gave up some of your hard-earned money to what?"

"I thought it would make you happy," I tell her honestly.

"You have no idea how happy I am right now." She lifts my hand and presses it against her heart. "Will you tell me why you always chew on your ankh when you're thinking?"

"Truth?"

"Yes."

"Because the ankh is supposed to symbolize eternal life." I begin to chuckle. "And then there was the fact I was trying not to flick some dick off who wanted to steal me away from Wildcard after I got it done. It took every ounce of my patience not to do it. Now, I'm not so sure I would hesitate."

Her smile is indulgent. "So, it became a habit."

"Maybe everyone just thinks I'm an asshole because I'm barely refraining from flicking them off?" I query.

"Nah. If I had to hazard a guess, it just adds to your total hotness," she teases.

The two of us laugh. And then regret spikes through me. *This. This is what it would have been like.* I want to tell her what I'm feeling, but instead I share, "Carys said Austyn's trending." Quickly, I explain everything that's happening back in New York.

Her fingers go slack on my hand, so it drops. I curve it around her hip. "Beckett, she's going to flip."

I chuckle. "I'd be surprised if she doesn't know."

"You're probably right." Then it hits her, much the same way it did when I was talking with Carys. "That means both of you will be going...soon?"

I swear ripely. "I don't have to do the Grammys, Paige."

The look she aims at me essentially asks me if I hear myself talking. I curse again. "All right, yes. I'm going to go do the Grammys. But I'll be back."

Her smile is tender. "No, you won't. You're going to get back to New York, and you'll fall back into your life."

I capture her by the nape of her neck and tug her back down. "I will be back as long as you are in this godforsaken town. I don't care what I have to do to rearrange my life; I'm not leaving you again."

"I can't ask you to do that."

"You're not asking me. I'm making a promise."

Paige doesn't say anything to validate my declaration. She just slides her hands up and cups my cheeks. Her lips meet mine. And that's when I remind her she's not too old to ride me out in the open regardless if there are security personnel patrolling her property.

Besides, who gives a fuck? She's mine. And she better get used to them being around.

PAIGE

Beckett Miller performing at the Grammys? Well, that's one way to shake a guy out of the blues and put him right back where his head belongs: rock 'n' roll.

— @PRyanPOfficial

I linger in the shower after my interlude with Beckett on the lanai, thinking about everything that's occurred since I came back to Kensington. As the suds sluice down my body, I'm left feeling more confused than ever. And at the center of it all is the swirl of so many questions of what's next?

I haven't felt a pain so acute since I was six months pregnant with Austyn and my father sat me down in his office chair before delivering the news that there was no news to give me about Beckett's location—that I was truly all alone. He'd left me, us. He'd broken his promise to love me when I'd given him all of me.

Sinking to a squat, I wrap my arms around my legs and begin rocking back and forth. I wonder if this time the emotions of what it feels like to be the woman left behind are going to be more devastating than those of the girl who was. My wet hair flies out in all directions as I shake my head. What am I thinking? I don't have to give it much thought.

It's going to be so much worse.

That's because the man Beckett grew into is so much more devastating to who I am. He already owned the largest piece of my soul I had to give, but his blunt honesty, uncomplicated generosity, and earnest affection for those he lets close snatched up the remainder.

In a few weeks, I've been so caught up in the crazy happening around me, I forgot to keep up my shields, and I did something so stupid I'm never going to recover.

I'm never going to stop loving him.

The first sob escapes. I duck my head so I can muffle the sound against my legs. The last thing I need is for either my daughter or her father to rush in here to ask me what's the matter because I can't answer that question without lying—or doing my damnedest to. Because love isn't just a word. It's a sound your mouth should make when your heart can back it up with real feelings.

And that means consciously keeping my feelings about Beckett to myself so he won't feel obligated when it's time to go. "This hurts worse than the first time," I whisper aloud. My chest is tight at the thought of losing him a second time, but then something stirs inside of me.

He was never mine to have. Either time.

At that realization, I fall back until my butt hits the shower floor. A man like Beckett Miller graces the planet because he was given a gift to share with the world. A small laugh bubbles out of me when I internally try to imagine how this would work out. "And here's my girlfriend. Paige who?"

"Try Paige everything," a dark voice growls above me.

My head snaps up to find a naked Beckett looming over me. I shove my wet hair out of my face and blink him into focus, squinting a bit. "What are you doing in here?"

"You've been in here an hour." Beckett steps directly under the spray before joining me on the floor.

I shake my head. "It couldn't have been that long."

He doesn't answer me, merely lifts my hand and looks at my fingers, which have shrunk down into prunes. "Oh," I respond inanely.

"Oh, is right. I was coming to tell you...never mind. What's going through your mind, bird?" And before I can open my mouth to say "nothing," he repeats, "And here's my girlfriend. Paige who?' Why don't we start there?"

"I was thinking," I begin.

His head immediately clunks back against the shower wall. "No conversation between us has ever gone well when you started it like that."

Indignantly, I poke him in his ribs. "That's not true."

He pins me with a look. "'I was thinking, we should skip school. Just one day.' Wouldn't you know that would be the day Mr. Roberts landed us with a pop quiz."

"I forgot all about that," I admit.

"'I was thinking, let's try sneaking into Rodeo Ralph's.'" But it's Beckett who laughs first. "Did you ever tell our daughter about that?"

"No! And you'd better not either. She's still underage."

He scoops me up so my legs straddle his. "'I was thinking, let's run away. Let's leave this all behind.'"

"Yeah. That plan didn't work out so well for one of us either, did it?"

He pushes my hair off my face where the weight of the water has shoved it forward again. "Not really. But that one's on me. You wanted to fly away long before I did, my little songbird."

I don't say anything because what is there to say. I did. I just wanted one thing out of this life: him. I swallow hard. "Not meant to be—at least not for me."

"Maybe not then. But now? What's holding you back?" he prods.

You! I want to shout, but the real answer is me. Slowly, I explain, "I'm what's holding me back because now, I'm afraid."

"Of what? Of me?" he asks incredulously.

"I was thinking, if I leave Texas, what do I have?" There a stillness in the shower despite the pounding of water from the dual shower-heads. "What do I really have, Beckett? My daughter—"

"Our daughter," he whispers.

"Our daughter is grown up. She's on her way to the kind of stardom you've spent your life enjoying. And tell me the truth. You love it."

"Are you asking me if I would change leaving?"

"I guess I am."

"Then the answer's no. God help me, Paige, that's the one thing I don't regret out of all of this is getting the hell away. But after that night, knowing what I'd have to endure to keep the secrets I held, there was no way I could stay and not begin to resent you."

I turn my head away so Beckett can't witness the exquisite agony he just seared me with. I smooth my hands up and down his slick skin and give him the last gift I have to give him. Forgiveness. "Once I knew the truth, I figured that out for myself. Don't..." I don't get to finish my sentence because his arms haul me so close we're pressed loin to loin, chest to chest, nose to nose.

And then our tragedy comes full circle when he breaks, "But I should have made damn sure I found a way to bring you with me. In my head, you were my only family, and I left you behind. What kind of man does that? And you were carrying our child?"

I can't respond. Beckett's own tears begin to fall. "You have me. You always have."

"That's just not true."

"In here it is. Everything I have, the man I am, is because you put him inside of me."

I rear back and snap. "Tell me this isn't some belated, misguided thank-you."

He rolls his eyes. "For Christ's sake, Paigey, you were just as diffi-cult to say the words 'I love you' to the first time."

My head spins. "Maybe I've been in the water for too long."

"Damnit, Paige, I'm trying to tell you I've always loved you. I've never stopped loving you."

I shake my head frantically. "It's not possible."

"Tell me why not," he challenges me.

"It's only been a few weeks."

"It's been years. Every damn night I dreamed it circled me back to here, to you. Don't try to deny it wasn't the same," he counters.

I open my mouth to do just that but am defeated by my own longings, my own wishes for this to be real this time.

"Say it." I open my mouth, but before I can get anything out, Beckett tramples right over me. "And don't you dare deny it."

"What makes you think you know me—this me?" I correct automatically.

He lifts my hand and kisses the palm hungrily. "Because on this planet, there's only been one person who ever loved me. *Me.* Not what I could do for them, but who I was. No one could love me the way you do because no one knew me. And that's how I know I love you." His hand cups the back of my neck, pulling me back into him.

I'm certain he can hear the pounding of my heart. "How?"

"Because I'm the only person who you ever let in. I'm the man who makes your heart sing, little songbird. I'm right, aren't I, Paige?"

God, I want to knock his arrogance down a few notches, but I can't. "Yes."

He pulls me back. Triumph shines in his eyes. "Then say it."

"B—"

He shakes his head. "That's not right."

I shudder. He's asking for me to lay my soul as bare as my body. And certain all parts of my body are shriveling into prunes, I repeat the words I said twenty years ago for the first time. "I love you, Beau Beckett Miller. I always will."

"And I love you, Paige Melissa Kensington. Forever, if you'll let me."

A sob bubbles up. "That's the problem. I know exactly how short forever really can be."

"It won't be this time," he reassures me.

"Beckett, our lives don't mesh."

"You don't know that. You can't."

"You left me! What happens when you find someone new?" I shout.

"That will never happen."

"How can you be so sure?"

"Because you're still my longest girlfriend to date."

"God help me, I'm in love with a madman," I moan. Then I groan louder. "And how do we explain us to people?"

"People?"

"Your associates. How do you explain *you* met someone as normal as a doctor?"

Unperturbed, he blows off my question. "I would think your bigger concern would be how we tell our daughter."

Horrified, I begin babbling. "No. Nope. Sex is one thing. How do I explain to her I'm dating her father?"

"Just tell her we had the longest breakup ever—that it didn't change our feelings for one another."

Water dribbles out of my mouth in a sputter. This man is going to drive me insane with a combination of laughter and insanity, I'm certain of it. "That it didn't change anything?"

"That's right."

"There's no way Austyn goes for that."

"Were you Daddy bashing when I wasn't in your lives?"

"Other than calling you a crazed lunatic, no."

"Then see? Everything will be fine. Now it's my turn to make plans for us."

I arch a brow. "Oh? And what do your plans involve, Mr. Miller?"

"Talking about where you fit in my life."

"Umm..."

His lips brush against mine once, twice, before he lingers over the next time our lips meet. I'm so lost in his kiss, it takes me a few moments to come out from the haze to hear what he says. "Nothing comes before you, Paige. Not music, not money, not fame. The rest of it—save Austyn—can go to hell. I've lived that life and..."

"And?" I can't keep the note of hope from my voice.

"I wrote that life for myself. I knew it could be better. I should have known the person I was supposed to write my life's music with was you and come back sooner. But I will never put anything before our love ever again. Nothing."

The intensity of his eyes fills the cracks of my heart. I scrub my hand through his beard and whisper, "I believe you. Okay. This time, you're in charge."

He scoots forward away from the wall, placing my face directly beneath the spray of the shower. "Damnit, Beckett!" I shout.

Struggling to his feet, he turns off first one nozzle, then the other. "First order of business is to dry off. I prefer my woman to be land-locked and not sprouting gills."

I giggle as he steps out of my enormous shower, eschewing the towels and heading straight for the master bedroom. "Beckett, you're getting water everywhere!"

"No, you are." Then he sends me sailing in the direction of my bed before following me.

I laugh from the bottom of my gut, the feeling so intense, it's euphoric. He wants me. He loves me. And he's committed to making this—us—work. He has to be.

We're his priority. Even beyond his music.

His words ring in my ears as he looms over me before we compose some of the most beautiful melodies of love heard.

BECKETT

Rumors no more. Wildcard Records has released an official statement. We are thrilled to announce Beckett Miller, Brendan Blake, and Erzulie will represent Wildcard Records by performing at this year's Grammy Awards. Set your favorite recording devices!

— StellaNova

Kane keeps a safe distance as I walk around the overgrown remains of where the place I should call home should be. "But it was never much of a home here," I finally conclude.

That's when I hear the footsteps behind me. Her arm wraps around my waist. I'm not surprised she's here when I need her the most. After all, other than the one time, she was always the person I turned to when things were the hardest.

Until I had to let her go for both our sakes.

I pull her tight against me, refusing to do that ever again. Breathing in Paige's scent amid the memories of rotten food, bugs, and rodents that were a part of my life here, I ask, "How did you get here?"

"I rode, of course." Her head moves up and down on my chest as she motions toward the foundation of her ancestral home about a half mile back.

"I should paddle your ass for walking through the field all alone."

"Really? Can we arrange a time for that?" The interest in her voice has my cock leaping to attention, but I refuse to give Kane a show.

"Later."

She hums her approval before settling in close, content to just be with me.

And that's when the tragedy of everything I gave up truly hits home. Paige would have been as content to have lived in a home just like the one I was raised in so long as she had me and our daughter. "And it would have been beautiful," I whisper above her head.

It would have been perfect.

"Beckett, what's wrong?" Concern laces her voice.

"I just got lost in a moment." It's the truth, only the moment is a vision of what our past would have been. I press my lips to hers, a sweet benediction of thanks to whatever god saw fit to bring us together again. I vow to donate buckets of gold to whatever deity did the trick. "What brings you here, Dr. Kensington?"

"Austyn said I'd find you here. I have some news."

Tipping her head back, I encourage her, "Tell me."

"I was approached by another audiologist about purchasing the practice today." A combination of nerves and excitement flit over her face.

"How soon?" Living in a world of contracts, I know these kinds of negotiations can either take place at the speed of sound or a snail's pace.

"A few months. Unless something falls through or there's some kind of complication, right about the time you're done with the Grammys." Her nose wrinkles. "Now, I have to find a job and a place to live."

Never in my wildest dreams, in the shadows of the place where I slept as a child, did I ever think I'd say these words as an adult. "Move in with me. Don't worry about a place to live."

The offer is impulsive, but it's from the depths of my heart. So, I appreciate when Paige gives it due consideration. But finally, she shakes her head. "Despite the last few weeks—which I've treasured, please don't ever think otherwise—we need time to adapt. All of us, including Austyn."

"She appears fine with us."

"Appears, Beckett. She's dreaming of Mama and Daddy being a family. Considering she's almost twenty years old, she needs to remember the things I taught her growing up."

"Which were?" A vision of Paige in a long white gown has taken root in my head, and now I can't get rid of it. And I'm wondering if I ever want to.

So it's no surprise I likely have a ridiculous smile on my face when she informs me, "That people share all different kinds of love. That it's their choice on how they celebrate it. And only part of that love is to respect their choices unless she's a part of that relationship. Then she has every damn right to demand everything from it."

I lean down and nuzzle my nose against hers. "Don't move an inch."

I pull out my phone and have a very quick, very heated discussion about how I'd be heading back with Paige. "No, you're not welcome to follow." I hang up in his ear before I grab her hand and start pulling her toward the hole in the fence, which is how I assume she slipped in.

It is.

"Did you just ditch your security detail, Mr. Miller?" Paige teases me.

"I did." I grab her hand and drag her to the one place we haven't been to since I got back.

Our place.

And now, I'm kicking myself for not bringing a blanket.

But when we get there, I find there's a blanket already spread on the ground not far from where her horse is tied up. And, much to my surprise, even her old backpack which I'd bet my penthouse has a bunch of our favorite snacks inside. "Paigey." It's the only thing I can manage to say.

"So, to celebrate, will you play for me, Beckett?" It's the same sweet request that used to haunt my dreams. Only this isn't a dream. It's my reality.

Thank fucking God.

I swoop her into my arms and carry her over to the blanket, the same exact way I did when we were in high school. And then I make love to the only woman I ever did.

And ever will.

✦

Hours later, wrapped in only the blanket while I wince as I hit another discordant key on the decrepit piano and sing to Paige, she murmurs, "I dreamed of this for years."

My hands hover over the missing keys. "Of what?"

"Of you. Wondering if you'd come back, look at me, feel the same. I mean, I'm me, and well, you're you."

Sensing we're treading onto sensitive ground, I feel my way carefully. "Paige, I'm still me. I just have more."

"No, you changed the moment you spit in the eye of this town. I only feel like that's just starting to happen."

"I disagree."

Exasperated, she rolls her eyes. "Beckett, you haven't been here."

"No, but who fought for her child to go to New York?"

"Well, of course."

"Who was determined to become a doctor?" I counter.

"It still was..."

"And who had our child? Kept her against all odds? Raised her and loved her? You don't think you've changed? And here I'm in awe of the woman you've become."

Shyly, she captures my hand and pulls it to her mouth. "Maybe our changes complement each other."

"I'd say they do." I trail my other fingers across the top of the blanket. "There is one thing we need to discuss though."

"What's that?" Paige asks. The blanket slips lower, barely catching on her turgid nipples to hold it up.

"Later," I say thickly. I can warn her later about how intrusive the press is in my life.

Right now I have better things to do. Like make up for lost time buried deep inside the woman I love.

✦

All too soon, the morning comes when Austyn and I fly back to New York. There's a pall over the entire house. At least there is until I drag Paige into the pantry and show her once more that she's mine, not giving a damn there are likely people who can hear us on the other side of the door.

But all too soon, my mood darkens again. I want to tell the Recording Academy, Carys, my band, and everyone else they can shove this appearance up their ass, and just stay here. I can't. I won't. That's because I won't let Paige down.

She's already moving heaven and earth to get her license transferred from Texas to Connecticut, where she found a job. She's put her house on the market. "I have to go through years of memories. I'm going to ugly cry, Beckett. It isn't going to be pretty. Go do the Grammys, and I'll see you faster than you can imagine."

"We'll talk every day," I promise her as I hold her by the front door. Austyn's already said bye to her mother and is seated in the back seat of the SUV. Kane is giving us a few moments of privacy before most of the team flies back to New York. Paige was both amused and dismayed when she realized that my leaving didn't mean security wasn't being called off. Hell no. She and Austyn are the most precious people in my life.

I'm not doing anything stupid to ruin my chances at my forever with them.

"Every day," she vows in return.

"FaceTime," I correct myself.

She rolls her eyes. "Beckett, if I'm out to dinner with my brothers, do you really want me answering a call on FaceTime, thereby telling the whole world who is calling me?"

I don't even hesitate. "Paige, you've become my whole world, so why would I care?"

Her lips part on a delicate sigh. I don't waste the opportunity. I pull her in and seize her lips in a kiss meant to remind her of everything: the past, the present, and our future.

Together.

Eventually, I do pull back. Her lips are puffy, and she's glassy-eyed. In other words, perfect. "I'll call you the minute we land."

That's when she does something so profound I know I'll remember it until my dying breath. She leans forward and kisses my chest. "Take care of my heart since you're taking it with you." Then she whispers, "I love you, Beckett."

I whisper, "God, Paige, I love you too. I don't know how I'm going to live without you."

Her smile is crooked. "Pray we won't have to find out. Now go before Kane storms up here to drag you away and realizes I'm not wearing any underwear because I couldn't find them behind the paper towels."

I wink at her, fucking ecstatic I have a lifetime to look forward to of mornings just like this.

And her to come back to.

BECKETT

Celebrity stylist Dee, whose credentials include stints at Gucci and Stella McCartney, was spotted leaving Beckett Miller's estate in Beverly Hills. The exclusive women's designer was mum when contacted about what she delivered. But it leaves us all to ask, who could he be escorting to this year's Grammys?

— Eva Henn, Fashion Blogger

"Beckett?" Austyn shouts. The sound reverberates off the walls in my marble tomb of a home in LA.

I fucking love it.

I bought the place because I was out here enough recording that I wanted a home base. Plus, Bristol said it was a great way to invest some of the money I had at my disposal. I've thrown parties here for hundreds—participating in some in my younger days, watching more often from the balcony from my master suite on the third floor. But never until my daughter stayed beneath the roof last night did this monstrosity of rock feel like a home.

Until now.

"In the kitchen," I yell back.

"Where's that? I think I'm lost," comes at me faintly.

Placing the chef's knife down on the counter, I go in search of my daughter, laughing.

I pass by the panoramic views of the Pacific Ocean just past my pool deck. I ignore security patrolling the grounds and call out, "Austyn?"

Then I find her sitting at the base of the stairs leading to the upper levels. "Mama always taught me it was safer to wait in place."

I chuckle, holding out a hand. "I was just about to make breakfast. Want some?"

"Do you know how to cook?" she asks warily as she clasps my hand.

"It was cook or starve," I admit as I tug her to her feet.

She's silent as she follows me to the kitchen. I immediately resume chopping peppers for the egg white omelet I was preparing. "Social media believes what they want to regardless of facts, don't they?" Austyn asks.

"In general or about me?"

"Both."

I contemplate her question. It's a tricky one. "I'm not perfect, Austyn," I warn her.

She snorts as she gestures to the coffeepot. "Help yourself. Cups in the cabinet above you," I inform her, lifting my own mug for a sip.

"Let's be real. I'm around the same age you were when you and Mama had me. I know just how 'not perfect' two people can be."

I choke as the warm liquid slides down my throat. "Christ. I don't want to think about you doing things like that!" I shout.

My daughter has the gall to laugh at me as she lifts her mug aloft. "Beckett, please. Mama already had these discussions with me when I was younger. Besides, she at least wasn't hypocritical."

I sputter. "It's not hypocritical. It's…"

Austyn takes a sip of her drink. "Hmm?"

"It's being a parent," I thunder.

She patronizingly pats my arm. "You're new at this. I get it. You'll get used to it. But please, try not to have a coronary over how much skin I'll be showing in my dress for the Grammys."

I open and close my mouth like a fish. "How did Paige do this alone for all these years? She deserves an award."

"At the very least," Austyn agrees as she hitches herself onto a stool in front of me. "Then again, when she was really frustrated, she would ship me off to Uncle Jesse and Uncle E."

I move the skillet onto the burner and begin sautéing the vegetables. "Cheese?" I ask, hating I don't even know if my daughter likes her eggs with cheese.

"Does a cow go moo?" she retorts.

"Thank God you're not going to worry that a few bites of cheese is going to ruin the lines of your dress," I mutter.

"Beckett, I say this in all sincerity, you've been dating the wrong women."

I couldn't agree more. But a little glow starts. "Paid much attention to my career?"

She shrugs. "Your music was okay. I had a total girl crush on Carly."

"Tell her that when you meet her later. She'll love it."

"Don't think I won't. Your music was good. Solid."

That glow spreads before it bursts into insane laughter.

"Thankfully, I didn't lustfully worship your bod the way some of my friends did..."

"That might have been a bit creepy now," I interject when I catch my breath.

"Right?" she emphasizes. "But due to my friends *totally* crushing on you—oh, God. My friends were creeping on my dad." Austyn begins making retching noises.

I grin before encouraging her to go on. "You were saying?"

"I still saw a lot of pics of you. You always seemed...detached... from whomever you were photographed with. After Mama told me the truth about you, about us, I searched for you online."

I pour in the eggs and let them sizzle before I reply. "I'd be surprised if you didn't."

"But that goes back to my comment from before. People just believe what they want to. They don't put in the time and effort to put the pieces together, to uncover the truth."

"There's a lot about me that's true, Austyn."

"And just as much that's not," she fires back hotly. "You were never in rehab; you were on tour. But the whole world believes you were because some no-name asswipe wrote about it."

A warmth steals through me at Austyn's defense. Indignancy follows close on its heels when she wonders aloud, "Do I have any brothers or sisters?"

"What? Hell no!" What Austyn doesn't need to know is any claims that might have been true were investigated and proven to be false long ago. I mentally perform the sign of the cross.

"While I wouldn't mind having siblings, I think it makes it easier for you and Mama to have this second chance."

I gape at her until the smell of burning eggs causes me to curse roundly. "Shit. Damn."

"Add in a fuck or two and you'll be the living image of a rocker dad—tatted up, making breakfast for his kid before sending her off to play for the day," she mocks.

"You're totally fucking with me," I accuse.

"Completely. For Christ's sake, Beckett. I have about a year's worth of questions to ask you, and we have no time before we have to fly back. Our schedules don't seem to sync up in New York. The only time we seem to connect is on airplanes."

I think about it for half a second. "I have an appointment this morning"—which is going to hurt like a bitch—"then Grammy rehearsal this afternoon. Why don't we stay a few days after? I'll show you around LA, and we can get to know one another without the time constraints."

Austyn chews her lower lip. It's an endearing habit I do as well. "I don't have any plans."

I toss the burnt eggs to the side. "Right. First order of business is to find something edible to eat. Go get dressed, and we'll pick up something through a drive-thru."

"In-N-Out? I hear their burgers are amazing." Austyn dashes through the kitchen in the direction of the stairs.

"For breakfast?" I shout.

"It opens at 10:30!" comes her reply.

I pick up my cell phone and text Paige. *How do you say no to Austyn?*

If you figure it out, let me know. Her text is followed by an evil smiling GIF.

Thanks for the help. I send her a laughing GIF of a baby falling over.

Of course. You're doing great, Dad. Miss you XOXO.

I think about the appointment I have that morning before typing, Not more than I miss you, baby. Every minute, every day. It's a permanent part of me.

Then I hear Austyn shout, "Do I need to dress up?"

I yell back, "To ride in a blacked-out car to get burgers? Get a move on, daughter!"

And I smile when I hear the clamoring of noise on the stairs. Yes, Austyn has brought life to this pile of stones just like Paige brought it to my heart.

PAIGE

Beckett Miller was distracted on the red carpet when escorting DJ Kensington. Although he normally takes time to socialize with as many members of the press as possible, he appeared eager to get inside. Perhaps he needed adjustments to his onstage attire, which was quite fitted. Although not for everyday wear, I can't deny it was visually appealing.

— Eva Henn, Fashion Blogger

"Damn, I always knew she'd look amazing on a red carpet." I whirl around, and a ridiculous smile takes over my face. This time, instead of the spasmodic ball of acid that fills my belly when Ethan points out Beckett's date, pride takes its place.

I lean against my brother as we watch Beckett's and my daughter saunter at his side down the red carpet at the Grammys. "You called it, sequins and all." I take a drag of my beer, one of the last I'll ever enjoy at Rodeo Ralph's.

"Wonder what you're gonna wear when he takes you? Something plum-colored and classy as hell."

The beer I just slid into my mouth comes hurling out at a rapid speed right onto Ethan's boots. "Are the computer screens sucking up what brain cells you have left?"

He pats my shoulder condescendingly. "Denial is such a lovely place to live."

"So is Connecticut, which is where I'm moving."

"And you think being a mere one state away—roughly sixty miles from Manhattan—is going to stop Beckett from furthering his courtship?"

"Stop it," I hiss, glancing around.

"You know, your gentleman friend who sent a bottle of champagne to you earlier. 'Wish you were with us. I love you.'"

"Jess is a dead man when he gets here," I vow, infuriated both that my older brother told Ethan about the champagne and that he read the card. Dead, I swear it.

"Your gentleman caller who dropped my name with the software company he wrote a certain jingle for to get my foot in the door on a contract bid?" he throws out offhandedly.

"He didn't," I breathe.

"He did," comes Jesse's voice. "And that same beau also offered to buy Dad out of the farm if I didn't have the capital out so Kensington would remain in the family."

"He's doing all that for Austyn," I protest weakly.

"Paigey, despite my concerns, you didn't see the way his eyes tracked your every movement over Christmas," Jesse chides me.

"No joke. The man is beyond halfway gone for you."

Absentmindedly, I say, "He mentioned using someone named Bristol..."

Both my brothers heave and choke simultaneously. "Brogan-Houde?" When I nod, Jesse manages, "She's only known on television as the 'Queen of Wall Street.'"

I shrug helplessly. "I guess? I don't think about his money." I'm too busy packing to be with him, responding to texts of songs being sent to me. And hot-as-hell FaceTimes that have me blushing.

Jesse's too shrewd not to notice. "She's hiding something."

"No, I..." But just then, a reporter stops Beckett and Austyn. We agreed not to disclose their relationship so Austyn would have a chance to make it all on her own in the music business. I tense, wondering how this is going to work.

The live closed caption reads:

[reporter] And who is this with you?

[Beckett Miller] My good friend, Kensington.

[reporter] The DJ?

[Kensington] Yes.

[reporter] Is this your first awards show?

[Kensington] (laughs) It is. But I hope it won't be my last.

[Beckett Miller] I'm sure it won't.

[reporter] Can you tell us who you're wearing?

[Kensington] Stella McCartney.

[Beckett Miller] Tom Ford.

[reporter] Well, thank you for stopping by. That was tonight's presenter of the Best Album of the Year award and last year's winner, Beckett Miller, as well as his friend DJ Kensington.

The three of us are silent a moment as we absorb the implication of what just occurred. I begin to laugh aloud. "Oh, God. Poor Austyn. Now she won't be able to go anywhere with her father without the paparazzi thinking it's a date."

"Do you think Beckett realized that?" Jesse asks with a wide grin.

I shake my head. "This is why he has a team of lawyers. Bless them. After tonight, he is going to owe them triple."

"Well, at least your daughter will provide a nice cover for you dating her father," Ethan points out.

I gape at my brother just as Jesse's hand connects with the back of his head. "You're a sick, sick man, E."

He lifts his beer in a toast. "I come by it naturally."

I can't suppress the giggles. "Too true." The butts of our beer bottles connect. "You know I'm going to miss you both ridiculously."

Jesse hooks an arm around me and the one holding his beer around Ethan. "Same goes. But if we didn't think this was the best thing for you, we'd tell you. You need to go, Paigey."

"And besides, we'll always be here." Ethan's arm wraps around me, completing our circle.

"I need to. I just wish I could take you both with me."

"You will. We'll be in the same spot you've had Beckett all these years—your heart," Ethan points out logically.

I squeeze them both before twisting my head and catching a last glimpse of Austyn and Beckett as they step into the theater, playing up to the crowd. I smile. Soon, I'll be there to witness their hijinks in person.

And I can't wait.

Moments later, I get a text from the man himself. It might be possible Carys kills me over this one, baby. If I go, you should know this is my official last will and testament.

She has every right. Even Jesse and E were commenting that A would make a great blind for us dating.

He sends me the vomiting emoji back. Sorry, no. And sorry your Grammy news is likely going to be filled with speculation about this.

I shrug. Beckett had warned me press about him was going to be ridiculously high tonight. *Then it's a good thing I'll be on a plane first thing in the morning to meet the movers.* I smirk as I press Send.

Then I face the television.

His head snaps up from the laissez-faire stance right to attention —back so straight it's almost militant. I want to double over with laughter over the little stunt I just pulled when he shows Austyn his phone and my baby girl's smile widens so huge the reporter asks, "What's the hot news, Beckett? A new album? A new collab? Come on, let us know!"

Beckett merely grabs our daughter's arm and starts stalking down the red carpet.

The little dots move, indicating he's typing. Then they stop as he and Austyn are ambushed. They pose.

"So, when are you telling Beckett you'll be waiting in Connecticut when they get back from LA?" Ethan asks me.

I nod toward the television. "I just did."

Jesse cackles as Mitch, my on-duty shadow, slips his cell from his pocket. His lips twitch, but he doesn't say anything. He just slips his phone back into his pants, and we all watch this play out on television.

Finally, Beckett and Austyn reach the last reporter. I can feel his frustration, and I'm halfway across the country. "This should be fun," I remark.

And it is. The reporter, from the glossy magazine StellaNova, asks what the hoopla is all about. Beckett replies directly into the camera, "I just got some news I'm thrilled to hear. Soon, I'll be able to share it with the world. Until then, I'm keeping it close to the heart."

"And he pulls out a save, ladies and gentlemen!" Ethan announces.

Jesse, always more circumspect, just starts applauding.

But I can't wipe the ridiculous smile from my face. Just a few more days and I'll pay for that little stunt.

I can't wait.

PAIGE
FEBRUARY

Ever since the Grammys, Beckett Miller and DJ Kensington are in each other's back pockets. Is this a potential collaboration or something more? I wouldn't mind more of either of them, if you take my meaning.

— Moore You Want

"You can move that hutch to the master," I inform the movers two days later. I blush slightly when I recall the conversation with the moving company where they said I could just leave things in there. Yeah, no. I put all my personal items into plastic bags before the movers came. Now, I want to grab everything tucked inside and begin loads of laundry before everything touches my skin again.

"Yes, ma'am."

It's been two months since I've seen Beckett. And now I'm counting down the hours until he's done showing Austyn Los Angeles so I can give him a tour of my new home. And I can't help but wonder if this won't just be a temporary stop to a more permanent one with him. The home we were meant to have together all those years ago if my father hadn't intervened.

I hear the doorbell ring and rush to go answer it. I glance outside the big bay window, and my excitement rises when I recognize the local cable company logo. I fling open the door. "Hi!"

"You arranged for a Comcast installation?"

I swing the door open wide. "Come on in."

My excitement continues to rise as more furniture and boxes are brought through the patio doors. I direct the movers to place things in particular rooms. Fortunately, I arranged for the home to be mostly furnished by the Realtor, so when I moved in, she had the necessities put away and it was professionally cleaned. The things being delivered are personal items and mementos as well as a few cherished items. I've made separate arrangements to store Austyn's piano until we decide what to do with it. But this also means I'll be settled in more quickly and able to dive headfirst into the life that's been waiting for me all these years.

I can hardly wait.

Deciding to leave the cable guy to it, I follow the movers upstairs when they enter with a wardrobe box. "To the master, guys."

"Absolutely, Dr. Kensington." We all trample up the wood staircase to the second floor.

I love the house that's a combination of a Tudor and a fairy's playhouse on the outskirts of Collyer. Painted a bright yellow, it's tucked behind oak and pine trees and has a trail of Pachysandra. "Hope you like gardening, ma'am," one of the movers said after I asked if he knew what the lush green plant lining the walkway was.

I pull out a pocket knife and quickly undo the wardrobe boxes. I hang my carefully packed suits up in the master walk-in, critically examining them. "Thank God I have a steamer."

Just then, the mover pops in with the very item I mention. I make a grab for it. "Thanks."

"No problem. The rest of the boxes are marked with an *A*? Where do you want those?"

"The third bedroom, please, Steve. Thank you."

He nods, leaving me to my unpacking. And daydreaming.

Pulling out a silk sleeveless walk-through jumpsuit I bought with an enormous bow as its only clasp, I wonder if Beckett's and my reunion will happen at a place where he'll have a chance to see me in it. And take me out of it. With a private smile, I hang it up near my suits and continue to remove items from the boxes. I dump out shoes as fast as I can, knowing I can arrange them later. Besides, I packed my new Louboutin heels in my suitcase, I reassure myself over my mistreatment of my clothes.

I just feel antsy. I don't know why. Maybe having my things spread around the space will make me settle down a bit.

I'm not sure how long I'm unpacking before I hear Steve call, "Dr. Kensington, the cable guy needs you a moment."

I squeeze past the box in my closet. Hurrying on bare feet down the stairs, I almost run into two other guys carrying boxes up to Austyn's room. "Oops, sorry, guys."

They both call back, "No worries."

I skid to a halt next to the cable guy. "What's up?"

"We're all set: downstairs television, computer in the office, and router for whole-house Wi-Fi. That is, unless you have a second television you want to hook up?"

"No, that's everything. Do I owe you anything?"

"It will be charged on your next bill. I do need to run through some things to make certain they work with you." He begins to drone on about logins, default passwords, and how to change them. In the middle, I have to stop him because Steve and his crew finish, and I do have to pay them. I give them all an extra tip plus bottles of water.

Offering one to the cable guy, which he gratefully accepts, we continue. "So, once I change all of that, my high speed is up and is secure for me to work from home."

"Yes, ma'am. You paid for the full-package support, so if you have any difficulties, just call." He hands me a card, which I slip into my pocket. "Now, let's just do a quick check of the television, and you'll be good to go."

He walks me through the steps to turn the television on and off using my new remote before calling it a day. I offer my hand and say thank you. "No, thank you. Welcome to Collyer, Dr. Kensington."

Soon enough, it's just me.

And sooner till, it will be us.

With that thought, I dash up the stairs, intent on getting my bras and panties in the wash with undue haste.

Later that night, I'm laughing over a comment on a new show on HGTV when my iPad pops up with a new notification about the Grammys.

I reach for it, laughing. "If I'm going nuts, Beckett has to be going crazy. He's already been on the Best Dressed lists, been speculated about with his relationship with Austyn enough to drive him batty, and has half the world wondering what his "news" is. If they knew it was me, they'd..." But my words trail off when I get an eyeful of what I'm seeing.

I blink, certain my mind is playing tricks on me. I refresh the page.

It's still there.

"This can't be possible," I whisper to the empty room.

Empty, because Beckett's on the opposite coast where according to this news alert, he's been spending quality time with Erzulie at his place in LA. It alludes to the fact she's always been special to him. Judging from their state of dress—or undress—I guess that's one way to interpret it.

I try not to jump to conclusions as I suck air into my lungs, but the picture blurs beneath me as the first tears plops onto the screen. It obscures their faces, but not those of his security team—particularly Kane, who looks grim to the point of angry.

I grab for my phone.

He answers on the first ring. "Hey, baby. We were just—"

I immediately go on the attack. "Who? You and Austyn? Or you and Erzulie?"

"What? Erzulie? What the hell are you talking about, Paige?" Beckett's voice, so warm when he first answered, angers.

"I'm looking right at it, Beckett!" I scream. Then I begin quoting, *"Is rock god Beckett Miller carrying indie goddess Erzulie away from the scene of the crime so his newest lover won't know? Shh, we won't tell. #tryst #life-withbeckett #grammys #tsk #wewouldtoo -@LFrederickShadowOfficial"*

I hear him ask Austyn for her phone. "Paige, I have no idea what the hell you're talking about."

All I can process is the tsunami of lies trying to suck me under one last time. I've been told so many by so many men, I feel battered by them. I can't find a way of separating them anymore. "I have to go."

"Paige! Don't go. Let's talk about this—"

I disconnect the call and race for the bathroom where I immediately vomit the baguette and brie I ate for dinner not a half hour before. In the distance, I hear my phone ring and stop before it starts all over again. I know it's Beckett trying to call me back, but I can't talk. I'm too busy crying and holding on to something solid, even if that solid is a piece of porcelain.

It might be the only real thing I've got left since I gave up everything else in my life to wait for a fairy tale that just isn't meant to come true.

PAIGE

Conversation starter: If you could fly away for a weekend to do anything with a celeb, what would it be and who? Keep it clean please! I reserve the right to remove any and all comments.

— Viego Martinez, Celebrity Blogger

My phone buzzes for the umpteenth time since the photo of Beckett and Erzulie hit the world's most prominent social media sites. My only saving grace is I've had the excuse of being able to push everyone off by letting them know I've been busy at the hospital, which for the last week has been the God's honest truth. Between the two-day mandatory orientation, being integrated with my new staff, filling out mountains of paperwork to satisfy my credential transfer, and staying late to take every mandatory training course slated for me for the foreseeable future, I've managed to successfully dodge my incoming calls.

Until now.

I'm clutching my phone in my hand as if it's about to bite me. Given the choice between tackling a Western diamondback rattler or answering this call, I question which I would rather face. I press the button to answer. "Hello, Austyn."

"What the ever-loving hell is wrong with you, Mama?" are the first words I hear from my child in a week.

Well, I guess she's as much Beckett's now as she is mine. Still, as much as she may try to justify what happened in Los Angeles to me, I'm still her mother. So, it's no surprise my voice comes out as cold as ice when I reply. "What a lovely greeting."

"If Uncle E hadn't tracked your phone, I'd have thought you were dead! This isn't who we are."

"What isn't who we are, Austyn?" Forget work; I'm not going to get another thing done. I start shutting programs down as quickly as the computer will allow. I don't even care if I lose my place in the training I was in the middle of being subjected to on sexual harassment. So, I have to take it again. So what? What else do I have to do to fill my nights?

Certainly not spend time with one of the two people I moved to this part of the country to be with.

Tears prick my eyes as I listen to my daughter rant about how irresponsible it was for me not to return her calls until finally I break in with, "Austyn Melissa Kensington, did you leave me an actual voice message to indicate there was an emergency?" Not that I've listened to any of the ones Beckett has left for me after the first—hearing his voice would have killed me. But Jesse left a frantic message urging me to return his call. Due to my father's ongoing medical condition, I briefly managed to connect with him. Once I found out all was well down in Texas, that he was merely doing his big-brother duties checking in on me, I stumbled out an explanation that I just couldn't talk about it yet.

Being the solitary man he is, he respected that.

But daily voicemails and texts for a conversation from Beckett have swamped my phone, even as pings of random love emojis from Austyn have decorated my screen.

I'm not ready to discuss my pain; will I ever be?

The air crackles between us before she replies sullenly, "No, ma'am."

"Then you might excuse me for not responding when I'm, oh, I don't know, settling in at a new job." It's a cop-out, and I know it.

So does she based on the fact she immediately declares, "That's not the reason you didn't contact me back. You just didn't want me to lecture you about possibly making the worst mistake of your life. You need to talk to Dad, Mama. Please, if only for me. Just talk to him."

I don't know how long I stand there holding the phone to my ear, wounds shredding me apart. I recall the words Beckett told me about how Carys went to war for him when the news was worth fighting over. And this wasn't. All this was worth was a voice message of "It's not what it appears, baby. Call me and we'll talk about it." Supposedly, neither was him leaving me behind twenty years ago.

Or at least that's what he convinced me.

I wrap my arm around my waist to hold in the scream that wants to erupt from the depths of the belly that carried his child. The same child that's now chastising me for not giving him a chance. "It's every mother's hope their child never lives through the same pain they experience."

"Mama..."

"Hush." My voice is a trembling whip.

And for once, Austyn does just that.

"Feeling like this isn't a choice; it's a sentence. I just want to know what I did so wrong in this life to deserve this. I alternate between moving around in a void and so much pain, I want to vomit. Again. This feeling is a wound that's not closing. There's no pretending it's tolerable. I have no defense against this because I didn't the first time it happened either. But back then, I had you nurturing my heart. And this time I don't." My voice cracks. "Because here you are pleading *his* case and refusing to let me be."

Her sharply indrawn breath is the only sign she's even listening. I whisper, "Not even on my worst enemy would I wish this pain. I'd have rather never found your father again to have lived through this."

With that, I pull the phone away from my ear. I can hear my

daughter squawking. I know I've said far too much that will for certain get back to Beckett, no doubt redoubling his effort to reach me. But right now, I can't care. I just need to escape for a few hours where I can lock out anyone who knows about the connection between me and Beckett Miller. Even if that escape is in my own mind.

Grabbing my briefcase, I throw the strap over my shoulder. I flick off the lights and make my way to the elevator. Punching the button with all my might, I do it again and again, the small but annoying task a singular vent for my frustration.

When the car arrives, I barely notice the other passenger as I step on. That is, until a deep voice says, "You look like you've had as miserable a day as I have."

I whirl around, startled. A man in a dress shirt and loosened tie has a small smile playing about his chiseled lips. Clinically, I'd label him as gorgeous, but as I've sworn off all men for the foreseeable future—as in forever—I give him a noncommittal "Hmm" before turning around and facing the elevator doors.

That doesn't deter him. "Bryan Moser. Dr. Bryan Moser. Head of Neurosurgery and Neurology."

I nod respectfully. "Doctor."

"And you are?" His eyes probe mine just before he sticks out his hand for me to take.

"Dr. Paige Kensington, audiology specialist new to the Otolaryngology department." I eye his hand but don't reach for it. Hierarchical protocol dictates I should accept his outstretched fingers, the seemingly benign handshake. Instead, my eyes don't leave his face as I continue to ignore his gesture before I fumble into my bag for my keys.

"New? And how do you like our lovely hospital?" His smile turns into an "I'm so irresistible" smirk.

Uncomfortable with him, with the situation, I clip out, "Well enough."

He braces his arm on the elevator door, the move so blatant under normal circumstances, I'd likely roll my eyes. *Oh, please.* "Is that a Southern drawl I detect in your voice, Doctor?"

"Texas. Born and raised," I reply shortly, shifting sideways in an effort to demonstrate my discomfort.

The elevator comes to a smooth stop, and Moser backs up. He places his thumb on the Door Closed button to prevent the doors from opening. "I don't suppose you'd be interested in grabbing a drink, would you, Paige?"

Counting to ten mentally in my head, I slip my house key between my index and middle finger. "No, I wouldn't."

"That's a real pity..."

"You see, Dr. Moser, if you don't release your finger from that button, I'm going to make you. And then, I'll be filling a harassment charge in my first week. After all—" I gesture to the cameras in the elevator. "—my new-hire training indicated these are operable."

His face flushes before he backs away. His finger lifts, and the doors begin to slide open. As soon as there's enough clearance, I step out. Once I'm on the other side, I whirl around before grinding out, "Like you mentioned, Dr. Moser, I've had quite a miserable day. And that was a considerable way to cap it off."

Someone in the crowd waiting to go up coughs to hide their laugh. Moser doesn't say a word.

I scurry away, not feeling victorious. Not feeling anything. All I do with each step away from that debacle is sink into the void I mentioned to Austyn earlier.

By the time I make it to my car, I'm so submerged in it, I can no longer feel anything. Which is exactly what I need to experience. Nothing. After all, it's better than feeling your heart breaking.

And I've had that happen twice as many times as I've needed to by the same man.

Listlessly, I shove food around my plate a few days later in the employees' dining room at the hospital. I know I need fuel, but I can't force myself to lift the fork and place it between my lips.

I'm just about to give up the farce and head back to my office when a tray is plunked down on the table across from me, startling me. So consumed by the loss of Beckett, by Austyn's inability to appreciate my decision, I didn't even notice someone approaching.

"Mind if I sit here?" a female voice chirps.

I must mumble something she takes as consent, because she drops into the chair across from me. "Dr. Alice Cleary."

"Dr. Paige Kensington. I just transferred here from Texas."

"Oh, I already knew that." I quirk a brow. Alice begins to chuckle as she unwraps a sandwich. "You'll learn quickly gossip makes its way around this building faster than the flu. And your little setback of Dr. Moser? Well, let's just say there are quite a few members of the staff who've been trying to bribe Security for the footage."

Thoroughly embarrassed, I grate out, "I'm thrilled to have boosted the staff's morale. Now, if you'll excuse me, I need to get back to my office." I start to shove my chair back when Alice's words have me freezing in my spot.

"I think you mistook me, Dr. Kensington—Paige, if I may? Certain members of the staff want to build a shrine to you. The man is a brilliant surgeon, but he's someone to avoid."

I don't know what makes me say it, but maybe it's her expression —completely guileless. "Right now, I feel that way about most men in general, so perhaps I was a bit harsh."

Her eyes narrow. Something in them shifts imperceptibly. "That's a fairly broad statement. I have some time if you'd care to discuss it? The hospital has programs for our staff..." She goes on to explain the mental welfare programs to alleviate stress in the doctors and nurses who work for the hospital while my eyes drop to the credentials pinned onto her lab coat.

I groan aloud. "Oh, hell. You're a doctor of psychology?"

"And sociology. Dual degrees." Alice appears unaffected by my reaction, taking a huge bite of her sandwich. She chews, swallows, and reiterates her offer. "The offer still stands. I don't have another patient for a few hours."

Overwhelmed, I find myself nodding. I can't handle another night of lying wide-awake any longer, seeing that picture splashed across my iPad. "Please."

Alice begins to rewrap her sandwich. "Why don't we eat in my office?"

"I don't feel much like eating," I admit.

"Then let's start there. Some friendly advice? Don't get the hot meal; the subs are much better."

And for the first time in days, a smile curves my lips. "Somehow, I don't think that's why I haven't been able to eat."

"Then we'll talk about it."

I swallow the saliva pooling in my mouth before I confess as we gather our things, "I have to be able to move forward beyond what I'm feeling. If I can't, I know my judgment will likely be impaired."

Alice's only reply is "I have stress balls and chocolate. Which one do you want first?"

I whisper, "Lead on. I'll decide along the way."

And for the first time since the picture of Beckett and Erzulie hit the media, I don't feel weighed down with each step. I feel like there might be a chance I can move on.

PAIGE

MARCH

Erzulie was spotted coming out of the Met. This genre-diverse singer may have been visiting for inspiration, but whatever she saw obviously spoke to her emotionally. We can't wait for her next album to drop so we can critique the song about it.

— Moore You Want

I pace back and forth in the tiny home I'm renting on the edge of Collyer. Working with Alice has given me a sense of self I've been missing since I was seventeen.

I spent the first session just verbally vomiting to Alice, who wasn't kidding about either the stress balls or the chocolate. By the time I was done, I was throwing one and voraciously consuming another. Beginning with our next session, we started to get into the whys.

Her words yesterday stuck with me. "Both you and Beckett had expectations as children which were blown to hell. It's unsurprising to me such a close bond formed between you both, nor that it lasted through decades."

"What was that?"

She tossed me a pack of M&Ms, which I eagerly accepted.

"Parental neglect. Children are born into this world with an expectation of being nurtured and cared for. Some do this by raising that child, some do it by giving that child up—it's often less cruel. But there are needs to be met as children. Your bond is incredibly strong because both of your childhoods occurred in a small town where you had no one else but each other that holds bittersweet memories."

I froze. "Are you saying that's the sole reason he claims he loves me? Why the emotions were so strong back in Kensington?"

"Don't be an ass, Paige. Do you only treat one symptom of a child?"

I couldn't help but grin. "No."

"There's your answer, then. What I'm saying is that bond is what brought you both together, and it's so incredibly powerful that being back where it started amplified it."

I relaxed before tearing open the chocolate. "That makes sense."

"But I think your father did a number on your issues of trust long before Beckett ever came back into your life. You're holding on to your anger with Beckett longer because—and I'm just speculating—you're still so angry at your father."

Her words shocked me to my core. Could it be possible?

"Did Beckett try to get you to listen to him? To explain?" she probes.

"So many times, I can't begin to count," I admitted.

"And your father?"

I open and shut my mouth, because there's no answer.

"Paige, during our sessions you've told me all about your past with Beckett, how he dropped everything to be with you and your daughter, and the catastrophe after the Grammys. I did some research, and yes, I've seen the photograph in question. But by not letting Beckett explain, whether it's what you want to hear or not, you won't ever heal. And you need to."

Now, it's time for me to place a phone call I've put off making since the last time she called when we did nothing but hurl harsh words at one another. For my own sanity, I've kept our conversations to text only since that disastrous conversation. Especially since I admitted to Alice, I overburdened my child with my emotions.

Much like my father did to me.

Pressing Send, I lift the phone up to my ear. Maybe she'll let it go to voicemail. Maybe she's preparing to go out. I don't even know...

"Mama!" she cries immediately upon answering.

The very first thing I do is what I swore I wouldn't: I burst into tears. "Baby, I'm so sorry."

And what does my daughter do? She starts laughing.

"This wasn't how I was predicting this call would go at all," I declare.

"Oh, Mama, you so should have. How many times growing up did I act like a total bitch when I was having guy troubles?"

"Do you want me to start back in middle school or when they started becoming serious?" I flop down on my couch. Resting my head back, I close my eyes and thank God for small miracles that I took this chance and reached out—that Austyn isn't going to hold this against me.

Her voice is gentle in my ear. "I just wanted to be there for you, chocolate and tears."

I blurt out, "I was talking with someone."

"You were? Who?"

Taking a deep breath, I admit, "A doctor at the hospital. Her name's Alice Cleary. As much as you wanted to support me, what happened devastated me, Austyn. I could barely function. I needed to speak with a professional."

There's a pregnant pause before a choked "Oh, Mama" comes over the line.

"It helped," I rush in to tell her quickly. "It truly helped. Alice helped me sort through so many different things. Including how to cope and go on." Because there's a lifetime of beats the heart has to pound out before the music of the heart is done playing. Even if Beckett's and mine weren't meant to be in the same band, there's still a beauty in the music we did play. I'm grateful for it. After all, we created Austyn from it.

"That's...amazing." Austyn's voice is subdued.

"What is it?" I catch the nuance immediately.

"Nothing. It's nothing. Say, how would you feel about a visit this weekend? I feel the need to wrap my arms around you."

The sigh my soul emits is audible. "I think that's perfect. Do you want for me to arrange for a car?"

"I'll get it covered," she assures me. "I'll be there Saturday. We'll catch up then."

"Good. I'll stock up."

"Perfect. And Mama?"

"Yes?"

"You need to know something." Her voice is unusually serious.

"Okay?"

"I'm glad you didn't go through that pain alone. Trevor—you remember my sound guy you filled in for at Redemption? Well, he kept telling me I was selfish—that I shouldn't take sides. I'm so sorry because I didn't just let you be, but I was so worried. And now, I'm so scared I did something to hurt us..." She rambles at the speed she normally reserves for her anxiety before a performance.

And that's another burden for me to bear: I did this to my daughter. It's time to set her straight. "Austyn, you are neither the cause for what happened, nor the effect. You..." I try to find the right words.

"Yes?"

"The joy you brought to my life outweighs any pain. Now. Always. You're my music, Austyn."

She sniffs on the other end of the line. "I love you, Mama."

"I love you too. See you Saturday." Pulling the phone away from my ear, I press End, feeling stronger than I have in a long while.

But I still have one more call to make.

Bolstered by the last one, I dial a number I've had memorized since I was a little girl. I don't press the button to connect the call.

For just a moment, I think about the ways I tried to make my father proud. From good grades and joining the right clubs to helping around the house and farm, I was supposed to be a child who made mistakes. I should have known—just as Austyn did—that I could turn to my father in my time of need.

Instead, systematically he's ripped everything I'd come to depend on. First, by causing Beckett to leave. Then by lying to me about him not being able to be found. And constantly by making me feel less. By not loving me the same because I came after my mother died.

Still, there's something my father needs to know.

I can't prevent the shudder that crawls through me when I hear his voice boom out, "Paigey? About damn time you called. This nurse won't listen to a damn thing. Anyway..."

I let him rant on about the round-the-clock nurse I hired to help him around the house while he recovers from his heart surgery. When he starts to wind down, he finally observes, "You haven't said much."

"That's because I only have one thing to say." My voice, thankfully, is calm.

"Then say it," he snaps.

I don't even hesitate. "I forgive you." Then before he can form a sentence, I hang up and immediately block his number. "But right now, I can't quite forget. Maybe if you loved me for me, I would have had enough confidence in me, in him." I glance down at a phone that hasn't buzzed in weeks. Not with a news alert, not with anything.

"I'll work on it though." And I pull up the hospital app to send a message to Alice to tell her how my conversations went before I check out the room I'd initially designated as Austyn's to see what I need to do to prepare it for her visit.

BECKETT

Something must be wrong. Normally, this is when Beckett Miller announces his spring tour, but there's nothing on his website. Don't let me down, man.

— @PRyanPOfficial

"So, I'm going to have to break the contract," I explain to Carys in her office. For the first time in forever, I feel like the aging rocker I actually am. I barely remembered to shrug on a coat on top of the sleeveless tee and torn jeans I've been wearing the last three days. Or maybe it's been longer? I don't know, and I don't really care.

I just want to get this business over with so I can go back to doing exactly what I did yesterday. Nothing. I figure if I do it long enough, I'll get lost in the moment forever. Then when I close my eyes, I won't see the wretched pain in Paige's.

She tries to argue with me. "Why don't I get an extension? I mean, it's not like Simon and Evangeline had a hard deadline in the original."

"Do you think I could compose anything right now?" I ask just as the hair along the back of my neck raises.

"Dad! Where are you?" Austyn shouts from beyond the closed doors. "I know you're here. I followed you from the penthouse since I've been blocked from seeing you!"

I leap from my seat and make it to the door before Carys even has a chance to respond to that. Flinging her door open wide, Austyn collapses into my arms. "Why are you panting like this? And what do you mean, not seeing you? We text all the time. Why the hell wouldn't I see you? I thought you weren't coming to visit me because of your mother," I growl.

"You try getting past your goon squad. Apparently you told them 'no visitors.' You didn't add the caveat, 'except my beautiful, brilliant daughter!'" Austyn snaps.

Suddenly, a ray of light pierces the darkness I've been living in. I gather her close, ignoring the gagging sounds she immediately begins to make. "I'm so sorry, kid. It's been a rough couple of weeks. I never imagined..."

"Yeah, well, you've got nothing on Mama. Your actions have done nothing but make you an ass," my daughter informs me.

I jerk back. "Excuse me?"

"Can you explain more clearly, Austyn?" Carys, bless her, steps in.

Austyn explains to us both how the social media photo brought out all of Paige's deep-seated insecurities, ones she never acknowledged she had. That it uncovered buried emotions Paige has been working with a doctor at the hospital to sort out. "She knows I love her. I even warned her there would be talk after the Grammys. Why would a simple photo of me and Erzulie at the Grammys do that?" I ask incredulously, rubbing my fingers over the ink at my neck, a tattoo I'd got for Paige. Not that she knows.

Carys slaps me upside the head. "Beckett, you ass. Did you even see it?"

"I asked Austyn to look it up when Paige called..." But my daughter shakes her head.

"I found the caption because it was everywhere but couldn't pinpoint what photo it was," she admits. "You were tagged with

Erzulie in too many by then to determine which one was the one that set Mama off."

"Then I couldn't find it after we flew back to New York. It was like they were all wiped, crazy as that sounds." I anxiously demand, "Carys?"

"It was the same damn photo you had me take down last fall. The one of you carrying Kylie out of the hotel when both of you are half-dressed because she's completely annihilated."

A dawning horror fills me. "I thought you threatened StellaNova with a damn lawsuit if they posted those photos!"

"I did! This wasn't StellaNova. And by the time I could find that out, the pictures were already taken down," she yells.

I take a step back and back right into Austyn. The look she exchanges with Carys frankly causes fear to skate along my spine. "Is there a chance I can fix this?" I can barely push the words out.

Austyn's cherished face scrunches up. "I don't know, but Mama deserves two things."

I'm afraid the ache that's spreading may eclipse everything else, including her. But still, I ask, "What are those?"

"A damn apology and for you to shower. Christ, Dad. You reek to high heaven. I might have to bathe after that hug." Austyn waves her hand in front of her nose in disgust.

Carys bursts into laughter even as I grab Austyn against my chest and hold her tighter. "Deal with it," I murmur against the top of her clean-smelling hair.

Her arms snake around my waist. She squeezes back tightly. "Gladly."

After long moments, we break apart. "Now, what are you going to do about Mama?"

Staring down into what Paige deemed was my most perfect composition, I announce, "I've been trying to explain, but now it's time to fight harder."

"And if she wants you to let her go?" Austyn asks me carefully.

I don't respond because there's no way in hell. I'm not losing the woman I've loved forever, not without one of us actually dying.

"Sue them. Sue the fuck out of them," I bark at Ward.

"Becks, it's been weeks. Besides, it was a picture they dug up on a slow..." Ward tries to placate me.

I whirl away from the windows and fling my phone on his desk. "Code ten, fifteen, twenty-seven."

He unlocks it and reads the text I had up on my screen. "Holy hell. Beckett, man. I don't know what to say."

I slam my fist down against the corner of his desk. "Tell me you're going to go after that twunt for every damn dollar she's made off of me and donate it to some charity—preferably one Paige would approve of."

"Not for nothing, but you were there, Beckett," Ward reminds me.

"It happened months ago! Not weeks ago! Not when the only woman my heart's ever longed for was moving across the country to be with me!"

"Is that how you feel about Mama? Really?"

"Austyn. Honey." I hold out my arm.

"She was devastated," Austyn tells Ward.

His eyes close in regret. "I appreciate that. But this might not work, Austyn. Just because your father said it wasn't so, the court of public opinion holds a lot of sway."

My daughter pulls back. "But it's not true."

"I certainly don't believe it is. But your mother has been let down by so many people lately, I'm not surprised she thought otherwise." Ward blows up the photo on his television-sized monitor, looking for something he can use.

That's when I feel her delicate fingers on the edge of the tattoo near my neck. "When did you do this?"

I turn as red as my shirt. "Not long ago."

Ward surges out of his seat. "Becks?"

"I...it's nothing. Okay? I just had some more ink added."

"When?" "What?" they both ask in unison before shooting the other sheepish looks.

"It was meant to be a surprise for Paige."

Austyn gasps. Ward curses.

"What? Is there something wrong?"

Ward drops back down in his chair. "No. When did you get it done?"

"Before the Grammys, not that it matters." Embarrassed, I run my finger over the lower edge of the ink. "It's why I wore an actual buttoned-up tux and shirts for the rest of the time we were in LA. I didn't want to spoil the surprise. Freaking-ass cravat almost strangled me. Why the hell can't the paps report on me wearing my shirt buttoned? Why didn't that make a slow news day?" And it hits me why he's asking. "The picture doesn't have my new ink. "Son of a..."

"Yeah, buddy. We've got them. At the very least, they'll be printing a retraction shortly."

Now, if only getting Paige back were that easy. I don't realize I've spoken aloud until Austyn hugs me. "Leave that up to me. I have an idea."

I relish the infusion of hope into my heart. But soon I know what it needs to survive.

Its other half.

And I'm not talking about music. I'm talking about the muse I realize I need to make that music. Otherwise, the world might have just heard the last of Beckett Miller.

Even if they don't know it.

PAIGE

Making a grocery list each week is key to staying on budget. Don't believe us? Statistics say you can save up to 25% of your grocery bill by making—and sticking—to a list.

— Fab and Delish

"Great job with those parents, Dr. Kensington," LaJuan, one of the PAs in the Department of Otolaryngology at Greenwich Hospital, compliments me.

"Thank you. Sometimes they just need a bit of reassurance. It's a difficult decision to put in ear tubes in an infant."

"Fourteen ear infections in the first year? Likely the right one."

"For them. For another family, maybe not. We always have to consider the patient's medical history," I remind her.

"Very true. Any big plans this weekend?" she asks.

"My daughter is coming up from the city. We're spending the weekend decorating my new place, and I'm certain she's going to eat me out of house and home. You?"

"Mine are on a break from school. We're planning on hitting the slopes. Do you ski?"

I add some extra drawl to my normal accent. "Not a lick. And as I've made it to my midthirties without breaking anything, I'm good."

We both laugh as we hit the doors back to check on my other patients.

Moving to Connecticut was a wonderful decision. I'm so grateful one of the winter graduates of the University of Texas wanted to purchase my business and was able to secure the loan to do so.

Here, I don't feel weighed down by the burdens of my decisions. I don't hear the ghosts of my past on the radio and remember a piano with our initials carved not so very far away. I arrived in the bleakness of winter and immediately started rebuilding my life from what I know to be based in fact. Like Carys said in her office all those months ago, that involved two things: my degree and my daughter.

Everything else is just supposition. Rumor. Innuendo. Or flat-out lies.

And I'll never deal in those ever again.

Regardless if it means shutting down part of the hope I've clung to for so long.

Finishing my check of my other patients, I head into the back and quickly shower and change into slacks and a warm sweater. After drying my hair, I slip my hospital ID around my neck before I meet my sleep-deprived eyes in the mirror.

Will Austyn know I'm lying to her about being happy when I'm clearly lying to myself? I wonder briefly. I turn away from the mirror before I give the thought more than the second it deserves.

Right now, I have to worry about hitting up the local Stop & Shop for groceries before they shut down the wine section. I'm still not used to Connecticut liquor laws shutting sales down by 10:00 p.m. And I have a feeling I'm going to need a glass once my daughter starts talking about her father.

Something I'm not going to be able to avoid.

No matter how hard I try.

A door slamming alerts me to Austyn's arrival the next day. The tiny cottage I rent on the outskirts of Collyer is perfect for me. The exterior is a bright sunny yellow with a white brick chimney. Inside, it's charming with wide floorboards, a fireplace in the living room, and a recently renovated kitchen. While much of my furniture from Austin easily fit, there were some pieces I sold because they didn't belong in this new life.

And fortunately, some of the new memories of Beckett didn't accompany them. It's hard enough dealing with the ones that did.

There was one thing I needed to ensure was shipped—Austyn's piano. I had that packed and sent directly to her apartment in New York. Fortunately, I had an excuse when she called me squawking. "I don't have room in my new place for it. If you can't fit it, well, contact your father." I ended the conversation quickly thereafter.

I frown when I hear two more doors slam before the *thump, thump, thump* signals Austyn dragging her bag up the flagstone walkway. Shoving to my feet, I move to the front door and fling it open.

My jaw falls open when not only is Austyn there, but Carys and Angie are right behind her holding enormous cellophane-filled baskets. The three of them yell, "Surprise!"

"That's one way of putting it. What are you all doing here?" I reach out and push open the storm door.

Austyn presses a kiss to my cheek, narrowly avoiding rolling her bag over my toes. "Which way to the washer and dryer, Mama?"

"Basement, kiddo. And before you worry about things like spiders and the like, it's a finished basement."

"I wasn't worried about them before, but now I will be. Thanks!"

"That's your punishment for not telling me we were having company," I call out to her.

"That's the concept of a surprise," she shoots back. She swivels her head left and right. "How do I get to the basement?"

"How about letting me greet my guests, you rotten kid?" I turn and find myself caught in a fierce hug from Carys. For such a tiny thing, she has tremendous strength. For just a moment, I let some of it bury deep inside so when I need it, I can pull it out. "It's good to see you both," I tell her as I pull back and give Angie a similar hug.

Angie's face is serene. After everything she's endured in the press in the last few months, I have no doubt why. "You too, Paige."

Austyn's dancing back and forth. Exasperated, I demand, "Do you need a bathroom or something?"

"No, I need to unpack my bag. I have something for you."

"Then just give it to me." I tap my foot impatiently.

"I think I'll wait until later. We have a lot of shopping to do." Austyn's eyes roam critically around the room. "What happened to all of your stuff, Mama?"

"Some of it's in the attic; some of it I sold. It was time to start with a fresh slate."

You might have announced I dropped a turd in a punch bowl. Carys brushes her hands together. "Right. So, we want style, but we're on a budget. You know where we need to go?"

"Where?"

"HomeGoods. There isn't a chance we won't find something there. Paige, get ready. This day is going to be one you won't forget."

"Do you want a tour first?" I offer.

Carys shakes her head. "Nope. Because there's always something unique to bring home at HomeGoods. And we're going to help you build your home around it."

"I love how that sounds." Is it my imagination, or do all three women relax a bit? "Let me get my stuff."

I'm halfway to the stairs when Carys calls out, "Paige, before we go, I need to clear the air."

I pause before facing her. "Okay."

"If I gave you my word that the photo wasn't what you think it was, would it make a difference?"

My eyes flutter as waves of despair wash over me. "No."

Her brow furrows. "Why?"

"Because how could he forgive me for doubting him? So, part of me hopes that's not what you're here to tell me today."

"It wasn't," Carys says.

"All right."

"I had to bring in our investigation team. They confirmed the photo was legitimate." A shaft of pain lances through me at Carys's words. "But it was from before you. Ward confronted the news source who originally took it to find out it was stolen from a disgruntled employee who was fired at StellaNova and sold."

I turn and sit on the stairs. "God, what did I do?"

Austyn rushes forward. "Nothing that can't be undone, Mama."

I brush her hair back. "You weren't on that call, Austyn. The things I said...the way I must have made him feel... Maybe today isn't a good day for this." I start to rise when Austyn does something she hasn't done since she was seven.

She sits on my lap, causing me to let out an inadvertent "Umph."

"Her shoes are by the couch. Jacket will be in the closet near the hall."

"Austyn," I snap. "What the hell are you doing?"

"Getting your head out of your ass, Mama."

I wriggle my butt. "It feels like you're molding yours to mine. Will you get up?"

"Not until you promise to go shopping."

"What is it about shopping?" I demand.

"We want you to know you're not alone, Paige. We know Beckett. We've been friends with him for years. Something happened to set you off, and it wasn't just some photo. It's our job to figure it out so it doesn't ruin the best thing happening in his life. Again," Carys says bluntly.

I relent. I haven't had many female friends, and I need some insight. But first, "Coffee. We have to go to the Coffee Shop and get some coffee. I won't survive much more of today without it."

Within moments, we're headed into downtown Collyer. Carys follows my directions and parks across the street. "This place is adorable," she announces.

"I love it. Food's terrific, coffee is a miracle. We might have to wait for a few as the place is mobbed on Saturdays."

"Who cares? God, check out that necklace?" Austyn drools over the beadwork in the dress shop next door.

I make a mental note to stop by later and pick it up for her as Angie swings the door open.

Like I expected, every booth is occupied, and Ava is spinning wildly, taking orders and issuing refills. I walk directly up to the to-go counter. Ava spots me and calls out, "Just a moment, Paige!"

"You got it, Ava."

Austyn comes up and wraps her arms around me from behind. "Already on a first-name basis with the locals, Mama? This bodes well."

"I'd say so. If your mother..." But Carys never finishes the thought. Instead, she begins making her way toward the back of the coffee shop with the same determined stride used the first day I met her. She walks up to a table filled with men and shoves one of them in the shoulder. Then she jabs the one across from him in the chest with her finger.

"Uh-oh. I'd better go see what that's about," Angie says before she flies after her boss and friend.

One of the men at the table leans slightly until his eyes focus on me. They're a deep penetrating green set in one of the most striking faces I've ever seen. His mouth moves, and within seconds, another devastating stranger whirls around, this one with dark eyes and dark hair. Carys slaps her hands on the table, and though her lips aren't moving, the flush riding her cheeks is getting darker. Green eyes slides out of the booth and shifts her to the side.

Before making his way in my direction.

"Keene, honey, do you need anything?" Ava calls out.

"Not quite done yet, Ava. Just need to talk with a few people." And judging by the way his stare hasn't left me or Austyn, I have a good idea of who he is. I slide her behind me and glare up at the taller man.

He notes the action before his bearded face breaks into a wide smile that softens every chiseled feature. "Dr. Kensington, Austyn, my name is Keene Marshall. I'm one of the founding partners of Hudson Investigations. It's a pleasure to meet both of you face-to-face."

My heart skips a beat. This man's company has investigated every nuance of my life from before I was born, and here he is, drinking coffee in *my* coffee shop. "Are you following me, Mr. Marshall?"

"Actually, no. My family and I live here in..."

I turn to Austyn. "Forget about decorating. I need to move."

"Dr. Kensington, if you would join us for a cup of coffee, Caleb and I would be happy to explain."

"Who is Caleb?" Austyn pipes in.

"The other founding partner in Hudson Investigations." Before I can reiterate my desire to move, Keene holds up his hand. "Please. Just a few minutes. We don't want you to feel uncomfortable in a community that has accepted us and our families."

All men can lie; God knows I've learned that. But maybe it's the way his face softened when he spoke of his family. I nod shortly. "Five minutes."

He steps back and gestures for us to precede him. "This way."

When we arrive at the booth, I'm so glad I did. There are children squished everywhere inside. "Daddy, did you ask Ms. Ava for more hot chocolate?" an adorable dark-haired, blue-eyed angel asks.

"No, Kaylie. I didn't have a chance. Can you monsters be nice enough to greet Dr. Paige and Ms. Austyn first?" Keene asks.

There's a cacophony of "Hi, Dr. Paige" and "Hey, Ms. Austyn" from what must be a set of twins on the other side of the table. The dark-eyed man holds out his hand. "Caleb Lockwood. Nice to meet you, Dr. Kensington. Let me do some quick introductions. My three: Laura, Jonathan, and Charles. Keene's three: Kaylie, Valerie, and Regina." He points as he introduces the children.

I wrap an arm around Austyn. "My one and only, Austyn."

Austyn bumps my hip. "Never say that, Mama. You're young enough to have more."

"That's what we call our Mama. Mama," one of Keene's youngest says in awe.

I loosen up enough to ask her father, "Is your wife from the South?"

He nods at Caleb. "*Our* wives' family is. We married sisters."

Carys grins, her earlier pique with Keene and Caleb obviously forgotten as she leans on the booth behind Caleb. "As a client, one of my favorite events each year is visiting the monstrosity of a farm you all live on and seeing how the family's expanded."

"You all live together?" I ask incredulously.

"Separate houses," both men say simultaneously.

"Probably because none of them could handle their brother-in-law for long stretches of time," Angie ventures.

"It would be like you all living with Beckett. And might I add, we consider our brother-in-law, Jason, a saint." Keene slants a wicked grin in my direction. "If you'd like to be nominated for canonization by my security team, fix whatever is wrong with Beckett. Please. The reports they're sending in is that he's a stinking mess."

Caleb throws a piece of toast at him. "Don't talk about one of our highest-paying clients like that."

But his words trouble me further. "I don't know if I can..."

Keene opens his mouth, but Carys shakes her head sharply. "We have to go. Don't scare her away from this town," she admonishes the men.

"All we have to do is introduce her to the wives. She'll never leave," Caleb reasons out.

"The wives?" Austyn asks.

"Amaryllis Events. Amaryllis Bakery. Amaryllis Designs," Caleb ticks off.

"Oh, God, Mama. Amaryllis Designs. Emily Freeman." Austyn shakes my arm so hard I think it's going to fall off.

"And you can wait for Christmas," I say firmly.

We all laugh when Austyn sighs like her world is ending. I turn to Keene and offer my hand. "Despite my earlier reaction, I'd rather know the truth. I am grateful for everything your team did to help me determine what was real."

He shakes mine firmly. "The truth can take a while, but it's worth it. I found that out myself. Wouldn't you agree, Caleb?"

I offer my hand to the other man who says, "It is. And welcome to Collyer. We'll have Cassidy reach out to have you over."

"Cassidy?"

Caleb grins at Keene. "My wife. We'll save the rest of the family explanations for a night you can join us for dinner."

"Now, before Carys stopped by…"

"Intruded. You can say it, Keene. But this is *huge*, Keene. We need to know."

"And when I find for certain, you will," he snaps.

"Keene, the kids," Caleb warns him.

"Sorry," Carys mutters.

"As I was starting to ask, where were you all headed to?" Keene asks.

"HomeGoods," Austyn volunteers.

For some reason that sends the men at the table laughing in hysterics. "Listen, if any of you finds something completely heinous for under fifty dollars, buy it. Carys, I'll discount your bill," Keene murmurs.

"Done," she agrees immediately.

"Keene!" Caleb starts indignantly.

"Listen, buddy, you weren't the one caught by a blogger buying our holiday white-elephant gift. When you are, you can argue with me."

Caleb thinks about it for a nanosecond. "Make it two."

After we step away, Carys fills us in on the Freeman holiday tradition of HomeGoods white-elephant gift giving. We're still laughing about the exchange when we finally manage to place our coffee orders and head back to Carys's car.

PAIGE

Listening is as important as talking. So much of what we process is noise and we forget to filter it out.

— **Beautiful Today**

"Do you want to talk about it?" Carys sidles up next to me while I'm inspecting a toilet paper holder at HomeGoods. I feel like my whole life has been inundated by crap lately, so I might as well get something nice to hold the tissue to wipe it away.

Austyn made a mad dash for the sheets, dragging Angie in tow to outfit her room once I set her budget after explaining I didn't pack her mix-and-match prints from home, which in no way reflects the woman she is now. Until now, I've been meandering around the store, half-heartedly poking through aisles of knickknacks.

Finding nothing special—feeling nothing special.

"Talk about what?" I hedge.

"Paige, we're so much alike it's scary. Case in point, I have this exact holder in my guest bathroom."

"Carys, I act put together, but I'm really not." Though I'm amused enough to put the holder in my cart.

She laughs softly. "And you think I am? I quit a ridiculously high-paying job because I was in love with my paralegal. I'm just glad he came to his senses and followed me."

It takes a moment for that to process. "David?"

"Yes. When I worked at Wildcard, I met him and felt my world tilt off its axis."

"And you didn't act on it why?"

"There was—is—a massive no-fraternization policy there. And one day, he slapped a picture of Becks down on my desk and asked if that's who I wanted to be associated with." Carys smiles fondly at the memory.

But I physically recoil at her words. "You...and Beckett?"

"Oh, no. Paige, he didn't tell you?"

"I didn't realize your...friendship...had been more." I fumble the words out while trying not to imagine this powerful woman in bed with the man I'll spend a lifetime trying to teach myself not to love. And fail miserably at the job.

She immediately reads me. "Never. Not ever. Not even a single real kiss."

That piques my interest and stills my movement. "A real kiss? What's the difference between that and a fake one."

"A kiss for the cameras that happens to be on the lips. Picture a kiss like one you'd give your daughter versus one you'd give your lover. The only way they're misinterpreted is if there's no brains behind them." She purses her lips so dramatically I can see her frenulum.

I immediately break into laughter picturing this overly puckered-up kiss meeting a similar one of Beckett's for the sake of the paparazzi. "Christ, Carys."

"What's funny is you immediately, as a normal, thinking human, went exactly where most of my affection with Becks did and does go—friendship. My husband? It took me ignoring him, quitting, and walking away for him to see me as something beyond his boss who was involved with some Lothario."

"That's one way of describing it." I say, understanding David Lennan's emotional gut check.

"Do you? Do you really think he's been involved with that many women? That he'd open himself up to that kind of emotional vulnerability after everything in his past?"

"If they're smart and intelligent, why wouldn't he give them a chance? He wasn't attached to someone."

"Wasn't he?" Before I can speak, Carys continues. "With you, he had all but buried the demons of his past. Not any of the women on his arm, not with me, but you. There were few of us who got to glimpse the heart beyond the man who stood on the edge of the stage. Now we know the woman who put it there."

I open and close my mouth before dropping the towel I'm holding. "I'm the reason his whole life has been damaged. How can you think in any way I'd be good for him?"

"Because with you he gives a damn about more than being the guy in the news," Carys tells me bluntly.

"Except you're trying to convince me he isn't that guy—that the last picture wasn't what I thought it was. What am I supposed to believe?"

"You're supposed to believe in yourself. Him." Her eyes sharpen. "How do you think Becks sees you?"

"That's just it. I don't know, not anymore. Not since that photograph." My voice cracks.

"A lover?"

"Yes. No. At least, not anymore. I mean, how could he? I'm nowhere near the caliber of women he dated—dates. See what this has done to me? I mean, just look at me." I step back and flick my hand from my long coat to my shoes.

Carys grabs my hand and drags me toward the mirror section. I protest about our purses. She just hushes me. Standing by my side, she asks again, "Who do you see yourself as, Paige?"

I open my mouth, but where I'm prepared to give her my standard answer, I whisper, "I don't know. So much has changed, I don't know who I am anymore."

"And you've fallen for a man it appears you don't know very well either."

I duck my head to the side, unable to deny the feelings Beckett brought back to the forefront in me. But still I try to push logic forward. "How is it possible to fall in love with someone I barely know? He's got this golden touch. His life is worth so much."

"If by worth you mean his mind and his heart, I agree. If you mean his assets, he works hard for what he has and pays dearly for it, often with his privacy and sanity. So many people who have the kind of wealth he does find it almost burdensome. And I also know he'd say you've given him something so priceless there is no value, something he'd sacrifice anything for."

"What's that?"

"Austyn. The rest of the world might not know who you are—thank God for small favors—but those of us who are closest to him do. You're a warrior, Paige Kensington. You are the kind of mother they write legends about."

Before I can protest that all I did was love my unborn child, Carys asks, "Do you want to know what I see when I look at you?" Before I can agree, Carys goes on. "I see the best kind of woman. Someone who is a force to be reckoned with. She's beautiful, wise, and resilient. She has a fount of power that will never dissipate. She's been wounded in battle, but she still fights with every ounce of energy for those she loves, for those who are needy."

"She sounds like Wonder Woman," I joke.

"She might as well be. She's a mother. In fact, she reminds me a great deal of *my* mother, who I miss a great deal. Maybe that's why Becks and I are such close friends—we were both missing the same kind of woman in our lives."

My chest tightens, and my knees start to buckle under the force of emotions. "God, Carys."

"Stop trying to think less of yourself than you really are. You're more valuable than that."

I just nod since I can't speak.

"Now, let Angie coach you about social media's love of all things

Beckett Miller. Let him explain about that stupid photograph. And for all that's holy, don't be pissed at us when you find your real housewarming gift waiting at your house when we go there in a few hours."

"What is it?" I whirl around and face Carys. I want to think about everything she said, but I won't have that chance until Austyn leaves tomorrow.

"Well, it's big enough that both Ward and David have to bring it out from the city. Ward and Angie are going to head on to their place in Brewster; David and I will head back to New York. Austyn said she'd be happy to accept a ride from us."

"I don't understand. She's supposed to stay until tomorrow."

"We figure you might want time alone."

A sizzling of awareness wells up inside me. "What did you get me?"

Carys squeezes my hand. "Who, Paige. And we're leaving him without his security team for you two to yell down the house."

Oh, God.

"Beckett. He's coming here?"

Carys looks at her watch. "Actually, by my estimation, he should already be here. Should we continue to shop for things, or do you want to go back to your place?"

The distance I shoved between us is enormous, and still he's trying to breach it. Slowly, I spin around and face myself in the mirror.

And I don't feel some revelation when I do. But the longer I stand there, the more ready I am to open up the lines of communication I shut down so abruptly. It's time to let me be me, for Beckett to no longer hide his true self, and let whatever will be happen.

The time for us is fast approaching.

I'm the best me I'll ever be. And if I find out that's not enough, then that will be Beckett's loss. Not mine. But I'll never know unless I give us a try. The two of us together is going to be hard enough without a self-imposed communication breakdown.

I meet Carys's eyes in the mirror. "Let's go."

Her crafty smile engulfs her face. "That's what I thought you'd say. Like I said, we're more alike than I thought."

⊕

On the drive back from HomeGoods, I received a crash course in Angie's job. "You mean you have to look at all the social media feeds for every client Carys represents every single day?"

"Yes. And let me assure you, Beckett can't wear a sock the wrong color without the bloggers catching it."

I begin to feel awful for him. "What must it be like to live under that constant pressure?"

Angie shudders. "It's awful. When Ward and I were first dating, I was terrified I would end up in the feeds."

Carys reaches over and pats her arm. "My brother did a fine job of keeping you out of it."

A luminous smile lights her face. "That's true."

"Is that because of what you do?" I ask curiously.

"Ahh, not exactly." Carys downshifts.

Angie blurts out, "It's because together the Burkes are almost as wealthy as Beckett."

"Angie!" Carys shouts.

"Well, it's not like she can't look up Ward and find he's edging out Beckett on some of the Most Eligible Bachelor lists."

Austyn raises her hand. "Umm, excuse me. May I ask a question?"

"Austyn, honey. You don't need to raise your hand," Angie explains.

"Though I love the idea and might instigate it at the office," Carys mutters.

"If you're so wealthy, why work?"

"An excellent question. Let me ask you a question. If you had all of your father's money, would you stop playing music?" Carys returns.

"No. Hell no. Music is a part of my soul."

"Well, I won't say defending your father against him being..." Carys searches for a word.

"Stupid? Moronic? Idiotic?" Angie supplies.

The four of us break up laughing, easing some of my tension as we get closer to Collyer. "Choose any of the above. I can't say that was part of my soul, but the life lessons our parents taught me and Ward were. The money's there. That's nice to know, but if I wasn't working, I wouldn't have met David. If I hadn't met David, I would have missed out on the most important thing."

"Love," I reply for her.

"Exactly. So, while it's different for everyone, I'd like to think money is the last reason we do the things we do. Love, passion, drive, need. You do the things you do because they feed your soul, not because you have to but because you want to," Carys finishes.

"And that's why Dad still plays," Austyn surmises.

"I think the world would be deprived of one of its greatest musicians if he didn't."

"I think it's sad," Austyn concludes. "The more he becomes successful, the less of himself he's able to just...be."

And Austyn's words strike me hard. They remind me of one of the texts Beckett sent to me that I tuned out because I was so wrapped in my own pain. Some days being part of the paparazzi feeding frenzy is worse than living back in Texas. Their stories can cut me to the core, but instead of it just being my parents, it's the world. And right now, it's you because you won't let me explain.

And I realize with simple clarity, if we're going to try to make it, we need to construct a place where the only thing that can penetrate the atmosphere is love. Where if we inhale deeply, we are enough, and when we breathe out, we expunge the stressors of his job, mine. Outside influences. We had that when we were young. It existed in a field on a foundation of love between two beds of lies. We just didn't know it.

Now we do.

And now we know how precious it truly was.

BECKETT

Wildcard Records has released a statement regarding the lack of Beckett Miller tour dates. "With full support of his label, Wildcard Records, Beckett Miller is working on a special project in conjunction with the Broadway community. Through the vocal prowess of Evangeline Brogan and Simon Houde, he will be bringing his incomparable talent to new fans of all ages." Bravo!

Now, what we'd like to know is who we have to bargain with for a seat at the debut performance, even if it's on the floor?

— StellaNova

"I've never seen you like this, even when we were trying to determine if Austyn was your daughter," David remarks in a calm voice, likely trying to not wake up his son, who fell asleep in his arms just a few moments ago.

"It's some of the best music you've written," Ward agrees.

I wave my hand. They have no idea the songs they heard me practicing are close to twenty years old. They're ones I wrote for Paige on the dilapidated piano at her family's original homestead. I'm not surprised they're the greatest things I've ever written; I had the best inspiration ever.

Love.

Feeling a tingle, I reach into my jacket pocket and pull out the tube of H2Ocean moisturizing cream. Moving over to the mirror behind the couch David and Ward are camped out on, I rub it over my neck, taking care to smooth it over every single inch of the sides.

"That ink is sick." Ward grins.

"Completely badass," David agrees.

I nod down to the bundle cuddled in David's arms. "So you won't mind if I take him for his first ink when he's older."

"If you take him before his mother agrees, you're going to die a slow and painful death. And it won't be me delivering it." David's swift reply is nothing but the truth.

"I debated getting one when I was younger," Ward admits.

"You didn't go through with it?" I ask curiously.

"No. There were a lot of things I never did after our parents died. Rebellion never appealed to me much. Who was I going to rebel against? Carrie? For giving up her whole life for me?"

"There's more reasons than rebellion to do it." David nods at the ink on my neck. "Becks has shown us that."

"One of the main reasons is love."

"How many of yours are because of that?" Ward asks.

I open my mouth to answer him but hear the crunch of gravel on the drive. "I thought they weren't supposed to be back for hours?" My voice is filled with panic. I race over to the bay window and peek out. Sure enough, Austyn pops out of the back seat. Then Angie and Carys, and finally, my heart thuds heavily as Paige emerges.

Her face twists toward me, as if she knows I'm hiding behind the closed blinds. "What the hell?" I snap.

Ben yawns and stretches in his father's arms. David murmurs to him, "Mama's here."

You would have thought the kid was told Santa was in the room. He snaps awake and immediately scrambles to his little booted feet. "Mama? Where?"

"She's outside." But no sooner are the words out of David's mouth than his son is racing for the door.

Fortunately, Ward catches him on the run because just as he's about to fly by, the front door opens. And in walks Paige.

My heart feels like my drummer's smashing against it. *Boom. Smash. Crash.*

"David? Carys said she's waiting for you outside. Um, Ward, the same with Angie." Paige hasn't met my eyes yet.

Both men push up from the sofa and head in Paige's direction where she's corralled Ben against her legs. After slipping on their outerwear, they both exchange quiet words with her. Words I can't decipher because I can't hear. I can't speak. All I can do is absorb the fact she's near me.

I'm shaken from my reverie when the door closes behind both of my friends. "I...uh...hi."

"Hi."

"I was hoping we could talk."

She steps closer to me. "You went to a lot of trouble for that."

Frantically, I search the room. It's filled with the flowers I never brought her. I try to find the words I wrote years ago—the music that says what I need to so much better than I could ever say. Spying them on her coffee table, I bend down to pick them up. When I straighten, she's within arm's reach. My breath whooshes out. "I need to tell you what happened."

She shakes her head. "Not right now, you don't. Right now, we need to do something for us."

Us. I relish the word, even as Paige shucks her coat and drops it to the floor. "What's that?"

"We used to have this place. There were no rules, no regrets. No lies, nothing but love. Do you remember it?" She reaches for my hand and cradles it in hers before laying it over her heart.

"I think I've spent far too long trying to get back there. But I ruined it. Again." My voice breaks.

"You didn't, Beckett. I swear. And neither did I. It's hard, but we keep letting other people in. For our place to be just ours, we have to stop doing that. It's going to be hard, but we have to try to find that place where only we can go. And I think I know where that is." Paige bends down and presses her lips to the tips of my fingers, fingers that have strummed guitars, pressed piano keys, and bled ink. And still been unfulfilled until I touched her skin again.

I drop the papers at my feet. What are mere words when I can speak to her in a language only she understands because she taught me it existed? I run my open hand down the side of her face, feeling the chill on her skin. "You undo me," I whisper hoarsely.

Her brow furrows. "I don't think that's right. We're supposed to put each other back together."

I bend down and lift her high against my chest before I move over to the couch and drop backward so Paige falls on top of me. "Undo me, put me back together. As often as you need to realize the heart inside only beats for you. It only ever has."

Paige's lips part, tempting me to push up and take them. "And that's where we're supposed to be. There. Just there."

"Where?" I'm confused.

"Home. The place that exists between your heart and mine. Will you forgive me? Will you let me back into our home?"

I'm flabbergasted. "There's nothing to forgive, at least not for you. But you have to let me explain. I've had Ward—"

Paige lays her fingers across my mouth. "Later. Right now, we're home. And I don't want to talk about work." She leans down, her eyes intent on my lips.

I flip us so she's on her back. I quickly remove her glasses and send them skidding across the end table. My hand rests on her hip. "Then what do you want to talk about?"

She tugs my face closer. I shift until I'm stretched out on top of her, and she lets out a happy sigh. "Now? Nothing." Then she takes my mouth in the searing kiss I've been hoping for since I knew she was heading toward the East Coast to be closer to me.

As my hands begin to play the melody in counterpart to the rhythm she's stirring up in me, I realize we have the composition down. We'll work on the lyrics to accompany it later because I'm not spending another night without the woman I love in my arms.

Not ever again.

After we made love on the couch, we stumbled up the narrow stairs to her bedroom where we went for another round. Now, she's spending an inordinate amount of time admiring my new tattoo that I finally got to show off. "It's the flower of life and seed of life. It's meant to represent you and Austyn. I had it done right before the Grammys."

"So, that's why you were in a wet suit when you FaceTimed me from LA." Her fingers dance over the swirls.

I nod. "I didn't want you to see it just yet. I hoped it wouldn't be noticed with that costume I put on for the Grammys, but then that picture came out in the paper." A surge of fury over the stupid social media site is dissipated when Paige presses her lips to the center.

"It's special."

"I'm going to have to mention it when I sue that site's ass off," I warn her.

"Sure, but not the meaning. Just that you had ink done, so obviously the pictures were from before that." Paige shrugs nonchalantly, as if our entire relationship didn't just hang in the balance.

I grip her shoulders. "I'm not in bed with a Paige-bot, right?"

She snickers. "A Paige-bot?"

"Invasion of the Paige-snatchers?" I become contemplative. "No, not that. I know you're..."

"Christ, Beckett!" she screeches.

"Definitely my Paige." Then with wonder, I whisper, "You are, aren't you? Mine. Finally."

She rests her weight on top of mine, expression solemn. "I can't say there aren't going to be times when I won't need reassurance, because I will. Emotionally, I've had so many highs and lows in the last five months. The things I put my faith in have crumbled beneath me. I honestly opened my heart to second chances: my father, my life, and you. God, especially you. Yet, we hit the first hurdle, and I tripped right over it."

"It was a pretty big hurdle, Paige," I allow.

"And I should have learned how to leap over them before trying to run away from the track."

"Are we still talking about the social media post?" I can't help but tease.

She thwacks me on the chest. "I can't apologize enough for blindly believing something I likely would never have given credence to had we not been involved. But never say I can't learn."

"God, love, let's hope there isn't another one of these." I shudder at the thought.

"For a man who is mentioned on average in forty-seven different blogs, social media channels, and news outlets a week, who has not one but fifteen separate hashtags, somehow I don't think they're going away."

"I think with the show, the coverage is going to...wait. Why do you know all that?" I ask suspiciously.

Paige lowers her lashes until I can catch just a hint of green. "Didn't you once say you thought my knowledge was sexy?"

"Something like that."

"Well, I'm taking the advanced course in Beckett U."

"What the hell is Beckett U?"

"Master's crash courses on how to handle the media and online relations taught by Carys and Angie. We decided Austyn should attend so she doesn't make the same mistakes her father made. Carys says she has visual aids."

I groan. "Christ. This is going to be a nightmare."

A wicked grin crosses Paige's lips that I'm dying to kiss away. "Angie says she's never sure who is going to trend more in the mornings—you or Ward. I can't wait to learn more about what that means."

"Stop. You're killing me."

"What's a LikLok?" Paige frowns in confusion.

"It's TikTok, and it's nothing you need to worry about." I immediately decide everyone at LLF thought they knew what work was before they should brace. Just wait. I'm going to make their lives hell.

Paige straddles me before leaning down and brushing her nose against mine. "Gotcha."

"What do you mean, 'gotcha'?" I ask suspiciously.

"Beckett, your daughter has one of the highest-streaming TikTok channels. You really should check it out," she informs me haughtily.

I flip her over onto her back. With a mock glare, I ask, "And the rest?"

Shyly, she dances her fingers over my new tattoo. "I'll just come home and ask."

I close my eyes and bask in the emotions washing over me. "I feel like I could compose a thousand songs right now. I feel...everything."

Paige lifts her head, and our lips touch. And in that instance, we whirl through time. I know years from now, her lips will meet mine just like this, and I'll still see her face the first time she kissed me amid the dusty fields of Texas when the only music I imagined making was making her heart sing.

I've sung for thousands, possibly millions. I've touched the souls of people whose names I'll never know or never remember, but hers is still the only one that matters. When our lips part, her eyes glow up at me. "Now, we do have one problem we might need some help with."

I frown. "It shouldn't be food. I prepared for that."

"That's good, but no. This is serious."

I roll to the side, tugging her against my body. "What's that?"

"I still don't want anything to impact Austyn's career, Becks. She's so determined to make it on her own. Plus, it's not like she's not going to be seen with you. What do we do?"

I chew on my lip for just a moment. Then my whole face smiles when the perfect idea hits.

"You figured it out," Paige guesses accurately.

"Yes."

"Tell me," she demands.

I reach out and cup her breast. She gasps, giving me an opening to take her mouth. When I'm done long moments later, I whisper, "Later."

She threads her hands into my hair, sliding her bare leg over my hip. "I just hope you can remember it."

Hmm. Good point. I start to tell Paige the idea, but the moment I do, Paige whispers something I can't resist. Something I've never been able to resist.

"I love you, Beau Beckett Miller. Always have."

Clutching her to me, I align myself before pushing deep inside and murmuring back, "And I love you, Paige Melissa Kensington. Always will."

BECKETT

SIX MONTHS LATER - SEPTEMBER

Broadway may be awash with cartoons, but it's historical musicals making a splash. With *The Golden Lady*, Evangeline Brogan's and Simon Houde's powerful voices lead us down a path of history all but a few tried to hide. The score, composed by Beckett Miller and DJ Kensington, will have you singing long after the show is over.

— The Fallen Curtain

Instead of wearing my trademark unbuttoned shirt for this event, like the Grammys, the buttoned-up collar on this getup I agreed to wear is so damned tight it's threatening to cut off my breathing. And I sure as fuck need that to hit some of these notes my co-composer wrote for this score.

On top of which, I'm not real thrilled about the fact it's hiding Paige and Austyn's tattoo.

Especially when I can see Paige from the wings and she's showing more skin than I usually do. I snarl a little bit when she shifts in her seat from the front row and the gold thread in her dress catches the overhead lights. "It's like a damn spotlight on her breasts."

I really hope she's not wearing much beneath it because I plan on fucking her in the limousine on our way back to Connecticut tonight.

A fatalistic sigh resonates from behind me. "Are you going to be able to keep your mind on the music, or will you be too distracted by Mama's boobs to actually play the music we've spent the last six months writing?"

I wince. "Christ, Austyn. Watch your damn mouth."

My daughter slides up next to me and wraps her arm around my waist. Similarly dressed, we're both in black-on-black tuxedos to avoid distracting the audience once the actors hit the stage. "What's the fun in that?"

I open my mouth to give her a lecture I'm sure Paige would appreciate, despite the fact I'll have to endure my own about hypocrisy when the child we made out of love over twenty years ago rests against me. "She's magnificent, isn't she, Dad?"

"She's incandescent."

Paige whirls around as Marco Houde taps her on the shoulder. She stands to greet him—and the curvy brunette who's now sporting his diamond—with a smile. She gestures to her left, and an older gentleman rises to his feet and holds out his hand.

Paige's father has spent the last six months working with a therapist. And while both Paige and I were less than inclined to forgive the man for the actions he took that separated us, it was Austyn who convinced us to let go of his transgressions. "In the end, he has to witness the love the two of you share. Isn't that enough punishment when he's endured a life without Grams?"

It's hard to accept all the moments I lost with Austyn. Which prompts me to say, "If I had a chance to turn back time, I'd give up every penny to my name to spend it with her and you."

And just as the house lights begin to flash on and off, signaling for everyone to take their seats, my twenty-year-old daughter whispers, "I know, Dad. Now, let's go kick a little ass."

I lean forward and press a kiss to her forehead. "Break a leg, darling."

She winks before reaching for the headset the stagehand is holding out for her. "You too."

As I slip mine on, we do a quick sound check. Then, the lights dim.

Three.

Two.

One.

First, Austyn slips out of the wings. Then, I follow her. Both of us head directly to center stage. This will be the one and only time I'll do this, so I have to make it count.

For all of us.

The noise is surprising. Even to someone who has heard propositions of marriage and solicitations of sexual acts, I'm surprised by how loud the thundering of applause is. And I'm grateful for it, not just for me, but for the prodigy at my side.

I wait for a slight lull before I begin speaking. "Thank you all very much. When I agreed to work with Evangeline Brogan and Simon Houde on a score for a Broadway show a little more than a year ago, I was asked to consider writing about the story of my life. What I didn't realize is that so much of the pain in my life had already been endured by so many others. Yet, so much had yet to be healed. Both are because of the same reason: a woman."

There's a tittering in the audience. I go on. "This woman encompasses more than the simple concept of past, present, and future; she's omnipresent. She is a healer, a warrior, and someone who nurtures those around her. Quite simply, she's composed of the traits that in history would have her revered as a queen. With my co-composer's help, we worked with Evangeline and Simon to bring modern music to a heartbreaking story of survival, theft, and justice. It's the true story behind Adele Bloch-Bauer, the muse behind Gustav Klimt's famous *Golden Lady* paintings."

There's a hum through the audience as Austyn and I move off the stage so we can come up beneath it and sing the songs I wrote about the love I have for her mother then, now, always, for another woman whose last remnants were left behind in the smoldering ashes of her life.

And yet, somehow, her legacy lives on.

That's what I want to give my child, I think fiercely as I sit down at the piano. Not wealth or fame but the richness of love. And as I feel Paige's eyes upon me when I lay my hands on the keys, I know I'll have her by my side to do just that.

I hear Austyn whisper almost soundlessly in my ear, "And a one, two, three..."

On four, I hit the first chord and let my fingers dance along the keys for a moment before I lend my voice to the melancholy notes. "*Is there more for a man like me? Each day gets longer, harder. I am worn. I am worn. So many days remain.*"

My head twists to the side, and I sing directly to where I know I last spied Paige. "Then Moses revealed you to me. Days swirl. Nights drift by. You remained in my heart. Always.

"*I became your disciple. Lived for you and me.*

"*Until a war they fought tore me apart. I knew I had to go. Don't make me go. The choice wasn't mine to make. So many days ahead. How do I go on without you when heaven's gate arrives?*"

Austyn's voice starts harmonizing on top of mine. First on "*Mine to make.*" And then, "*Heaven's gate arrives.*"

The first time Austyn heard me sing the title song of the Broadway show I scored titled "Mine to Make," she said her mother was going to cry. But when I try to find Paige's eyes in the audience, it's her father's face I find.

And he's wiping a handkerchief beneath his eyes, nodding slowly.

Keith Richards said music is a language that doesn't speak in particular words; it speaks in emotions.

I always admired the man for his music. Now as I finish singing a song I wrote right after I left Paige, I realize I admire him for his wisdom.

Wrapping up the song to a ridiculous amount of applause, Austyn and I slide right into the opening number, and Evangeline Brogan steps into the spotlight, belting out the opening words to "Secret Garden." Moments later, Simon Houde joins her onstage.

And just like that, *The Golden Lady* becomes Broadway history.

"So, what do you think?" Simon yells as he hands me a glass of champagne.

"About the show?" I lift my glass to toast him. "I think the number of curtain calls you received should give you a good idea how it's going to be received."

He grins. "No, I meant about backstage at a Broadway cast production. Is it different than what it's like at your shows?"

"There's no comparison." I take a sip of my drink.

"Why's that?"

Seconds later I feel a body jump onto my back and arms wrap around my neck before a smacking kiss is laid upon my cheek. "Do you really think this would happen at one of my shows?" I twist my face and find Austyn grinning at me. "Well, hey there."

"We killed it!" And before I can say anything, she reaches over and yanks my glass out of my hands before draining it.

I just sigh. "Please tell me your mother is around here somewhere."

"She got waylaid by Linnie and her husband. She and Gramps are making their way over." Austyn starts to teeter a bit as she tries to nab a glass from a passing waiter.

Simon snatches two fresh glasses while I boost my daughter higher against my back. Then he hands each of us new glasses. I try to sip my celebratory drink while Austyn keeps on the lookout and chokes me at the same time, spilling champagne on my shirt.

Like I give a damn.

"I have to say, I'm finding your bodyguards awfully useful, Beckett," Simon's wife, Bristol Brogan-Houde, comments.

I glare down at my longtime financial advisor. "Good, take them off my hands. You're rich enough to afford them."

She grins. "I just meant that for once I can enjoy my husband at one of these after-parties without being closed off in a dressing room that smells like cilantro and moldy cheese."

I bark out a laugh when the flush rides the Tony-Award-winning actor's face. "Your sister started it."

"Actually, darling..." Bristol starts to contradict, but Austyn yells. "Here they all come!"

Kane and Mitch separate away from the entrance to the VIP area to allow Paige, Tyson, Evangeline, and her husband to enter. Austyn slides off my back to run to her mother while introductions and greetings are exchanged by everyone else. Then finally, finally, I have Paige where I need her.

With me. Next to me.

But before she can say how she felt about the show, Tyson is holding out his hand. "Congratulations, Beckett. You—both of you" —he gazes down at his granddaughter, who is standing next to him— "created magic out there tonight. Being able to sit in that audience will be among one of the greatest moments of my life."

"What were some of the others, Gramps?" Austyn asks. Before he can answer, she teases, "Does bailing me out the clink for sneaking into Rodeo Ralph's with a fake ID count?"

He bops her on the end of her nose and informs her, "No. That wasn't even in the top ten."

I murmur to Paige, "You didn't mention that."

"Fortunately, Ralph just called the sheriff to scare her. He didn't press charges."

"Uh-huh." I think about the way Sheriff Lewis openly admired Paige, and I growl.

She turns and pats my stomach before promising, "We'll take care of that later."

A stupid feeling of euphoria lances through me. *Yes, we will.* Then I tune back in to what Tyson is saying.

"No, the things I'm most proud of are your Grams, your uncles, and your mother. They've been the greatest joys—and sorrows—of my life. But like you and your dad showed me tonight, you can't earn the strength of such love without equal measures of pain sometimes. Both have always been mine; I just didn't handle one well." His eyes find mine, before he dips his chin in acknowledgment and a silent apology.

For just a moment, I hold on to the bitterness, but then I see Austyn next to him. Paige shifts restlessly next to me, and I realize I can support them giving him a second chance. Not only because I have the rainbow and the pot of gold at the end, but because if something happens, I'll be there if they fall.

I'll always be here. That will never change. Not ever again.

"That's in the past. Let's move on," I hear myself say. "What was your favorite part of the show?"

Paige's body bucks against mine in response. I just hope she's not crying. She'll be pissed if we face the media out the stage door and her makeup is ruined.

"The music. Best part of the whole show." Tyson wraps his arm around Austyn and kisses the top of her head.

Evangeline leans into her husband before surprising the hell out of me. "I agree. Never before have I ever sung a score so brilliant. Becks, Austyn, I think you both have a whole new career path ahead of you—if you want it."

Huh. Something to think about for another day. "We can talk later. Right now, I need to get my fiancée something to wipe up these black tears."

Paige groans. "Great. Another photo where I look like '90s goth."

"A great time in music history," I comment absentmindedly as I dab at her eyes with the tissues Simon passes me.

Everyone in our group laughs except Paige, who swats at me.

I lean forward and press a soft kiss to her lips.

It's not possible I could have composed a more perfect day. After all, Paige is by my side.

That's all I need. That's all I've ever wanted.

EPILOGUE
BECKETT

FIVE MONTHS LATER

February

Paige has four days off from the hospital, so we're spending them at my penthouse in the city instead of her home in Connecticut.

"Ward and Angie do it every weekend. Why can't we?" I love the atmosphere in Collyer, so much so I'm debating buying another piece of real estate there.

"And what happens when the schedule isn't as flexible as it is now? What if we can't be as flexible as we are now? You won't find it too confining? Too...rustic?" She frets over her morning coffee.

I pause with my own mug halfway to my mouth. "Why this sudden concern? We're getting married. I told you before I needed exactly one thing for my home. That's you, remember?"

The diamond I slipped on her finger months ago winks at me. It's enormous. I really think Paige may have carpal tunnel from lifting it on her hand when we're ninety and in side-by-side rocking chairs. After we made love and I slipped it on her finger, she pretended to let her hand fall to the floor like it was holding an anvil.

Of course, she's been followed by as many media crews as I am these days. Her security has been upped as a result. At first, she felt more than a little confined at not being able to zip off to grab a cup of coffee in her pajama bottoms without it being reported on some blogger's Worst Dressed List.

As for me? I'm completely unrepentant. I want everyone to know she's mine, finally and forever.

"Yes, Beckett. But I want to be certain Collyer is where you want to make our home." She chews on her lower lip.

I put my tablet down from where I've been looking at larger properties and reach for her hand. "What are you thinking so hard about over there, baby?"

Her head swivels first left, then right, doing everything but looking me in the eye. "We're almost forty."

I reply cautiously. "I know."

"I went to the doctor to check about my birth control because I wasn't sure if I should renew it." This time she bites down on the inside of her cheek.

"Why not?" We'd long dispensed with condoms once I'd had a physical that I think even checked for toe fungus to satisfy my Paige.

"Because of my age! I'm reaching a point where..."

I break in. "I'll start using condoms again. I'm not risking you." I'll never risk losing Paige again, not for anything.

"No, Beckett, you don't understand." She moves between my legs and takes my hand. "We have a window—it's a small one, but we could...if you wanted to..."

"If I wanted to what?" Then it hits me harder than any punch I ever endured from my father and sweeter than any kiss from Paige's lips. She's offering me the chance to experience fatherhood all over again from the beginning. My lips are frozen just at the moment when she needs me to speak.

But she just presses her lips to me. "Don't say a word. Just when you're thinking about buying a house, factor that in. The home might have to be a little bit bigger than you planned if you decide that's something you want."

If? I'm about to tell her to chuck the birth control when my iPad dings. "If that's the real estate agent, she has really shitty timing," I growl.

Paige tries, and fails, to suppress a smile. "Did you have something else on your mind?"

I grab her hand and pull it down to my iron-hard cock. "Yes. It involves the way one and one make three. And it's not nice to...what's wrong?" I demand when she snatches her hand away like it's just been burned.

She just hands me the tablet. Then she dashes away into the bedroom.

I scan it before roaring, "Shit!"

Rumors are swirling around Grammy-Award-winning artist Beckett Miller. How long has he known that a composition he wrote long ago resulted in a melody of a different sort—the nine-month variety that wore adorable booties? And what does his new woman have to say about it?

— StellaNova

I knew it was just a matter of time with the way she kept slipping up in public, but damnit, I was hoping we had until after the wedding. I fire off a quick text to Carys to let her know the news has broken about Austyn on StellaNova—and their implication she might not be Paige's.

Then I race behind Paige to gear up for war.

⊕

Thankfully, Kane pulled the car beneath the building for us to clamor into an hour later. I've spent that amount of time listening to him remind Paige about how to address the reporters, though I'm certain the reminder is more for me than it is for her as she's sitting quietly staring out the blackout windows. I'd never know her anxiety if it wasn't for the way her diamond is cutting into my hand.

This is what love is all about, I realize with startling clarity. I'd willingly stay lost from her life forever, or I'd absorb the pain of a thousand cuts—whatever it took to spare her a moment of pain. The most worthwhile love is worth sacrificing one's soul for. That's why poets and musicians write about it.

We're getting closer to Rockefeller Center when I spy the gaggle of reporters and cameras outside of Carys's building. I'm about to open my mouth to reassure Paige when I get a good look at her face. Without a second's hesitation, I pull her toward me before pressing my lips against hers.

When I let her up for air, I tell her, "I want our next daughter to have your same fierceness even if she makes me old before my time." And that's when I fling open the door and step into the vortex of flashing lights. I vaguely hear Kane cursing.

Paige slides out right behind me. For a moment, we hold court. Everyone's shouting questions and over and over on repeat. *Did you know Beckett got some poor girl pregnant years ago?*

And that's when Paige becomes social media gold. She addresses them, one and all. "I became pregnant when I was seventeen years old. It was my choice—as it is every woman's—to decide what to do with that pregnancy. I was fortunate enough to have the support to carry that pregnancy to term and the resources many in this country don't have to raise my daughter at such a young age while pursuing a career.

"I have also been fortunate enough to have fallen in love with the same man twice. And the man I chose to do that with is Beckett Miller. It is none of your business if my adult daughter now feels such a deep abiding affection for him after not having a father her entire life that she chooses to call him 'Dad.'

"He'll help her continue to grow as an independent woman, helping her stand up again after she makes her own mistakes. He'll be there to celebrate her joys—which we both hope there will be many. He's going to despise every man she dates, because they will never be good enough. And, God willing, she will ask him to walk her down the aisle one day. Hold her children. And why? Even if she wasn't his, he'd do it because she's mine. He didn't need a reason beyond that. And frankly, you don't need one at all. But there. Now you have it. Now, may the father of my child and I please pass?"

Concluding Paige's diatribe, I grab her hand and drag her through the throng of paparazzi to the doors leading to Carys's office.

She hasn't said another word, merely tipping her chin to security as we approach the elevator. I don't get any words out because the second the doors open, she drags me into the elevator.

After slapping the floor for Carys's office, I press my body against hers until she's backed against the elevator. Her eyes are burning into mine. Chest heaving, heart racing where I can feel it under my fingers. "When, not if, I give you a second child, I want you to remember this moment right now."

"Why?"

"Because here, now, you made us a family. And no vow we take together will be sweeter than that."

Confusion knits her brow. "I already told you yes."

"I know. I just didn't understand how deeply you meant it. It's more beautiful than any music I've ever heard." I lean down and press my lips against her forehead.

"Any music composed about love is beautiful."

"And I love you, Paige. That's never changed."

The elevator doors open. "Let's go see what the crew thought of your impromptu press conference," I urge. I try to prevent the smile flirting with my lips, but I can't quite manage it.

Paige groans but takes my outstretched hand. "Carys is going to strangle me."

I fling open the door to LLF, and Paige is partially correct. Carys does go for her throat but only to wrap her arms around her neck for a gigantic hug. "You were brilliant, Paige!" she shouts. She only lets up to smack me. "Why can't you be this articulate with the press?"

I extract my fiancée only to wrap her up tightly. "Somehow, I don't think that will be much of a worry in the future."

Ward and Angie come bursting through the door. Angie exclaims, "Why is everyone just sitting around out here? We saw the alerts and came in."

Knowing the two were taking a few days off for their honeymoon, I'm about to thank them before the door slams open again.

This time, it's Austyn. Her hair is a wild mess. She looks like a twister has torn through her hair and she slapped her clothes on in a hurry. I mentally warn myself not to go there before I demand what —or whom—she was doing. I send silent prayers heavenward. *Please, Lord, give me strength.*

"Mama? Dad? Is everything okay?" She rushes right toward us.

I let Paige go just enough to catch the final piece of us.

"We're fine," I soothe her.

"Damn right, you are." Angie's voice is filled with awe. "Stella-Nova has Paige's statement word for word. Are you certain you didn't do a stint in PR?"

"Right? I was hooting as E! streamed it live," Carys declares triumphantly.

"Mama? What did you say?" Austyn asks in confusion

"You'd have been proud of your mother, honey," I murmur into the top of her head.

"That's where you're a bit off, Dad. I always have been." Austyn lets me go to hug her mother hard.

It's then Paige bursts into tears. I reach down and wipe them away. "Baby, why are you crying now?"

Just then, David walks into the office. His feet come to a complete standstill. "Oh, God. You heard the news about Erzulie."

And the tension that had left all of us refills the room. "What happened to Erzulie?" Carys panics.

David quickly explains. "I don't think the media has it yet."

"They wouldn't after Paige's declaration." Carys races to her office.

I pull out my cell and call down to the security team, ordering them to Erzulie immediately. I snap, "No, I won't leave the fucking premises. Just go get her to a hospital, Kane. I'll clear it with Colby."

Paige tips her head back and presses a kiss to my chin. "You're a good man."

"I don't know what I'd do if something happened to either of you." I turn to our daughter. "You're getting permanent security." Just as Austyn starts to protest, I hold up a hand to silence her. "Don't argue. Not right now. Please."

One heartbeat. Two. Then Austyn relents.

"Whatever it takes," she readily agrees.

Then Paige lightens the burden on my soul when she murmurs, "Maybe a boy this time around."

Later that night, Carys texts me. Look up the hashtag I created for Paige.

Groaning, I pull out my phone.

"What's wrong now?" Paige demands as she makes dinner for the three of us.

"Nothing. I hope." I type in the tag into my search engine. I then sit down to read.

#DrPaigeMD, you're my new #hero

No one should be ashamed #DrPaigeMD #hero #lifegoals

Way to go, Paige! #DrPaigeMD

Not your business. Leave them alone. #beckettmiller #Kensington #DrPaigeMD

Over and over, I read pages of support from fans and critics of mine in the industry supporting Paige. I'm still reeling from it when I feel her fingers sift through my hair. "Come on. Dinner's ready. This can wait until later."

Then she turns and heads back to the kitchen, where she cracks a joke with our daughter about burning the perfectly golden grilled cheese.

And my hand cups the ink around my neck. I'm a lucky bastard and not because of the things around me but because of the people who surround me.

Huh. Quickly, I pull out my phone and jot the line down. That might make a good song. I'll work on it when Paige and I get back from our honeymoon.

When I go to toss my iPad on the table, a final alert pops in that has me calling out to Paige. "Honey, the news about Erzulie just broke."

Paige pops out from the kitchen, wiping her hands on a dish towel. "Then we'll be her support the same way everyone was there for us. But there's nothing you can do tonight, Beckett—as much as I know you want to."

"Yeah," I agree, but I've done all I can.

For the moment.

Erzulie—always believed to be folk-award-winning singing sensation Kylie Miles—was proven this evening to be her identical twin sister, Leanne, when she was rushed to the emergency room.

Leanne isn't available for comment.

— StellaNova

Perfect
ORDER

TRACEY JERALD

Leanne's story is available now!
To order her book, go to my website
https://www.traceyjerald.com

ACKNOWLEDGMENTS

First, to my husband who sings to me in the car. Best voice in the world, in my opinion. It sends shivers down my spine every time.

To our son. I can't wait for you to start music classes this year, baby. I hope you love them as much as I did.

To my mother, who encouraged me to play a ridiculous number of instruments.

To my Jen. Even when I lost the ability to sing decently, you've always encouraged me to keep on—just like with everything in my life. I love you!

To my Meows, so much love. And think of all the music we've shared between cruise ships, karaoke, parties, and table dancing. Please, God, destroy the videos.

To Sandra Depukat, from One Love Editing, for all the love notes that play through my manuscripts. They completely keep me going.

To Holly Malgieri, from Comma Sutra Editorial, for the final check before my books go on "stage."

To Deborah Bradseth, Tugboat Designs. You made my rock 'n roll dreams come true with this cover!

To photographer Wander Aguiar, Andrey Bahia, and model Clayton Wells, I have to say it again; this photo was pure magic. Thank you all!

To Gloria Landavazo at Blooming Books. Thank you so much for not only being a brilliant artist, but permitting me to have Beckett recognize that as well in the story. XOXO

To Gel, at Tempting Illustrations, you're the first image everyone sees of the books and it's always beautiful. Thank you!

To the fantastic team at Foreword PR, there's not enough ways to thank you! I could try singing it, but...

Linda Russell, my world is absolutely a better place because you're in it. Thank you for always pushing me to be a better me.

To my Musketeers. Little did we know when we started this journey what we would discover. #unbreakable

To Susan Henn, Amy Rhodes, and Dawn Hurst, my dream team! I don't know what I would do without any of you!

For the amazing individuals who are a part of Tracey's Tribe, thank you for being a part of my world!

And for all of the readers and bloggers who take the time to enjoy my books, you are the real stars. Thank you.

ABOUT THE AUTHOR

Tracey Jerald knew she was meant to be a writer when she would rewrite the ending of books in her head when she was a young girl growing up in southern Connecticut. It wasn't long before she was typing alternate endings and extended epilogues "just for fun".

After college in Florida, where she obtained a degree in Criminal Justice, Tracey traded the world of law and order for IT. Her work for a world-wide internet startup transferred her to Northern Virginia where she met her husband in what many call their own happily ever after. They have one son.

When she's not busy with her family or writing, Tracey can be found in her home in north Florida drinking coffee, reading, training for a runDisney event, or feeding her addiction to HGTV.

Connect with her on her website (https://www.traceyjerald.com) for all social media links, bonus scenes, and upcoming news.

CPSIA information can be obtained
at www.ICGtesting.com
Printed in the USA
BVHW041818090422
633354BV00005B/16